THE LIGHT A BODY RADIATES

01 02 03 04 05 22 21 20 19 18

Caitlin Press Inc.
8100 Alderwood Road
Halfmoon Bay, BC V0N 1Y1
www.caitlin-press.com

Text and cover design by Vici Johnstone
Cover image © Jonathan Cruz
Printed in Canada

Caitlin Press Inc. acknowledges financial support from the Government of Canada and the Canada Council for the Arts, and the Province of British Columbia through the British Columbia Arts Council and the Book Publisher's Tax Credit.

Library and Archives Canada Cataloguing in Publication

Whitty, Ethel, author
    The light a body radiates / Ethel Whitty.

ISBN 978-1-987915-61-7 (softcover)

    I. Title.
PS8645.H59L54 2018   C813'.6   C2017-906534-3

THE
LIGHT
A BODY
RADIATES

ETHEL WHITTY

CAITLIN PRESS

This book is dedicated to Shanthi and Kieran, who
provide so much light in my life

1

On a day when I still thought our family could never be wounded, my older brother, Francis, played a favourite game with me. He and my brother Joe cradled my eight-year-old self in their arms and threw me back and forth, each time taking a step back to see how far they could make the toss. Francis was sixteen and Joe fifteen, both past their growth spurt and tall for their ages.

It was five o'clock and already dark, so we had to rely on the light from the verandah. Snowflakes wandered down from the sky, and the night before there'd been a silver thaw. Every inch of the crabapple tree was covered in glittering ice, dusted with the light snow.

When one of them released me into the air the stars sped by overhead until I landed with a thump against one of their thin, hard bodies. I wanted to squeal but knew that if I did my mother would come running out and put an end to it.

They never dropped me. When the toss became risky, Francis said, "I think that's far enough."

"Come on," I begged, "one more. You won't drop me."

"What if I did and you cracked your head?"

"*Nooo*, you won't."

"I'd have to tell people I had a cracked sister. I wouldn't like that."

"You're mean."

"Yes, I am."

He held the back storm door open so we could all pile into the kitchen. We dragged in quite a bit of snow and Francis snatched a rag from the counter to mop up our puddles. Even so, when Mama came into the room and saw the mess, she sighed, as she often did, "Every house in Cape Breton has a back porch except this one."

My sister Stella, fourteen, stood in front of the kitchen mirror curling her hair around rollers the size of tin cans. Francis looked from her to me until he was sure he had our attention and then held his hands up by his sides and made his wrists go limp. Stella rolled her eyes skyward and turned back to the mirror. "Oh shut up," she said. There was a bit of laughter in her voice, so I climbed up on the stepstool, hoping they would practise rock and rolling to the radio.

Stella finished rolling up her long, straight hair while Francis watched. She was the only one of us with light brown hair. Mama told me that when Stella was small she had blond hair like our small brother Murdoch has now.

Francis could pass for older than his years, although he was still very thin and didn't have his mature weight yet. He had wide brown eyes and his curly hair never lay flat. I thought he was a handsome brother, except that his ears seemed too big for his head. My mother had promised me he would grow into them.

A friend of his sat next to me at the rink one Saturday and stared before he said, "Are you Frankie MacPherson's sister?"

"Yes, I am," I said.

He laughed out loud. "You're a dead ringer for him."

It was good to think I looked like him.

That night, Francis and Stella danced to a tune called "Tutti Frutti." I thought the words were babyish for people their age. It had a chorus that went, "A-wop-bop-a-loo-bop-a-lop-bam-boom!" Halfway through the song Francis motioned to me.

"Come on, Eileen. Get down. You can dance."

I jumped down and he held my hand above my head and twirled me around. I wasn't much good at it. When the song ended, Francis said he had to get ready to go out and Stella kept dancing on her own.

"Fifty cents she doesn't show up," she said. "What kind of girl would come get the guy?"

We knew Mama was nervous about the girl coming to pick him up after supper, so Stella and our younger sister, Iona, and I sat with her at the kitchen table, drinking tea while we waited.

"It's the state of the house that bothers me," she said quietly, not wanting our father to hear her complaint. "I don't need a big fancy house but I'd like a finished one. What kind of house has stacks of wallboard in the hall or no railing on the stairs and plywood on the floor?" We'd heard this question before and no one offered an answer.

The girl who picked him up in her car an hour later looked older than Francis. She came striding into our house through the front door, wearing spike heels, with her black hair done up in a beehive. Francis stood close beside her so we could compare.

"Do you see that?" he said. "She's taller than me." He seemed awfully pleased by her height and smiled as if he couldn't stop himself.

Stella looked at her shoes for a moment while adjusting to the fact she'd lost the fifty-cent bet. When she turned back to the conversation she took a deep breath and made an effort at nonchalance.

"Nice shoes."

"They're five inches," the girl said, smiling in a way that conveyed how pleased she was with them and with Stella for asking. Stella really had no choice but to smile back.

Mama was a tall woman herself but I never saw her wear spike heels and her auburn hair was tied back in a loose bun, so she had no height advantage there. I didn't know a woman could be taller than Mama. After she said, "Come in. Sit down. Would you like some tea?" the girl thanked her and sat at the kitchen table. Mama smiled. They all seemed so drawn to her, especially Francis, and I wasn't sure I liked it.

When I pulled my eyes away I saw my father standing in the doorway of the kitchen. He was taking in the whole situation while my little brother Murdoch squeezed between his legs, running in circles around him. After a moment he put his hand on the top of Murdoch's head in a way that made him try to squirm away and then stopped him from moving. Everyone noticed when the riotous running quieted and they turned, seeking the sound. Seeing so many eyes upon him, Murdoch buried his face in our father's pant leg.

Mama said, "Neil, this is Nancy MacKay." He lifted his hand off Murdoch's head, then picked him up and stuck him under his arm like a football so he could come forward and shake Nancy's hand. Murdoch didn't object and stared at the girl. Francis piped in, "Her father works at the plant."

"Would that be Danny MacKay in the rail yard?"

"No, my father is Carl. He works in the office," she said with that smile. This left my father speechless. He nodded as if he understood something, set Murdoch on the floor and went to the sink for a glass of water. Soon after, he left the room.

Once Francis and very tall Nancy were gone, my father came back and sat at the table. He looked at my mother with raised eyebrows.

"That McKay is not a friend to workers."

"He must be in the union."

"No, he's not."

"He's a clerk," said Mama.

My father closed his eyes, rubbed his face with both hands and sighed.

"Why is it always something?" she asked.

I knew what she meant by that. Francis so often displeased him. There was not as much yelling as there had been in the past, but now whenever they were in the same room, they seemed to always be looking somewhere else. When Neil told him to do his chores or to come home early, Francis glared at his shoes and Neil got red in the face. Mama always got him a glass of water when that happened, as if he might be too warm. He retreated to the basement at those times and we tried not to disturb him while he worked on some piece of carpentry or repair.

"He seems happy," she insisted as she poured a cup of tea and set it with a biscuit on a plate in front of Neil.

He lifted his head and looked right at her, "At least it's good to see him with a girl. I was beginning to wonder."

Mama looked at us smaller children sitting there.

"Bedtime," she said.

That night our bedroom windows were covered in an eighth of an inch of frost. When Mama came into the room my younger sister, Iona, and I had our fingers pressed against the glass, making holes through the frost so we could look out. She pulled us both away, "The air will be colder if you make holes in that." Once we were in pajamas, she held the covers high while we leapt into the bed and lay flat on our backs with our knees pulled up. She let the covers fall, then tucked us in, pinning our blankets down with the five-inch pins that were used for the fronts of kilts. She held her tongue in her teeth when she made the effort to push the big pins through the bedding.

Finished, she sat on the side of the bed, one leg folded under and her body twisted around to better look at us. She told a story about an artist who came and painted the beautiful swirling patterns of frost on the windows to keep us warm. I always thought it was Mama who did that.

Stella slept on the other side of the girls' room but she wasn't in bed yet. The sound of the radio wafted up from downstairs where she was doing her homework at the kitchen table. It didn't seem right that she was missing the story.

When Mama said goodnight, Iona closed her eyes and mumbled, "See you in the morning." Mama's reply, "God willing," floated off her tongue the way a person would say "sleep tight" but it caused a sharp pang of anxiety and dread to travel from my heart down to my stomach.

What if God was not willing? And what would make him decide, in the middle of the night, that he'd had enough of us?

Murdoch was asleep in a crib outside our room. It was a good, warm place for a baby right beside the chimney, and there was no room anywhere else. We heard her footsteps stop beside him after she left us and when she reached her own room we could hear her pull a book from the bedside table.

After some time Murdoch let out a cry in the night and I wiggled out of the covers. The soles of my feet touched the floor as softly as possible and I shuffled out to the hall with small, quiet steps. I hoped I could soothe him before Mama would have to rouse herself. He was walking around his crib looking for his special monkey. I found it under the covers and gave it back to him. Still, he was disturbed by something, so I danced for him to music that only I could hear. It seemed to fascinate him enough that he eventually fell from his standing position to a small sleeping heap in the crib. After covering him up, I squeezed back under the pinned-down covers beside Iona and pressed against her warm body. She didn't wake but murmured in a way that echoed the music I had danced to, as if it were a song we all knew that emanated from the rafters of the house.

I lay awake a long time then, or at least I think I did. Stella came in quietly; I could hear her undress in the dark and flop into bed. When Murdoch squawked again, Mama called out quietly, "Never mind. I've got him." I squirmed out of bed anyway and padded through the hall to her bedroom. The door was ajar. I could see her lying on her side with her back to the door and curled around Murdoch. He was already asleep.

"I need a glass of milk," I said.

"Fine. Be quick," she whispered without turning.

Downstairs, my father sat in his chair reading one of his magazines that told how to fix everything electrical. He looked up. "Don't dawdle." I took my time pouring the milk and on the way back said, "Goodnight, Neil," and kept going. There was a short outburst of breath behind me, which I took to be a laugh but may have been exasperation.

I called him Neil from the time I learned to talk. Stella took exception to it when I was about three or four years old. I came running in from outside and couldn't find a place to sit so I squeezed into my father's chair and said, "Move over, Neil." Stella was holding Iona on her lap and said, "Don't say that in front of the baby." I looked back and forth from

Mama to Neil. Mama looked at him and he pretended not to hear. He never said, "Don't call me that," so I kept on doing it. Mama didn't try to correct me. I heard her say quietly to Stella, "He gets a kick out of it."

When she spoke of him she always called him Neil or "your father." When he spoke of her, he called her Mama, not her real name, which was Jessica. I don't know how the older ones ever figured out to call him Dad. They must have picked it up outside the house.

When I got back to the girls' room, Iona's breathing was punctuated with an occasional sigh or throat noise but nothing that would suggest anything other than sleeping. She was curled up in a ball in our bed, so I lay down and put my arms around her the way I'd seen Mama do with Murdoch. Stella was awake but she pretended not to be and rolled over with her face to the wall. I could hear the radio whispering in the boys' room across the hall. I knew that Francis's bed was empty.

Nothing moved or changed for a long time until I heard a car stop outside. Luckily for me there was a knothole in the unfinished floorboards of the upstairs hallway and no plasterboard on the ceiling below. If there was a light on anywhere down there a beam escaped into the upstairs. The hall was dark when I made my way toward the end near the stairs but, once I was right over the hole, I could see some light that must have come from the kitchen. I lay down next to it, knowing I could easily hear what people said and, with one eye, could catch more than a glimpse of their movements.

Francis quietly opened the door and just as quietly closed it behind him. Neil stepped out of the living room while Francis had his back turned and put a heavy hand on his shoulder in a move to turn him around. Perhaps Francis didn't know it was him and swung his fist impulsively. It happened so fast I hardly saw him do it. The force of the blow knocked Neil's head back. I heard the crack when it hit the wall or the door frame or something else I couldn't see.

For one frozen moment I feared Neil might be terribly hurt. Francis seemed to be paralyzed as he stood in the one spot, staring. My father gave his head a shake, stared blankly and then lunged at him. He easily knocked Francis's feet out from under him and threw him to the floor, landing him flat on his back with a loud double thump when he bounced. I could see Francis's face for the first time. His curly hair blended into the patterned linoleum floor and his eyes were open wide, looking straight up at the knothole. Heat rose in my face to my scalp and I thought I might throw up.

Now I heard Mama's feet hit the floor. I couldn't pull my eyes away from my view of Francis through the hole. He blinked a few times, then rolled over and sprang up with his fists raised. Mama yanked the door open and flew into the hallway, almost stepping on me. "Get back to bed!" she hissed as she started down the stairs. Through the hole I could see Neil standing straight, with his arms at his sides and the blood running down from his nose. He said, "You think about it before you do that, boy."

By that time Mama was at the bottom of the stairs. "Francis, go to bed!" He was staring at Neil but she interrupted his gaze and he jerked his head to one side. Then he turned and headed up the stairs without looking back. When he got to the top he didn't notice me lying over the knothole. At least I didn't think so, because he kept his eyes on the floor when he went into his room.

I could see the tops of Mama's and my father's heads standing facing each other and heard her say to him, "You promised."

"It was him who lashed out!"

"I'm sure he just walked in and bloodied your nose for nothing!"

"Don't you be saucy to me!"

"I'm not one of the children," Mama said.

"All I did was put a hand on his shoulder."

"Not quite all."

"Alright then. Leave it."

"*You* should leave it."

By this time the others were awake. Joe stayed with Francis, but Stella came out of the room and pulled me up from the knothole. "What happened?"

"Neil and Francis were fighting and Neil has a bloody nose."

"We'll finish this conversation in the morning!" my father's voice came up the stairs. I didn't know for sure if he directed that at Mama or Francis or at me. Perhaps all of us. They moved into the front room and we could no longer make out what they were saying.

Murdoch started fussing in Mama's room. Stella whispered, "Go get him and put him in with Iona." I was glad to be released from the commotion and went to Murdoch, whose two-year-old face was crumpled and wet with tears. He reached out his arms and as I picked him up and put my face in his neck, I caught the scent of his baby smell. When I carried him back to our room and squeezed him under the covers beside Iona, she didn't even wake up.

Mama came up the stairs quickly and opened the boys' room door. "Are you all right?"

"He hates me," said Francis. "I'm the only one he hates."

"No, he doesn't. Something overtakes him sometimes."

"You always say that!"

"He knows and he can't stop. It's himself he hates. I thought this kind of thing was over. You have to talk to him," Mama said.

"I never will again."

"You can't say that!"

"Yes I can."

"Try to sleep. We'll talk in the morning."

When she left his room, I saw Mama put her hand on Stella's arm for a second before she went back downstairs.

Stella came back into our room and picked up Murdoch and put him back in his crib. Then she told me, "Get back in bed and stay there," and went back to bed herself. I tried to listen but there was only murmuring to be heard.

In the morning the holes Iona and I had made in the frost on the window were covered in as if we had never been there. I wished that she would wake so we could whisper. She was so still, her curly hair all messed from sleeping. She had a cold and was breathing through her mouth.

"I want to get up," I said out loud.

Stella thought better of that. "Wait until she calls us." Finally Mama yelled up the stairs, "Breakfast!" Iona blinked her eyes rapidly, then sat up straight and looked around the room as if deciding where she was. Within a few moments we'd all gathered our clothes and ran down the bare wooden stairs that bounced a little underfoot. We pushed and nudged until there was a place for each of us to stand in front of the wood-burning jacket heater that sat to one side in our main room. The scurrying and the heat and dressing in front of the stove were usually a good way to begin the day and when Iona, who was often known to be forgetful, rushed back upstairs, Stella took the opportunity to tease, "Aw, forgot her shoes again."

The silence in the kitchen told us that the conversation of the night before had not been finished. We were eating breakfast when Mama admitted that Francis had already gone to school. "He looked to me like he didn't sleep at all."

"Don't encourage him," Neil said. "He still has to answer to me tonight."

Mama had already been up for hours lighting the fires and making the porridge. Now she was packing my father's lunch can with sandwiches and making breakfast for the rest of us. Not looking directly at him, as if trying to control her own anger, she said, "It's not for the purpose of goring the lambs that horns were put on the sheep."

To which my father replied, "Who are you confusing with a lamb?"

She spoke quietly, without looking up from the stove. "He says he may have a job to go to."

"He has school to go to," said my father.

"Maybe he should go," she said. "Your arguments are hard on all of us."

I couldn't believe she was saying this. It felt terribly wrong to let him go so easily. We all knew he was Mama's favourite and no one minded. It seemed to be an honest compensation for his contentious relationship with our father. I wanted Stella or my brother Joe to say something but they just sat there looking at their porridge.

I stared at Neil and blurted, "No! Tell him you want him to stay."

He looked directly at me when he said, "It's not my fault. He's not going to run this house as long as I pay the bills."

I climbed down off the chair and went to hide in the boys' room closet where I thought no one would look for me. Francis's and Joe's clothes hung down in front of me and made a cocoon as I sat leaning on the wall at the back. Before he went to work, Neil came upstairs. He looked in the girls' room and then in the boys' room, and then stood in the hall for a minute wondering where I could be. I was hoping he'd think I'd disappeared somehow. Gone. After a moment he crouched down at the door of the closet and pulled the clothes aside.

"Come out of there now. You have to go to school," he said quietly. He didn't ask what I was doing.

 ✺

When Francis arrived home that day around four, he came in the front door, paced the length of the hall quickly, and sat abruptly in a chair at the kitchen table. Mama was drying her hands on a tea towel and didn't have time to even put the kettle on before he said, "A man is coming to pick me up after supper. He has work for me."

"What kind of work?"

"He sells bibles."

She nodded slowly before asking, "How long will you be gone?"

"A while, I guess."

At supper my father never looked up from his meal. The silence made my ears ring. I could hear Iona chewing her food and gave her a hard look, but she didn't notice and kept on. Afterwards, when Francis stood at the door to say goodbye, he wore a black suit that hung loosely on him and he carried a suitcase. He didn't put it down when my mother hugged him goodbye but he hugged her hard with one arm. Then he curtly nodded to my father, who was standing at the end of the hall in the same place he'd stood the night before. Neil dug his wallet out of his back pocket, selected the only twenty-dollar bill it held and offered it. Francis looked for one moment before waving the money away.

"Go on. Take it," my father said. "You're going to need it."

"No I won't," Francis said. "I won't need it at all."

A black car that was all angles and fins pulled up outside. The man who drove it never got out. My brother pushed open the door and was gone like a puff of air.

After the storm door slammed and the car drove away, my father sat down in his chair, picked up his unlit pipe and knocked its dry contents into the palm of his hand. But then, instead of filling it from the pouch on the side table, he sat still, staring at the old spent ashes.

Mama told Iona and me to go outside to play, so we pulled on our boots and coats and went out into the night. After standing on the verandah for a few moments, we both walked down the step and lay quietly in the snow.

The black sky was filled with sharp pinpoints of light, and we slowly moved our arms and legs against the snowy ground. I recognized one of the constellations that Mama had shown us. It was the twins, the ones she called Gemini. They seemed to be reclining against the dark sky in almost the same positions as we were against the snow—a mirror image of us. I reached over to hold Iona's hand and sat up, signifying that we should try to stand without damaging the snow angels. Iona counted to three and we sprang up together without lifting our feet at all. They were perfect. Iona looked at me and then back to the snow angels before saying, "I'm smaller than you and I'm not crying."

2

The arctic pack ice arrived with a thump and slid along the coast from the North Atlantic, bringing another six weeks of winter to the island. We passed the harbour on the way home from school and jumped on the enormous floating chunks that clogged it as if the ocean had frozen over. When we got closer to home I spent time kicking at the ice in the ditches trying to break it up while Iona walked slowly ahead and called back to me. "What are you doing that for?"

It was a terrible spring. There was a blizzard on April 15. All that day my mother stood at the window, watching the drifting snow and worrying about Francis, thinking he might be caught outside.

"Dear God, I hope he's in a motel room."

The departure of her eldest child took a heavy toll on Mama. It sounds so melodramatic to speak of my brother leaving home as if it was some kind of tragedy. After all, we all leave home one day. It was the way he went that left us living as if we sat around a crater of an unknown depth. He left quietly, formally you might even say. He wore a tie and I had never seen him dressed that way. The only time my father wore a suit was when he went to church wearing his brown tweedy one. Francis's suit was roomy but you could see he'd grow into it.

On the night of the storm, the phone rang after bedtime. My mother grabbed her robe and ran down the stairs, each tread bouncing in its known pattern. Afterwards she said she rushed because she didn't want the telephone to wake the baby, but when we'd peeked out our doorways we'd caught a glimpse of her dread that something might have happened to Francis.

When she returned to her bed, I heard my parents' muffled conversation through the walls. "Where is he?"

"He's in Toronto. He says he might get a job at a radio station."

My father shifted in the bed. "Oh, for God's sake."

I didn't speak for several days and found I could go totally unbothered as long as I responded with a nod to requests like, "Please set the table, Eileen." Or "I could use some help peeling these potatoes." And I could always have my head in a book and people would assume I was barely conscious of the world around me. It became a kind of experiment. If there were two of us gone, would anyone notice?

Aunt Effie came for a few days to buy dresses that she picked up downtown and brought home to get Mama's opinion. I saw her coming up the walk, barely able to see over her stack of boxes, and rushed out to help her. When we got them inside she asked, "Help me try them on?" She knew I loved the showing off of dresses.

I grabbed a couple of the boxes and ran up to Mama's bedroom with Aunt Effie in tow. There were half a dozen of them and we laid them all out on the bed at once. She let me choose the order and I helped with zippers and flew up and down the stairs with her to watch while she twirled around in the living room so we could see them from all angles. Her red hair and freckles made her seem more like a girl than a woman. She looked at me for a long moment at one point, expecting me to have an opinion. When the last dress was admired and the choices made—a red seersucker shirtwaist and a navy blue sheath with sleeves for church—Mama suggested that I probably had homework to do. I left the room but didn't go very far and she spoke to me through the wall.

"Eileen, go do your homework."

I moved from the dining room into the kitchen.

They lowered their voices then but I heard Aunt Effie bringing my silence to Mama's attention. "She hasn't said a word all day."

My mother responded, "She'll talk when she has something to say."

"Do you talk to her?"

I couldn't see the look Mama was probably giving her but I could imagine it: head to one side a bit, eyebrows raised. "I talk to her every day."

"I know you do."

"It's not as if anyone around here is talking much at the moment," Mama admitted.

It was surprising they let it go on that long without at least trying to tease me out of it. Francis wouldn't have let that happen.

No one lay on the single beds in the boys' room. They were pushed against opposite walls under slanted ceilings with a window at the foot of each. Between the windows the four-foot-wide bookshelf that held all of their belongings was crammed with schoolbooks and paperbacks, a protractor and calipers and other geometry tools. The previous year's shop projects—a lathed wooden lamp and a small rough box—were set on the top shelf. The room was as messy as usual, clothes and comics spilling off the beds onto the floor.

The exception to that were the records. Francis had always insisted that they be put back in their jackets. I could almost see him there, squatting on the floor with the records spread out around him while he talked about them. He'd grab one and say to me, "Okay, tell me what you think about this one," which always made me laugh because if he loved it, I knew I would love it.

So I'd say, "It's pretty cool."

He'd laugh then. "I appreciate your opinion. We have similar tastes."

Whenever he slipped a record out of its cardboard jacket, he held it at the extreme edges only, and then carefully set it upon the deck of the small record player on the bottom shelf. He was very patient when he showed me how to put one on the turntable.

"Put the needle down very carefully just at the edge. Never let it scratch the record."

Not quite so patient when the needle skittered across the record with a grating shriek.

"Okay, not quite ready for that," he said as he held his hands over his ears.

I felt very sorry to disappoint him at the time and I never touched the records again when they were out of their envelopes.

From the doorway I could see that the one called "Sunny Side Up" was right on top in its red jacket. It drew me to it and when I picked it up I saw Elvis Presley was just underneath. I liked both of them and so did Francis.

I could see him sitting there with his head bobbing up and down to the music he said was called bebop. I never heard Dizzy Gillespie anywhere except in this room. Francis said it wasn't the kind of thing they played much on the radio. I liked the name as much as the music.

I turned the sound low while I lowered the needle so I'd hear no scratchy sound. Then I slowly turned it up until it filled the room. I pretended that no one downstairs could hear me, but of course they could. They probably needed to hear it as much as I did.

There was another small stack of 45s that were mostly fiddle music. He played them when he was practising. At first when he was learning

I thought it sounded like hens screeching. After he'd practised a while the slow tunes had a feeling of sadness and the fast ones felt like running downhill laughing.

His fiddle wasn't in the room and I didn't know if he had it with him when he left or if one of our parents had put it away for safekeeping. I wished I had a record of him. He had his own way of playing and the tunes sounded different than they did on the radio. With his head lowered to the chin rest and his eyes closed when he played a slow, mournful tune, it looked as if he was praying.

He had always practised in this room and once, while we all listened from the living room, our father had put his paper down on his knee and looked out the window. He said, "I hope he sticks to that." Francis probably never even knew he noticed. Maybe Neil didn't know he'd care.

Looking around for something to read, I picked up a book lying open on Francis's bed. The title was *On the Road*. The very first line I read promised some explanation of why he'd left: "What is the feeling when you're driving away from people and they recede on the plain till you see their specks dispersing?"

I read for as long as I could but soon I ran into some pages where I had no idea what was going on, so I went downstairs to show it to Mama. She was in the kitchen making cod cakes for dinner.

"This book is about a trip. I understood the words in the beginning but now I don't know what he's talking about at all. I can't even sound out some of them."

She gently took the book from me and leafed through, reading some bits of it here and there.

"Where did you get this?"

"On Francis's bed."

"Better find something else, honey."

She stood on tiptoe and placed the book on a shelf between two crockery bowls where I could never reach it.

"We'll go down to the library tomorrow," she said.

I stood behind her, watching her back for some time before saying, "I want it."

She turned and looked at me with some pity.

"It's too old for you!"

"I won't read it. I won't read it. I promise. He's in the middle of it. He's going to want it when he comes back."

She sighed. "Fine, then." She retrieved the book from the shelf. "Don't even open it."

I nodded. "I'll put it back on the bed where he left it."

In the following weeks the kitchen became my place of refuge. It was where Mama could always be found. She had a wooden counter with a sink in it and a stove with a full coal scuttle beside it. The shelves under the counter were hidden with a pretty blue print curtain that she always kept clean and pressed. There was a table and a pull-out bin for flour, so it was easy to cook and bake. Best of all was the homemade daybed that sat along the wall opposite the counter. It was raised at one end and had big cushions that you could lie down on when you were home sick from school or just hanging around Mama. We called it a chaise lounge.

One day after school I lay reading one of Joe's comic books and became so absorbed by the exploits of Millie the Model that I forgot Francis was gone and I laughed. Mama looked up from where she was cutting biscuit dough with a baby food tin and the surprise on her face reminded me. I didn't want her to be disappointed or think I didn't care so I said, "Francis would laugh at this if he was here."

"Out loud?"

"Yes, he would."

She smiled and went back to cutting the dough.

We both had forgotten that it was after four and startled when we heard the back door open. My father came in and put his lunch can on the floor before he looked around and saw me there.

"Hello," he said. "Can you let your old tired daddy lie down?" I jumped up so he could use it to rest like he always did after work, and he said, "Relax a bit. I have to get these dirty clothes off first."

He made his way slowly up the stairs and I knew he would spend many minutes trying the clean the coal dust from his hands and under his nails. I hadn't spoken to him since Francis left but I wasn't sure he noticed.

When my father finally came back and lay on the chaise, he asked my mother, "Were the children any trouble today?"

From my spot on the back step I could still hear but not be seen.

"Oh no," she said, "no trouble at all."

"I must start on the railing on the back step," he said. "I'm afraid someone is going to fall off."

"It would be good to have that done before next winter. I guess there's no need of building a bunk bed in the boys' room anymore."

"No, there wouldn't be now. But you know I would have done that. There was room enough for him here."

I didn't hear Mama make any reply.

That evening, a batch of big, soft, molasses cookies cooled on the counter. We called them "crybaby cookies" because if you put one in each hand of a crying baby he will stop right away. Experimenting with Murdoch had proved it. As the cookies cooled, Mama started on a batch of bannock. I loved the careless way she scooped the flour out of the bin under the counter and threw it into a mixing bowl. The process of throwing ingredients together, and coming up with something altogether different, seemed to put her in the mood to talk.

I listened as she sifted through stories of her own childhood while she kneaded bread in that competent, brisk way she had of shifting the dough, or delicately spreading a layer of warm, cooked dates on a sweet oat base in the pan. Later, when I ate the date squares or the fat pieces of warm bread layered with butter, I could taste the stories in them.

You might say I was always hungry for stories. Like a baby bird with its mouth open, whenever a parent came into view, I devoured whispered fragments of conversations and stories overheard. The grown-ups nurtured me in this way and I think they knew I'd be the keeper of the story we all came to believe.

"At the time, Cape Breton wasn't tethered to the mainland by the causeway, so we were more on our own. The island felt bigger." She pressed the bannock dough into the pan. "My mother didn't want me go away to teach. She thought I was too young, and managed things so that there was a place for me in the school at home. God knows how she did that. Check the thermometer, will you?"

I had to open the oven door to see the round thermometer that stood like a small alarm clock on the shelf. It was so obscured by layers of baked-on grease that I couldn't really read it. "Hot enough," I said.

"At one time, Uncle Donald and Aunt Effie were both my students."

"You were their teacher?"

"Yes, I was."

"Did they like you?"

She laughed. "As much as ever I suppose."

"Did they get in trouble?"

"Oh no, Donald was in grade eleven. He only came when there was no work to do at home. Effie was ten and she helped me teach the smaller ones."

"What happened to your other brothers and sisters?"

"Well, Uncle Angus is one of them and you know what happened to him. I had one more brother, Malcolm. He went away to work in Boston with my father when I was ten, and he stayed there when my father died."

"How old was he?"

She thought about that for a brief moment and then raised her eyes to meet mine. "He was sixteen."

"Did you ever see him again?"

She placed the pan in the oven before she sat down in a chair on the other side of the table and leaned toward me. "No, I never did, but it was different times. Francis will come home."

"What was different?"

"It was 1933. There was only the train for travel and it seemed when people went, it was too hard to come back. Malcolm stayed on to work. He was older than the rest of us." She rose abruptly from the table. "Better clean up these dishes."

While the sink filled with steaming soapy water, and she piled in the bowls and cooking spoons, I went to stand beside her with a drying cloth and watched her face to try to read her thoughts. There was a smear of white flour on her cheek that she didn't brush away.

"Did you miss him?"

She looked at me as if trying to think what to say.

"I worried more about the ones closer to hand. Donald took our father's death very hard. He blamed himself even though he was only a child when it happened."

She was interrupted by the sound of yelling in the living room, my father shouting, "I should have gone to live alone in a shack in the woods!"

Joe yelling back, "I'm just no good at it. You know it never turns out!"

"Go, then. I don't need your help!"

Joe came into the kitchen and disappeared out the door with a backward look at my mother. I expected my father to yell after him as I remembered him shouting at Francis from the door, for the entire world to hear, as he ran off down the street, "No one will miss you if you don't come back!"

Watching from the verandah on that earlier night, I saw the way Francis almost stumbled when he heard that. When he recovered his balance, he ran faster.

Neil stayed where he was in the living room and as the back door slammed shut, I put a hand on Mama's elbow to make her look at me. "Go get him," I said, holding her eyes with mine.

"Don't worry, he'll be back." She didn't look to me as if she believed it, and suddenly I had so many questions they all came out in a jumble and had to be whispered so my father wouldn't hear. "Why is he always so cross? Why does he always say that mean thing about the shack in the woods?"

Mama dried her hands on a dishtowel and seemed to be absorbed in its checked pattern.

"We trail more than clouds of glory."

"What does that mean?"

She looked up as if she'd forgotten I was there.

"When I met him he sang all the old Gaelic songs and played harmonica. He's just tired all the time now. The house is too much for him and the only one who can really help now is Joe."

The map was not a map of the world but it was all the map I needed. Instead of doing my homework, measuring the distance between capitals and converting the inches to miles, I was working on a different calculation. "How many days would it take to walk to Toronto?" It was early morning and I was tracing the route west from Cape Breton while Mama scrubbed a pot in the kitchen sink.

"When you leave home, I'm sure you can find a better way than on foot," she answered.

When I looked up I couldn't see her face, so I said to her back, "I'm never leaving home."

"More likely wild horses couldn't stop you when your turn comes."

"Do we all have to go when we turn sixteen?"

The pot she was cleaning clattered in the sink before she turned around. Her eyes seemed filled with tears. "No, darling. No. No, you don't." She grabbed a dishtowel to dry her soapy hands and rushed to put her arms around me.

At breakfast that morning Joe sat at one end of the table eating his porridge and reading Louis L'Amour. Neil sat at the other end quietly eating his eggs and bacon and didn't seem to even notice Joe was there.

I kept waiting for the fight they'd begun the night before to start again, but Joe got up to go to school. He said, "I'll be home by four to help with the wallboard." Neil kept cutting up the bacon and didn't look up when he answered, "Good then." Then he looked up at Mama as if he was asking her a question, and her eyes smiled back at him.

Iona and Murdoch lined up to kiss him goodbye after Mama handed him his lunch bucket. I had to go to the bathroom right then. Then we all stood at the window and they waved while he clambered up the six-foot snowbank left behind by the plow. I didn't wave and said to Mama, "I thought Joe wasn't coming back."

"Joe isn't going anywhere. Don't worry about that. He'll leave home in his own good time."

"It wasn't a good time for Francis."

"Time will tell."

I stayed in the front window to watch Stella and Joe tackle the snowbank. For Stella it meant wading through the yard and then shovelling out a small opening to the level road. She was in high school and not allowed to wear pants, even under her dresses. In between shovelfuls she was muttering, her anger fuelling her work.

"You'd think the nuns would like pants. Covers more of you up."

Joe was sixteen by then but that didn't stop him from leaping and running up and down the walls of the bank just for fun. Stella glared at him occasionally, as he surveyed her work from above. It seemed to be enough to make him decide that, as King of the Castle, he should probably be helping his sister, who was struggling in her skirt and short boots, knees covered only with stockings. At least that's how it looked to me. He jumped back down into the yard and reached to take the shovel from her. When she resisted and grabbed it closer, he stepped back and looked at her. "It's not my fault," he said. She gave the shovel up with a shrug and Joe waved her back.

The sparkling hill became lumpy and uneven on two sides of the narrow path to the road as Joe repeatedly lifted the full shovel and threw its heavy load to one side or the other. Stella stood behind him with her hands up the sleeves of her coat and stamped her feet to keep warm. When he finished opening up the bank she conceded, "Not bad for a kid." He let out a short laugh that could be confused with coughing. She moved toward him and gave him a little sideways hug of thanks. They both trudged through the hole he'd made and I couldn't see them anymore. There was an empty shimmering space where they had been.

3

My father went out and bought a television set. It came in a cardboard box, and two men wearing blue shirts and pants left it like that in the middle of the living room after shaking Neil's hand and nodding and smiling at Mama. Neil carefully cut the box off so as not to scratch the cabinet and moved it into its permanent place in the corner. When he turned it on all we got was a grey fuzzy screen. He said, "I'll get it going tomorrow when I have the time." The next morning when Mama was stirring the porridge she said, "He thinks it will lift the gloom and make us forget our troubles."

Joe had a job at the department store downtown on the weekends and he helped Neil buy the TV on an installment plan. The job had belonged to Francis and after he left, Joe went down to see if he could have it. They said sure, so, like Francis had, he carried furniture and big boxes in and out of the trucks when they arrived at the back of the store. They paid him enough to take his girlfriend to a movie and to buy a good shirt sometimes. He bought nice things for Mama too, like a pretty vase on her birthday.

Before we got the TV set, Joe had come home one evening with a large framed photograph of a dirt road meandering off into the distance under a canopy of overarching trees. He hung it over the sofa, making sure you couldn't see the nail, and then stood leaning on the door frame of the living room. A huge smile began to spread across his face until he pulled himself together and pushed his hair aside.

While Neil put the antenna up on the roof, Mama washed the kitchen floor and we all did a chore. I didn't like to have to fill the coal scuttle. That had always been Francis's job and I thought I was better suited to vacuuming. Stella vacuumed because she was the best at that, even though I liked it. At suppertime she helped Iona set the table properly and Murdoch said, "Is someone coming to visit?" Mama laughed because she could see why he thought we were getting ready for guests.

That evening we all gathered in the living room while Neil fiddled with the rabbit ears to try to make the picture come into focus. Mama wanted *Don Messer's Jubilee* and there wasn't much else anyway, so we had nothing to argue about. There were only five children—because Francis was gone—but there still weren't enough seats in the living room for all of us to watch the thing at the same time. There was a chesterfield for the kids and two armchairs for my parents. Murdoch had to sit on Stella's lap and I sat on the back of the sofa above Joe's shoulders and combed his hair. He always had a quarter or a dime for small favours like combing his hair or scratching his back.

Pretty soon he sent me to the store to buy MacDonald's extra-strength cigarettes and a large bottle of Coke for all of us to share. Stella poured the Coca Cola out in equal measures. The rule was that whoever poured had to let all of the others pick their glass first. She asked Mama and Neil if they wanted any but they said no.

I shook my head to indicate I didn't want any either, fixing my face to show no feeling. Stella looked at Mama then back at me, and said, "You're a very strange child."

Mama said, "Let her be."

⁂

I was more than happy when the television went on the blink. A late snowstorm took out the roof antenna one day and we got to sit around the table after supper to talk for an hour without even getting up to clear the dishes. At least some of us did. My father went to read his newspaper or maybe *Popular Mechanics*. Stella went to do her homework because she was very studious. Iona read at the table and Murdoch was entertained with a paper and crayon. At least there was my mother and Joe to talk. He loved to talk to Mama, just like Francis did, and if he engaged her enough he could avoid his dreaded homework.

Joe tilted his chair on the back two legs while he listened, and when Murdoch tried to copy him he fell backwards and hit his head. When he got up, he held his eyes really wide and didn't cry. We all laughed. Mama held him on her lap because she could see he was struggling to be brave.

Joe looked at me and at Mama and put a hand out to Murdoch, "Hey buddy, want to go look at the stars?"

When Murdoch nodded seriously we all flung our coats on and raced outside to a still world blanketed in white with a clear night sky revealing all its wonders.

Mama pointed out Orion and the Pleiades and told us that the hunter would forever chase the seven sisters across the sky. Iona asked her why they didn't stop to wait and she said, "Oh, they have their reasons."

My favourite constellation was the one she called Bernice's Hair, because it was so hard to see it that part of the seeing was imagining it, and it took a summer night lying on the grass beside her to do it. The summer sky was my favourite for this reason and because it was full of heroes and swans and music. This night we had to make do with Gemini and their Little Dog.

"How can we see them if they're so far away?" I asked.

She looked at me as if pondering the weight of the question and then looked back to the sky. "The light a body radiates is measured in energy and time."

I really had no idea what she was talking about and thought she meant our own bodies, so I looked hard and long at everyone around me, trying to measure the amount of light they shed. Perhaps if I concentrated I might see light flow from a person's fingertips in a graceful arc whenever they waved hello or goodbye.

As we all stood together staring skyward, Joe wondered aloud, "How many do you think there are?"

Mama thought a moment before saying, "Impossible to say… the light takes a long time to get here. Some of them have died and left the light behind."

When I looked back at the house I could see Neil looking out from the upstairs window. The house looked very small against the background of the night sky. It was really more verandah than house. My father had always wanted a verandah and my mother joked that when he started building it, he built that first. Inside, the house was not finished but the verandah was perfect in its symmetry and grace. If you sat in the crabapple tree, looking down on it, the house looked like a jewel box, each window in line with the others and with perfect little dormers like wings that were holding us aloft. It looked snug and tight and there was no way to tell from the outside that there was no insulation and that the rafters and boards of the roof were exposed without any inside plaster or wallboard. My father meant to close it in but he was always too tired after a day at the steel plant to take up his tools and carry the heavy wallboard up the stairs to finish a job he had started so many years before. And Mama said that most weeks when he came home with the pay envelope and gave it to her to manage, there was just enough for the food we ate or maybe a much needed pair of shoes or a coat, let alone building supplies.

Luckily for us, the nails that were holding on the roof stuck through the rafters and, in winter, gathered frost and formed pinpoints of reflected light that we fantasized were stars. Many nights Iona and I made up our own constellations. Stella pretended she didn't care what we were saying and only wanted to go to sleep. One of our favourites was when we had Orion playing the Lyre for the Seven Sisters. We hummed a tune that went with it and had no care at all that we were mixing up the summer and the winter skies.

Once the noisy TV set was repaired, it banished these long, glorious conversations forever. Sometimes I had no idea what to do with myself. For weeks I imagined getting up in the night, dragging the heavy television to the brook and watching it sink to the bottom of the frog pond.

Mama spent a lot of time on the phone with her friend Wilma, telling her of all her plans to fix the house. "I'd really like some wallboard in the main hall at least. I'm embarrassed to have people in for bridge," and after some commiserating murmurs from Wilma, "No it's not normal at all. We've been here for ten years." A pause and then, "There's no pretending anymore that we're just a young couple starting out and building as we go along."

It was while listening in to one of these conversations that I heard her say, "He always has to have it his way." When she noticed me in the room she held her mouth thin before saying, "Well, at least he never drank," which I understood to be some kind of mitigating factor in their argument.

While Mama spent her time imagining an improved house, I took to building a private road, a good six inches wide and lined with stones, leading from the back door of the house. The plan was for it to meander away through the woods and down the hill to the brook that lay below us at the base of a long slope. It avoided the main path that I often travelled along on my visits to the frog pond. I had no idea what the road to Toronto looked like but there was a dirt track that led out of town on the way to the goat farm up the road, the same road that the black car with the big fins sped away on. I decided to model it after that.

It was a way to stay outside in the lengthening evenings without raising anyone's alarm. In a short space of time it became a passion. I collected stones and pieces of glass that could be used to delineate the road and cleared everything else in its path. It was just as well they were so busy watching the television because if Murdoch or Iona came out and absent-mindedly kicked the rocks aside I became quietly furious and wouldn't even look at them until I had repaired the damage and added a length of road for good measure.

There came a morning though, a Saturday, when my father was up early as always and I watched from the bedroom window as he carefully skirted the road and followed its length away from the house. I heard my parents talking about it after he came in for breakfast, when they thought we were all sleeping. He laughed and said, "Maybe it's a good thing. The next time the government changes she can get a job on the highway."

He came out to the verandah before supper and sat down to watch as I worked in the yard. It had rained the night before and the path was no longer smooth so I was combing it with a broken red comb that Mama had given me. The comb was the same width as the path and was actually the perfect tool for the job. Even the missing teeth in the comb worked well because it made the marks it left look like a tractor or a big truck had been through.

After a while Neil said, "That comb makes a nice little toy."

I pretended not to hear.

He watched while I sat back on my haunches and studied the road as if that was all that mattered to me.

"I didn't mean to disturb your work," he said. Then he rose from his seat and disappeared into the house.

I would have liked to tell him about the large heavy thing in my chest that made it hard to breath. It was a worry but how could I let him comfort me when he wouldn't comfort Francis?

By June the road had reached its destination and I could follow along beside it or even walk right on it if I carefully put one foot ahead of the other. It was always cleared of grass or pebbles and I made sure to lay a dirt bed on it that was smooth and even. Clover was in bloom so I sometimes put clover flowers on the top of the stones that I thought of as boulders. I didn't mind taking the time to do that, even though it slowed the building and the next day the clover had to be cleared because it was brown and dried and no longer beautiful. I thought it was worth it for a holiday atmosphere once in a while.

4

"Bring some cards in case of a rainy day. We're only going for three weeks now. We'll come home for a week and then go again for all of August, so don't worry if you forget something."

The steam from the iron rose and curled wisps of Mama's hair around her face. She lifted her head from her work and smiled as she looked for my response.

She planned to come back in mid-summer to check on Neil and Joe because they weren't coming with us. My father never came up the country to stay, and this time Joe was staying home as well because of his new job.

"Is Francis coming?" I asked.

She bent her head back to her work.

"No, dear. Francis is in Toronto. How can he come?"

"What if he comes home and we're gone?"

"He's not coming right now. He'll come sometime," she said. "Go get ready." She went back to her ironing, making her voice soft and light. "Only one doll. You won't be playing inside much."

I stood motionless in front of her. She put the iron back on its stand and looked at me in the way that meant there is no more to be said.

"I'm not going without Francis. There's no point!" I said.

"Of course you are. Uncle Donald will be here in an hour. Help Iona pack."

"I'm staying here with Neil and Joe. When Francis comes home we'll go up on the bus."

"Eileen! Francis is not coming home right now! And you are coming up the country with us."

She didn't stop me when I rushed from the room and from the house, letting the door slam behind me. The branches snagged my clothes and the birches made quivering shadows on the path as I ran hard all the way to the brook.

The pond the brook flowed into lay perfectly still and I sat on my heels at the edge, carefully scanning the surface. I wondered why the frogs had not come when I'd built the perfect road for them to travel on.

I picked up the bucket we'd left behind to scoop up tadpoles and started digging for no reason at all, ignoring Mama's calls.

31

She loomed above me in no time.

"Don't you ever ignore me when I call you. I have more things to do than chase around after you. Get going."

All the way up the path she flicked at my arm with her fingers.

When I slunk through the kitchen door Stella was making sandwiches for the trip and everything else was set to go. She said, "It's lucky for you Uncle Donald is late."

Back out on the verandah, Iona was kneeling over her suitcase, with the contents spread out around her, repacking it. Her eye had been caught by the comic book she pulled from the bag and her dark curls covered her face as she bent to read it. When Mama saw that, she sighed. "Go get your bag," she said to me.

At noon we were still waiting while Mama tried to keep us from getting bored and wandering off. Murdoch and Iona played Snakes and Ladders, and Mama and Stella read. We were all hungry so we ate some of the egg sandwiches.

"He must have some business to attend to," Mama said, but she sat on her hands on the top step of the verandah and stared out into the empty road. She noticed I was watching her and swung her arm around me.

"Don't worry. He's coming."

"Sure," I said.

The verandah was reduced to a quiet buzzing. I squirmed out from under Mama's arm and went to the kitchen to lie face down on the chaise, tracing the light with a finger as it fell in diamond patterns on the kitchen floor. The light moved in a wide arc as the back door opened when Donald came in.

He sat down facing me on the side of the chaise.

"Say ahhh," he said. He pursed his lips and nodded as he peered into my open mouth. We played this drama of him as the doctor and me as the patient as if I had a sore throat, even when I didn't, because I so often did have one. He acted at being very serious when he urged, "Don't be showing those tonsils to any doctor. They'll be taking them out as quick as look at them."

Our voices drew Mama into the kitchen. "Oh, you're here, are you?" she said as if we hadn't been waiting at all. Their tall frames resembled each other but the sun coming through the windows did not glint off his hair with red highlights as it did with hers.

He shook his head, apologizing, "I had a flat tire. Had to hike back to the gas station."

Mama said, "I'm surprised you got here at all."

"You knew I would come," he said.

"Sorry. We're all a bit out of sorts."

He looked at her with a question in his eyes. She looked back at him with a smile that was hardly there. Then they were all hustle and bustle getting the bags into his grey and white Plymouth.

"A little more room this year," he said. As if we should be glad of that.

Usually on the trip to the country I sat on Francis with Joe and Stella crammed in beside us in the back seat of the Plymouth. Iona would be in the front beside Mama, who held Murdoch on her lap. But on this day, with no Francis and no Joe along, Murdoch fell asleep on Stella's lap, leaning on her with a bit of baby drool wetting her neck. She made a disgusted face but she didn't wake him.

In my mind I was already on the path that ran in a wandering circle through Gran Isabel's property, and at every turn I saw him. He stood up ahead with a flat blade of grass, he and Joe both trying to make the thing whistle. When I asked him to show me how to do that, he knelt on both knees and picked a wide blade to hand to me.

"Hold it taut between your thumbs," he said. "Keep your thumbs as close as you can get them and then blow with all you've got."

I focused with an intensity I rarely had experienced and the result of my work was a blasting trumpet sound that surprised us all. Francis sat back on his heels and grinned at Joe and then at me. "There you go. You can do anything." And I thought perhaps I could.

With the memory of that, the hard lump at the base of my throat began to soften.

As we neared the end of the day's journey, a winding curve revealed an open field running down to the sea under a sapphire sky, and the newly paved road stretched around the landscape like a black ribbon on a blue and green dress. "That would be a magnificent painting," Mama declared to no one in particular, but in the same voice she usually saved for our father.

The weeping willows lining the dusty track welcomed us with waving arms as we drove up the lane to the house. Grandma stood at the end of the gentle incline, one raised hand shielding her eyes from the setting sun, and peered toward us down the lane. Even at a distance the contrast of her hair and her eyebrows was striking. The hair was white and tied back in a bun but the eyebrows above her blue eyes were still brown and full. The juxtaposition made it feel as if I was looking at two different people at the same time. Mama noticed Gran's furrowed brow even at a car length away and through a dusty windshield. "I wonder how long she's been waiting."

The moment the car glided to a stop, Gran was talking to us about food while inviting us to pile out. "Finally! I hope you didn't stop for tea. I have it all ready."

Mama was gathering bags and belongings from the front seat of the Plymouth but she stopped and looked at her. "We didn't stop at all," she said. "Donald had a flat tire and took some time to get it repaired." Gran nodded in that way she had of gently flicking her head up. She turned to welcome the rest of us as we spilled into her yard, but it was Iona who headed for her outstretched hands. With her arms around Gran's waist and her head buried in Gran's bosom, I noticed how similar they were: the same muscled limbs, the small stature. When it was my turn she held me away from her at arm's length and said, "I see you're planning to be tall." As if it was a choice. She hugged me with her strong encircling arms and I yearned to be released into the fields.

She turned to Uncle Donald. "There is something wrong with the pump. Muriel has gone into the village to get some part of it."

"I'm sure I could fix it in a minute."

"There was no minute of yours to be had. We were making supper."

"I'll have a look at it." He turned and hurried to the back of the house, glad to get away perhaps.

Inside the door of the parlour our bags clattered to the wood floor. Mama shushed us. "It's just as easy to put those down quietly."

"I don't know what is wrong with young people these days. They can't seem to stand a little noise," Grandma remarked.

Mama tilted her head to one side, looking away from her mother.

"Where are the children?" she asked, meaning the children of Uncle Donald and Muriel, who all lived there.

"The boys went off to the swimming rock. You took so fearful long to get here we thought you weren't coming. Isa is gone with her mother trying to find a part of the pump."

"You think Isa will be any help?"

"If Muriel wants to have her baby with her every minute, it's not me who'll interfere with that."

Mama glanced at me and nodded toward the grey divan at one end of the large room, so I pushed Iona and Murdoch ahead of me to sit down. The springs were not exactly sharp but I could feel the round outline of each one against my legs. Stella sat opposite on a footstool embroidered with green thistle on a black background. Above the wood-burning heater that sat to one side in the room was a mantelpiece on the wall with pictures of various groupings of family past and present. My favourite was one of a large group of people of all ages sitting in front of the house before grass or trees had grown around it to anchor it to the land. The picture was taken from some distance and there were no weeping willow trees to be seen. The men wore farm clothes with jackets over them and the women wore long dresses. Gran was a child, standing at the knee of her own grandmother, who looked awfully dour to me. In the picture Gran was the only one smiling. The first time she saw me examine it, she'd said, "We were meant to not smile but the man with the camera covering his head looked so ridiculous I couldn't help it. I was just a kid."

Now Gran raised her voice to be heard from where she sat at the far end of the room. "Stella, jump up and get the tea. We'll have to make it supper, it's so late. Bring the meat first, dear."

Stella glanced in my direction, with a twitch of her eyebrows, as she moved toward the kitchen. I envied her age. It so often gave her reasons to escape.

"Eileen, come help me," she called from the other room.

We returned with plates of ham and devilled eggs and steamed Swiss chard cut up and laced with butter and vinegar. After we'd had our fill, eating from plates on our laps because this was meant to be tea, not supper, and Gran was satisfied we'd had enough, she nodded toward the kitchen and we rushed to bring in the fresh bannock with cinnamon, just the way Murdoch loved it, and banana bread and date squares and creamy tea.

As we ate, Grandma watched and motioned to Stella to replenish the plates when we finished anything. We'd all been warned by Mama not to take the last piece but sometimes it was hard to remember.

"It will be a strange summer without the boys," Gran said to Mama.

Francis was not only the oldest child; he was the oldest grandchild.

"I can't imagine what Neil was thinking letting him go like that. Stella, you'll have to take care of the little ones."

"Oh, I will."

"I'll help," I said, looking for more responsibility, as a nine-year-old will.

When we were dismissed after tea, we bunched up at the door waiting to be set free by Mama's one instruction to "Stay away from the marsh." When I looked back, she was leaning toward Gran, talking quietly and seriously to her. I would rather have stayed to hear.

The path to Aunt Effie's led in a wandering circle connecting all the houses and barns and doubling back, lower down in the field, just above a wetland that was forbidden to small children. In case Iona and Murdoch were unaware of that, I insisted they hold hands as we walked single file along the well-worn earth.

The first time I was allowed to make the trip through the field and across the creek to visit Gran, I was three years old.

Pale green silky hay rose on either side of me. I was in a shimmering, shifting tunnel with clear blue sky above and I was alone. Never mind that my mother stood at one end of the path and waited until she saw Muriel's hand open the screen door. Nor was I aware that she had rung ahead and warned them of my coming. I was out in the world on my own and that feeling of pride stayed with me and anchored me whenever I had to step into the world alone.

By measuring my height against that of the August hay on both sides of the path, I can always determine my age in any particular memory of the farm. In the earlier recollections, I am walking through walls of softly waving grass and cannot see above the hay at all. When I am slightly older, I can catch a glimpse of the land when I stop, and jump up as high as I can, to peek above it. That summer I turned nine and, walking slowly along the path, I could see above the hay perfectly and the field fell away and stretched below me like a great inland sea.

On our way we ran into Effie's husband. He was tall and his hair was white too, although he didn't look old. He picked up our heaviest bags and motioned us ahead of him. As we passed under the arch of his raised arm, he said, "What took you so long? I have to go tomorrow. I was afraid I'd miss you altogether." I was sorry he was leaving. He was a carpenter and he often worked away. When he followed us into the house he caught Aunt Effie's eye. "Here's your company. You won't even notice I'm gone."

Aunt Effie had no children but her home was built as if they were expected. The ceilings were high and it was newer than Grandma Isabel's. The porch at the back could hold all the coats and boots that we and other cousins would bring, and it had proper iron hooks on the walls instead of the nails used at our house. I ran to sit in the broad window seat in the kitchen that would be the place to settle for a good read.

Aunt Effie began assigning rooms. "Stella, you can have the little bedroom off the kitchen by yourself."

Stella was so happy but she tried to keep her face straight. I understood that she needed to get time alone. She had no private road.

"Iona and Eileen will be in the front bedroom and Murdoch will go in with your mother. You might as well settle in now. There's no light left to spend any time outside."

There was no point in arguing so we went to wash our faces in the pantry basin.

The next morning a sweet, milky smell embraced me like a friend when I wandered into the barn and sat in the soft hay piled in one of the stalls. Light fell in beams, through swirling hay dust, from high, thin windows near the roof, and lit up my feet. Small barn creatures could be heard scuffling and scurrying, living their lives somewhere just out of sight. Thinking I'd heard a bird in the roof somewhere, I climbed the ladder to the loft full of loose, fresh hay, tossed there in the days before.

After jumping for a while and covering myself with the hay, I fell into a kind of trance remembering the last time I'd played there with Francis. We threw hay at each other and he showed me how to move from one loft to the other along the beams in the roof. With him along I was brave enough to do it.

Together we'd gathered up large bundles of hay to throw on the barn floor below until there was enough for him to jump in it. I was only eight then. "You'll have to wait," he said. "You're still too small. Next year."

Realizing that it was "next year," it occurred to me that I was old enough to jump, so I threw hay down until I'd built a small haystack on the floor below. The heap looked substantial to me, as I lay above it, leaning over the edge, and deep enough to receive me if I jumped. I backed off and took a running leap, free-falling through air just as Mama and Aunt Effie entered the barn. It must have been a shock to see me hurtling out of the rafters that way, but they didn't cry out.

Landing at their feet, in a seated position, with a thump on my tailbone, I couldn't speak even though I wanted to. My mother put her arm out to hold Effie back from scooping me up, and said, "It's okay, she just had the wind knocked out of her." She knelt closer and said to me, "You did well. That was very high. You made a good cushion for yourself." Then I knew I wasn't hurt at all and nodded so she'd know I was all right.

"Donald and I often jumped from there," she said, "but usually there was a whole load of hay here when we did it." Then she pulled me up and started picking the hay off my clothes, but not before I'd had an image of her in my mind as a child in this spot where we were standing.

We walked back to the house in single file along the hay path in silence. I was sore but I felt quite proud that I'd survived and that Mama seemed to understand me. I hoped she'd tell Francis I did it just the way he showed me.

Sometime earlier, Iona and Murdoch had fallen asleep playing hide and seek and when the house grew quiet Mama had noticed I was gone and came to look for me. When we got back she showed me where they were sleeping in the closet under the stairs. She opened the small door carefully and we peered inside. Murdoch was curled up with his head on Iona's shoulder. I thought she must have been telling him a story. They were covered with a blanket and looked comfortable enough, so we quietly closed the door.

The verandah was on the north side of the house and we sat in the shade, watching the road at the other end of the tree-lined lane, listening to the sounds of Aunt Effie making lemonade, the hiss of the kettle and the clink of chipped ice. When she came back outside, Murdoch trailed behind her with sleep-spoiled hair and one side of his face red from having slept so long in one spot. "Is Iona still asleep?" Mama asked when she saw him.

"She's reading. I'm going to Gran's to see the baby."

"Perhaps Eileen will take you."

"No," he said. "I want to go alone. I'm big now."

"You can't go all that way alone," Mama said. I looked at her with raised eyebrows. She raised her eyebrows back at me and said to Murdoch, "Fine then. Come in and comb your hair and we'll walk you to the path."

Aunt Effie took him to the porch sink to wash his face and Mama turned the crank on the wall phone to call Aunt Muriel. After a moment she said quietly, "Murdoch's coming to see you on his own. I'll watch at this end."

"Everyone is looking for adventure today," she murmured as we watched him go.

That evening Mama talked to Neil by phone and, from my hiding place on the stairs, one thing she said stood out.

"She came flying out of the hayloft today and knocked the wind out of her. Not a word of complaint." There was a pause while she must have been listening to Neil.

"I'm worried sick about her, but I can't very well keep her out of the loft. She'd be broken-hearted."

In the middle of summer, when we came home to see how Neil and Joe were doing, Uncle Donald's son, John, came along because his fiddle needed repair and there was a good man in town to do it.

Mama invited them in. "Don't be in a hurry now," she said. "You know Neil would like to say hello."

"Of course I'm coming in," Donald replied.

We scattered upstairs to our rooms to make sure everything was the same as when we left. Usually Neil did some work on the house while we were gone. It was a relief to see that nothing had changed.

When I ran back down, Donald and Neil were clapping each other on the back and punching each other on the arm. They pushed through the bags of vegetables and milk and pork, which we'd brought from the farm, to go out to the verandah where they could sit undisturbed.

In the kitchen I quietly asked Mama, "Why do they do that punching thing?" Something about it felt dangerous.

She smiled. "They used to box together. For some reason, after the war, it helped both of them to have an adversary who was a friend. Your father had some episodes in those early years when the war would reach out and clutch at him as if it was some kind of evil spirit. Donald didn't react in the same way but he understood it better than the rest of us, having been there. He took care of Neil for a while until he mostly got over it. So sometimes they pretend to punch each other a bit. Like children would do."

I shrugged to pretend it was no big deal, but I still didn't like it.

"You know that Donald introduced us?" she asked.

"You never told me that."

"I assumed you knew that. Everyone else does."

"People don't tell me things," I said.

"If you ask me, people tell you quite a lot of things."

At that point I didn't agree.

Moving as quietly and unobtrusively as I possibly could, I went to sit on the verandah step. They noticed me right away.

"Did you draw some good pictures?" Neil asked.

I quickly shook my head.

"Well… that's too bad."

Donald spoke to cover the silence. "You know your father and I played at the dances before you were born. I was on the fiddle and he played harmonica. We were quite a hit."

"If you say so," said Neil.

"We met in the middle of a brawl," Donald said to me.

"Now don't tell her things she has no business knowing. She takes note of everything."

"Your father was a painter then."

Neil moved his head in a kind of sideways nod.

"A brawl?" I asked Donald. They both looked away.

"Never mind about that now. We're both better men than we were," Donald said.

On Sunday we went to church, walking the distance, with Neil and Mama walking ahead and all of us behind. There'd been a big fight trying to get Joe out of bed in time to go. Ever since Francis left, Joe didn't seem to want to go to church anymore. Neil had to yell to get him up, so everyone was out of sorts.

We were late and had to sit at the back. When the nuns who kept blocking my view moved, I could see the virgin standing with her foot on the head of a snake while she held her baby. Silently I asked her, "Will you please ask God to send Francis home? We need him."

She looked right at me but I wasn't sure she was listening. Mama always said it was better to ask the virgin to ask God for you, but I wondered if I should ask him myself.

Neil arrived at the end of the pew with the collection basket. He tried to catch my eye, but I pretended not to notice.

When we came down the big front stairs after the mass, one of the women waiting at the bottom asked Mama, "Have you heard from Francis? We heard he went to look for work."

"Yes, he did," Mama told her. "Hopefully just for a year. He'll try to save some money and come home."

I never heard that theory before.

But then the woman said in a joking way, "The next thing you'll hear he has a girlfriend and wants to stay."

"God forbid," said Mama. "He's only seventeen."

"That's what happened to mine," the woman said. "Comes home once a year is all."

Mama looked down at me and just gave her head a little shake with half-closed eyes, as if we shared an understanding.

Late in the afternoon, when the clouds were scudding across the sky, casting shadows that ran away before me and turning the world alternately light and dark, I went out to check on the road. I was planning to replace flowers that had faded and any stones that may have been rolled out of place by a stray animal. We lived at the edge of the town and the woods covered a vast area of a hundred square miles behind us. Sometimes the deer came into our yard in the early morning or at dusk and stepped on my road.

It was perfectly intact, although somewhat soggy from the rain. I loaded on some buttercup that was blooming nearby. It was five thirty but, as the days were quite long, there was lots of time to visit my favourite rock, a small outcropping. It took the shape of a cat and had a pointed spot that looked to me like the cat's nose. After my cat, Blackie, had been hit by a car, I'd watched from the upstairs window and saw my father pick him up and throw him into the woods with a long arching pass. For years I thought the rock was his petrified remains. Although I told myself I'd outgrown this belief, I still went there whenever I needed to be alone with my thoughts.

Near the edge of the woods grew a beautiful undisturbed blueberry patch with very large berries. I picked and travelled and picked as I went, and eventually lost my bearings completely. I will never know why I didn't scream for help while I still might have been in hearing distance of my family. I think it never even occurred to me because I was so sunk in my silence.

After running in all directions and not returning to the cat rock or finding any sign of our house, my heart was racing and I was breathing so quickly that I made myself sit down on my heels. A house sat on a hill some distance away and I hoped to find some help there, so I started in that direction, pushing branches and small trees aside.

The woods were thick and wet from the recent rains, and it was hard to make my way. I think I managed to stay on a straight path but, after half an hour or so had passed, I was so deep in wood that I could no longer see the distant landmark I was using to guide my way. Instead, I came to a small clearing that I realize now must have been a sleeping place for deer. Leading out of this clearing was an animal path that I decided to follow because at least there was some comfort in thinking it might go somewhere.

There were places on the path where I could not stand up and had to crawl. The ground was damp and the knees of my pants were soon wet. I worried that I might meet some animal head on, as I was on all fours, but at least it was continuous and there seemed to be no going back. The only creatures I met were bugs and a small garter snake who slithered away from me.

I was standing again and able to travel quickly when the path completely vanished. It ended in a meadow ringed by forest and left me with no sense at all of which way to turn. I knew I could go back on the deer path but that led back into the woods and the sun was sinking. I decided then to begin yelling. "Help me! Help me!" rang into the silence of the field, but there was no returning sound, not even an echo. There was only the sound of my racing heart and somewhere the babble of water.

Perhaps only ten minutes passed, although it felt much longer, as I stood at the edge of the field gathering courage. Eventually I decided to walk along the perimeter and try in some way to get my bearings. If I could have seen the ocean I would have headed in that direction, knowing I'd find someone there. But all the trees at the edge of the meadow looked the same. There was no way to tell how far I'd travelled. The setting sun stayed in one place so *that*, at least, was comforting.

When I stopped again it occurred to me that I might be there all night and I started to scream again. "Mamaaaa!" In the silence that followed, the sound of running water seemed to call louder in return. What if it was tricking me? What if I got into the woods and the sound disappeared?

The lupins growing in the field nodded to me and I saw that I could pick them and lay down the petals behind me at least for some way into the woods. The blooms snapped off easily, so I gathered all I could carry and started into the dark forest, dropping them behind me every few feet and making sure I could see the one I'd dropped behind it. The water sound did not diminish and before long I came to a high bank where I could see a stream running below. My heartbeat slowed to a pace where I could breath more easily. I decided it must be the brook that ran behind our house, although I'd never been that far along it before. This spot was obviously upstream from home because beyond us the creek wound its way through an open field.

To follow it, I had to climb down the high bank. Some of the way there were trees to hang on to and sometimes I had to slide on my bum. I slid and scraped my elbows at one point but there was no real damage done. Soon I was sitting a few feet above the water on a steep slope. I could see I would have to make my way by walking through the stream because there was no path along it. So I jumped and landed in cold water up to my knees. Before long I slipped on the smooth stones in the creek bed and fell, soaking my clothes completely but not hurting myself at all. I was wet and cold but had passed out of fear and into a strange determination to survive. Now that I had found the brook I knew I could even survive through the night, if I had to, and was convinced I'd find my way in the morning. But before I had gone far, I heard a whistle and my name being called. "I'm here!" I yelled and heard my father's voice calling back to me, "Stay in one place and describe it to me. I'll come there."

"I'm in the brook!"

"Good. Keep talking!"

"There are tall white birches on the bank and I can see the sunset through the leaves. It's pink and orange."

"I know right where you are. Stay there!"

I could hear him crashing through the bush when I looked down at the water running over my red sneakers. "The stones in the brook are grey and white," I hollered. He came into view then and waved his cap to me as if he was at a baseball game and the favourite team had just hit a home run. He half stumbled and half ran through the brook until he reached me and then grabbed me by the shoulders and looked me in the eyes, not saying a word. I was both relieved and concerned because I expected him to be angry, knowing I was very late. He took me by the hand, silently, and we walked in the stream bed through the cold, clear water until we came to an opening in the bushes that I recognized as the path up to our home. My own road ended there.

As we climbed the hill, the red roof of the house came slowly into view above us. Gathered in the yard were a number of neighbours who had been searching and had heard our conversation and our thrashing through the woods. They were all laughing and smiling and my mother came leaping down the hill toward us with her hair escaping its pins and flying out behind her. She picked me up in one scooping motion to carry me back to the house.

We were all safely back in the kitchen and I had my feet up on the oven door of the wood stove, Iona standing behind my chair and everyone talking at once above my head, when my father crouched down beside me and said, "The next time you go in the woods, leave a trail of crumbs, will you."

"Francis needs a trail of crumbs too," I said.

He said. "I see." And then, after a pause, "Were you looking for him?"

"Of course not. I know he's not in the woods."

"Sorry," he said quickly.

Later I heard him tell my mother that he thought I had needed to be quiet for a while, the way any wounded creature makes itself still while it's healing.

Neil played harmonica for us that night as a special bedtime treat for the first time since Francis left. He sat on a straight-backed chair in the kitchen and we sat around him cross-legged on the floor in our pajamas. None of us understood the Gaelic song he sang but I loved the sound of it anyway. "Did you learn that from your father or mother?" I asked. It was the first attempt I'd made to draw him into a story in some time.

He lifted his head to look directly at me. "When I was your age, I didn't have a father." It was the first time I'd heard that, but he immediately took up the harmonica again so there was no opportunity to ask for more of a story. Instead, I made one up that went along with the movement of his foot as it tapped out the rhythm of the song.

When I was older, and finally given access to all of the pieces, a story emerged that we all understood to be true.

5

Neil's breath followed a chaotic rhythm, as difficult to expel as to inhale, as he watched a hay wagon, carrying a plain pine box, travel slowly away from his home. A small group dressed in their best black Sunday clothes followed beside. Dust rose behind the wagon and obscured both the people and the hayfields growing up to the edges of the road.

He sat on the front step with a roundish woman with white hair whom he barely knew, because his mother said he was too young to go to his father's funeral. She left him at home, like a baby, being looked after by a neighbour. His brother Frank was only seven but she took him with her. He did not cry. Not even when they disappeared from sight.

The same box had sat on the floor the night before with his mother sitting beside it on a kitchen chair, holding him in her lap. He studied the way her tears flowed in steady rivers all the way down to her collar. She stared at the box as if it might speak.

He prodded her, "Open it, why don't you?"

"I don't want to disturb him," she said.

He fell asleep in her arms wondering when his father would wake up.

In the morning he woke in his bed to the sound of unknown male voices and the movement of furniture in the adjacent room. He jumped from the quilted cover and hurried to them, knowing he'd see his father among them, awake and laughing, slapping the other men on the back in his friendly way.

Instead, some of the men were strangers to him and they were lifting the box all together and carrying it out of the house. He looked around for his father and spoke to his mother, who sat on a kitchen chair without making a move to stop them.

"Is he still in the box?" he asked.

"Yes, he is," she replied with her eyes fixed nowhere.

"When is he coming back?" he asked.

"He won't be coming back," she said.

"What do you mean?" he yelled. "He said he was coming back!"

His brother Frank stood up then and also yelled, as if Neil would otherwise not hear him, "He's dead! The coal fell on him." His mother grabbed at Frank to hold him back.

Neil wasn't yet four years old but he knew what dead was. When the sheep died he never saw her again, and when the cat disappeared they said she was dead. He ran to his mother's side. "When is he coming back?" he demanded to know.

"He wanted to come back." She spoke as if she was talking not to him and Frank but to some unseen person who also needed to understand what had happened. "He only meant to go into the mine for a few weeks to make some wages. He loved us and he wanted to come home."

She stood up as if to go, then stooped to put her arms around him. "He's gone to heaven," she said. "You'll see him there some day."

As he clung to her skirt he heard her voice, "You stay with Mrs. Fraser. We'll be back soon."

"No! Take me!"

She turned to the round, white-haired woman. "Should I?"

"He won't be able to make sense of it," she said.

After Neil and Mrs. Fraser had watched the wagon recede from their sight, he would not speak to her or even to admit she was there, and soon she slowly raised herself from the step and went inside.

An ant was building a hill of sand at his feet. After a while he picked up a stick, spread out the sand and drew a picture of a man and a boy with the man waving his cap in the air. But in Neil's mind there was an ocean behind the boy, rushing at him, and it was his father waving the cap and calling out, "Run to me, Neil, run to me!" while he rushed toward him, finally scooping him up in his arms and saving him from the wave.

"You'd have had a good soaking," his father said, laughing and holding him upside down. "Maybe you still will." Neil shrieked and hollered, safe in the arms of this big man he knew would always save him from the wave.

Looking at the picture he'd drawn in the sand he was reminded of the blue carpenter's chalk he'd seen his father use to mark wood when he was building a new bed for his mother. He knew he could find it in the shed where his father so carefully kept his tools and yes, there it was, shimmering in the darkness above the workbench. He had to climb to reach it.

When he ran back out into the light, the emptiness of the field and the oppressive way the sun shone down on it made it feel as if the world had become absolutely vacant and the only thing left was the cool, blue chalk in his hand.

For what seemed a long time he drew another picture of the man and the boy waving to each other on the outer wall of the shed. He made them so large he had to jump to reach the father's height. The faded wooden siding was rough and splintered. He had to go over the lines many times until they were thick and blue and strong. When his mother and brothers returned he was still working the silhouettes, which towered above his small frame. His mother stood a long time staring at the drawing, then turned to him and said, "I should have taken you."

She reached out to hold him but Neil shook her off, being sure in that moment that his father was the only one who'd really known his feelings or cared for him.

The drawing stayed intact for days. Every morning he went out to look and they were still there. Weeks later it rained and some of the chalk washed away but it lasted until the heavy rains of fall. He felt he had at least done something to mark his father's passing even if his mother thought he was too small to feel it.

The following spring a young fellow delivered a cord of wood, a gift from the neighbours, and stayed to chop it for Neil's mother. The family stood on the verandah watching him there in the yard piling one split log upon the other. Neil remembered the previous winter when the wood had run out and they had all gone to the woods looking for loose twigs and pieces of fallen branch that they could haul home together in the hope of keeping warm. In this, they had no great luck.

The man's name was John Fisher; they called him Jack. The next time he came he brought his fiddle. Neil thought him an unlikely fiddle player, with fingers so short and broad. Everything about him was wide: his shoulders, his head. He sat in the kitchen, playing a jig, with his fedora on the table beside him. When he finished the first piece he said loudly, "Does no one in this house dance?"

The boys were both delighted and surprised to see their mother jump up and say, "They certainly do." Neil was too young to remember the kitchen dancing that had happened there before his father died, but Frank was not. His mother grabbed them both and pulled them to their feet. She said to Jack, "Play another." Jack delivered a wide grin and launched into a reel. Neil had never seen his mother step-dancing. Her legs and feet flew around her body with the toes gracefully pointed, a contained kind of wildness in it. Frank could make something of an imitation of her movements, but Neil was awkward and flailed around, finally choosing to sit and watch. All the tightness seemed to evaporate from her face and he could see that she had once been a young girl.

When Jack stopped playing she sat down, a bit breathless.

"I could sing now," she said.

"Well, do it then," Jack replied.

She sang a Gaelic ballad about a wife who waits in vain for her husband to return from sea. Neil saw, for the first time, that sadness could be a beautiful thing. It sobered them all, and Jack rose, saying he had to get back. She rose quickly as well and said, "I'm not always so dour. Come again."

In November, on the day Jack Fisher came to collect them for the long walk to the church where he and Neil's mother were going to marry, he brought each boy a bag of penny candy. Neil and Frank sat on the grey wooden stoop, shrunken inside their jackets to retreat from the cutting wind, while Frank ate the peppermint and licorice silently. Neil could not bring himself to open the bag of candy as long as they sat there looking at the frozen dirt road. He took it behind the barn and ate a little of it, but something about it made him want to cry. After a while, when he went back into the kitchen where they were all seated drinking tea, he handed the candy to Frank.

"I don't care for sweet things," he said when Jack took notice of it.

Jack responded with a grin to his mother, as if they shared a joke. "Well, you needn't worry. There won't be too many sweet things for you."

Neil searched his mother's eyes for meaning but she looked confused herself. She smiled and shrugged as if it meant nothing but when she looked back at Jack, Neil could see she had some worry.

She said, "Perhaps the boys should stay home. They'll be all right on their own for the afternoon. It's so bitterly cold."

Jack would have none of that. "And have them miss the most important wedding of their lives?"

They started out along the shore road that led to the church some miles away, Neil and Frank walking behind their mother and Jack. The sleeves of Neil's coat were short and he had no gloves but he jammed his hands deep into his pockets to keep warm.

He thought it was a good thing when he heard Jack say to his mother, "We'll buy them new coats with my next pay." He saw the way her hand, in the crook of his arm, tightened on the muscle and when she sighed in relief her breath became a soft cloud of mist they passed into and through.

The snow beneath their feet was wet and heavy, unmarked by other footsteps, so they all bent their bodies to the task and spoke little. The silence was only broken by the shrill sound of the wind racing across the open fields on either side of the track.

At the door of the rectory, the pastor's housekeeper drew her breath in alarm when she saw them. "Come in, come in. Have you walked all the way from the shore? The boys will have frostbite."

Neil was grateful for the gentle way she spoke as she took their coats and hung them on hooks in the hallway. "Take your boots off to warm your feet by the fire. I'll tell the pastor you need a few minutes."

"No need," said Jack. "We won't make any trouble for you. We just want to get this done quickly and be off home."

The woman looked to Neil's mother while she kept a hand on his shoulder. "Will you be moving to a new home?"

"Oh no, Jack is new to these parts. He's moving in with us."

The woman raised her eyebrows in some kind of question and Jack intervened. "It's a bit small but it won't be long before these two are gone off and the house will be plenty big enough for two."

Frank drew closer to Neil, and their mother said with a light voice, "Don't worry, you won't be going anywhere soon."

The housekeeper drew them into the parlour and the pastor was slow to materialize, so they were somewhat warmed by the time the marriage vows were given. Neil never took his eyes off his mother's face as she answered the questions. He was surprised by her promise to obey this man. He still seemed like a stranger to Neil, and he was most uncomfortable when the pastor said, "You may kiss the bride." Jack burst out with, "Finally," took her by both shoulders and pulled her to him to kiss her on the mouth. Neil and Frank exchanged alarmed but silent glances.

After the signing of the book, with the housekeeper and her husband as witnesses, they began the long journey back under a darkening sky. The children were bundled in scarves and gloves given to them after the ceremony and the whole trip seemed to go faster when they knew they were headed for home and had the wind behind them.

Nevertheless, Neil was relieved when they arrived back in their own kitchen and his mother rushed to the stove to build up the fire. He slid down beside the door and watched as Frank fed her the kindling from the box beside the stove. She was bent over, pushing the pieces into the firebox, when Jack came up behind her and put his arms around her waist.

"Leave that," he said. "We have more important things to do."

She continued with the task. "The boys are half frozen."

He grabbed her wrist and she dropped the piece of wood she held in her hand. Frank bent to pick it up.

"That's right," said Jack evenly. "You're old enough to light the fire by yourself."

"He's never done it."

His voice became tighter. "It's going to be a sorry marriage if you can't even put me ahead of them on our wedding night." He turned his head to take in the boys with a tight grin. "You fellas wouldn't want that now, would you?"

Neil's eyes were fixed on the way he still held his mother's wrist in his grip, bent over her, not letting her stand straight.

"You're hurting her!" he yelled.

Jack let go of her with a push so that she stumbled against the stove. In a second he was crouched in front of Neil with his big hands crushing Neil's shoulders. His angry words were spoken in a low hiss and so close to Neil's face that he felt the flying spittle that came with them.

"Don't you ever speak to me that way, boy. I'm the man of this house now. If you ever forget that I'll put you out that door at any time of day or in any weather I please."

He let go and stood up, grabbing Neil's mother again and leading her to the bedroom off the kitchen. "Fine example to be giving them," he said softly to her as he pulled the door closed behind them.

6

It was already dark and the playing had started when we arrived back at Gran's. The music wafted out over the field and into the dancing willows as we approached. They were all in the sun porch and, with the lights on, the screen could not be seen. So it looked as if they were sitting on a verandah, two with fiddles and the others nodding their heads and tapping their feet. We got closer and, when she saw we were within grabbing distance, Gran opened the screen door of the kitchen.

"Get in! Get in! Don't let the bugs in."

Once we were landed, she held my hands and looked me in the eye, "Still growing."

Then, when Iona came barrelling past me, Gran put her arms out for her to run into them. "You," she said, "on the other hand, have a lot of catching up to do."

She and Mama held each other crushingly and quickly let go.

"Never mind all that. Leave that now. Come sit," she said, waving her hands at our luggage and then catching sight of the fiddle sitting on top of the bags.

"What's this then? Who's playing it?"

"Neil sent it along in case someone wanted to play it," Mama said. "He's hoping Donald can teach Eileen a few things."

"He can certainly do that," Gran agreed on Donald's behalf. "Don't leave it there now," she said to me. "Bring it in." So the fiddle became mine to carry into that place of music. I was terrified I would be asked to play.

In the sun porch, the two boys kept playing as we quietly filled the room and all its corners. Iona squeezed onto the arm of a sofa chair next to Gran, and Murdoch found a small, square wooden stool that he pulled close to Aunt Effie. She put her hand on his head and kissed his hair. He wriggled away and smiled shyly. When a slow Highland dance tune they called a strathspey came to a logical conclusion, Donald announced, "We'll take a little break now. I believe we have some folks who need tea."

We all crowded back into the kitchen for tea and biscuits with strawberry jam, and I got to sit beside John, who was the best fiddle player now that Francis was gone. At least that's the way I saw it.

He picked up the fiddle from where it sat beside me on the bench. "I'm surprised Francis didn't take it with him."

"I'll take care of it," I said.

"You will. Are you going to learn to play it?"

"I doubt it."

"That's what everyone thinks at first."

I wanted desperately to learn to play Francis's fiddle but it seemed a terrible lie to pretend I could.

⁂

I hadn't seen it since Francis left and I was surprised that morning to find it lying in its open case on the kitchen table. I looked around quickly to see if Francis came with it. The light from the open door fell on the warm blond wood of the instrument so that it glowed the colour of honey. I gently plucked one string, looked up as its gentle tone filled the room and saw Neil filling the doorway.

"Sorry," I said.

"No no," he said. "That's why I brought it out. I thought you might want to learn it."

I was astounded to hear him say that. I was nine years old and a girl. He couldn't be serious but he pretended to be and so I did too.

"Perhaps Iona would get along better with it."

"Iona is a fine singer. But there's more than one gift of music in this family."

"You mean Francis."

He stopped for a moment.

"You love music as much as he does."

"The way I love it is different, and this is Francis's fiddle."

"This was my father's fiddle. He wouldn't mind."

This was brand new information for me. I didn't remember any of this kind of talk when he first gave the fiddle to Francis, but perhaps they had an understanding they didn't share with the rest of us, although it seemed unlikely.

"He didn't teach you to play it?"

"I was far too young for that before he died. My stepfather played and I was about your age when he discovered my father's fiddle at the bottom of my mother's wooden trunk. I don't think he really wanted me to play. He put it on the table and he said, 'There now. That's for you.

Don't say I never gave you nothing.' I didn't know what to do with it and couldn't be sure he was serious that it was to be mine."

"I can understand that," I said.

Neil laughed. "'Try it out,' the old man said, but I would have liked to be alone the first time I tried it. I thought I might remember what my father looked like when I picked it up. Irrational thinking but... when I held it and dragged the bow across its strings, the sound was a terrible yowling. Jack laughed until he couldn't breathe and when I put it down and refused to pick it up again, he hit me across the back of the head."

Neil paused for a full minute but he still looked like he was thinking, rubbing his hand on his forehead, so I didn't want to interrupt. Finally he said, "Maybe he really did want me to play. Maybe Jack didn't know how to be a father."

"Francis learned," I said.

"Yes, he did. It was a good thing he had Donald to teach him."

"You gave him the fiddle."

"Only good thing I ever did for him, I guess. Take it up the country with you. Donald's boy John will show you."

Being given Francis's fiddle and being told I was not only allowed, but could become competent enough to play it, was overwhelming. When I wrote to him to say I learned to play it, would he care?

"It's just a fiddle," my father said. "It's not his life I'm putting in your hands."

∂⊙

At a word from Donald we all drifted back into the sun porch. Iona and I took our place sitting on kitchen chairs closer to the musicians so we could sing when our turn came. Iona and I knew one of the old songs and whenever we sang it Gran said it made a person want to weep.

It was a song about the longing for the land left behind, and when we finished it on this night I heard Gran say, "Those mournful songs are so much better sung with the fervor of youth."

"As opposed to the indifference of age?" Mama asked, with her eyebrows raised.

"Never mind that now," said Gran.

∂⊙

The next day John found me in the barn, sitting in the loft, trying to play just one acceptable sound.

"Do you want me to show you something on that?" he called up to me.

"No thank you," I called down. "I'm fine."

"Come down here. I'll show you how to hold it."

That sounded simple, so I climbed down the ladder from the loft with him watching me and passed him the fiddle when I was halfway down. He knelt in the hay and showed me how to hold it properly under the chin and then passed it back to me. It was very awkward and kept slipping out.

"You need a shoulder rest. Those are not very padded shoulders you have there." He paused and looked around. "Come in the house with me. You really can't learn to play the fiddle in the barn. It's too dusty and you need a piano to tune it by."

An hour passed with him showing me how to hold the bow and how to tune the strings. Finally he showed me how to play some notes and how to draw the bow across the violin with one even stroke. The first time I tried it, the note rang true. The next time it was awful.

"I think that's enough for today," he said. "It takes a long time."

I struggled to find private places to make fiddle noises for the next few weeks. John helped me when he could take a break from chores. I didn't seem to have a natural leaning. I remembered that Francis did not play well at first either, but I didn't remember it being this bad.

A steady rain pattering on the roof woke us in stages. The others ran back on the path to Gran's for breakfast but I pretended to still be sleepy so that I could have some time alone. The two houses were within sight of each other and it was easy to travel along the path at a moment's notice if a person wanted a change. Instead of running, I walked and trailed my fingers through the hay with the large, warm drops of rain splashing off my bare arms.

The kitchen was already filled with the smell of sweets and butter biscuits when I stood dripping at the back door, wet right through my yellow cotton print dress. "Sit at the table close to the fire," Gran insisted. She came back from the pantry with a towel and quickly rubbed it all over my head. I could feel her bony fingers through the softness of the towel.

Uncle Donald came from upstairs just as this happened and, when he noticed the state of my hair and dress, he saluted, "I'm leaving you in charge, Private." Gran almost smiled but caught herself in time to click her tongue instead.

A yellow slicker hung from a hook by the door and Donald grabbed it and slung it over his head so he could slide both arms inside it at once. He fastened every toggle before he nodded at the rest of us, opened the door and bowed his head to face the sheet of rain. He closed it behind him with a decisive tug.

I surveyed the table to see where I could squeeze in. Aunt Muriel was feeding porridge to her baby girl. Isa looked like a smaller version of Muriel with her pale skin and her curly black hair. Her brown eyes examined us from her perch in her high chair. When I said, "Hello, darling, how are you?" she buried her face in her hands.

The kitchen and its table were a decent compensation for being rain bound. The southwest-facing window framed the field, and a low valley, set with elm trees, gradually rose to the low hills beyond. We spent the day playing cards or drawing and watching raindrops bounce off the pond that lay between the house and the barn. When Aunt Effie stopped to look at the drawing I'd made of a house with a curving walk and a boy somewhere along its path, waving, she asked, "Is he coming or going?"

"Neither one," I said. "He's just out there."

In the evening, when the rain stopped, Isa surprised us by squealing and pointing to the window. There was a burst of rose and purple streaking all the clouds in the sky.

꿈

On a dry, grasshopper-clicking day, when the grass was hot to touch, before the hay was mown, we went out to the far reaches of the path to pick blueberries. I took the fiddle with me so I could practise in relative privacy. Murdoch and Iona didn't mind if we stopped, and I made some scratching notes while they picked and ate. When I got discouraged I put it carefully back in its case. The hay was tall enough to brush my shoulders so I bent to put my arms around Murdoch's waist from behind and hoisted him up so he could see the fields and the marshland below and the elms and the hills beyond. Iona's eyes were just below the top height of the hay, but when I offered to pick her up she said, "I'm not a baby," which caused Murdoch to scowl.

"You can get on my back then," I said.

She shrugged her shoulders but when I crouched down she scrambled up and wound her wiry arms around my neck. She was almost seven but small for her age so I could carry her for at least a few minutes before tiring. I wanted to do something to show that I was older and could take care of them. Francis had taken me to an old house on the upper path once. I wanted to see it again and tried to bring them along with me.

The path switched back and forth up a fairly steep rise. In previous summers, Francis led the way, sometimes getting out of sight and yelling back, "Keep up! There'll be hell to pay if I lose you," then stopping and waiting, rolling his eyes. "Come on!"

Francis was my leader and I gladly followed him.

I did not inspire the same confidence in Murdoch and he started to complain of the heat and the climb. Iona jumped off so I could pull him onto my back. She sang "Row row row your boat gently down a stream," under her breath. The grasshoppers clicked in response and the birds called out to encourage us, so we found no need to talk or even to think. We turned back without finding the old house.

On the way home, we came across the fiddle case sitting in the middle of the path where I had left it. When I saw it there I was flooded with anxiety and shame. *What if I had lost it? Who would be more disappointed in me? Neil or Francis? Or myself?* Iona looked from me to the fiddle and said seriously, "It was safe there. What could hurt it?" I carefully picked it up and cradled it in my arms as we continued home.

That evening I asked if I could pump the water at the pantry sink while Gran washed the dishes. "Sure you can. Pull up the stepstool." I pushed down on the pump handle and water gushed from the tap. Light reflecting off it from the kerosene lamp attached to the wall made it look as if thousands of stars spilled and bounced into the basin.

"Oh, you're good at that," she said.

I thought about telling her what I'd done with the fiddle, when we'd gone for our walk, but couldn't get the words out. Instead I asked, "Is the little house on the upper path still there?"

She laughed. "I do hope so. It was, the last time I looked."

"Did you know the people who lived there?"

"Yes, I did know them."

"Where are they now?"

"Gone."

I pushed on the pump handle and waited.

"They were people from the Hebrides, dropped on the shore in September with no provisions to speak of. If the ones who belonged here hadn't helped them, they'd have starved."

She looked through from the pantry to the kitchen. Iona was sitting alone at the table. Everyone else was in the screened porch listening to Donald and his son play the fiddle. Usually Francis would be with him and they'd practise and play together, urging each other on to be faster, or sometimes one would play a tune that seemed to float slowly on the night air. The summer before, Mama would have got up and danced, but she sat quietly smiling and watching now.

"We should sit down with the others for this." Gran dried her hands and headed to the table, stopping to lift the teapot off the stove as she passed. When she'd poured her tea she looked up to see if anyone else was coming in from the porch.

"Never mind them," I pleaded on Iona's and my own behalf.

She studied our faces, back and forth, before replying and then started into the kind of story we so looked for.

"There was a child among them when they first arrived, a girl of eight. Her name was Catriona, her hair was coal black, and under her blue wool dress her body was thin after their long journey. When they were ferried from the ship to the shore in a small rowboat, she knelt, leaning back on the bench with her elbows, surveying her new world. She had lived all her life on the shore but had never seen one look so forbidding with the trees running right down to the narrow beach.

"One image floated above all others she remembered. It was that of her small brother's fevered body in his mother's arms as the ship pitched and rolled. It broke her heart that he went stiff and cold before she was allowed to touch him. She would have liked to say goodbye.

"Despite the hard journey, her mother was not sorry to see the wildness of the place. When they had boarded the ship in South Uist, there were men in English uniforms walking among their trunks and bundles of tools piled on the dock. One of them came near, so she drew her children close to her and held their hands as if they might be taken from her. When the soldier passed he stopped abruptly, looking directly in her eyes. She refused to lower them.

"'No one wants your little savages,' he said.

"Remembering this, the mother crouched down beside her daughter and said, 'Look at the colour of the sky. Isn't it just the same as the blue sky in North Uist?'

"'And as my dress,' Catriona said.

"Her mother hoped this child might throw a life buoy when her own grief threatened to drown her. The child hoped the same. They were not entirely successful in that."

Gran stopped for a moment, lost to us. It was with a question that we knew she could be re-engaged.

"Did they want to go back home?"

"Oh yes, sometimes they did. The mother spent every free moment she had wandering the shore and staring out to sea. She knew what lay on the other side far better than she knew the dark, damp place where they'd landed. In spring her husband took her away from the ocean and they settled here and built the old house."

"How do you know about her? Did you meet her?"

By this point Iona was sleeping with her head on her arms on the table. Gran paused a moment and her voice dropped a notch. "Catriona was my own grandmother and she passed on all of her stories to me. The only way to keep a story alive is to tell it. You have to make the stories your own. That's the way with stories. People either don't tell you the whole thing or different people tell you stories that contradict each other. If you're a storyteller, it's your job to make it a story that wants to be told. Where we come from, the one who keeps the stories is always the grand-daughter." Then she murmured, "You can be that granddaughter to me." In response to the confusion she read on my face, she continued in a less conspiratorial tone, "Don't worry, they'll be good stories."

I knew they would be good stories, and I have spent a lifetime re-cording them, but at that age I feared I was not capable of being this person she implied I could be.

"What if I don't remember?"

"If it's a good story, you'll remember. If not, you can forget it. Take your sister off to bed now."

In the bedroom, the curtains were off the windows for washing, and after the hour when everyone slept and there were no more creaking boards or murmuring voices to be heard, an unusual light bathed the walls. I quietly left the bed I was sharing with Iona and crept into the darkened hall where I could lean out the second-storey window at its far end to survey the field.

The moonlight was reflecting off a bank of fog that lay evenly on the land like a floating flannelette blanket. I never saw such a thing. It drew me to it and I padded downstairs, searching in the back porch for my new white summer sneakers. When I opened the door I could see there was a light on in Gran's kitchen, but as I walked toward it on the path it occurred to me that if anyone was up they'd send me home.

The hayfield was on the side of a rounded hill. In the dark, and through the stubbly hay, it was not easy to run with such abandon but somehow I did. Now I think of it more as flying because I have no memory of my feet touching the ground. Perhaps I was blinded by the fog or else I'd run down this hill so many times I knew every dip and rise.

Three-quarters of the way down I was completely enshrouded in the billowing fog and felt myself cross the lower path. We were not allowed to go below it to the marsh and, although I couldn't see in front of me, I knew the marsh was there. People say you can get caught, as if in quicksand, and that no one will hear your call for help. But I could feel the ground beneath my feet so solidly that I kept on running.

When I stepped into the water I noticed that my feet were wet and cool, but I was only standing in an oozy inch or two of water. It still held the warmth of the day and was the same temperature as the mist brushing my cheeks as it wafted by. The white cotton pajamas I was wearing covered my limbs so that I could not see them while I walked farther out into the wetland. The cloud blew over me and my disembodied hands floated before me.

A flicker of movement in the cloud drew my focus. A dark-haired girl in a blue dress walked at some distance away, and she turned to look at me with what seemed to be a kind of longing. She raised a hand in recognition before the cloud drifted between us again. I wondered if I followed her where we would go. I could see she was one of our own.

It's hard to know how long I stayed there. It could have been hours or minutes. When Mama's voice began to call to me from up above the field, I made my way back up to find her. She was racing back and forth, turning in all directions and calling my name in the mist. I called out, to comfort her, and when I ran into her outstretched, grasping arms she held me closely, demanding to know why I had left the house in the middle of the night and where I had been.

I whispered, "There's no quicksand in the marsh. You never have to worry that it will suck us up again."

She pulled back from me, her face uncomprehending, and said, "What are you doing out here?"

"I couldn't sleep so I flew down the field and took a walk in the marsh. It was like walking in heaven."

"I told you not to walk there."

"It was safe, Mama…. I saw…"

Her inquiring eyes waited for me to finish but I couldn't tell her about the girl in the blue dress. "I just knew," I said.

Mama closed her eyes for a moment and then she opened them. "If I see you walk into unknown water again, you will be one very sorry little girl. Do you hear me?"

"Yes, Mama."

She sighed and nudged me ahead of her back to bed.

I suppose I was some trouble for her.

The next afternoon Gran and I sat side by side, resting on the far side of a rise in the field, where we couldn't be seen from the house, she in her cotton dress and me in my thin cotton shorts. The hay was uncut and we'd laid a swath of it to sit on, facing the late sun, the field warm and dry from its daily baking.

"Ask me something you want to know," she said.

"Why did Catriona's family leave home?" sprang out of me.

"There you go. That's an important question." She patted my hand and looked into the distance. I knew I was in for a good story then, and I was pleased with the way it began.

"*Gu gnothuichein a thuigsinn,'s coir toiseachadh aig toicheach.*"

These were the first Gaelic words Gran taught me. I only understood much later that they represented a lofty ideal, one impossible to reach.

"*In order to understand things it is best to begin at the beginning.*"

She plucked a piece of dry grass and twisted it into knots. "Every generation seems to have their own battles to fight. It's always something. One of our own was banished to the south and when his wife returned, alone, her head covered in black, rough linen, she was left almost speechless at the memory of what she'd seen: her husband tied to a stake, with thick brush built up around him, and the flame licking at his feet before she turned to run."

"What was happening?" I asked.

"Those barbarians were burning him alive."

She noticed my silence while that information searched my mind for some place to rest.

"It's just a story I'm telling you. No need to mention I told you about the ones burned at the stake."

"So that's why they came?"

"And other reasons. They were reduced to nothing. Catriona's father was a literate man. He could have gone anywhere but this place was made to sound like a dream: one hundred acres for each man, your own fields to plow. So he brought the whole lot here."

"That must have been a relief."

"They may have felt a kind of relief, but there was no joy in their leave taking. When Catriona came down to the wharf with her mother and father to board the ship, she saw some who flung themselves on the earth and wept with no constraint at all.

"The voyage was forty days long. It was hardest on the little ones."

"Were they sorry they did it?"

"You'd think so, wouldn't you? You'd think that people who were forced to leave the home they love, and come to some godforsaken place, would never settle. In the end they belonged here. It was theirs and they were among their own. We're a loyal bunch. You can always say that for us if you're casting about for a compliment."

"Is Francis not loyal?"

A light seemed to skip across the blue ocean of her eyes when she turned her attention to me. "Stories of leaving and being left behind are all stories of survival. He's as loyal as the rest of us."

She paused and looked out over the field as the rolling blue hills beyond it flooded with an orange sunset. When she looked back and noticed I had a broad piece of grass in my hands, trying to make a whistle with it, she said, "Never mind. We're up to the present more or less."

I jumped to my feet and offered a hand. She took it, but I felt no weight when she rose from the field. She continued to hold my hand as we turned our backs to the sun and started home. When I looked up, her face crinkled and her teeth showed. I caught a glimpse of the girl in the photo on the mantle.

"Remember who you are now," she said.

I had no idea how a person could forget that but smiled a little to show agreement.

Of course I forgot to keep my mouth closed and the next morning at breakfast I told Stella about the man tied to the stake and set on fire. She told Mama I was frightened. But what I really said was that it was a frightening story. Those things are different.

That night I heard the murmuring voices of Mama and Gran downstairs. We were already in bed so I told Iona to stop singing and listen to what they were saying.

"Why on earth do you tell her those stories about burnings?" Mama asked.

"Because I want her to know that they may have said we were wild and uncivilized but that our people would never have done that. How is she supposed to know anything about us? Neil, with all the Gaelic you were so proud of, hasn't taught them a word and neither have you."

"What would she do with Gaelic?" my mother said gently.

"She'd know what kind of people we are. I want her to know we take care of our own."

"She knows it anyway."

7

Stories of leaving and being left behind lined the bookshelves of Isabel's mind. Her husband, Duncan, went away to work in Boston when Donald was ten and Jessica was eleven. The morning Isabel shared bad news with Duncan, he was shoeing a horse in the barn. She watched him for a moment before speaking. "Donald needs his tonsils out, the doctor says."

He set the horse's foot down and stood up.

"I better find some winter work. A few things will go wanting if I don't."

She nodded once, her head tilting upward.

"I'd like to plant some willows before you go. The front lane is not very welcoming."

Very soon after that he dug the holes and Isabel planted three-foot twigs that she had gathered from another family's tree. As she held each one in the ground while her husband filled in the holes, she said, "This is a good place for them. The creek will satisfy their insatiable thirst."

Her husband lightheartedly replied, "It's your insatiable thirst these trees will be quenching."

"I have no idea what you mean."

He stood and put his arms around her.

A picture of Duncan and their eldest, Malcolm, standing on the wide verandah of a large and finely constructed, but still unshingled, house arrived in a letter with the Christmas packages. Isabel carefully put it back in its envelope. "Put this in the china cabinet, Jessica."

Jessica pulled it out to look at once more before tucking it away. Her father held a carpenter's square and Malcolm held a level, and they were smiling. There was no question of who was building the house. The snowdrift in the picture was just like the one against their barn. She put the letter between two teacups on the shelf.

On Christmas morning the whole family sat around the perimeters of the parlour, waiting for a sign that they could open presents. Their mother sat with them while they stole glances at the packages on the sideboard. Eventually she rose to retrieve them and put a box wrapped in red tissue paper beside Jessica on the divan and another one beside Donald, who sat cross-legged on the floor. Then she put a box wrapped in brown paper on the seat of another chair that their older brother, Angus, would occupy as soon as he'd washed up after milking the cows. On Effie's lap she placed a neat square box with a red satin ribbon.

"The best things come in small packages."

Effie looked at Jessica and squirmed a bit in her seat.

Finally their mother set one gift on the table beside her own chair. The children darted curious looks at it because usually their parents didn't get presents.

"As soon as Angus gets in here, you can open them," she said. Her eyes showed strain as she looked from one to the other of her children, searching for reaction. Jessica wanted to put her arms around her mother and lay her head on her shoulder. She could see that her mother was trying to be festive because it was usually her father who provided the levity. He often worked away but had always before made it home for Christmas.

The back door opened and was slammed shut by a cold blast of wind. No one spoke while they waited for Angus to appear. When he did, with his red hair windblown and dusted with snow, he stopped a moment considering where to sit. Isabel motioned him to the chair normally occupied by their father.

Effie, the smallest, was allowed to go first and found a miniature china doll wrapped in layers and layers of tissue to keep it from breaking. It still sits in her cabinet, years later, in a place of honour alongside her best dishes.

One by one, Donald pulled out a set of small wooden horses, each one different but perfect, and a note that he was old enough to be keeping his own stable now. Every Christmas for the next four years he would round them up and place them under the tree in exactly the same positions. He said they were wild horses stampeding.

When it was Jessica's turn, she undid the green ribbon and wound it on her fingers while she kept her eyes on the box. There was no tear in the tissue after she unwrapped it. The winter coat she found inside was a reddish brown, much the same colour as her hair. She slipped it on and stroked one sleeve, the velvety wool fabric so soft under her hand. Isabel told her to go see it in the long mirror in the hallway. She was pleased to have a chance to admire it in private and decided that it made her look more grown up.

"It seems to fit," she said when she returned to the room and saw they were all watching her expectantly. Her mother smiled slightly and Angus spoke as she reluctantly pulled the coat off. "It looks good. The colour is right for you."

She folded it carefully, put it back in the box and left it under the tree where she could keep an eye on it. A few days after Christmas, her mother told her to put it away. "That coat will get dusty if you leave it there much longer. Let me see you in it again."

Jessica pulled on the soft coat, grateful for the chance to feel its weight and the approval in her mother's nod.

She was gathering up the wrapping and gift box to store it away when she discovered a thin packet of white paper folded many times over. As she carefully unfolded it, the size became unwieldy. With her mother and Effie trailing behind her, she travelled to the kitchen as if holding a great sail in front of her and set it down on the table, smoothing out the whole width and length of it.

A note fell to the floor. Isabel picked it up and saw it was addressed to Jessica, so she passed it over. Jessica read silently, "Get everyone out in the field at 9:00 on Christmas night. I'll stand in the middle of the street outside the boarding house. We can all look at the same stars together." She stood staring at the note.

"We missed it. He must have been there all alone."

"Where was he all alone?" asked Effie.

"Let me read that," said Isabel. She scanned the note and looked quickly back to Jessica. "Perhaps it would be all right if he never knew that."

Jessica nodded. She wished for a chance to tell him she regretted the mix-up and ask if they could try that again, but she knew her mother must know better.

They turned their attention back to the piece of fine translucent parchment that covered the table's length. It was a carefully drawn chart of all the stars in the northern sky. Isabel remarked, "You'd almost think he drew it himself, although it seems unlikely." Jessica never doubted that he did.

She imagined him in a library, looking at books about stars and copying their pages at a long wooden table. She wondered where he got the parchment. Was it in a shop that sold it for carpenter's plans from long rolls hanging off the walls? Did he bring it to the library rolled up under his arm?

That evening she wrote to him by the steady, warm light of a kerosene lamp.

> Dear Papa,
>   Your gift of the night sky is one I will always keep close. All of us enjoyed finding the constellations. It must have been a lot of work. The coat is beautiful too. Mama says I could weather any kind of storm in it.
> Your grateful daughter,
> Jessica

ᗡᗞ

On an unexpectedly warm day in April, Isabel saw her brother, Fraser, coming across the field with his eyes downcast on the path. As he got closer she saw he was carrying an envelope. She ran out to meet him, yelling, "No, no, no, go back. The children are here." When he reached her, Fraser put a hand out to her and she steadied herself and tried to catch her breath before he handed her the telegram.

> Papa has passed away Stop I found him this morning lying on his bed fully dressed Stop I am sending his body to you but staying on to work as we have promised to complete by June Stop I will send the cheque at the first of the month Stop Your loving son Malcolm.

She returned to the house in a panic, desperately trying to think what she could say to her waiting children. When she crossed back over the threshold and saw their expectant faces, she could only manage, "Your father… is not able to come home," and fought an inclination to run out into the field as if she was being chased. Instead, she gathered them to her for reassurance.

Donald stood in the barn for hours the next morning silently watching the horses. He unfolded the note from his father that had come with his present at Christmas.

> When I saw these little horses they reminded me of you. I guess you'll soon be old enough to be keeping your own stable. Take good care of Diamond. You're the only one who understands her as I do. I'm happier here knowing she's in such good hands. I'm depending on you now. Don't be giving her

too many treats. When I get home we'll go for a ride up the mountain first thing. Your Papa.

When Angus and Fraser came in to saddle up the horses, they didn't notice him in the half-light of the barn. It was only after they hitched up the wagon and were settled in the seat that he yelled out to them. "I'm coming!"

Fraser pulled up on the reins to wait for him and without a word he climbed up on the wheels and then to the seat. Angus looked to Uncle Fraser, who exhaled a long breath before speaking. "He's best here. All of the women in the house are helping your mother, and the girls are comforting each other."

On the trip to the station, Donald wore a blue woollen scarf wrapped around his neck even though the ground was thawing and there was the beginning of warmth in the air. Most of the people they met on the road had impatiently and delightedly thrown off their coats onto the wagon seat beside them, but Donald would not part with the scarf. In the long night between the telegram and the trip to River Denys, he had made raw red scratches on his neck, tearing at the place where he'd had the operation.

Fraser signed a paper at the counter in the station saying they'd received the body. The box was heavy and they could have used more men to load it on the wagon, so a couple of the porters helped them lift it. Donald sat beside the box on the floor of the wagon on the way home, with one hand on top as if to steady it.

Late in the evening, Jessica sat curled in a corner of the divan in the parlour watching Donald sitting beside the coffin, silently setting up his toy horses in different arrangements. Effie sat opposite in her mother's lap, unable to control huge gulping sobs. Her mother encircled her with her arms but looked at the dry-eyed Jessica as she repeated, "Shush, there there now, shush." Then she said, addressing no one in particular, "I don't believe the cows have been milked."

Jessica had completed that chore in the early morning. They were usually milked again after supper but now it was close to midnight and they could be heard lowing in the barn. Isabel thought Jessica looked taller when she picked up the kerosene lamp and left the room to quietly tend to them.

One of the cows was moaning softly and when Jessica entered the stall she gently put a hand on the animal's rump and slowly lowered herself to the stool. It took an extra measure of patience and gentleness to coax the milk from the two cows, but she was able to do it. While she did she wept out loud, thinking no one could hear her, but when she returned to the house with her full pail of milk, she could see by the sorry looks she received that she was mistaken.

The day of the funeral was fine and bright and the wind blew lightly but steadily on the hillside overlooking the lake. The Bras d'Or looked as big as an ocean that day. Donald could not hear the words the minister spoke. The gaping hole they had created yesterday looked deeper and the mound beside it diminished with the earth dried out somewhat and the wind having blown it about.

His eyes were fixed on the box when it was lowered. He heard the first handful of earth, thrown down by the minister, make a solid thud on the wood below and he broke from Isabel's hand and ran toward the box, meaning to throw himself into the grave. Several people started after him but Angus got to him first and held onto him while he screamed, "No! No! No! Stop! No!" until Uncle Fraser came and scooped him into his massive arms and held him while he flailed and finally, thankfully, cried.

After the funeral, Isabel sat in the kitchen with one of the aunts, who said, "It was very hard on him to be keeping it all in."

"I can't get his attention at all. I'm afraid he's never going to recover."

"Of course he will. It takes a year to get over the grief sometimes."

Among themselves, they said they'd never seen it go so heavy in a child.

The summer passed with everyone doing a portion more than his or her share and then realizing that, in fact, this now was their share. Fraser helped with the calving and organized Angus and Jessica to take over the chores that would have so easily been done by their father. Malcolm sent a large cheque that fall. The note read, "I've had a good season. Moving down the coast now to South Carolina where the weather is good enough to work in winter. Most of the hurricane season has passed. I'll write again at Christmas."

In Malcolm's pocket, at the time he wrote the note, was a newspaper clipping he'd been saving since the spring. It described an incident of a carpenter falling from a ladder after climbing to the roof of a new house to install a weather vane on the peak. He was fairly near the top of the ladder when one of the rungs collapsed beneath his foot. When he felt himself slipping he grabbed at the side and pulled the ladder away from its resting place on the roof. His son, holding the ladder below, was unable to steady his weight. The article said the boy likely saw and heard his father's body hit the road. The son raced to his side and crouched there, then held his head in his arms while he bled.

Malcolm believed that no one at home had seen this piece. It was a small paragraph in the back pages of the daily paper. However, Isabel's sister, who lived in the state, sent her a copy of this newspaper. Although Isabel hid it away, she could not bring herself to destroy the last news of her husband. There were not so many good hiding places in the house, except for her bedroom, and the children did invade there when they could. Nevertheless, the telegram was placed in the bible as a record of his passing and no one ever spoke about the clipping.

The day they finished putting the hay in the barn, Angus found Donald sitting in the hayloft, throwing hay down to the floor.

"What's that you're doing?" he asked.

"Picking out some good pieces for Diamond."

"Oh, I think they're all pretty good."

Donald didn't look at Angus at all when he said, "I'm the one taking care of her."

"Yes, I know."

Angus worried about Donald and wanted him to laugh uncontrollably as he had in the old days or to describe every detail of some project with excitement and passion. He thought to himself, "He needs a distraction," and decided a new saddle might do it.

The sound of Donald's excited voice and his glowing eyes when he returned from the first trip round the field on Diamond, with the new saddle, proved Angus right. Isabel paused her cheese making in the pantry and let out a long sigh of relief. Jessica came from the back porch where she'd been cutting the churned butter to stack in the icehouse, and put her arms around her mother. "He'll be all right now, Mama."

Isabel was surprised by having her mind read, but spoke casually without raising her eyes. "And what about you, Jess? Will you be all right?"

"Well, seeing as I'm the only other woman in this family, I guess I'll have to be."

Isabel looked up and found Jessica smiling. As they both went back to their work, she thought about how everyone had so praised Angus for becoming a man so quickly and had scarcely noticed the coming of age (at twelve) that had happened to Jessica. She did all of the milking without a complaint, even if she took longer than she should.

Her mother had no idea that Jessica kept the star map in the barn. In the early morning, when she finished milking, she pulled it down from a shelf above one of the stalls. By the light of the lamp she opened it randomly to one small section and found a new constellation to make note of in her mind. Then she stood in the yard outside the barn, rotating slowly, matching the map to the stars as they lay above her head.

8

"You have to make things in the distance smaller. The things closest to you are not only bigger; they have more depth because you can see them better." I looked up and Neil's eyes met mine. "That's what they call perspective," he said. He leaned over the table and sketched on another piece of paper with his labour-swollen hands to demonstrate his meaning.

Iona and I were drawing at the kitchen table and he had stopped on his way to the basement to see what we were doing. The picture in front of me was of a curving road leading away from a house with a smoking chimney, the same one I always drew. Trees with red leaves lined the road. There was a boy the same height as the house standing out along the road and waving.

Mama was standing behind Neil in the open kitchen doorway, silhouetted by the red maples, surrounded by their crimson light. Iona was sitting opposite me and had stopped drawing to listen. She resumed her drawing and seemed to be absorbed in it when she spoke. "I'm close to you. Why not put me in the picture?"

There was a chance to watch her carefully, the very next day, as she sat on the ground using a flat stick to dig out a hole that was round and even, the size of half a baseball. Her attitude was one of concentration and devotion as she finished scraping it smooth. She jumped up and sat cross-legged on the grass holding open the green cloth bag of marbles that she'd been given for her birthday, so I could see what she had. I'd looked at them many times before but showing them was a rule that Stella insisted on when she first taught us the game.

The marbles were all about half an inch in diameter and were a mix of marbled glass and cat's eyes. There was a single white one. I had a bag of ball bearings that our father brought home from the plant. We called them steelies. When I opened my bag for inspection, Iona said, "Those are small but they can do a lot of damage." The steelies were heavy and could rocket toward an unprotected marble.

After choosing a blue cat's eye, she sat on her heels with her knees spread and studied the lay of the land. Then she got down on her hands and knees and carefully shot the marble. It came to an easy stop inside the hole. When she got up, her dress rose above her bare knees and she brushed the tiny pebbles off, revealing indentations they left behind in her skin.

When it was my turn I decided to crouch but as I bent, Iona asked, "Who's that?"

There was a girl around our size walking along the road toward us on the other side.

"Don't stare. It's Genevieve."

This was a girl who lived not far up the road but she went to the Protestant school and we went to the Catholic one, so we seldom crossed paths.

Eventually she stopped directly across from us. We both turned to face her and stood side by side.

Iona called out, "I like your dress!" referring to the red cowgirl dress Genevieve was wearing. She brushed her straight blond bangs out of her eyes and said nothing. Then I saw that she was clutching a bag of something to her chest.

"Would you like to play?" I called over.

She took a step and then looked carefully up and down the empty dirt road before running across to us. She stood there silently.

"I'm Eileen and this is Iona."

"I know who you are."

Without another word, she opened the pull string on her purple whisky bag with the gold tassel to show us what she had. Her marbles were three times the size of ours and seemed to be truly made of marble.

"I should get three of your marbles for each one I win. These are worth three times as much."

"That's fair," I said. "You go next."

The girl probably thought she had an advantage and was careless in how she launched her marble. That was all I could think of to explain why it bounced a bit and slowly made its way across the grass, never reaching the target. I took some time lining up my steelie and shot it with a flick of a finger. It had just enough weight and speed to shove her marble into the hole on top of Iona's, but not hard enough to propel it over the opposite edge.

All the marbles were in the hole.

I yelped with joy but when I bent to pick them up, Genevieve started screaming. "That's cheating! There's no such a thing as steelies!" I looked up to see her purple bag before it collided with my head. It knocked me back to the ground. When I opened my eyes the world looked sharp and at the same time distant. Sweat trickled down my forehead and when I wiped it away there was blood on my hand.

"She's bleeding! You hurt her!" Iona leapt up and threw her arms around the girl's neck from behind. Even though her feet left the ground, the girl couldn't shake her off and began screeching as if she'd been stung. Neil heard the commotion and came out to investigate. "Get off of her now!" he yelled.

Iona released her hold and the other girl ran away from us, yelling out so everyone in the neighbourhood might hear, "You're crazy! No wonder your brother ran away!" Neil rubbed his forehead as if it was all too much for him, but he didn't make Iona go inside. She knelt beside me on the gravel shoulder and grabbed my hand.

"Are you okay? Are you going to be okay?"

"He didn't run away," I insisted to no one in particular, but sought confirmation in my father's eyes.

"He's coming home. We know where he is."

Iona's tear-filled eyes were staring at the blood oozing from my minor wound.

Mama came out to assess the trouble and Neil said, "You better take over. This is out of my league."

Iona cried easily, but this time it was not lost on me that I was her object of concern. I began to appreciate her passion in a way I never had before. She was usually happy in a generous, inclusive way but when she was upset she would most likely be weeping or shouting. In the past I'd found her a bit hard to comfort.

That evening, when Neil was playing the harmonica for us while Mama was out at her card club, Iona sang "You Are My Sunshine" with a clear and beautiful voice. She looked and sounded so sweet that Neil stopped and laughed out loud. When he did that she scowled and stamped her feet. This he found to be very funny and his laughter caused her to wail, so finally he said to her, "I'm not teasing you."

"Yes you are," she said and set off on another round of weeping.

"Go upstairs if you need to make that much noise."

She pushed back from the table and ran up the stairs.

To me, our father said, "Go figure her out, will you?"

I went upstairs and sat on the bed with her while she cried. "I'm not silly! I'm a good singer." All I could figure was that she didn't like to be funny, or maybe she was tired from the excitement of the day.

It was bedtime anyway so we played together with our dolls even though I knew I was getting too old for it. I was the mama and she played the child with all of the dolls as sisters and brothers. When I tucked myself in with them, and lay facing her, she said, "You're my best friend now." I could see the way her eyelashes brushed her face and her hair drifted into her eyes. There were miniature reflections of myself in both of her brown eyes. Her hands, pulled up to her chest, still showed the dirt under her fingernails from having dug the hole for our marbles game.

When she folded into sleep, I lay there and thought about the way she was when Francis left. We lay in bed together that night and she didn't seem sad at all. She wanted to play bicycle, one of us at each end of the bed, feet on the other's feet, pretending they were pedals.

"That's no fun," I said, realizing that I would never want to play this childish game again.

She pulled the wool blanket over her head. "Do you only love Francis?" she asked. At the time, as I sat in the bed looking at her as a heap of red wool blanket, it seemed to me she only thought of herself but now I could see she was asking me not to forget her.

We were all in the kitchen, waiting for it, when a call came from Francis that Mama had especially arranged. She picked up the receiver on the wall phone when it rang. "Hello! Yes, we're all good... How are you now?... Good. There's a lot of people here want to talk to you. I'll pass you on and then come back to me."

She held out the phone to Neil. He held up a hand like a signal to stop and walked out to the backyard saying, "I'm just going to check the barometer."

When it was my turn to talk, Francis said, "I've been lifting weights so when I come home Joe and I can still toss you around."

"Did you run away?"

There was silence at the other end.

"Would I be talking to you right now if I ran away?"

"I don't know."

"No. When you run away you're gone."

"You're gone," I said.

"Do you listen to my show?"

"Only once. Mama says it's on too late."

"You're not missing much," he laughed.

"How do you know what to say about all that music?"

"They tell me. They give it to me on a piece of paper before each show."

"Are you allowed to say anything else?"

"Sure, if I think of something."

"Can you say hello?" I asked.

"You mean to you?"

"Or to Iona."

"Of course I can. I'll play you something special tomorrow night and I'll say hello."

In the kitchen we played cards, after Murdoch went to bed, and waited for the show to come on. Stella was out at one of the parish dances, but Joe stuck around to play for a while. We were so absorbed in our game that we were surprised when we heard him speak. "You're listening to *Late Night Classics* and this is Francis MacPherson." The voice was different than his old voice. It was deeper and smoother and he sounded like he might be from anywhere. I wondered if that was his choice or if they told him how to sound as well as what to say.

"I'm going to play something a little different tonight. This is for my lovely sisters, Iona and Eileen. They may be only eight and ten, but man, have they got rhythm."

The first song he played was by Nat King Cole. "Straighten up and fly right. Cool down, Papa, don't you blow your top."

Mama's back stiffened a bit as it always did when she felt she might have to defend someone. I looked around to see if Neil was near, but he wasn't, and she just shook her head at me. Iona didn't seem to notice but Joe did and tried to divert attention.

"Is there a call-in line for this show? We could call and tell him to straighten up himself."

There was relief in Mama's face and we all broke into wide, toothy grins.

The next one was also a Nat King Cole. "There was a boy, a very strange, enchanted boy… They say he wandered very far, very far…"

Joe rolled his eyes, "I suppose that's him."

There were other songs that swung around us in a way that meant something, as if they were a conversation with him and he could tease as if he was right there. There was one about a thieving rabbit.

Yeah everyday I'm tryin' to avoid it.
What do I do, I know that I enjoy it.
Really and true, I'm beggin' momma's pardon.
All the time I'm headin' for the garden.

It wasn't really a children's song but we could pretend it was. The best part of all was the way Mama threw her head back and laughed with her teeth showing. By the time we went to bed our cheeks were sore from smiling.

He called the next day.

"They loved it! The boss wants me to do it again. When I cued up the show for you and Iona, I completely forgot to ask the new boss until I saw him pass the window wall and go into his office and close his door. So I had to get my nerve up and go knock. The boss is not bad but he's not the friendliest guy in the world, and when he yelled 'come in' he had his back turned, looking out the window, and didn't even turn around.

"I couldn't just say I wanted to play something for my sisters so I held up the Mingus and kind of jabbered at him. 'I think this would wake people up a bit. Get their attention, you know. The guy is a genius.' So he turned around, looked me up and down and said, 'You don't have to convince me. Do whatever you want. If it's bad, you're fired.'"

Francis laughed that hooting laugh he had.

"Now I get to do whatever I want."

This was the beginning of an era and for years we thought of the saxophone pieces and the piano solos or the a cappella voices, the songs he sent home to us through the radio, as "Francis music."

It's easy to idealize a disembodied voice. I suppose that's what we did. We knew him, in the same way many strangers did, as the voice of this late-night radio, a voice that comforted me even if a long time passed without laying eyes upon each other.

On weeknights we went to bed early and couldn't listen, but on a night when I came down for water, and stood very quietly in the hall, I saw Neil leaning with both arms folded over the radio and his head resting there, while Francis told stories about songs. At another time, if you asked Neil, he would say he never listened to that kind of music.

I wondered if Francis could feel him there and thought perhaps Neil was hoping he could.

Back upstairs, I stood silently beside Mama's bed until her eyes flew open. "What?"

"When is he coming?"

She took a long deep breath and let out a short sigh before pulling herself up on one elbow.

"He'll come as soon as he can. At least now he knows people."

"How do you know?"

"I talked to him last night."

"He called?" How could she have not told me?

"He always calls on Thursday. I believe you know that."

"You didn't tell me that."

She sounded exasperated. "Every Friday morning I tell you he called last night."

"Not this week."

"Well, okay, that's true. Anyway he said he has good friends there now."

"He has a girlfriend?"

She looked as if she was searching for an answer somewhere in my face.

"I don't know. I hope so. Go back to bed."

Iona was sleeping in a curled-up ball when I crawled back into bed so I wrapped myself around her and buried my face in her hair. The house cracked and moaned a little before it settled into sleep.

The next time we played a game with her dolls, she handed me her bear and said, "You be Francis. I'm you," holding up the goldilocks doll that was meant to be me. Then she pretended to speak in my voice. "Iona and I are coming to see you when we get big."

"Maybe I'll come to see you soon," I said, trying to mimic Francis's new radio voice.

"It's okay. I have Iona to play with," she said as me.

"I hope you like my radio show," the Francis bear in my hand offered as an extra bit of small talk.

"Oh, I like it a lot," the Eileen doll remarked, "and Iona is learning all the songs so I can hear them anytime I want."

She made me laugh. "I can learn them! Why are you laughing?"

"I'm not laughing at *you*! I'm laughing at myself, remember?"

Morning came early. We were near the solstice, and we all knew my father never slept after the first rays of light entered his room. At that time of day he could be seen in the backyard standing facing east, if you had to get up for some reason and happened to look down from the bathroom window.

I ran downstairs in my pajamas, glided across the grass barefoot, and stood beside him. His eyes never left the horizon. I looked to see the light as it bloomed across the sky and watched for several long and quiet moments.

"It's cold out here," I said.

"Go in then. Don't be cold."

"Aren't you cold too?" I asked, wondering why he did this, but feeling that it would be impolite to ask and hoping he would see the question on my upturned face.

"I like to meet the day on my own terms," he said. "Go on in now."

I climbed in with Stella when I got back to our room. My feet were freezing and she pulled away when I tried to warm them on her bare legs. For a while we lay side by side listening to Iona's sleepy breathing.

"Why does he do that?" I whispered.

"Francis used to say he practised some kind of sun religion," she replied.

I gave her a friendly little punch so that she'd know that I knew she was kidding. My mind filled with Francis like an umbrella popping open in a phone booth and leaving no room to even open the door. Stella noticed but she may have been a bit weary of my preoccupation with him.

"Bigger things happen. You'll see him again. You have to get over it."

"Like just forget about him? Like who cares?"

She rolled her eyes.

"You could write to him, you know," she said, with a look she rarely gave that meant she felt a bit sorry for me.

"Would he write back?"

"Yes, he would."

I was afraid she might be wrong because I knew he was busy and had a lot of friends and because he never wrote to me.

After my father left for work and while we ate breakfast, I asked Mama why he was standing in the yard at dawn examining the sky.

She looked at me for a moment before answering.

"When he was nine, and his brother Frank was twelve, his stepfather started using a shaving strop to beat them awake in the morning. He couldn't remember much about his own father but when he asked Frank if his father ever beat them he said, 'No, never.'"

"Is that the first thing he thinks of every morning?" I asked.

"Yes, I guess it is."

Writing the letter felt more like writing to an imaginary friend. I couldn't think of a thing to say and sat at the kitchen table searching my brain for something that would compel an answer. It seemed impossible to forget what Mama had told me. The memory of another time pushed its way into my mind. Joe and Francis, only ten or eleven, were arguing and pushing in their room. Neil put a stop to it by swinging his shaving strap. Most of the strikes landed on Francis. It all happened above my height and in a dark room with Mama shouting, "Neil! Stop!"

When I was able to focus on the letter again, I wrote:

Dear Francis,

Hope you are doing well. We're all fine.

Thanks for playing that music. We missed it after you left.

It's almost summer and soon we can go swimming. Stella will never let me go in deep enough to swim though.

This morning when I saw Neil practicing his sun religion I asked Mama why he did that. She said it was because he felt bad that he hit you. Is that why you left? You've been gone a long time. Do you think you'll ever come home? I hope so.

Your favourite sister,

Eileen

It didn't matter that Mama didn't say exactly that. It was still not a lie.

A week later I sat on the bottom of the back step waiting for the mailman to arrive. He seemed to be only about Francis's age.

"Collecting the mail, are you?" he said.

"I'm waiting for a letter from my brother in Toronto. I wrote to him a week ago."

"Well, it could take a while. He probably just got it."

So I sat there, waiting, every day. We had a warm spell that week and once he arrived with sweat dripping off his face. He wiped it with a blue handkerchief he dragged out of his pocket and asked for a glass of water. After that, Mama always gave me a pitcher of water for him with ice in it.

The day the letter arrived, it was in a large, thick envelope. "Here you go," he said and poured a glass of water for himself. "I hope you have other letters to wait for."

After he left, I sat for a few minutes just holding it and looking at the address in Francis's handwriting. Mama opened the door a crack.

"Did you get something?"

I nodded and didn't move so she came out and sat beside me on the step.

"Are you going to open it?" she asked.

I nodded again and started to tear it, but she said, "Wait, I'll get a knife. You don't want to tear it."

She came back with a butter knife and neatly ripped the end. When I looked up at her without opening it, she understood.

"You go ahead and read that. I'll be in the kitchen."

Inside was a letter written on yellow lined paper and a map of southern Ontario with Toronto at its centre.

Dear Eileen,

If you look at the map that came with this letter, you'll see that Toronto is a lot of small towns clustered together. I pinpointed my house on the map. Follow the red line from the right. And there I am.

It's too hard to explain why I left. But yes, I'll come home some day.

I'll be sorry to miss the swimming. Please don't drown.
Your big brother,
Francis

I wished someone would tell me what happened. Was it my father's fault? Or did he just want to go?

With the map spread out on the landing of the porch, I traced the highway route into town with my forefinger. I couldn't tell how far it was but I figured I could walk anywhere if I had enough time.

At that very moment, Aunt Effie came around the corner of the house and up the path, her arms full of dress boxes.

Mama came back out on the porch to greet her and saw me looking at the map. "Eileen is planning a little trip," she said to Effie. She looked back to me and smiled. "It might be delayed a few years but there's no harm in planning."

"Why are you laughing?" I asked.

"I'm not laughing!"

"Yes you are!"

"Eileen, I want him home as much as you do. He's his own person now. We can't make him come home." All the laughter had gone from her eyes.

At dusk the next evening, before Aunt Effie went home to the farm, I slid out the back door and around to the verandah and sat perfectly still on the bottom step. She and Mama had dragged kitchen chairs outside and they were talking about when Mama left home for the first time. I thought it was likely because they'd been discussing Francis leaving. I regretted not coming out earlier to catch all of it.

"The morning I decided to leave I climbed the big tree in the field in front of the house just as the sun was rising," she said.

"You mean the big elm?" Aunt Effie asked by way of encouragement.

At that early point in the story, the cat wandered up the dirt path to the bottom of the steps and sat in front of me, purring. I tried to quietly shoo her away with my hand but this drew Mama's attention and, with a quick intake of her breath, she said sharply, "Eileen! How long have you been sitting there? Announce yourself when you come into a room."

"I'm pretty big now, Mama. You'd think you'd notice me."

At which my mother laughed, "Yes, you'd think so, wouldn't you?" Then she paused. "We were just talking about when I left home. I'm sure you aren't too interested in that."

"Yes I am!"

They exchanged looks that were hard to read.

"Well, all right then. You can stay."

I scrambled up to the top step to be closer, and Mama resumed her story.

"It was the big elm and you remember how the morning fog makes its upper branches disappear. No whisper of a breeze. I knew I couldn't be seen from the house and although I could see the branches well enough, I couldn't see a thing beyond and nothing below. Just sat there and thought about what I wanted to have happen in the rest of my life. I imagined children at the edge of the field, laughing and waving and calling, 'We're out here. Come out to us.'"

As she talked, she mimicked the children who were waving. Then she dropped her hand and laughed. "One of them must have been you, I guess," she said, smiling at me.

I couldn't believe she thought she saw me before I was even born. It was unusual for her to think something so unlikely. I almost told her about the girl in the blue dress in the marsh but thought better of it.

She continued in a more normal vein. "Of course, when I got back to the kitchen our mother said, 'Aren't you a bit old for that?' and I said, 'I'm a bit old for quite a few things.'

"You know how she always had a premonition if comings or goings were imminent."

Mama looked directly at me. "I'm assuming you can keep this confidential. I wouldn't want my mother to know I was telling stories on her."

I nodded expectantly.

"It was a canning day, and while I was thinking of what to tell her about my plans, taking my time chopping the beans, she thought I was dawdling too much. 'Beans are not that delicate,' she said.

"So I just blurted it out. 'I'm taking a teaching job in Sydney.'"

"'You are not,' she said.

"'You don't need me here,' I said. 'Lots of women are out in the world doing all kinds of jobs; they say there are even women working at the steel plant.'"

I interjected a question to Aunt Effie. "Where were you?"

"I was already gone to nursing school."

"This was just after Donald and Muriel married," Mama continued, "so I felt free to go. They were going to have the farm. I was only twenty-two. I wanted to do something with myself and so many of the men were still oversees. Of course, this was unthinkable. She'd already tried to get me married off closer to home."

She play-acted both roles, her own and her mother's, when she told the rest. Her mother spoke in a more sombre tone, and she tried to make herself seem cheerful and sensible.

"'If it's a man you're looking for, I don't know what's wrong with Duncan MacLennan.'

"'I hardly know him.'

"'He asked you to marry him, didn't he?'

"'Yes, because when he started looking around, I was the nearest one.'

"'He has a very good house and a beautiful field.'"

"Literally grasping at straws," Aunt Effie interjected.

"Oh, and then she tried, 'It's so dirty in Sydney that when you go shopping your slip has a ring of black on the bottom when you get home.'"

"You were the only one able to stand up to her," said Aunt Effie.

"I was stubborn. That's for sure. I went anyway."

There was a pause while they both remembered that, so I asked, "Did you live with Neil?"

I wondered what their exchanged smiles meant, so I said, "What?"

Mama said, "I rented a room from Wilma Currie. She was a widow at the time and the children were small.

"That's enough for tonight. That story is not going anywhere."

9

Jessica stepped through the doorway of the Ukrainian Hall to get some air, just as a car pulled up to the front. She recognized it as belonging to her brother Donald. He knew she'd been going to dances there on Saturday nights since living at Wilma Currie's place in the Pier. He didn't look at all surprised to see her standing on the steps.

He grinned when he rolled down his window and yelled up to her, "I'm just going to leave Neil MacPherson here. He's a good fella. Be nice to him."

She had never met his friend Neil but she'd often heard Donald talk about driving places they never should go in the backcountry, stopping on narrow passes with a steep drop on one side so that Neil could paint the landscape. He'd come home late and explain that his friend had to be taken home because he'd consumed more rum than he'd intended. Jessica knew that it was not only his friend who drank too much.

She bent to see who was in the passenger seat just as Neil opened the door of the car and stood up on the other side.

She stood up and had a bird's-eye view of him.

To Donald she said. "Tell Mama I'm coming up on the weekend."

"Good enough." He gave her a quick wave without looking, put the car in gear and skidded away.

She lightly stepped down a few steps to avoid the moths and insects drawn to the light above her head. The music wafting out behind her was a familiar strathspey. Her brown silky dress shone like copper in the light of the moon.

Neil stood for a few minutes gazing at her, a good-looking man, not as tall as her brothers but more muscular. Jessica felt as if she recognized him even though she knew very well she did not. He took her off guard when he stepped forward and said to her in Gaelic, "I believe I've come for you."

The lilt of her mother's language made her well disposed toward him but she replied, "I think you've come for another drink and you'd be better off going on home."

"I was hoping you'd marry me," he said, "but I didn't expect you'd be taking care of me so soon."

"There is no accounting for what men will say when they're drunk," she said.

"There is no accounting for finding the love of one's life on the doorstep of the Ukrainian Hall."

She tilted her head to one side. "I'm going back in now," and she turned away.

"Will you dance with me?" he called after her.

She turned back and said softly, "Ask me someday when you're sober."

When he followed her inside she was surprised that so many people offered a hand or spoke his name and welcomed him as if he was a favourite son of the place.

That night Neil dreamt of an inky ocean beneath a cobalt blue sky. The silver stars were reflected on the water as perfect golden counterpoints of light. When he stepped into the dream the world became animated and the waves began to dance.

He spent many days recreating it on canvas: the perfect balance between light and dark filled him with an unreasonable hope.

The next week at the dance, he was there when she arrived. He came to her with cap in hand.

"Could I try again?" he asked quietly.

Jessica thought to herself, *Here's a switch,* and said out loud, "Are you sober?"

"Never been more."

Over the following few months they exchanged stories the way people do when they fall in love and wish they'd known each other all their lives. He said he had been looking for her since he was a little boy. She told him she'd never marry a man who drank. And so he didn't.

He spoke to her of his childhood in a mocking sort of way, as if it was all a great joke, and she didn't quite believe his tone when he talked about his father dying when he was four years old.

"My father dropped dead in the field, but I want to assure you I don't come from one of those families where the men are forever doing that."

The only time his voice thickened up a bit was when he spoke of his mother, who lived on the mainland with her brother's family. He never mentioned Frank except to say he had a brother who died in the war, and she didn't press him for more.

Even his war experience was reduced to stories of crossing the ocean singing songs while watching the reflection of the moon on the water. He didn't tell her anything at all about the shameful episodes he thought of as his night terrors, choosing instead to say he was a bit of a sleepwalker and making fun of himself for sometimes waking up standing in the field in the middle of the night. She became very quiet then and asked, "Are you sure it's not alcohol that does it?"

"Oh no!" he exclaimed. "Happens when I'm dead sober. Most people have the good sense to wake up when they find themselves running away from something in a dream." She wondered what he might run from on these nocturnal journeys, but didn't want to pry this information from him and assumed he would tell her in his own good time.

The first time he sang for her in Gaelic was on a fogbound winter morning when he picked her up at Wilma's in his friend's car and drove out to the garage. An eagle watched them, from the highest branch in a nearby tree, as they flung open the doors and climbed out simultaneously, rushing toward the ocean.

The waves struck at the shore with great force below where they were stopped on the bank. He stood beside her, looking out to sea, and in a clear, unfaltering voice sang a familiar song about a young girl who is in love with a boatman and constantly seeks him on the shore.

> *Thug mi gaol dhuit, 's chan fhaod mi aicheadh.*
> *Cha ghaol bliadhna, 's cha ghaol raidhe,*
> *Ach gaol a thoisich 'n uair bha mi m' phaisdein,*
> *'S nach searg a chaoidh, gus an claoidh am mas mi.*

I gave my love to you and I can't deny it.
It's not a love of years or seasons,
But a love that began when I was a child,
And it'll never wither till death overpowers me.

Sometimes she thought it was presumptuous of him to love so grandly and with such patience. But she was moved in a way she had never been before. She knew him through the song, a response as much to him singing in Gaelic as it was about the meaning. The fact that he spoke better Gaelic than most of his generation, and certainly better than others would admit, made her regard him as more complete than other men she'd met, as if there was a family template that a person had to fit before having any meaningful chance of becoming part of her life. She was sure that her mother would approve of a man and a family that valued the language as much as she did.

The garage he worked in backed onto the water and faced a great expanse of open sea. The owner had poured a slab of concrete where you could park a couple of cars but Neil had set it up as an outdoor studio, and there were several paintings done in oil on donnacona board. There was a piece set up on the easel of a starlit sky reflected in an animated sea.

"Where is this?" she asked?

"It's from a dream," he said. Standing there, she felt a kind of connection with him that she never had before. "There's some kind of magic in it," was all she said.

Looking around, she saw that there were other paintings in the same unfinished state. "Do you think you'll ever finish these?"

"I think so. I hope so. Most of the pictures I have in my mind are only partly coloured in. I'd like to finish this one, though," he said, indicating the painting of a wagon carrying a pine box on a narrow dusty road that stretched away toward the horizon. "If I had my way I'd live in a shack in the woods and paint for the rest of my life."

"Do you not want children?"

"Oh, at least ten." He glanced down at his feet to hide any expression that might display his desire.

Although that pleased her, she said, "It would need more than a shack to house a family like that."

He looked up. "I know that well. Don't you worry. I'll take care of my own."

The physical work he did for a living, along with the training and sparring in the boxing club, gave him great strength. He could easily pick her up in his arms and thoroughly kiss her before setting her down again. She liked it when he flexed his biceps for her. She thought there might be something wrong with how much she loved the way the colour rose in his cheeks when he talked about boxing. She knew she shouldn't associate violence with pleasure, but he was extraordinarily beautiful in that animated state.

They both tried to keep their emotions in check when they took leave of each other in June. At the train station, they spoke casually the way people do when they know it will not be long before they meet again.

"See you in a few weeks!" Jessica had no way of knowing that he was terrified to see her go.

He arrived at her mother's farm, intending to take her on a picnic, one day when she was in the village. Isabel, who knew him by description right away when she opened the door, drew herself up to her full five-foot height.

"Well, you're quite the one, aren't you? You have nothing to offer and you come here looking for my daughter? Just what do you intend to do with her? Live in a shack in the woods? If you have any respect for her at all, you'll leave her alone and let her get on with her life."

"Mrs. MacPhail, surely your daughter is old enough to decide for herself who she does and doesn't care for."

"Surely you are old enough to understand I'm telling you to leave my property. When you have some of your own you can invite us to visit you there."

He felt deeply wounded, as if every fibre of his body had been put at risk. His stomach roiled but he had no choice, really, except to leave. When he got into his borrowed car and drove away, he ducked his head and pretended that he couldn't see her standing in the doorway, watching.

Isabel and Muriel were seated at the kitchen table in front of the big window when Jessica returned. Muriel's teacup clattered when she set it down.

"What is it?"

No response from Isabel. Muriel looked up.

"Neil was here."

"Where is he now?'

"I sent him away," Isabel got up to go to the stove and rattle the burners as if she was tending the fire. "He has a lot of nerve coming here with cap in hand. If he wants you, he'll come back with a better offer."

Six weeks went by and always the same question at the small post office wicket, "Anything today?" produced the same response.

"Nothing." The postmaster looked over the top of his glasses with a question in his eyes but he never asked.

She was afraid he'd been thrown off too easily and that his love offered no security after all. Her brother Donald tried to comfort her. "Let the whole thing blow over. Neil is probably just waiting to see you in town."

But with the summer almost passed and no word from him, Jessica weakened when the teacher in a nearby village school married, leaving her post open.

Neil was stunned when she didn't return. He spent weeks at the boxing club hammering away at the heavy bag, not knowing how else to respond. Some nights in desperation he sat in his room and tried to write a letter telling her how he felt, but words seemed inadequate to convey his feeling. The whole autumn was passed with a sickening anxiety. In January, he ran into Donald, who was in town having a drink with some friends and in an outgoing frame of mind. He slapped Neil on the back and said, "What happened to you? You look half alive."

"I'm holding up all right." Then after some moments of silence, he asked lightly, "Is Jessica happy in her new job?"

"Go ask her yourself. Surely to God you aren't going to let my mother run your life, are you?" Neil almost rose to this bait with an angry retort, but when he looked up all he saw was the face of a friend.

That evening, at the small table set in front of the narrow window in his room, he watched the ocean while he struggled to compose a poem that begged her to ignore the wishes of those who could not possibly understand the strength of their love.

> Let not those dark antipathies
> Sway life from the path it wends
> Nor courage lose, when hazards rise
> To make us aught but friends.

He crushed it in his hand.

The day of his journey, he straightened his room and carefully put away his canvases as if she might be coming back with him, or as if he might not be coming back at all. He wore the best clothes he owned, a pair of grey flannel trousers and a tweed jacket with a felt fedora. He wished he had a tie but at least his shirt was clean and white. The day before, the garage owner had given him the keys to his car when he heard where he was headed, so he wouldn't have to take the train and hitch a ride.

"I suppose I'm going to lose you now?" he asked.

"Don't put any money on it," Neil mumbled in reply.

The elation she felt when she saw him drive into the yard provided a chaotic emotional contrast to her despair. She was boarding with friends of her mother's and had given up hope of his coming. *Take it slowly*, she thought to herself. *Don't let him know how much this means. He may have come to say he's sorry, but under the circumstances…* She threw on a sweater and edged through the doorway and down the steps to meet him. There were awkward hellos while they both tried to pretend nothing momentous was about to happen.

The yard was soft and muddy with an early spring approaching.

"It's awfully wet here underfoot," she said.

"Well then, let's just sit in the car for a bit."

She nodded.

As he opened the door, he was relieved he'd cleaned it so thoroughly.

Even with her seated beside him, he seemed to be having a hard time finding words. Finally, staring straight ahead, he spoke, "I miss you too much, Jessica. When I think about the rest of my life stretching ahead of me without you in it, my stomach turns over."

Jessica's relief burst out of her in a gasp of laughter.

"But I said I'd marry you! Why did you stay away so long?"

"I didn't think I had a choice. After your mother chased me off the farm I never heard a word."

"Why didn't you write to me?"

"I have no property."

"Neither do I."

They both turned to look at each other then, understanding for the first time what they were about to promise.

"I was trying to think what to do," Neil said.

"What did you finally come up with?"

"This!"

The paper he handed her had been crumpled in a ball at some point, but an attempt had been made to straighten it out and it was folded neatly in four. She didn't laugh then. She'd never seen him at such a loss for words or knowing what to do. In their brief months together he'd always been so competent and self–assured, and it was often she who felt like a child beside him. It surprised her that he came to her so humbled. They sat for a moment contemplating each other without a word exchanged until she said, "It will take more than four lines to make up for such a long absence."

"How many will it take?"

She held her forehead in one hand for a moment, and when she looked up she put the paper in her pocket.

"I'll save this. We might need it later."

The mixture of astonishment and relief displayed on his face would always be etched in her mind as a turning point in their lives.

They married in Sydney a month later in a formal church with only her brother Donald and his Muriel as witnesses. Their vows echoed in the vaulted ceilings of the church, creating a sense that they were miniatures in a cavernous world. Isabel claimed illness, and in fact was very sick at heart. The only thing she really had against him was that he would always be subject to the whims of an employer. The fact that her own land was not very fertile and that half of it was mountain outcrop did nothing to displace her Gaelic pride that they had escaped the interlopers in their homeland and come to a place free from landlords and chiefs. She wanted more than serfdom for Jessica.

The letter she received from Lake Ainslie, where Jessica was finishing out her contract, did nothing to assure her.

Dear Mama,

I have married the man I love. I hope you will understand the wisdom in that and forgive my impatience. I will always be your faithful daughter in every other respect.

With gratitude for all you have done for me,

Jessica

10

The leather sole of my shoe had come loose from the upper, as if the stitches holding them together had a lifespan and died all at once. It was undone all the way to the heel.

Mama's hair fell over her face, while she sat at the kitchen table, examining the problem. She didn't raise her head or push her hair back after she set the shoe down on the floor. I hovered behind her and when she turned around to look at me, a mixture of frustration and regret passed over her face before she softened it to one of caring.

"I had to carry them and walk home barefoot," I said, showing her the dirty soles of my feet. "Mrs. Chisholm passed me and looked a bit worried. I just smiled and pretended I liked walking barefoot."

I could tell by the way her shoulders reached for her ears that it was the wrong thing to say. She looked again at the black loafer sitting lifeless on the floor.

"It's spring," I tried. "I walked on the grass instead of the sidewalk."

She turned and looked up at my face then. "I won't have money to get it fixed until payday," she said.

So we both examined the shoe for a while, at a loss for what to do.

"We could wrap them together with electric tape," I said, thinking that was fairly innovative. She looked at me with that considering look she had sometimes, her blue eyes searching mine and her head tilted.

"Wouldn't you mind?"

"No," I said, "I don't care at all as long as they stop flapping." So I put the shoe on and held the sole to the upper while she wrapped the tape round and round very carefully. The tape was the same colour as the shoe and I really thought it looked good.

Mama looked at me, biting her lower lip. "You can wear them around home but you can't go to school like that."

"I don't think anyone will notice."

"Some people will and I'm afraid they might make fun of you."

"Why?"

"It will look as if we can't afford to buy shoes."

I sat looking at the perfectly neat shoe from an entirely new perspective.

"Are we poor?" I asked her.

"There are people much worse off than you are! Are you ever hungry?"

"No, but why don't we have a car?"

"We can't afford a car."

"Other people do."

"Your father would rather build us a house, even if it comes out of his paycheques bit by bit. He said we would own our own home and we do."

I was lost for a response because it had never occurred to me that the reason we were so much at home and didn't go to the movies or take piano lessons, like some people did, was because we were poor. I just thought they liked to have us home and that seemed good enough because there was usually someone to quarrel or play with.

"Well then," I shrugged. "I guess I'll have to stay home until payday."

She laughed. "No, you won't. I'll think of something." A thought occurred to her and her eyebrows sprang up.

"Stella left a pair of shoes upstairs that she doesn't want. They'd be big but you could wear some wool socks in them."

This was a perfect solution, I thought. Better to have shoes that were too big than no shoes at all. And better for me that they were Stella's.

"Do you think she'd mind?" I wondered.

"No no, she said to give them away. She bought herself a new pair when she got paid. I put the loafers under my bed thinking you'd grow into them, but I guess we're not going to wait for that."

There was a very small smile at the corners of her mouth. "Run up and get them," she said.

Stella was eighteen and working and could afford things like shoes. She'd spent a lot of time in the previous summer tanning in the field behind the house with her friends, listening to a transistor radio and singing along to "Downtown" or "We Gotta Get Out of This Place." You could kind of tell what she had on her mind. The two friends piled into the living room in their bathing suits and danced and sang along with the radio to "Catch Us If You Ca-a-a-an!" They sounded so sure and so excited about what was going to happen in their lives now that school was over. Mama looked in to watch and then came back to her baking.

"People say that forty is the prime of your life, but in there it looks like it might be eighteen," she said.

One of them planned to go to nursing school and the other to teacher's college but Stella took typing in high school so she was all set.

The day they left, in September, she came down all dressed for school and said, "I'm going out to get a job at the airport."

"Are you now? asked Mama. "How will you get there?"

"There's a bus from downtown goes right there."

"I didn't know that."

This was a revelation to me as well. I liked the airport but was always dependent on some neighbour or relative to take us out there for a Sunday drive if we wanted to watch the planes coming and going. Now I realized that with a couple of bus tickets, a plane ticket and a sandwich in a bag, you could go all on your own from our house to Toronto just by doing it. It was expensive, but if you saved money you could do it. Probably anyone could.

When Stella came home she was looking too pleased with herself. She held out her arms as if we were to check out what she wore, and said, "Ticket taker. Air Canada."

She grinned and her voice softened to almost a whisper, "I think I'll be able to graduate to a stewardess soon."

A stewardess was known to be a privileged and coveted position, flying all over the place. Everyone knew you had to be young and beautiful, and I could see that with her dimples and long thick hair she had a good chance.

When she noticed I was wearing her old shoes, she said, "Next time I get paid, I'll buy you a pair." Mama took a deep breath and patted her arm.

Early in the following year she brought a fellow named David home to dinner. We knew he was from away and we did a lot of tidying up before he arrived. He seemed awfully formal in a suit. I wondered if he'd just got off work.

Over the course of dinner we managed to glean some important bits of info about him and his origins. He was from away—only Halifax, but that seemed a long way—and already a manager. He was older, maybe twenty-five.

"Are your parents still in Halifax?" asked my father.

"No, my parents died in a car accident when I was ten."

Mama and Neil exchanged glances. Losing your parent as a child was something they both knew a lot about.

"I grew up with my mother's sister's family. I go home to see them all the time."

I wondered if Stella had told him what to say. His answers couldn't have been more perfect.

It was after midnight when she came home that night, and Iona and I were already in bed. Mama was waiting up, of course, and we could hear them talking, then exclaiming and laughing. We got up and ran downstairs. When we reached the hallway, Stella was standing in the hall, the widest possible grin on her face, with her left hand held conspicuously out and a diamond ring on her finger.

"I'm moving to Calgary," she said.

"Right now?" I asked, remembering how another late night incident in this hallway had torn Francis away.

"Nooo! I have to get married first."

She still shared a room with Iona and me, so over the next few months we got to hear endless plans about the wedding and the honeymoon in Montreal where they were going to stay in a hotel. She never talked about the fact that they were going to live in Calgary. No one else did either.

"I want the real thing for a wedding," she said. "Dinner and a dance at the hall just before Labour Day when everyone will be home. The girl's parents are supposed to pay for it, but I'm going to pay for it myself. No one will know."

"Are you inviting Francis?" I asked her one night.

"Of course I am. He has to be there. All of David's family will be there, and his friends from college."

There was a theorem in her statements that I couldn't understand so I changed the subject.

"Why doesn't our family go to college?"

She shrugged. "I don't know. It's expensive for one thing. We just aren't college people."

The most important thing to me was not that Stella was getting married; it was that Francis would come home for her wedding. He was our oldest brother. Stella believed he would come. I could barely contain my excitement and everyone gave me credit for being happy for Stella. I was. But I was doubly happy because I missed Francis and I wanted him to see me almost all grown up.

When Joe came home one evening and found me tidying up his books and old comics and dusting his room, he asked, "What are you doing messing around in here?"

"Thought I'd make it nice with Francis coming home. You know."

"No, I don't know. Who said he's coming home?"

My stomach clenched tight when he said that, but I had no response.

I waited as long as I could and a few days later asked Mama.

"Did you hear from him?"

She just shook her head. She was sewing the bridesmaids' lilac peau de soie dresses at the dining room table, with pieces of silk and pattern pieces all in disarray, so I could see she had a lot to concentrate on, but I wanted more of an answer.

"Did you call him?"

"Stella did. He said he'd call when he decides."

My hands tingled and flexed as if they felt like strangling someone or something—possibly Francis. There was no reason for him not to come home. Not even for his sister's wedding? That was just selfish, I thought.

The screen door slammed behind me with a justifiably jarring sound as I flung myself into a chair on the verandah and pulled on one of Mama's sweaters for warmth.

The face of the man in the moon was easily discerned that night and I took to talking to him as I sat there in the cool evening air.

"He's twenty-one. If he doesn't come now he never will."

"Call him," the man in the moon said to me.

I did it the next evening when Mama was out at Wilma's getting some advice with a sewing difficulty and everyone else was watching TV. I dialed the wall phone in the kitchen very quietly and sat on the kitchen stool, hoping he would answer, and was surprised when he did.

"Eileen!" he shouted when he heard my voice. "Are you all excited about the wedding?"

"I don't know. We've spent hours making those tissue carnations so she can drive off in a pink cloud of glory," I said. "At least as far as the hotel."

"That's a bit cynical for a twelve-year-old."

"Thirteen."

"Sorry. I knew that."

"Stella seems a bit cranky actually," I told him.

"Just nerves I'm sure."

"I don't know. She caught me looking in the mirror the other day and she said, 'You look as if you're checking to see if you're still there.' I've been thinking about that and I think she was right."

I could hear Francis smiling. "She didn't mean anything by that."

"Everyone is asking if you're coming. It's as if you're famous now."

"It may seem that way from there. But believe me, Canadian radio is a very small stage to appear on. And you don't even appear."

"But you like it."

"Yes, I do."

"Are you coming to the wedding?" I asked in an offhand way.

There was a pause while he considered his answer.

"It's hard to get away from here."

"So you say."

"I have a present for her. Well, for them, I guess."

"Stella will feel bad if you don't come."

"No, she knows. She and David are stopping in Toronto on the way to Calgary. They're going to come by."

"Stella knows? When did you tell her?"

"Just recently."

"Why do people hide things from me?"

"Who hides things?"

"Everyone. You all think I'm some kind of baby."

"What do you think we're hiding?"

"If I knew, it wouldn't be a problem, would it?"

There was nothing to do but leave it at that.

The wedding was only a few days away when Iona and I walked in from school and Stella burst into tears. She'd been washing the kitchen floor and the sight of her with tears running down her face while she banged the mop back into the pail, crying and talking at the same time, was confusing.

"You open the door and walk right in when I just mopped there! I'll be so happy to get out of here," she half cried out.

"What happened?" Mama called out from the dining room.

"Nothing happened. Nothing ever happens. It's just going to go on and on and I'm going to be far away and no one will even notice. You'll all be so happy I'm gone."

Mama showed up in the doorway then. She looked back and forth between us until her eyes rested on Stella, who had started to jam the mop up and down in the bucket again.

"We'll all miss you terribly," Mama said.

Stella threw the mop down and flung herself into Mama's arms, crying.

"What if I'm not happy?"

Mama held her. "You'll be happy. Maybe he'll get transferred back here again. You never know what the future holds."

This comment didn't seem to help, as Stella started crying again.

"You can always come home for a visit," Mama said, looking at me over Stella's shoulder.

Later, speaking with her friend Wilma on the phone, Mama said, "It's hard to let her go but there isn't much I can do. He's got work there. I'm hoping one or two of the others will stay. But there's no promise of that!"

꩜

The day of the wedding, I snuck away to visit the pond. It was the only place I wouldn't be found and I desperately needed some time on my own. As I travelled the main path to the brook, remnants of the path I'd built so carefully five years before were still visible to one side. Leaves had fallen and obscured most of it but there were places where two lines of stones six inches apart could be seen rising through the buttercups.

Below the house, where the brook opened out to the pond, was the place where Francis taught me to scoop a bucket full of tadpoles to take home to watch. At thirteen, I was too old for that kind of concentrated inactivity and was more focused on the birds.

My boots slid on the path when I stopped at the bottom, making far too much noise for a birdwatcher. I stayed perfectly still for a few moments and the birds began to sing and call to one another again.

But there were no goldfinch calls that morning. It was a sound I'd come to know well on my solo forays to the brook, splashing through the marsh, watching butterflies alight on the thistle at its edge. The goldfinches seemed to be playing all the time then, looping and chasing each other and making a sound like lilting laughter.

It was not until August that they'd started to build a nest. The female flew in and out of the tree carrying construction materials like bark or small twigs and fine grasses to line it. She seemed to be the architect but the male stood by, offering moral support and encouragement with his song. If he sometimes brought a piece to add, it was she who packed it firmly into the nest. They worked at a deliberate and steady pace, taking long pauses to fly around and play their game of tag.

Working my way around through the brook carefully and silently, hopping from one flat rock to another and hoping to keep dry, I came to a place directly under a branch of the tree that arched out over the water. It was in the fork where that branch and another met that the finch's nest was still cradled. There were no birds flying to and fro or adding necessary bits that day, so I thought perhaps they were out of sight, sitting on the nest to keep their babies warm.

The August sun, filtered through the ripening leaves, glinted off the silver-pink bark of the tree and raced all over my body in warm flickers of light as I shimmied out along the branch to examine the nest. Enveloped in its soft compact centre were five perfect eggs, all about the size of large peanuts, pale bluish white, with a few scattered specks of brown. The whole nest was lined with thistle down and held together with something that looked like spider web and caterpillar silk. I slowly shimmied away and dropped as quietly as I could to the base of the tree. I stayed for a long hour, waiting for the mother's return, then walked up the path, lost in my plan to save the abandoned eggs.

The wedding was a sit-down dinner for a hundred people. I felt as if I attended from a long way off. Stella's bridesmaids looked good, as bridesmaids do, in the lilac dresses it had taken Mama weeks to sew. Aunt Effie was there, Grandma Isabel, the cousins, everyone but Francis. I was starting to forget what he looked like unless I saw a picture, and even then I knew he didn't look sixteen anymore.

David's mother, who was slim and wore her blond hair in a French twist, said she'd heard his show and was sorry not to meet him. She seemed to be younger than Mama and she and her husband danced well together, like royalty or someone you'd see in a movie.

One of his good-looking friends talked to me for some time and I never let on I was only thirteen. When he asked my age outright, he seemed surprised and left the table immediately. I wasn't going to be flirting with some older man but it occurred to me that I might meet him again when I was older and wondered if he'd remember me.

Murdoch tagged behind Stella as she made the rounds of all the guests, shaking hands and expressing her gratitude, her dark eyes lighting up as she spoke to each one. "So kind of you to come. I hope you're en-joying yourself. My mother loved meeting you." She stepped back and onto Murdoch's toes as he stood directly behind her. "Murdoch. I didn't see you there."

He'd carried her train up the aisle, wearing a suit, as if he was going to his first communion, and didn't stop haunting her steps for the rest of the day. The devastated way he looked at her felt familiar.

"Come with me," I said to him. "We'll get more cake."

"No," he said. "I'm part of the wedding."

"Okay, then I'll go get you some."

The cousins played fiddle in the next set. By the time I got back to the table, they were playing a reel and Neil was tapping his feet. When I sat beside him he said, "I wish my mother could see this. No matter how hard things got, or whether we'd eaten nothing but potatoes, if someone came into our kitchen with a fiddle, she forgot it all. She would dance as if all of her life was a joy and sing with a beautiful despair. She was a very fine singer, my mother."

He leaned over to confide in me. "We should have had her sing at our wedding but your mother and I made a very quiet affair of it."

11

Jessica and Neil stood side by side at the tall window of their second-floor apartment, watching the night sky, while the neon light of the store below flashed intermittently on their faces and clothes. *Kozy Korner* in orange and blue ran down the length of their bodies. Neil bent his head and whispered to her as if it was a secret he wanted her to know. "Our life is a work of art." This made Jessica grin and she nudged him with her elbow. He nudged her back. They shared an intimate silence that held all of the secrets they kept from each other.

They were grateful he'd managed to get out of the coke ovens and into the machine shop. He would never tell Jessica that the beautiful sandwiches she made so carefully with lobster, lettuce and mayonnaise for his lunch box tasted like a combination of cast iron, dust and machine oil by the time he ate them. And Jessica never told him how much she missed her name. Even the other women called her Mrs. MacPherson. She was suddenly no one except whoever she was to him, with no family behind her at all.

That evening she sat on her bed, propped up on pillows with her hands folded on top of her enormous belly and her legs stretched out in front of her, contemplating the way the sunset was reflected into the tiny room off the windows of a nearby building. The walls of the room were covered in swirls of red and gold like some kind of southern aurora borealis. The light recalled the colours of the half-finished canvases that were no longer a part of their lives.

Through the door of the bedroom she could see Neil bent over the newspaper at the wooden kitchen table, and she called out to him, "Do you dream about painting?"

"I never think of it," he said, not looking up from the paper. "I have you now."

Jessica was then, and would always be, both thrilled and embarrassed by such overt expressions of affection. Sometimes it seemed too much to be believed, but when she searched his face at those times she found no cynicism or teasing there.

"I'm as big as a house," she called out. "Not exactly dream material at the moment."

Neil pushed his weary body up from the table and came into the room, ducking to avoid the door frame. He crawled onto the bed beside her and put his arm around her shoulder as if they were in a movie theatre and the sunset on the wall at the end of the bed was the feature.

"Painting may have saved my life, but the difference is that now I know what I was saving it for."

"That's laying it on a bit thick, don't you think?" she asked.

As answer, he pulled her closer.

The thought of having a child of his own recalled memories of Frank and him as small boys. He told her a story about the time he climbed to the roof of the barn to rescue Frank even though Frank was older, because he was not afraid of heights. She took it as a sign of health that he was moving on to happier memories. "I'm sorry you never met Frank," he added quietly before he turned to go back to his paper.

On his way home from work, Neil picked up small gifts on the shore and presented them to Jessica, hiding his hands behind his back and getting her to choose which one he would open first. When he held out the palm of his hand, it held something like an interesting piece of coloured glass or a unique stone of some kind. They would examine it together, remarking on the colour or the line as if it was a precious jewel. Jessica would later say that there was no way to know, then, that they would never be like this again.

A porcelain cup and saucer he brought home was of the finest sort, a white translucent artifact of an imagined time when life was genteel and people had the time and inclination to drink tea out of such a beautiful vessel. The woman who ran the grocery store had given it to him when she heard he had married. She said it was a piece that had been given to her by a woman whose children she had cared for, and that it was very old.

Their bedtime tea took on an air of ritual as Jessica poured hers into the cup and, after she had a sip, she said, "It tastes the same but the difference is that when you lift it to your mouth the light passes through and makes the tea glow. It's like drinking something luminous." She placed it in a visible spot in the front of her cupboard and said she'd use it to read tea leaves.

It seemed to be a promise of better things to come.

The wind howled the night before she went into labour. She told Neil it reminded her of the night her sister Effie was born. The doctor who had come to tend her mother had worn an enormous fur coat that extended all the way to the floor, and he seemed to her to be some kind of huge bear. She tried to hide herself in the clothes cupboard but her father had found one small foot sticking up and had gently drawn her out and told her that the doctor was an angel of mercy. She said, "For a time there was some confusion in my mind between bears and angels."

Neil awoke in early morning with the light spilling around the edges of the blind covering the tall bedroom window. It looked like a halo around a movie screen that might soon display their life story. Jessica had her back to him and his arms encircled her enormous belly. Although she hadn't stirred he sensed she was awake. There was a great peace filling the room and he was not prepared when her muscles contracted strongly and roused her so that she pushed him away and sat upright.

"I think it might be time," she said.

"I thought it was next week," he whispered. That brought a short huff of a laugh to escape from her lungs before she whispered back, "If you can convince the baby of that, I'm all for it." She immediately had another contraction.

He threw his clothes on and ran out into the snow, fearful that no taxi would be there on a Sunday morning, and was relieved when he saw a cab waiting at the stand. When he opened the passenger door, a man he knew from the boxing club was sitting in the driver's seat reading his paper. Neil blurted out, "My wife is in labour."

"Get in, then," the man said, resigned to his cab becoming a moving emergency ward where anything might happen. As they skidded around the corner he asked, "Do we have time or is she going to have it in the car?"

"We have time."

"That's good."

When they got back to the apartment, she was already down at the door leaning against the dark terracotta wall, with her hair of almost the same colour blowing back against it, while she closed her eyes and held her roundness as if it was a weight she didn't want to drop. Before he got to her she collapsed in a crouch and let her hair fall forward to conceal the pain.

Neil was relieved he wasn't allowed to be present for the birth. He was quite sure he would show weakness.

When he tentatively entered the hospital room, he could see Jessica sleeping on her side with her back to the door. The nurse gently pushed him into the room and walked away after whispering, "He's in the bed. Have a look at him."

The baby was sleeping in a basket by her side. The railing was up on that side of the bed to ensure that no accident would send him tumbling to the floor, but the child's exposure to the world filled Neil with alarm. He leaned over the railing to touch Jessica's hand and she woke easily, looking up at him and then at the baby. "Do you want to hold him?"

"Not right now," he said, lightly touching the baby's head. He didn't want to admit, even to himself, that he was afraid he might hurt him somehow.

He got off work at four on a Friday afternoon and walked to the hospital, wading through drifts of snow. As he and Jessica walked down the stairs he felt an overwhelming responsibility. The baby was wrapped in blankets and a raincoat. Jessica looked as if she had never been so happy or so anxious.

They spent the whole weekend together lying in bed and watching baby Francis breathe. If Jessica slept, Neil stayed awake, hovering over the basket. He napped sometimes when she was feeding.

Once Neil went back to work on Monday morning, it was usually just Jessica and the baby at home alone together. Francis noticed every sound and flicker that passed over him. She saw the delight in his eyes as they followed the light moving along the wall when a cloud passed over the sun. But he resisted sleep as if some great danger awaited him on the other side of a precipice he felt himself slipping toward. Jessica spent hours walking back and forth with him, singing and rubbing his small back, and he sometimes fell asleep and let her put him in his bed without startling. Other times, his eyes popped open before he began to scream and the whole cycle started again.

Neil began spending a great deal of time in union meetings and was often out at night. When she asked him not to go, he said, "I have to. There are only a few people organizing this thing. I made a promise to see it through."

"Have them come here."

This surprised him. "They smoke and they swear and are rude to each other."

"I'm so delicate I couldn't handle that?"

He stopped to consider how to answer her. "These are strategy meetings. All the talk is about how to grow the union and not get caught. They're very private."

"Please don't get caught."

He nodded. "Don't wait up."

She knew something had to be done about his scanty wages. If she could just go back to teaching, it would be fine, she told herself. A strike was such a drastic option when they had no savings at all.

The evening a decision was made, Neil came home in a sombre mood.

"We'll be off the job in a week if they refuse to give us any increase. It could be a long one."

Jessica threw up after rushing out of the room, barely making it to the toilet. When she had regained her equilibrium and reappeared in the kitchen, she said, "I'm pregnant."

After a brief silence, he asked, "How far along are you?"

"Over four months."

They both sat motionless until they heard Francis stir from his sleep. She picked him up and gathered him into her arms and then went back to the place she'd been sitting and assumed a motionless vigil while he sucked. None of them changed position until the baby had to change sides. After they settled again, Neil spoke, "If it keeps on a long time you'll have to go to your mother."

"Would you mind?" she asked.

He looked for a long time at his auburn-haired wife with her baby on the breast and said, "Yes, I would."

When they finally walked off the job, all the excitement he'd felt when they'd been scheming and planning was dampened by the way the men left the grounds. The silence was almost eerie and they each looked a long way into the distance. He thought it might be the way people always look when they are walking away from their only source of security in the hope of finding a better future. Perhaps they had walked this way when they left their own crofts to board an immigrant ship, or when they walked inland from the shore where they'd been left, to find a piece of land on which to hack a farm out of the forest. He knew what it was to leave behind that farm. Perhaps it was their fate to always walk away.

Ten days later they received the letter from Isabel.

Dear Children,

    I've heard about the strike. Please put aside whatever differences we have had in the past and come home to us.

Your Loving Mama

"Loving Mama, my eye, but I know you have to go," was Neil's response.

Jessica was almost six months pregnant, and food was running low, when her brother Donald came to pick her up to take her "home."

He shook Neil's hand. "We're all behind you," he said.

"Your mother too?" Neil asked.

"I wouldn't even give that a thought."

Neil stayed behind in Sydney burying the blow to his pride by organizing the picket line. A month later, Jessica insisted on boarding a train with Francis in order to visit him. As she packed up the baby and made sandwiches for the journey, her mother hovered and worried about the trip.

"You'd think he could come here. It's not as if he's working."

Isabel insisted on going with them to the station to pay the fare and waved at them for a long time down the track.

The next time Jessica made the trip, she left Francis with her mother, who denounced the journey as taking chances with her unborn baby's life. She was close to delivery and in fact had the baby in Sydney with Neil by her side. He was eternally grateful to her on this account and sure that she had planned it just this way. He would prefer to have the ground swallow him whole than have to go to her mother's home to visit his newborn child.

They both understood that she would have to go back, so he spent his afternoons at the hospital, soaking up the time with her and the baby as if it was the sun nourishing his skin. He sat beside her on the bed.

"Do you think your mother was right about me?"

She watched his face for a moment to find the right answer before she said, "She thinks you're fine."

"She thinks I can't put food on my family's table and she is right."

"This is what families do. They help each other."

"At what cost?"

"None at all."

He only nodded in reply.

The late August and September storms made travelling impossible for some time after and they had no further visit until the strike was over. On the same day it ended, he posted a letter to her.

Dear Jess,

The strike is over as you may have heard by now. If I had the fare I could come to see you today, as the trains are running just fine, but I have to work a few months to pay the back rent and put in food and coal. Do you think you could stay a bit longer there?

Love to you and the babies,

Neil

Writing those words caused him to experience both physical and spiritual vertigo. Jessica understood this and wrote back to him.

Dear Neil,

I'm sorry not to be there to make the sandwiches and light the fire. I'd rather be with you than anywhere else on the earth. We'll stay a few weeks.

Weeks stretched on as Neil tried to make the homecoming as perfect as it could be. While he was alone, he painted, setting up a makeshift easel by the kitchen table. He wrote to her about the pictures he was making, mostly of the sky at night, a thousand stars bursting over the water.

He wanted them back but he had grown used to living alone. There was a peace in it that he knew would not be possible when she came home with their babies.

One of the women who cleaned up at the train station ran over to their apartment to tell him to collect his family when they arrived unexpectedly in December. When he reached the platform, his heart was pounding. There she was, surrounded by large canvas bags of produce and milk from the farm, carrying one baby, with another standing behind her hanging on to her coat and peeking out at him. He scooped Francis up and held them all together in his arms, and when the children squirmed and squawked he just laughed and kissed Jessica more.

There was great clomping of feet and dropping of bags as they occupied the apartment. The kitchen took her completely by surprise. The canvases transported her back to the garage and their carefree days by the sea. She looked at him in wonder. "You still want to paint."

"No, no," he said, "I had to do something to occupy my mind while you were gone." He started picking them up and stacking them together against the wall. "I'll get these smelly things out of here. No one should breathe this stuff," he said, "especially the kids."

She grabbed his hands as he turned to pick up another and pulled herself into his arms.

"You could still paint."

"I don't even want to."

He held her close and she couldn't see his eyes.

Every week for the following few months, Isabel sent letters and small gifts for Francis. He began to look for and depend on these for his happiness. On one of Isabel's visits that fall Neil came home to find Jessica, Isabel and Francis baking biscuits in the kitchen. Francis was standing on a chair using a small milk tin to cut perfect rounds in the dough. Jessica and Isabel were drinking tea and waiting for him to finish.

"Come set the fire in the grate," Neil told Francis.

He knew this was a favourite task, so Francis's reply surprised him. "No, I want to make biscuits." He felt betrayed, and then he felt childish and didn't know which was worse. He admitted to himself that he couldn't warm up to the boy, who seemed too attached to his grandmother, and he felt entirely unable to live up to his own limited idea of what a father might do with a son.

On a day when Isabel was in the house, he made a special trip to the beach alone with Francis. For a few good moments he watched the child face the surf with the wind blowing his hair and a look of wonder in his eyes. Without thinking about it, he picked him up quickly and held him upside down above the waves, pretending he would drop him. This was a game he fondly remembered his father playing with him and did not expect the screaming and weeping that Francis continued long after he put him down on the shore. Eventually he paid more attention to Joe, who was a friendly and contented baby.

When Francis turned four, Isabel sent him a letter wishing him a happy birthday.

Dear Francis,

Here another year has rolled by and you are having another birthday. I hear you are quite a big boy now and going out to play but you must be very careful and not go out on the street or you might get hurt. How are Joseph and Stella? I know you are good to them as you are a big boy now and can take care of them. Coax your mother to come up this summer to spend time with her old Mama and take Joe and Stella with you. I'm sending you a dollar so your mother can buy you some small gift.

Lots of love and kisses to you and some for Joe and Stella.

Gran

Jessica read the letter out loud to all of them and after they blew out the candles on the cake, she handed the dollar to Francis. He took it and looked it over and then got up from his seat and went to stand beside his father's chair, trying to make a connection that would elude him for most of his life. He held out the dollar and said, "You have this." But Neil was so closed to Isabel that he said, "Keep it. I don't need Isabel's money."

Francis's face fell and he went back to his seat and left the dollar by Jessica's plate. She said, "You're a very generous boy. We'll buy a treat tomorrow with this," and stared at Neil rather pointedly. He looked at his plate then picked it up and carried it to the kitchen. She heard him settle in the living room to read the paper. Francis took a similar attitude, copying his father's downward looks and refusal to meet eyes.

Jessica contemplated him for a while. "It's your birthday. Should I read the tea leaves and tell your future?"

"No."

"Come on now. It's just a game. I'll get out the beautiful cup. What do you think, Joseph?"

Joe was enthusiastic. "I pour the tea!"

"No, I'm the only one who can handle the tea or the cup. But you can look and listen."

Getting out the special cup was hard for Francis to refuse. It was the prettiest one they owned and the favourite of both his mother and his father, although they never used it.

"Can you really tell tomorrow?" he asked.

"I can't tell everything but I can tell some."

"Okay."

She picked Stella up from her high chair and carried her to the playpen in the kitchen. "You two sit at the table," she said to the boys. Only after she was sure they were settled did she retrieve the translucent cup from the pine cabinet. It shone softly when she set it in the middle of the table. "Nobody touch." With a spoon, she pulled the tea bag out of the glass pot warming at the back of the stove and stuck it with a paring knife so she could spill its contents into the simmering water. They watched as the soft, wet tea separated and slowly swirled to the bottom of the light-filled cup. She let the leaves settle before carefully pouring the liquid back into the pot.

Reading the pattern of the leaves left at the bottom of the cup was similar to reading clouds. Jessica studied what they had to say before relaying it to the boys. "Hmmm," she murmured. "I see you in the field by the railway track. Look at that. It must be the picnic we're going on tomorrow. You're kicking the ball with your father."

"No! I don't want him there." Francis's face was closed, his eyebrows pulled down.

"Oh look. He's kicking the ball right to you. It'll be great fun." She got up to pull the cookie tin from the cabinet, hoping something sweet might soften his anger.

Francis peered into the cup and then picked it up to look more closely, as if he might really see the game that he would play with his father on the next day's planned walk in the country. When Jessica turned she had no time to warn him to be careful before she saw it slip from his hands. It fell in slow motion and cracked into three large, neat pieces when it hit the tiled floor. They sat together like a broken eggshell and the handle remained intact on one of them.

There was the sound of four or five footsteps and then Neil was in the room. He bent to pick up the pieces without looking at anyone. He held fragments of translucent porcelain in his hands and stood in his spot for one brief moment, looking at Francis still seated at the table, before he spoke. "That was no accident." Jessica watched him retreat to their bedroom where he would carefully set the pieces on the dresser until he could repair them.

She recalled the morning she'd climbed the elm tree on the day she had decided to leave home. The vision of the future she'd seen so clearly through the breaking fog had revealed only her and her children. She wondered if either one of them knew what a father should do.

On the day of the last walk in the country, Jessica and Neil piled the two little ones in the carriage and Francis walked beside them holding Jessica's hand. They travelled on a dirt road that climbed away from the edge of the town to an area of forests and fields. Neil had to push the carriage because it was such heavy going to get up the hill and because the wind was blowing against them. Jessica carried a picnic lunch they would eat in the large, rolling field of a farmer who knew them well. Usually, if the farmer saw them passing, he would invite the children into the barnyard to visit the goat, which had to be tethered on a long rope to keep it from wandering or jumping the fence. Francis loved to hear that sometimes it chewed through the rope and had overnight adventures of its own before being discovered in the morning destroying some other farmer's lilac bushes. They didn't see the farmer at all that day.

At the top of the hill the road dwindled away but not before it crossed a railway track that ran through the field. The bed of the track was wide enough for a single path on either side of the rails. The family veered off there, looking for a place protected from the wind where they could stop to eat their lunch. As they walked, the high aspect of the land gave them a good view of the town, and to the east they could see the ocean and the harbour several miles away. They could never have traversed the field with a baby carriage without the level train bed because the land undulated away from them and kept bumping into itself in gentle folds. There was one place where the track was built five or six feet higher than the land for quite a long piece, and this part of the journey worried Neil. It was not as if they were crossing a bridge and might get caught if a train passed. He knew the train schedule and he knew that if he heard an unexpected whistle he could scramble down the side with the carriage to get away into the field. But there were three children with them and he felt a great responsibility for all of them, as well as for Jessica. He worried that he might not cope well if one of them went sliding over the edge and was hurt.

On this day the sun was shining and the wind was blowing just enough to be a source of laughter when it lifted Jessica's skirt. Francis wanted to run ahead, as children do, and Neil said, "No, stay with us," but Jessica looked across at Neil above the child's head and motioned with one upheld palm to the expanse of field and track ahead of them as if to say, "We can see for miles." Neil gave a quick twitch of his head and said to Francis, "Alright then, go, but stop and come back when I tell you to."

Jessica smiled through bits of her hair, loose from its pins and whipping across her face, while the wind pressed her cotton dress against her girlish body. They quietly went along for several moments, watching Francis fly along the path ahead of them until he slowed and finally stopped to look at something on the track. Even from that distance Jessica could see his small body shudder. He turned and ran back to them, screaming as if he'd been hurt, and when he reached them he couldn't catch his breath to speak. He stood there, his shoulders heaving with great gulping sobs. Neil put a hand on his head and told him, "Be still, I'll go see what the trouble is." He grabbed Jessica's hand and placed it on the handle of the carriage so it would not slip down the side. Jessica raised her eyebrows, but when she caught his eye he shook his head distractedly and rushed away.

He ran until he saw something lying on the tracks ahead, slowed down a bit when he saw it looked like a body, and then carefully approached the gory remains of the goat. It was mostly intact except for one gouged eye and looked as if the train had dragged it for some distance. Its white coat was almost entirely soaked in blood. He bent down to touch it and came away with a hand full of wet blood that he wiped on the front of his jacket.

When he turned to look back at his family, he froze in silence. He was in a different country altogether. The sun, with a haze around it, was burning above a line of blue mountains. There were gunshots at some distance and then complete silence as men reacted to the horror of their position being strafed with bullets. Everyone crawled or slithered, trying to find the trench. He stumbled through the landscape, white chalk streaked with blood. Another burst of gunfire sent him reeling to the ground. Ahead of him he saw Frank stand to support an injured man just as the sun flashed off the barrel of a distant rifle pointed in their direction.

The stench of the gunpowder stung his nose and eyes. Terror grabbed his heart with a thudding, rising beat. He broke into a run, with his head down to protect himself, yelling the whole time, "Get down! Get down!"

Jessica had never seen this kind of daylight panic before and looked around quickly, trying to assess and react. She held the carriage tightly on one side and Francis's hand in the other. Neil continued headlong and when he reached them he grabbed Francis roughly and lunged for the ground, Francis falling underneath him while Neil let out a wild animal howl of pain.

Jessica began screaming, "Neil! Neil! Stop. What are you doing?"

He looked at her and then jumped up and stepped away from them all. She let go of the carriage and pulled Francis up from the track and pushed him behind her. He grabbed her skirt with one fist.

Neil's face grew paler and began to glisten while he stood in one spot, shivering. She said, "Where are you, Neil?"

"What's going on here?"

"You're taking your children for a Sunday walk."

"Are they hurt?"

"No, they're not." Suddenly Francis ran toward his father and flung himself around his legs, but Neil grabbed him and threw him off, shouting at Jessica, "Take him. Get him away from me!" Francis became even more hysterical and the other children joined him in a shrill cacophony of baby cries.

Jessica turned the carriage and told Francis to hold the handle. She said, "We're going home." Then she turned to Neil and commanded, "Follow us."

Although it was not the first time that Jessica had witnessed this type of episode, it was the only time it ever occurred in daylight and the only time the children ever saw it. Usually it was at night and coming out of some kind of nightmare that he would rise up halfway from the bed and shout at some unseen enemy.

On a night soon after they were married he had crawled beneath the bed after one of these shouting incidents and lay there wide eyed, staring out at her, so she got down on the floor and lifted the bedcovers to check on him. When she spoke to him softly, so as not to further frighten him, he gave no sign of understanding. She pulled the blankets slowly off the bed to cover herself and lay there on the floor, watching him until she fell asleep. In the morning she woke to him gently stroking her back. When she looked up at him he asked, "Did we have a bad night?"

"Not so bad," she said. "You went after the scary thing under the bed and fell asleep there." He lay beside her on the floor and wrapped his arms around her, saying over and over, "You're everything to me. You're everything."

On the day they found the goat, he went to bed in silence. Jessica woke around 3 a.m. Beside her, the bed was empty. She tentatively went to investigate his whereabouts and found him sitting in the kitchen with his head on the table. When she spoke to him—"Neil?"—he sat up and rubbed his eyes and his face with his open hands.

"Would you like some tea?"

"Yes, I would," he said.

She touched his back but he made no response so she busied herself at the stove. He struggled to rise and stood, arms hanging loosely by his sides. All he could say was, "I am so sorry."

She spoke without looking at him. "Can you talk to me about what happened up there?"

"I would if I knew."

"Did you see something?"

He thought for a moment before saying, "I saw Frank get shot. His head…"

Jessica became very still.

"I'm sorry," he said, "it will never happen again."

"How do you know?"

"I'm telling you it never will," he said, and slowly turned and walked out the kitchen door into the dawn.

It made her feel lonesome. Who could she tell about such a thing? How could she explain what happened to Francis? What sense did he make of it, she wondered. It was bad enough that he saw the remains of the goat.

12

There were no warning signs on the day our lives were changed; no whimpering dogs running to and fro, no shattered mirrors or other portents. There was only Donald standing in our back porch in his red plaid jacket and his brown cap with the black fur earflaps. He was tall, slim and straight, and completely covered in snow from having waded through our as yet unshovelled walk. The sun glittered off the snow behind him and my mother swept him with a broom as if he was a small child and she his mother.

The snowplow had gone through that morning after Neil went to work and left behind a sparkling white bank, six or seven feet high, lining the road. It left no point of entry to our path. For Iona and Murdoch, this was an opportunity to scale the walls in whatever dream of adventure they inhabited. As I watched from the window they were up and over the side and on their way to school.

After they left, I lay on the kitchen chaise under a layer of heavy blankets, with a sore throat I was hoping would last for a while. The house was perfectly quiet except for the sound of Mama slapping and kneading the bread dough on the kitchen table. I watched her fold it over and then shove it down and fold it over again. The bread breathed a sigh of relief every time she touched it.

Two short knocks and the sound of retreating feet surprised us. Mama opened the door only to have a snowball lobbed through the opening, sliding and crumbling across the newly washed kitchen floor. When Donald poked his head around the doorcase, she burst out laughing. If anyone else had done it she might not have found the fun in it so quickly, but for her brother Donald some special reserve of wholeheartedness always floated to the surface. I liked it when he came to visit. She got younger and quicker in his company.

"Eileen, are you expecting a snowman?" Mama asked.

"No, I wasn't, but if you don't close the door I'm going to be one."

She looked back to Donald. "She always gets a bit saucy when she's sick."

"Fairly astute, I'd say," Donald replied.

She swept the snow off his clothing with long, even strokes of the broom. "I seem to recall our mother taking a broom to you once."

He ducked his head down and to one side a bit. When he hung his snowy coat on the handle of the shovel and left it outside on the back step to drip, she said, "Oh bring it inside. It will get cold."

"No no, it'll make a puddle. I can't stay long anyway." Then he sat on the stool by the door to take off his overshoes and put them carefully side by side on the black rubber mat. When the family was at home the mat was covered with a jumble of boots, but all it held that day were Mama's and mine.

Finally he folded his long body into a kitchen chair and sat on his hands to warm them. Steam rose from the cup of amber tea that Mama placed on the table in front of him. "Put your hands around that," she suggested. We waited patiently while he took his first quiet sips, hoping he had some exciting or at least interesting news. Still, when he began to speak he didn't tell us right away why he'd come. Instead he talked about the goings-on at the farm and the way the snowdrifts had reached all the way up to the hayloft window on the barn. Eventually my mother's curiosity could no longer be contained.

"Now what brings you into town today?"

"I came especially to see you, Jessica."

"You did not."

He laughed and launched right into it then.

"The lake is frozen as hard as a rock. Minus ten for two weeks! And the wind did most of the work clearing the surface. This morning I found the cleats in the barn. Haven't seen them for years. We're going to race the horses on the ice on Saturday."

"You're not! You're teasing me. Is it solid?"

"Solid? That ice is so solid you could build a house on it and it would still be there next winter."

"Well wouldn't I love to see that! Do you remember the time you won?"

He turned to me. "That's like me asking her if she remembers having you." Then to her, "Yes, I remember and I was thinking you might come."

"On these roads?"

"They're *plowing* the roads," he said dryly, and then raised his eyebrows and spoke sideways, "You tell your mother you want to go, Eileen, and bring your skates."

My mother had told me stories about the racing on the ice but I thought it was something that belonged to another time and would never be part of my world. That I might get a chance to be one of the young ones skating at the edges of the lake, while the grown-ups would visit with each other and make small wagers, made me feel as if time had stopped short somehow. I looked at my mother and could see she was soft on it.

"We'll see," she said. "We'll see how it looks on Friday night."

Donald rose to go. "Good enough then. I'm off. Try to come, Jessica."

And more quietly, pretending he didn't want my mother to hear, "Don't take no for an answer, Eileen."

What I loved about him was that he always spoke as if I understood the world as he did or as if we shared some secret, although I rarely spoke a word to him. We could have a whole conversation, with only him talking, and at the end of it I'd feel as if he understood everything I'd said.

He waved at us before he disappeared on the other side of the snow-banks after making one more attempt to shoot a snowball through the open door we were waving from.

"Donald!" My mother yelled, "A grown man!" She looked at me. "He's an awful brat for a man his age. I don't want you taking him as any example." We both smiled at that.

At supper a smile still hovered around the edges of her mouth as she served the steaming beans to our plates from a crock on the table and remarked, "Donald is still a fine figure of a man."

My father, in his deliberate way, replied, "Yes, he's come a long way from the man I used to stumble home with."

My mother's back stiffened a bit. She didn't like to be reminded of the dark time of his or Donald's early life.

"He's forty-three. The same age as our father was when he died. His shortcomings would be understandable to any discerning human being." She looked back at Neil. "As would yours."

Neil became very busy salting his food and buttering the molasses bread.

In the next days and weeks, I tried to be discerning, putting the stories that family members told me together with conversations overheard and making up some pieces that were missing. All the pieces I'd stored in the nooks and crannies of my mind were pulled from their places and laid out before me, and I hoped the puzzle would show its picture and a larger story would emerge.

There was no racing on the ice at all that year, other than on the seventy-five miles of frozen highway from our house to the farm, my father tightly clutching the wheel, refusing all emotion, and my mother staring straight ahead, ignoring the large wet tears coursing down her face. Occasionally she murmured something about the horse. "I should have known it would be the horse," or "Of course the horse was his undoing," as if it was she who had dropped the reins.

On the day before the race, a few days after we'd seen him, Donald decided to ride down to the lake just to get a feel for the conditions. Muriel told Aunt Effie, who told me, that Donald had felt he could almost go from the place his father had left off and continue the life he hadn't had the chance to live.

He was elated by the conditions but Muriel suggested that it might be better if John, their fifteen-year-old, drove the horses.

"No, John can drive later if the ice holds. This first one is mine."

She said that when he left, he looked like a man at the zenith of his life.

When we arrived at the farm the next day, we found him lying in an elaborate coffin in the front room, with only the top half open so that he looked somehow nestled there and protected. Muriel sat in an armchair on one side of the room, her eyes never leaving his face. She didn't stand to greet us, as she normally would do. Mama rushed to her and they hugged awkwardly, one standing, one sitting. She looked up, saying, "He never meant to go that far." Mama held her for another moment, then moved to take a seat beside the coffin, first standing and touching his hair. I stood watching, feeling an acute pulse of pain from both within and without.

There were people quietly milling about everywhere, and over and over the muffled words, "Sorry for your trouble," were being repeated to my mother and to Aunt Muriel and almost, it seemed, to anyone who'd listen. Uncle Angus sat rigidly by the box that held his brother. He was wearing his minister's collar and his eyes were swollen and red. Grandma Isabel sat on a straight-backed chair, rocking herself slightly. Her gnarled and still competent hands darted out of their place on her lap when her small namesake, Isa, ran by and then it was only to fleetingly touch the reddish curls on Isa's head.

The best escape, for me, seemed to be to follow three-year-old Isa.

We sat quietly together on the outside steps for a moment, watching the horses frisk around the field, before she said, "Daddy's going to heaven but he's having a sleep in the front room first. Come see." Then she jumped up, grabbed my hand, and led me back to where I belonged.

That first afternoon was a blur of too many adults, murmuring voices, date squares and potato salad. It was only when late evening came that the house settled. With only the family left to hold vigil, the story began to be told. Uncle Angus spoke first, his eyes on his mother.

"We could tell what happened from the tracks they left. He would have been about half an hour from shore when the wind started gusting from the northeast. The heavy snowflakes must have brought an early dusk. With the squall, and in the wet snow, the horse lost her footing and she fell. I'd say he was thrown. At that point he must have been all in one piece because he struggled to help her regain her footing. It would have taken a great effort on both their parts to finally have her standing."

"He had no cleats," Muriel offered. "He only meant to skirt the edge."

Uncle Angus turned his gaze to her. "There was a thin crust of snow on the surface of the ice there. It made the going easier and he wasn't planning to run the horse. Lightning was so sure-footed."

The pain revealing itself in Muriel's face caused him to avert his eyes.

"There was no sign of the storm when he left," he said.

Muriel bowed her head and put her hands over her face. Mama asked if she would like to go up to bed. "No, I won't be sleeping and I need to hear."

Angus finished telling his part. "It looked like they'd only gone a hundred yards, with Donald walking beside her when she fell again. It was perhaps only three thirty but, remember, it was dark by then.

"By the time they were on the way, they would have both been laden with snow, but you know what a hopeful and determined man he was. He would never give up. You could tell they came to a dryer place on the ice after a while and were likely able to travel a little faster. He probably wasn't prepared when they hit another slippery patch. He must have gone down fast, because he damaged his ankle. After that he couldn't walk. He made some effort to haul himself up onto the horse's back, but the tracks suggested that her hind legs kept slipping out from under her.

"So he tied up her reins and slapped her on the rump the same way he always did when he wanted to send her home for some reason.

How many times have I seen him do that? He'd say, 'Go home Lightning' and off she'd go. It looked as if she trotted and then turned back to him before walking more carefully away.

"He began to crawl on his hands and knees, probably to save the broken ankle. Perhaps he told himself he'd keep warmer this way and that we'd come for him when Lightning alerted us.

"The horse did the best she could. She made it to shore and her whinnying brought the attention of old MacEachern. She came right up to his door. When he saw her he knew right away and got on the phone to the operator. She was the one who called us. By the time we got to the shore, there were a dozen men rolling out long ropes and fishing twine. There was not a lot of snow but it was blowing in a hard horizontal line by then. We attached ourselves by means of these lines to someone standing on shore, knowing we could be lost in minutes, then travelled along the shore and ventured out onto the ice, one man anchoring all the others by what seemed like fragile threads compared to the fierce power of the blizzard. It wasn't until morning that we were successful. John was with the group of men who found him."

I didn't think John was going to tell us anything at all. He was silent for some long minutes, examining the pattern in the parlour rug. Finally he spoke with a tear-swollen voice. "His red plaid jacket made him an easy target to spot. We knew before we reached him that we were too late. He was in a frozen position on his elbows and knees, with his head hanging down, as if he was searching for some small thing he'd lost."

Then he unfolded his long, flexible body from the chair, as I'd seen his father do, and walked upstairs without a word. When he returned, he carried the last letter that Donald had received from his father, when he was ten years old. It was a soft, handled, often-folded piece of paper written in carpenter's pencil, quite faded but still legible. We passed it among us as a jewel to be examined. "When I saw these little horses they reminded me of you... Take good care of Diamond... I'm depending on you now... Your Papa."

"He'd be glad to know Lightning survived," John said.

It felt like a gust of wind had blown through the room. It caught my breath. I think as the time went on, it caught us all.

We stayed up as late as we could. After midnight, it was Aunt Effie who had the grace to softly approach the coffin and gently close its cover. "We should all try to go to bed now," she said, looking at Muriel. Iona had already fallen asleep beside Mama, who was trying to gently wake her by touching her hair. Neil gathered a sleeping Murdoch in his arms and silently led us up the stairs to the bedrooms of this house we knew so well. At the top, he looked around slowly, wondering which rooms were ours to share. Perhaps he had never been up there before.

In the night I woke to coldness in the room. I recalled a dream that seemed more like a memory, of Donald on the ice.

The next morning, the smell of breakfast coming from the big sunny kitchen made it feel like we were on one of our visiting holidays, so it was alarming when I looked into the front room. Isa was sitting on her father's chest, having mussed up his hair, and was attempting to open one of his eyes. I ran to get Aunt Effie, who seemed to have more fortitude than anyone else, and told her what was happening. She explained that they had all talked and had decided that Isa was too young to understand matters of decorum and they would not make her feel that she couldn't touch her father. All that day she climbed all over Donald and, if she opened his eyes, Effie made it her business to close them again. Then Isa would go back to her musing as she sat on top of the coffin attempting to understand the mystery of her father's inactivity. On the second and last evening, the closer members of the family were sitting in the room with Donald, in a suspended silence, knowing this was the last of their time with him. For five or ten minutes, no one had spoken and the only sound was the howling of the wind and the patter of rain that had brought with it thawing temperatures. Isa was perched on the closed bottom half of the coffin, with her hands folded in her lap, and into this silence interjected, "That's the longest I've ever seen Daddy with his mouth shut."

Everyone in the room broke into relieved laughter, but even after this had subsided, Muriel and Jessica laughed and laughed, and cried, and laughed and cried.

13

A period of bright and bitter cold descended in the following winter, as if to remind us of the racing on the ice. A year had passed but Mama had never regained her peace of mind. It seemed that whenever I brought Francis up, it made her even sadder, so I didn't. I know he still called her at night once in a while and she said that was a comfort.

The washing often froze on the line until the pants and shirts became so stiff they could stand on their own. One afternoon, Mama sat at the kitchen table, pretending to read the newspaper and twirling a piece of hair at the base of her neck, when her head jerked up as if she was startled. "The clothes. Shoot!"

The blue wool sweater she pulled over her cotton print dress dragged a few stray pieces of hair from her pins. She brushed them back with one hand as she glanced in my direction. I was home from school with the ever-persistent sore throat but was well enough to feel excitement and to welcome the distraction. "We can play 'invisible,'" I said, shedding my slippers and putting on my shoes. She looked at me through her distraction as if she didn't know what I meant. Then she took a breath and nodded.

"Fine. You hold the door open just enough to drag in one piece at a time. Get your jacket on too. It's cold."

"I don't need it for just a minute."

"Yes, you do."

She waited while I put on the red quilted jacket that was my favourite in the spring and far too light for this February day.

She considered me for a moment. "Get something warmer." I grabbed a navy wool jacket from a hook by the door. It belonged to one of the boys and fit over the red one. I presented myself again.

She nodded. "Don't let the door get away from you in the wind." Then she pulled open the door and squeezed through the smallest opening she could make. I came behind her and kept it open a crack, holding the handle tightly against a gusting wind that threatened to throw the door open. Once she got to the edge of the back step, she braced herself with a wide stance and unpinned each piece, handing it back to me, turning and swooping, without moving her well-planted feet. Each time she did this I opened the door wider and accepted the frozen garment. We repeated this dance step a dozen times before she said, "That's enough. You've been in the open door too long," and turned to come inside.

Different kinds of pants were piled in a stack behind me: the khaki work pants of my father, the small and large blue jeans of children, and the skinny black pants that Joe wore. They all froze equally well, although the black ones were lighter fabric and didn't hold their shape as well when you placed them in a particular position. The shirts were equally varied and, luckily, there were a couple of blouses among them. All in all there were enough shirts and pants for about six people. That made three people each to arrange. We got to work quickly, placing them on chairs or leaning them against the cupboard or the sink. We sculpted their presence with folded legs or an outstretched arm draped on the back of a chair, in the most natural of poses, so that they resembled the invisible clothed. The names we gave them were based on their posture and how well they wore the garments, and they were always some other family from Boston or up the country somewhere.

I gave one of them the black pants and a blouse. The blouse was already beginning to warm up and was slumping. "A tired tourist," I said. "Florence is her name."

Mama tried to suppress a smile. "Just came to take a look, did she?"

"She's nice. She says she likes it here except there are no landmarks."

"This fellow looks a bit tired too," Mama said, considering her farmer in khakis and plaid shirt. "These people aren't going to last long."

"They never do," I said.

The smile she offered then had a flicker in it that must have been sadness, but a dark cloud had covered the sun and darkened the room, so perhaps I was mistaken.

The ringing of the phone disturbed the game.

"Should I get it?" I asked.

"No, I'll get it. It's probably Wilma. Turn the light on will you, dear?" She turned and picked up the receiver on the wall phone, "Hello… Muriel, I can't hear you," and listened for a few minutes more. She had her back to me and I couldn't see her face, but soon she held the phone away from her ear and examined it, then held it closer again as if it was a sea conch and all she could hear was the ocean. The sound of Aunt Muriel's panicked voice, emitting in small bursts from the phone, was impossible to follow. Mama spoke into the receiver slowly. "That can't be true…

Oh God, when?... What happened?" As she listened to the urgent murmuring, she turned in my direction but she didn't seem to see me. She said, "No, no, I have no phone number but I think I have an old address for him in California. The operator can find a number for us."

She hung up, promising, "I'll call you back."

The drawer of the pine china cupboard slid out quickly and she fingered its contents as if not really seeing them. Then, with some agitation, she pulled it completely out of its place, and dumped the contents on the kitchen table with a clatter. She bent her head and carefully picked through the elastic bands, pencils, buttons, tape, shoelaces and scissors, the usual items to be found in any kitchen junk drawer, but it was bits of old notes or receipts that she pulled out and examined closely.

"What are you looking for?" I asked.

"My brother Malcolm."

"What happened?"

"My mother died."

I saw all of the room at once: the frozen people slumping in their chairs, the contents of the upturned drawer spread on the table, Mama devouring the details of some ten-year-old note before discarding it.

With a great gasp of air, she abandoned her search and moved to the sink, where she leaned forward on the edge and held her face in her hands for a brief moment. Then she dug her hands into her hair and lifted her head. Through the window above the sink I could see the birches swaying wildly in the four o'clock dusk. Her hands floated slowly down to the edge of the sink. "I'll take in the rest of the clothes."

"You should put on a jacket, Mama." She didn't seem to hear me. This time, when she opened the door and stepped on to the deck of the back steps, the storm door, which was hooked open so it wouldn't bang itself around in the wind, tore loose from its hook and slammed shut and then swung wildly. Watching through the slim opening of the heavy wood door, I saw the wind take Mama over the side as if she weighed nothing, her hands grasping wildly for a railing that didn't exist. She landed with no sound other than a sickening thud. I let the inside door go and ran down the steps, tripping and falling and landing without injury in a drift of fresh fallen snow.

The snow was thigh deep in places so I plodded through to her, stepping high and sinking deep over and over again. When I reached her she was lying flat on her back with the snow collapsed under her. She was making no effort to get up and her hands were spread upon her rounded belly.

The blue sweater and the dress beneath it had settled on her body in a way they didn't when she sat or stood. The late pregnancy she'd been so carefully hiding from the neighbours was exposed for all to see.

I said, "Are you okay? Can you get up?"

"Go find a neighbour. Try Mildred first. Tell her to come over."

"Mama, you'll freeze there."

"No, I just need something for my head." She looked sleepy.

I negotiated every slippery step back into the house with great caution and called an ambulance. The woman who answered told me to slow down when I said, "My mother fell outside and is freezing to death." She wanted the address and then my name and Mama's name and even after I'd given her all of these details she still wanted to keep me there.

"How old are you?" she asked.

"I'm fourteen."

"Okay, dear. You should wait here on the phone with me until the ambulance comes."

"I can't. She needs a pillow and a coat." I hung up and rushed back to Mama.

When the ambulance arrived, the medics looked at my bare legs and double coat and asked, "Are you home alone?"

"Yes, for now."

"You better come with your mother then. Get some pants and come quickly."

I sat in the ambulance with her, watching from a corner while the medic kept taking her pulse and putting a large hand on her shoulder. At the hospital they left me out in the hall on a chair for an hour. No one in the hallway looked happy and it was a relief when I was allowed to go in to see her.

She had a bruise on one side of her face, as if she'd been hit by something.

"I can't smile but I'm in no pain. There's nothing broken. I just have to stay until they make sure everything is fine," she said. "Can you go home on the bus and let the others know? I have a feeling Neil is working a double shift."

"All right then."

"Take the keys in case they locked it." She rummaged in her purse. I accepted the keys without a word.

The wind whipped around me as I waited for the bus. The double layer of coats turned out to be a blessing. Iona and Murdoch were sitting on the verandah, huddled together to keep warm. The ambulance attendant had used the keys to lock up the house even though Mama never did that.

"Where were you? Where's Mama?"

"She fell. She's okay but she's at the hospital overnight while they check her over."

When I opened the door there were damp, abandoned shirts and pants all over the kitchen floor. Iona seemed as much dismayed by this as by the news that Mama had fallen. She opened up the clothes rack and picked up the clothing to spread it to dry. She looked at me and started a question. "What were you…?" then thought better of it and turned back to the clothes. She probably guessed we were playing invisible. It was a game we'd played with Mama as children and I knew she would have liked to be included.

Neil was home soon after and when he heard the story he went out to look at the back step in the dark. For a moment I feared he also would fall, but he came back in without mishap and rushed upstairs to change, muttering, "Damn, damn, damn, damn," under his breath. He came down wearing a sweater and a pair of slacks instead of his work clothes and hurried back out to the hospital.

When Joe came home from his job and heard the news, he paced back and forth in the kitchen.

"Should I go see how it's going?"

"Neil said no."

"I'll turn on the TV, okay?

So we huddled around *Bonanza* and never talked about the fact it was a motherless family. When it was over, we all went dutifully to put on our pajamas and lay in bed waiting. Joe read comics with Murdoch, I tried to read too, but Iona cried and feared that Mama was not coming home.

Neil came home from the hospital very late, opened the door quietly, and walked down the hall into the kitchen. We heard the scrape of his chair as he pulled it out to sit down at the table. He turned on the radio and a table lamp. One by one we populated the kitchen, wearing pajamas and t-shirts and nightgowns, Joe the only one still dressed. We felt diminished without Stella and Francis, but especially without Mama.

Neil looked at each one of us once we'd all gathered. "She's fine, a little bruised. She'll be right as rain in a couple of weeks."

"When is she coming home?"

"They're going to keep her a few days and make sure everything is good."

Joe anxiously paced back and forth behind us. "Can we go see her tomorrow?"

"Best to just let her rest. She's coming home in a couple of days. You'll see her."

When he got up from the table, he looked at us as if we were a great puzzle. "I guess it's bedtime," he said. Everything around me seemed to be in sharp relief as we made our way upstairs, every crack in the stair treads, every knot in the wood, every splinter coming loose. When we trailed into our rooms, like ghosts in pajamas, he shut the doors behind us and switched off the light in the hall. Then he stood, quite immobile, in the dark. All of his movements were clear to us by listening to the house. It wasn't much of a wait before he spoke, just loudly enough to be heard, "I'm sorry to say she lost the baby," and after several seconds of silence, "Goodnight now. Go to sleep."

He turned then, opened the door to their room and walked a few steps to their bed, where he lay down. We could hear the springs as he settled.

Iona was sitting on the side of the bed with her shoulders slumped. She looked out the window to the street as if the lost baby might be found there. She reminded me of how tired the invisible looked. I tiptoed out our door and went to stand outside the boys' room.

Joe called out, "He's in with me."

At first I didn't understand why we weren't allowed to visit. I thought perhaps she was hiding the bruise on her face from Murdoch and Iona. In the end, I knew it was just the way Neil wanted it. The morning he went to pick her up, we were all so tired of missing her and wanted to go with him but he said, "No, it will be quicker if I just go on my own. She'll be here in minutes."

I couldn't stand to wait a moment longer.

"She's going to have things to carry and you might have to help her walk."

"I can manage on my own."

"She asked me to come help her when it was time to come home."

He looked at me as if he knew this was a lie but nodded anyway.

It was hard to keep up with him on the way there. If I hadn't been with him he'd have been running. He raced up the hospital stairs two at a time and when he got to her room he pushed back the curtain surrounding her bed as if he was afraid she'd be gone. She was fully dressed and laid back crosswise on the bed, with her legs dangling off the side.

Their exchange has entered the realm of family lore.

"I lost my mind somewhere. I'm hoping it's at home," she said.

"You don't need it," Neil said. "Thinking isn't going to help much."

Aunt Effie arrived in a taxi the next day and struggled along the path carrying a suitcase that banged against her knees. They were up late the first evening, drinking tea in the kitchen, even though Mama was still bruised up and should probably have been in bed. I listened through the knothole in the upstairs landing and caught most of the story. She told Mama all about how Lightning escaped from the stable and got mired in deep snow on the same day she fell. Muriel and Grandma Isabel were alone with Isa on the farm and Gran insisted on rescuing him even though none of the boys was home to help. They shovelled out a path for him back to the barn, with Muriel alternately working and pleading, "Isabel, stop. You'll get too tired," while Gran worked at a furious pace.

They managed to get the horse back inside the stable and themselves into the kitchen before Isabel lay down on the kitchen sofa.

"I feel something very heavy on my heart," she whispered.

It was not only grief to which she referred. When Muriel bent over to look at her, the pallor in her face suggested more than emotional distress. The doctor in the village came as quickly as he could, considering the conditions of the road. Muriel held Grandma's hand until he arrived although it had gone limp sometime before.

She phoned Mama right away and of course that was the call that precipitated her fall.

They talked about the baby too. "I hate that expression, 'lost the baby,'" said Effie. "I don't know why people say it that way. He wasn't lost, he was taken."

"He just went away. It was probably foolish of me to try again but you know how a baby will sometimes draw people together."

When she said that, her eyes were fixed on some far place inside herself. I wondered what people she meant.

"I don't really know that," Effie said.

The conversation jumped from one loss to the other, in an effort to change the subject, but the subjects of which they spoke—Donald's family, his Isa, their own mother, their father, Effie's childlessness—all led to the same emotional place.

⁂

We tried in our own ways to cheer Mama. On a Sunday in March, after her bruises had healed, Iona suggested, "Walk to town with us, Mama. The stores are closed but we can window shop."

She looked at me. "Do you want to do that too, Eileen?"

"Yes, that would be good."

"A walk would be nice." It was the first time she'd been out so far away from home since she'd fallen six weeks before.

The sidewalks sparkled in the afternoon sun but they were still patchy and uneven with brittle snow and ice, so she decided we would go through the park where the walkways were nicely plowed. Her breathing was a bit laboured and she struggled to say, "All that lying around has left me short-winded." Small puffs of white steam escaped our lungs. It made me feel grown up when she put her hand through the crook of my arm.

The paved walkway in the park sloped down toward a pond. It had been ploughed and salted. There was no ice but she stumbled in her square-heeled pumps, and went down on one knee. I grabbed frantically and managed to steady her. We gripped each other and I feared if I moved she'd fall down. Gradually she was able to balance on one leg so we managed to hop and half walk to a bench a few feet away on the side of the path. She settled on the bench for a moment, then raised her head to look at me, "It's all right. I think my leg has fallen asleep. I'll sit for a minute." She spoke calmly as if there was nothing to worry about.

It was lucky that the pond had great melted pools in the ice. It gave room for the ducks to swim, and watching them gave us an excuse to be sitting on a park bench in the middle of winter. Murdoch sat beside her on the bench, leaning on her for comfort.

A long time went by and the feeling in her leg didn't come back. Eventually Murdoch laid his head down on the bench beside her and fell asleep. "He's going to get cold there," she said, but she made no move to lift him, so I pulled the scarf from around my neck and put it under his head.

Iona sat beside her the whole time and never took her eyes off her face, but I wandered back and forth on the path, hoping someone would come to help. Mama fished around in her purse and brought out a five-dollar bill. "Get some ice cream cones from that store on the corner and ask the man there to call a taxi for us. Take Iona with you."

"Can you get up now?"

"I will when the taxi comes."

Iona ran ahead as if she wanted to get the job done quickly. When I caught up with her she was standing by the pay phone, just inside a wooden door, urging me on with her eyes. The store had a dark interior and it was not easily detected that a boy of about ten years sat behind a wooden counter further in, watching us.

"I want to call a cab and get two cones," I said, feeling uncertain on which side of the boundary between child and grown-up I lived.

He wrote down the number for a cab. While I dialed, he and Iona negotiated the flavour of the cones.

We were just a few minutes inside, but when we came out into the day again, clouds filled the sky and darkened the day.

"We better hurry," I said. "I don't want it to snow on the ice cream."

"It's frozen anyway," Iona said. Her brow wrinkled as she contemplated where to start licking. She looked as if she might cry.

I hurried along the path, knowing she would follow, and left her and the ice cream in Mama's care. "I better go stand at the road in case he can't find us."

She nodded.

The cab was black and white and the driver was thin, wearing a fedora and black-rimmed glasses. He was not prepared for the cold weather so he was none too happy when I said he had to come into the park to get Mama.

"They can just come out here," he said.

Mama was right on the other side of the hedge that lined the sidewalk, so I tried to speak in a more confidential way, not wanting her to hear me.

"There's something wrong."

"Sounds like you need an ambulance, not a taxi."

"She said she'd get up when you arrive, but we need help."

He gave in and said, "Fine, lead the way."

When we reached them at the bench, Iona was still licking her cone and Mama was holding the other one out straight, so it wouldn't drip on her clothing. They looked tired and cold and the driver relented. "You can't eat that ice cream in the car."

"Please give us a minute," Mama said, handing the ice cream back to me. "I've lost the feeling in one of my legs and can't walk any further." Behind the glasses, his brown eyes took in the whole scene: Mama sitting with one leg straight out in front of her and Murdoch still sleeping on the bench.

"How long has your leg been asleep?"

"It's been an hour," she said, looking directly at him.

"I better take you to the hospital."

"No, no, my husband will be home from work soon and he'll worry if we're not there. I'll call the doctor when I get home."

"Fine then. Let's try to get up the path." She was a bit embarrassed when he had to steady her by placing a hand on her waist, but at least she was able to stand on one leg and hop on the other with an arm around his neck.

She turned. "Eileen, will you wake Murdoch?" I tried to do it gently but he wasn't ready and it made him whimper, so I picked him up and half dragged his thin eight-year-old body along the path to the street. When we reached the car, Iona scrambled into the back seat and I dumped Murdoch in on top of her. She yelled at him, "Get off me!"

The taxi driver turned around to look at us. "Here's the thing. If you are very quiet, I won't change my mind."

Mama raised her eyebrows and nodded once.

We travelled home in silence.

All the rest of that day, Mama lay on the chesterfield with a dark green and navy blue plaid blanket loosely draped over the length of her body. It rose in small hills where it covered her feet and her breast and fell into a small valley at her waist. The white pillow raised her head enough that she could see around the doctor, who was seated blocking our view. He had come to look in on her to be sure she was fine. She smiled to reassure us.

"Give the doctor some room," Neil said.

Iona pulled my hand to go outside to the verandah and Murdoch followed behind. Joe and Neil were the only ones who stayed nearby and heard the doctor say, "We're going to have to do some tests. I believe what you need, more than anything else, is complete bed rest for a month. I wish you'd stay in hospital."

"I can rest here."

"You'll have to stay in your own room where it's quiet."

"That's fine."

Neil came in from the hall where he'd been waiting, and he stood beside the chesterfield. "We'll be alright here. Lots of people to wait on her. The kids won't mind missing a few days of school."

The doctor shook Neil's hand and picked up his hat.

"Let me know if anything changes."

And to Mama he said, "No heroics. Stay in bed."

My father sat on the side of the chesterfield and hooked his arm through Mama's in a way that helped her sit up. Then he swung her legs around and helped her stand on one leg as if this was something he'd always done. She hopped and was half carried up the stairs in a jolting pattern. We crowded back into the hallway and watched her go. Even while we listened to the sound, we knew we would never forget it.

It was after nine that evening when Neil came downstairs and asked, "Did you fellas get anything to eat?" We were all surprised by the question. None of us had even mentioned food since they had gone upstairs, but once it was raised, we found we were hungry.

I could hardly believe I hadn't thought of getting food for the others. I slapped pieces of bread down on the counter and slathered them with peanut butter. When it came time to serve it, we all sat in silence at the dining room table.

Murdoch pushed his plate aside, "I want supper."

Neil intervened. "Eat that. Every bite."

He did.

In the middle of the night Iona started whimpering. Eventually she woke up but kept sniffling. She said, "There's a prisoner of war camp and in the middle of all the pain and torture, I have to be good and sweep the floor." She held her arms around herself and stared intently at the floor while she spoke. "It's not the first time I've had this dream and it always makes me cry."

I tried to joke her out of it, "Maybe you were a saint in another lifetime," but that didn't seem to cheer her.

In the dark, and from her room, Mama called, "Are you alright?" Iona lay down in the bed and said, "Yes, we're fine." I did the same and lay beside her with our elbows and feet touching.

The next day at lunch Murdoch and I went in to see Mama. He carefully carried a plate up the stairs and quietly set it down on her bedside stand. Then he sat in the corner chair, staring at his shoes and moving one foot. He looked as if he hoped to become invisible before we were tempted to tell him what the trouble was.

She tried to chat with him about the weather. "It's a beautiful day out there, isn't it?"

"Yes, it really is," he said without raising his eyes. She looked over at me and shook her head once. She let him go with, "You should be out in that. Another few days and it might be too cold to be out."

Neil arrived home on the Tuesday with a wheelchair for her. One of the wheels was slightly out of alignment and made a swooshing sound on the wood floor as he twirled it around in the living room. We could hear him promoting it when he went up to see her. "It's a great rig. All the kids want a ride."

"I'd rather die than be an invalid the rest of my life."

"What's the rest of your life got to do with it? You want to be down-stairs now."

"I need to walk."

She was sitting on the side of the bed, so he sat beside her and put his elbow out for her to hold. "Let's go for a walk then." She stood, with his help, and they walked three steps across the room.

She lowered herself into the chair, "You know why people laugh when someone falls down? They're embarrassed for the person because they're of no use."

"That's ridiculous."

"I'm not using that chair. Not today."

The next morning she was at the table drinking tea when we arrived in the kitchen for breakfast. Her steps were halting and uneven when she got up to fill the bowls, but everyone pretended not to notice. We sat still as she served us our cream of wheat.

That evening I heard her telling Neil, "Falling makes you fear being left behind. In primitive times, it must have been a disaster if you fell when you were running with your people. Whatever was chasing you might catch up. I think that expression 'a fallen woman' means a woman who is no longer considered good for anything. I'm ashamed."

"Don't say that. It makes no sense," said Neil.

We listened to Francis together that night. They even let Murdoch stay up.

"Are you going to call him?" I asked Mama.

"He'll call on Thursday. No need to worry him," she said.

It was a slow recovery, but by May she decided we needed a bigger garden and enlisted all of us to help, organizing who would prepare the soil and what we would plant. When it was finally warm enough to start digging, she sat in the garden on a straight-backed chair with another chair in front of her with a cushion on it so she could put up her leg if she wanted. From there she could direct the action.

Neil and Joe dug out the sod and turned over the earth beneath so that somehow it filled the space where the sod had been. The yard stunk of manure for a few days but Neil thought the soil needed it. Joe raked the beds flat and made perfect ridges for planting seeds. Murdoch had a round stick he used to make a hole in the earth and patiently placed the seeds, one by one, exactly the right distance apart. Iona and I came behind and covered them up by gently pushing the earth into the hole and tapping it lightly. When I checked to see if Mama was watching us, her eyes were closed and her face was tilted to the sun.

The garden was in full bloom by the time Mama's birthday came around in late August, and to most of us the accident was just a memory. Mama was picking some vegetables for dinner and I followed her outside. She walked through the paths and bent to examine the kale that lay in a row below the clothesline. A fan of air swept her forehead. When she looked up to catch the breeze, I noticed that her eyes fell upon a small number of orange butterflies nestled on the purple milkweed. She nodded and perhaps forgot that I was a few rows behind her when she asked, "How do you know where you're going?"

14

Mama sewed a dress for me, the colour of the ocean. It was made of silk dupioni, with the warp and weft of different hues so that it shimmered aqua blue with a quivering of sand when the fabric floated and twirled around my legs. It recalled the sea on a day when it rushes and spills against the shore and disturbs the earth beneath it.

The memory of the dress lives more in my solar plexus than in the recesses of my brain, and the amount of meaning I give it is a mystery when I think about the magnitude of everything else going on in the world right then.

Millions of workers were on strike in France and students had burned down the stock exchange in Paris. The Vietnam War and all of its atrocities could be watched in our living room almost every night. I found it so difficult to understand why people were doing the things they were. Iona had more opinions than I did, but Mama said that if I didn't know how to reply when some older person asked me what I thought, it was perfectly acceptable to say, "I don't know anything about that."

She said, "Imagine how mortified you'd be if you were caught pretending to know something you do not."

"Those poor buggers," my father said, watching airplanes drop bombs and soldiers and civilians running for cover or shot dead in their tracks.

"Who are the ones causing it?" I asked.

"Oh, they'll tell you it's the communists or the radicals but you'll never really know unless you're there."

A boy I had met at the parish hall asked me to the Spring Dance. Foolishly, I said yes, even though I didn't want, or even plan, to go with him. In those days I really didn't know how to say no to anything that sounded like a reasonable request. It wasn't that I didn't like the boy. I liked him quite a bit, but he made me very nervous. I confided to my mother one night while she was reading the paper after dinner. I didn't talk about how I felt about the boy; I wouldn't think to mention that.

"A boy asked me to the Dosco Ball and I said yes."

She looked over the top of the paper at me. "I guess you'll need a new dress."

"I'm not going."

"Why would that be?"

"I won't know what to say."

"Who is he?" she asked.

"Robbie MacLean."

"What's he like?"

"Blond hair," I said.

"Wasn't exactly what I meant," she said, tilting her head to one side.

"Oh well, I don't know, he seems nice."

"So there's no reason to go back on your word then."

The department store where I worked after school had a good fabric section. Maisie Cochrane, who was somewhere between my mother's age and my own, was the boss and was thought to be stylish. She wore green eye shadow and Parkhurst sweaters, some of them cashmere. I remember her as not being very wordy. She would point at you with her pen and, with only the slightest suggestion of impatience, say things like, "Fold sweaters," or "Take cash."

Mama came in one day after school and asked her for permission to borrow me for a few minutes. I noticed that Miss Cochrane spoke in complete sentences to her. She led us over to the part of the store where the most beautiful silks were perfectly wound on cardboard rolls and Mama held the cloth up to my face to judge the colour. She said it was easy fabric to cut and sew and if I bought it she'd make a dress for me for the dance. I was thrilled because ever since I'd started making my own clothes, she'd stopped sewing for me and she was so much more competent than I was. We bought an extra yard even though it cost so much.

"Just in case we make a mistake," she said, "there might not be any left when we come back."

"What do you mean 'we'? I thought you were going to make it."

"Don't be a smart aleck," she said. "You can do some of it."

"I think you mean a Smart Eileen, don't you?" I suggested.

After a brief pause she replied, "I mean pretty much anyone who thinks she can take her mother for granted with no repercussions."

Maisie Cochrane gave me a direct look and raised her eyebrows so that the green eye shadow became a broader band of colour stretching upward to her forehead.

For some reason, the richness of the colour of the dress calmed me. It made it easier to go to the dance without Iona. As if I would still have an ally, a friend.

In the previous fall and winter, Iona and I had gone together every weekend to one of the parish halls to dance. Neither Mama nor Neil had much to say about anything we did. They wanted us to be happy and not to be weighed down by the sadness that had crept into their lives. In any case, this is what I secretly decided to be true.

Neil made us choose between Friday and Saturday night, as if dancing was something that could ruin your health. He felt he had to do something. Likely the fact we were thirteen and fifteen figured into his thinking, although that seemed irrelevant to us. Come to think of it, he may not have been too clear on how old we were anyway.

The whole thing about dancing was really Iona's idea. The thought of having to be lined up waiting for someone to ask me to dance in full view of all of my peers made my stomach jump.

Iona loved to dance. Her way of being taken seriously was to become extraordinarily good at everything she tried. If we had grown up in a time and place where children were engaged in extracurricular activities, which extended beyond tree climbing, I suppose Iona would have taken up ballet. Overcoming the pain required to create a thing of beauty would have appealed to her.

She developed a grace on the dance floor that survived even the twist and the monkey and all the other fish and animal dances that came later. When I compared my own dancing to hers, I saw a perfection that I was sure my longer and more awkward limbs would never achieve. There was more muscle rippling under the smooth, tight skin of her arms than girls usually had in those years before women "worked out." My mother used to say she was made of some steely kind of rubber, and some nights when she accidentally kicked me in her sleep I felt the truth of that.

On the day we were first given permission to go to a dance, she rushed into our bedroom. "We're going!" she said. I was surprised because I'd never gone to a dance myself. She explained that she'd been dropping comments to Mama for weeks about how good it would be to have company at the dance and that if they didn't let her go now I might be gone away before she got to go with me. She said she didn't see how Mama could deny her the pleasure of the memory of going to dances with her sister. The whole time she was telling me this she was making little motions of clearing away earth and planting seeds.

Iona was not what you would ever call a diminutive person, but this had more to do with her personality than her physical stature. Something about her made me want to protect her, even if I thought I needed her more than she needed me. Her glossy black hair and her unusually small size in a family known for its height could have accounted for some of our focus, but there was something more that inspired dedication. She seemed to strain against the restrictions of being a child, as if her body was too small for her spirit.

The parish hall was lit up against the night and music blasted out the door as we arrived on our first excursion. Stella had told us about the dance and made it sound like a big party of some kind. As we drew closer, I hoped Iona had taken in more of the details. She certainly seemed eager to join the crowd. Some people, boys really, stood around outside smoking. They looked us over as we went in. I pretended not to see them and Iona smiled and nodded.

Once inside we were a bit stunned by the scene we encountered. The dancers were in the middle of the floor, and walking around them was a procession of all of the young men in the room—a never-ending, revolving parade of boys. The girls stood at the outer edges of the circle, waiting to be asked to dance, some of them talking to each other and others scanning the crowd as if they sought one special dance partner. We took our place at the edge of the floor where they stood, sometimes two deep, waiting to be chosen.

The music was deafening and there was no opportunity to talk, but we were unprepared for the solemnity of this silent group of young men circling and inspecting. When a girl in front of us was asked, Iona stepped quickly into her place at the very edge of the dance floor. Almost immediately a tall, good-looking boy stopped and asked her to dance. She said no. He looked offended as he quickly moved off, so I leaned over and put my lips to her ear. "Why?"

"Too old," she said.

Lots of boys asked her and she accepted many of them. She announced to each and every one of them that she was only thirteen. She liked surprising them and now I see it might have been her way of warning them that she was still a child. The line usually kept running smoothly, but at times it bunched up a bit in the corner where Iona was standing, as if she was a magnet and the boys were metal filings.

I was proud of her and at the same time I watched her closely to try to learn her method. She spoke in the same engaged way to everyone and didn't seem to know how much of a stir she was causing. She assumed that the same unspoken understanding she shared with me could be shared with all of them. If you looked at the boys surrounding her you could see the wisdom in it. It also became apparent she was beautiful, although I'm not sure she understood that. Which may have been part of the charm.

Later in the evening, the first boy she'd turned down asked me instead, and I said yes. This was Robbie MacLean. He was embarrassed he'd asked Iona to dance when she was so young, even though she didn't look it. He was eighteen and didn't want anyone to think he was robbing the cradle. He said, "I'll walk you both home if you want." It was raining and I said, "No, we have to run."

When we stood in the doorway of the hall and watched the rain spilling in a sheet of water along the overhang, Iona said, "If you run, the same amount of rain hits you because you are covering twice the territory in the same amount of time." We laughed wildly at this ridiculous idea and ran without stopping to our home a mile away. We were soaked through and breathless but very warm when we arrived.

When we lay in bed that night, still sharing even though the second bed was empty, Iona told me she loved boys. She thought it was charming when they got so hot and flushed when they were dancing close, and took it as some kind of compliment when one of them wanted to kiss her neck, even if she wouldn't let him.

"I'm not sure they're all so charming," I said. "Don't let them touch you. You don't want to get a reputation."

I was afraid she'd forget that all of our body parts had to stay intact. "When they're getting too friendly just think about what happened to Mary MacDonald." This was to remind her of a girl who had to go away to the home for unwed mothers and who was never able to come back. We were told she'd been sent to live with an aunt in Montreal.

"I'm not going to do that!" Iona said emphatically.

The next weekend we tried the dance at the YMCA. We weren't really supposed to, because they were a different religion, but when we left home on Saturday night, replying offhandedly to Mama's inquiry, we knew she would never guess the truth.

"Where are you off to?"

"The dance."

There was no stag line at the Y. Groups of young men and women stood around in a casual way and occasionally one was asked to dance. This seemed to be a more relaxed atmosphere unless boys surrounded one girl, as happened to Iona that night. I could see that the equality afforded by the more formal system at the parish halls at least avoided a situation where one girl might feel the wrath of many. Or in this case, two girls, because she wouldn't let me leave her side. We stood side by side with one arm around each other when a confident and very clean-looking boy with a blond crewcut asked, "Are you from here?"

Iona replied, "Where else would we be from?"

He said we looked like we might be from the country and I wondered what he meant by that. Then he asked, "How old are you?" and Iona quickly lied and said we were both sixteen and that we were fraternal twins, all the time looking at me to insist that I back her up in this deception. I didn't have much choice but to go along even as I wondered how it was she'd changed her mind about announcing her real age all the time. She was perhaps a bit intimidated. As a way of making conversation she casually threw out that her brother was Francis MacPherson who had the radio show. The boy gave a kind of whistle in appreciation. "That's great. I guess you know a lot about music. Who do you listen to?"

I named Jeff Beck because I'd listened to Francis talk about him just the night before as I lay in bed.

He said, "Oh yeah, I heard that show last night too."

So I countered, "What about you? Who do you like?"

"No no. You were going to tell me about Jeff Beck."

I searched for anything to come to mind that Francis had said about him, but realized I'd been listening to his voice and not to what he said.

"Jeff Beck is brilliant," I offered.

There was something dismissive in the boy's snicker. "You two are full of shit. You don't know anything about music and," he pointed at Iona, "you are not sixteen." Then he turned and left as if we'd done some disgusting thing and pulled the other boys away with a flick of his head. He looked back with a bit of a sneer but spoke as if to one of the other boys when he said, "I hear there's a lot of fairies in Toronto."

I'd heard the word used that way before and knew what it meant but it made me feel a bit squeamish when he said that, as if it was a personal insult.

The other boys broke away, some reluctantly, if you could trust their backward glances. They formed smaller knots with other girls, which should have been a relief but wasn't.

Iona and I had always listened to Francis's show but now we listened harder to his preambles. We took this on as a self-improvement project and tried to remember some of the major and minor jazz players and at least one thing about their music. We learned names like Miles Davis and Keith Jarrett. On Saturday mornings we tested each other before we got out of bed.

My favourite was a bossa nova album. We worked up our own routine: dancing side by side, with swaying hips and swivelling shoulders, faster and faster until we collapsed on the chesterfield, laughing at missed steps and our own audacity. Iona loved Lambert, Hendricks and Ross and could even sing along to their crazy rhymes and musical jokes. That's about as far as we got in terms of the jazz lexicon, but I figured it was enough to get us by if we ever ran into someone like the boy at the Y again. When my energy waned, Iona reminded me, "We have to learn this stuff or we'll always look like idiots." Underneath that careless attitude, we liked the fact that jazz was big enough for each of us to love a different style and both still claim some intimacy with it.

We decided to investigate the local radio station to get an idea of what kind of place Francis worked. I thought he might even like working there. It was a two-room walk-up over a storefront on the drag. One summer night the announcer, who was nice to all the high school kids, invited us to visit him when he played records on air. We knew we had a special "in" with him because of Francis. He gave us the name of a singer and a song and let us take turns using the microphone to announce it any way we wanted. I went for a kind of Marilyn Munroe breathiness. Afterwards he said we sounded very sexy, and if we wanted some work we could come back and do a few ads with him. We never did go. We didn't think it added up that a man with such a big job would be bothered with us. Not that we talked about it. We just had a mutual understanding.

Sometimes we had to work at those. At the dance one night Iona said, "We think *he's* good looking."

I replied with a non-committal, "Maybe."

"Really, look at him, he's beautiful."

"Beauty isn't necessarily all it's cracked up to be."

"Oh sure, I suppose you'd rather someone ugly."

Mama approved of our closeness but still made some attempts to keep a difference between us that recognized the gap in our ages. She insisted on this when we discussed the spring dance one Saturday while we helped her paint the linoleum in the kitchen with glossy green and black squares. The original colour had rubbed off the floor after so many years and so much traffic, so she had masked it all with tape and enlisted us to help her paint it by hand. The next day, when it was dry, she paste-waxed it heavily, and when we came home from school she handed us big wool socks to put on our feet so we could slip and slide all over it to shine it up. While Mama slid around the floor with us, Iona took the opportunity to say, "I was asked to the dance today. Can I go?"

Mama took some time before she replied.

"There's a time for everything. Sixteen is the right time to go to this kind of dance. Your time will come and, when it does, I'll make you a beautiful dress too. You can start planning it now if you like."

I noticed that her cotton dress had smears of black and green paint on it and hoped she knew that the gift of a beautiful dress was not taken for granted.

A few days after we painted the floor I came home from school and found her lying on the beautiful green and black painted squares, with the almost-finished dress spilling all over her. She'd pulled it down off the table when she'd fallen from her chair. Her eyes were open and watching, but she couldn't move and she looked as if she might be drowning in a sparkling blue sea. I quickly bent to touch her, and then ran to the phone to call the doctor without letting my eyes leave hers.

The doctor sent a car because he was afraid she'd had a stroke but I knew that wasn't it at all. There was no diagnosis the last time she'd fallen, but multiple sclerosis had been murmured and wondered about. I was alone, waiting with her, and hoped Iona and Murdoch would not arrive before the car came.

The ambulance driver and his partner smoothly and delicately picked Mama up as if she might break.

"I'd go with you, Mama, but I have to wait for Murdoch." I nodded for her. Murdoch was ten and very attached to her and I was pretty worried about how he'd react. I knew Iona always took the long way home so she could talk to the other girls at their respective corners. I'd have a moment alone with him before she got there.

"They'll be frightened if they get home and there's no one here."
Nodding again for us both, I stepped away from the ambulance door.

When they closed it, I was afraid I'd never see her again.

A while later, Murdoch came up the back stairs and burst into the kitchen to throw his books down and grab a baseball bat. He turned to run out again without even saying hello.

"Hang on a sec," I said.

He looked back and stopped while he scanned the kitchen. "Where's Mama?" he asked.

"She's in the hospital. She'll be fine. She fell down."

"What did she hurt?"

"Not sure. They'll check her out and we can go see her later after Daddy gets home."

"Why are you calling him Daddy? You always call him Neil."

"I don't know."

During the following week I was in a daze a lot of the time, feeling at a complete loss to make sense of the world. At home we were unable to talk to one another at all. At school, when Sister McLennan started the morning by saying, "We're all going to take a moment to pray for Eileen MacPherson's mother, who has fallen seriously ill," I wished I could become liquid and melt onto the scrubbed hardwood floor and out under the closed door of the room.

Francis worried enough about her that he called one evening and spoke to Neil.

"Is she going to be okay?"

"Oh yes, I think so," Neil told him.

"I should come to see her."

"I know she'd love to see you."

This was before she had regained her strength and while she was still convalescing at the hospital. Neil told Mama that Francis was coming to visit, so she wrote a note to him and another, saying that I was to read it to Francis on the phone. I phoned him that night after supper and read it out clearly to him, "Don't you dare come home right now after all this time. What good is a hospital visit? Wait until I'm at home."

"You sound exactly like her," he said.

It was a message I was both happy and sorry to deliver. I didn't want to think that the first time I'd see him in eight years would be in such unhappy circumstances. I missed the way he laughed out loud and looked you in the eyes the whole time, so that it was impossible not to laugh even if perhaps you had no idea why. I was afraid there would be no laughing at all if he came at a time like this, all the while feeling guilty to be so selfish and thinking that if she saw him it might make her well.

On the day of the dance, I put the final stitches in the dress and modelled it for Mama in her hospital room.

"You look outstanding," said Iona. Mama didn't say anything but her eyes were bright and I knew what she was thinking. Iona planned to stay and keep her company for a while, so I changed back into my jeans and carefully folded up the dress in tissue paper and put it in a dress box. I walked home carrying it in front of me as if it was a large cake that had to remain flat. On the way one of the neighbours fell into step with me, saying, "What do you have there?"

"It's a dress that Mama sewed for me."

"Dear God, you mean you still have her at the sewing machine even in her hospital bed? Small wonder the poor woman is sick." She abruptly turned off at the next corner and left without letting me explain.

It was not the first time it occurred to me that we might be the reason Mama sometimes collapsed with exhaustion. I would have happily foregone the dance that night but I knew I had to go. The dress was her gift of beauty to me.

When I got home my father was waiting for me at the door.

"How is she?"

"She's pretty good," I lied.

"I started supper," Neil said, and I could smell something burning. When we went into the kitchen a thin line of smoke was leaking from the oven, so he opened its door, grabbed the pan with the charred roast and roughly flung it onto the back porch to cool down.

"I was planning to make hash anyway," I said, and pulled some leftovers out of the fridge. With Stella married and gone away, there was just me, Iona, Joe and Murdoch left at home. While we ate, Neil sat in his place at the head of the table with his hands curled in fists around a knife and a fork, held upright as if he'd forgotten how to eat.

"I found it really warm today," he murmured. Murdoch picked up on that theme and said, "Yes, it was really hot when we won the ball game today."

"You won, did you?

"Seven to four"

"Well, good then. You beat the other guys. I'll have to tell your mother that."

There didn't seem to be anything else to say until we'd wolfed down the last of the supper and Neil spoke again, "You boys are doing the dishes tonight. Eileen has to get ready." They protested that they'd never done them before and didn't even know how, but I believe they broke a plate and a cup more out of resistance than clumsiness.

That morning Iona and I had cleaned the house and got everything put away that normally looked messy, like all the shoes and boots cluttering the front hall. We threw out the stacks of newspapers that had gathered on all the chairs and pulled the overflowing ashtrays out from under the chesterfield where my father had tucked them as a way of tidying up. Then we washed and pressed the blue print curtains that hung around the kitchen sink. We even found a nice wool blanket to put on the threadbare chesterfield and washed and waxed the linoleum carpet that covered the planks of the living room floor. That evening, when I finished dressing and came downstairs, I was proud and satisfied with how clean and homey it looked. Even the plywood lying against the stair rail looked fine, as if there was a new job to be done and we were in the middle of it.

The boys were watching boxing on television with my father. I stopped to look and could see that two men, one of whom was called Tiger, I think, were smashing each other on the head. My father was sitting at the edge of his seat, his feet shuffling in front of his chair, and one fist kept jabbing out involuntarily. When the man called Tiger got a good punch in, they all cheered and laughed.

It took them a while to even notice me, and when he did my father said, "What did Mama think of the dress?"

"She thought it was beautiful," I said.

"Well, she's always right about that," he agreed.

Then the man named Tiger knocked the other one out and they all went crazy.

I closed my eyes and pretended that the wild cheering of my brothers was intended for me. The feeling of standing inside the dress surrounded by their noisy and joyous applause is one I draw on still, when I want to remember what beauty feels like from the inside out.

When the cheering had subsided, my father sent Murdoch out to the store for a bottle of coke to celebrate. I had to refuse a glass because I was afraid I'd spill it on myself while I sat on the edge of an armchair waiting for my date to arrive. There was no way to get more comfortable without crushing the dress. I wished Francis was there to make me laugh.

I could go on and on here about the next two hours and the waiting and the watching out the door, but the only thing to say, really, is that Robbie with the curly hair and the blue eyes never came. Around ten o'clock, when I could no longer pretend and neither could anyone else, my father started pacing around and the boys got up every few minutes to go to the fridge or look out the door.

"I'll wait out here," I tossed over my shoulder nonchalantly as I headed to the verandah for refuge. A fog had begun to roll in, the kind that has a slight breeze behind it so that you can feel it as it brushes your face with its fingers. The last time I'd seen a fog so thick was in the lower field below the path.

By the time Iona arrived home, the dress was carefully hung on a hanger on the bedroom door and the boys were talking in hushed tones while I was out in the back field pretending to look at the stars. She came out and stood beside me. I said, "He didn't come."

"I know." If I had asked her then how she knew, she might have told me. Instead my eyes started leaking and she put her arms around me and just kept saying, "I'm sorry, I'm sorry."

I finally said, "Don't be so sorry. It's not as if you were out dancing with him." I was afraid she was getting too emotional, and in the end might feel worse than I did, which I was not prepared to let happen.

That night as we lay in bed with our backs touching, she asked me to tell her a story as I used to do when we were much younger. I told her a long and complicated version of the time when I went walking in the bog in the lower field. I knew she liked it. I intended this to be a light and funny telling of the story, but when I ended it I thought Iona was sleeping so indulged myself in melancholy.

"I guess this is unknown water."

She wasn't sleeping after all and whispered back, "You're the only person in the world who could see a ghost in the fog."

I suddenly thought, and said aloud, "Do you think something could have happened to him? Do you think he could be hurt?"

There was a long silence before she said, "We can only hope."

I kicked her gently. I believe it was the last time we ever lay like that.

The next evening we visited Mama. I told elaborate stories about how much fun I had at the dance. "Everyone loved the dress, even the nuns." She managed a smile worth every lie. When we kissed her good-bye I didn't feel so broken-hearted.

It was still warm at dusk as we stood near the chip wagon on the main street in town with a clutch of girls from school. We already had our boxes of home-cut potatoes, sprinkled with salt and vinegar, in our hands. One of the Margarets (there were three of them in the circle) asked why I wasn't at the dance. I'd expected that and was ready. "Food poisoning. It was awful."

She looked from me to Iona and said, "Ohhh… I saw you playing pinball with Robbie on my way to the dance and I couldn't figure out what the heck was going on."

Iona turned a fiery red, so this was apparently the truth, but in that moment loyalty to our shared place in the world trumped anger and surprise.

"Oh yeah, when he came for me, I couldn't even come out of the bathroom, so I asked Iona to take care of him." I smiled, amazed at my ready duplicity. "She's embarrassed because she's not allowed to play pinball." Turning to Iona and dropping the artificial smile, I said, "We should go. I'm still not feeling so good."

When we got out of earshot, she tried to permeate my burning fury with, "I saw him there on the way home from the hospital and I went in and he said he just couldn't go to the dance because he was too unhappy and he knew you'd have a terrible time with him." She told me they'd talked mostly about what a fantastic person I was, and that she'd make him say I didn't go to the dance because I was sick and I agreed. Engaging him in this humiliating fiction had to be done or he'd go off telling some other story and everyone would know the truth. In the end, all but the most suspicious and wise among us accepted this story.

I wouldn't speak to her and created as much distance between us as possible. Crowell's became a place to hide from my embarrassment and anger. They were willing to have me work every day after school at the cash register in the glove department. The fine leather gloves were in boxes beside the white evening gloves in cellophane. I spent a great deal of time dusting and lining up the packages. Maisie Cochrane kept an eye on me but didn't bark too often. She knew Mama was sick.

On the way home I stood watching the boats in the harbour for a while so that I could avoid having dinner with everyone else. Some days the waves were small laps against the shore, but there were days that June when the wind approached from the sea with a thin wavering scream and pushed the waves into sharp peaks that broke against the steep shore. Sheets of water rose up like angry ghosts as the ocean met the sharp resistance of the rocky bank. The spray drenched my clothing. I enjoyed the edge of danger that I felt in its assault.

I made up for coming home late by washing dishes without complaint and blamed it on my job so that Neil wouldn't know I was sulking. I refused to go to any more dances for fear of running into the boy, and because then Iona couldn't go either, her being too young to go without me. She would come into a room where I was sitting and stare at me until I would finally have to get up and go elsewhere.

We didn't tell anyone else about our distress. Mama still thought I'd gone to the dance with Robbie MacLean. Our father and brothers, conveniently for all of us, put our silences and distance down to some strange female business they couldn't possibly understand.

The day Mama came home from the hospital we were embroiled in a foolish tussle over who she loved the most. Iona had actually suggested that Mama told her she loved her better than me. I wouldn't allow that Mama would ever say such a thing but Iona insisted she had.

"She was just trying to make you feel good that day." This rang hollow even in my own ears and didn't phase Iona one bit. By the time Mama walked through the door I couldn't talk without weeping. When she asked what was wrong, I blurted out the gist of the thing and she looked from one to the other of us and seemed to decide that fear must be the source of our competition because we were far too old to be having this kind of argument. She put her arms around the two of us and said, "I love you both the same and fiercely."

Having her at home did not alleviate my sorrow and embarrassment at having been stood up for the dance. In some ways it made it worse because I had to pretend that everything was fine. She could tell something was wrong. "Did that boy hurt you?" I was glad to be able to truthfully say no but I couldn't tell her it was Iona I was mourning.

One Friday night, when I had turned up my nose at the mention of going to the dance with Iona, and she had gone off to the chip wagon alone, I sat in the kitchen listening to Francis on the radio. Mama was well now and he could easily have come home. I wondered if there was something wrong with him that he couldn't make the journey so many others made almost every year. We were at the kitchen table listening together, so I asked her, "Why doesn't he come?"

"It's expensive and it takes a lot of time. I think it's hard to get away from his job."

"Do you want him to?"

She looked at me for a long moment before saying, "You could call him."

"Why don't you call him?" I said loudly enough to bring Neil into the room, where he stopped and retreated when we both fell silent. The tears that welled up then were tears of shame that I could be so foolish and so dependent on my family, that I had no other real friends, and tears of rage that I could no longer count on them to fill the gaps in my world as they always had. The tears took her by surprise. Faced with a daughter who seemed unaccountably sad and angry, she had no idea how to respond.

"Can I go see him?" I managed to say. "Just for a few days?"

This was an unthinkable thing for me to ask when she had so recently come home from the hospital, and my head sank to the table and rested on my arms.

"Forget it. That's a bad idea." I said as I turned my face away from her.

She easily read my mind.

"I'm fine now. I won't get sick again for a long time."

Her permission to go was shocking. She was usually protective in the manner of a mother cat who picks up her kittens and hides them in a closet, not intending to limit their life's possibilities but rather to expand their chances of survival. The table was wet with tears when I raised my head to look at her, so she went to get a cloth to wipe them away.

In the middle of the night, with the moon throwing some light in the back door window onto the checkered linoleum floor of the kitchen and illuminating the wall phone just enough to make out the numbers on the dial, I called him. I knew he would still be up because he always prepared the next night's show after he signed off at eleven.

He said, "What's wrong?"

"Nothing. I just can't sleep."

"Mama's okay?"

"You could come to see for yourself. People come home from Toronto all the time."

I didn't say that I wanted to see him or that he'd said he'd come home when Mama was well.

He brushed that off like dust on his shoulders.

"Sooo. Can't sleep. Do you have a boyfriend?" he asked.

"Absolutely not. Do you have a girlfriend?" I tossed back.

"No, I don't."

I didn't believe him. I'm not sure why.

"I have nothing to do for the summer," I said. "There are no jobs here."

There was a long silence at the other end.

"Maybe you should come up here for the summer," he suggested. "I see signs looking for waitresses."

I could hardly believe he'd said that.

"You're inviting me to come to stay with you?"

"Yes, I am."

"Okay… I'll call you back…"

"Talk to Mama about it."

"Okay. I will. I'll do that. Thanks."

Afterwards I lay on my side at the edge of the big bed in our room with my hands tucked under my face. I could feel my own heart beating a bit too fast. Iona snored softly in the smaller bed across the room. Light from the street lamp glinted off the nails poking through the rafters. I thought about the silk dress Mama made for me and decided that if I went to Toronto I would take it. Perhaps it was intended for some greater occasion than the spring dance and I was fortunate to never have had the chance to wear it.

15

A songbird trilled in exultation, a solo sung by one who yearned for more. The sound of my mother shuffling the burner covers from place to place as she lit the fire in the stove provided sharp notes of percussion against the steady beat of my heart. I understood it was the beginning of an era and lay there for some time composing a new melody for my life.

Iona lay in the opposite bed, breathing quietly. I wanted to wake her and tell her about this new life I was embarking on but quickly put that thought aside in case it threatened my resolve. A door slammed and the car in the driveway revved into life, so I knew Mama would be alone in the kitchen. I slipped out from between the covers and silently stepped into the blue jeans that were sitting on the bedroom floor with the pant legs folded up into cuffs. Iona pretended to sleep.

Fiddle music wafted quietly from the radio and sunlight lay on the kitchen floor in the pattern of the screen door. Mama poured tea into her cup at the table and held the pot up to ask if I wanted some. Even with only her in it, the kitchen managed to be full of life.

"Yes, please. Where's Neil?"

"Out under the car." She poured my tea and set the pot back on the stove.

"Is it broken?"

"Oh, there's always something."

The words that I'd been practising since I woke burst out of me, "I think you're right. I'd like to go see Francis."

She swivelled around. "Would you now?"

"Yes I would. I'd like to go today."

"Oh now, how can you do that? You need a ticket. You need to pack. You can't just pick up and go like that."

"I saved the money for a ticket."

She turned back to the stove to shift the teapot from one burner to another. "Have you talked to Francis?" Her voice sounded muffled.

"Yes, I have, and he says he can get me a job for the summer."

"I wasn't really thinking you'd go for the whole summer. A week or ten days would be enough."

"If I could work there, it would be like a paid vacation."

"Crowell's will have hired someone else by then," she protested.

"I can get another job when I come back."

"It's a big city…"

"I won't be on my own. I'll be with Francis."

She turned to face me then.

"Francis has his own world there. He's a lot older than you. Who will you spend time with?"

It was not easy to meet her eyes when I was unsure of my answer, but I persevered.

"I didn't say I was leaving home! Anyway, I'm the same age that Francis was when he left and he did okay."

This was met by silence at first and then, "Wait another day so we can see you off properly. I'll go talk to Neil."

From my seat at the kitchen table, I saw her bend to speak to the legs protruding from the car. The legs shimmied out and Neil appeared and stood, looking toward the house. She talked to him in a low voice, and for a long time, holding his arm.

When they came through the door he headed for the stepstool, where he sat with his arms folded, looking at the floor. Mama went back to the dish sink. Raising his head, he spoke. "I can't give you permission to go."

"Because I'm a girl?"

"Because it isn't safe."

"What's unsafe? I'll be with Francis."

"No, you'll be wandering around a big city on your own half the time."

"I want to go."

"I will not stand in the doorway to stop you, but you don't have my permission."

I stood up. "I'm going then."

"That's a fine thing!"

The look in his eyes surprised me. Hidden among the disbelief and concern was a fragment of admiration.

"Sleep on it," he finally said. "You may feel differently tomorrow. If not, we'll take you to the train."

I nodded.

The temperature dropped suddenly that day and the wind whipped billowing dark clouds across the sky. Thunder and lightning were the supper excitement, the rumbles following closely after each flash. They seemed to be directly overhead. Mama remarked on the temperature. "We could use a bit of a fire."

She knew how much I loved to light the furnace and I didn't hesitate. She was the one who usually got it going in the morning before everyone was up, and banked it at night so there would be a small fire to keep the main house warm, but if she didn't get to it in time after supper, she appreciated my help in going down to build it up again. Over the past few years it had become a friend of mine.

Sitting at the open door of the furnace on a small stool, I twisted newspapers from a large stack we used for just this purpose, and then carefully put the finely cut kindling on top of that. A huge mound of glistening, jagged lumps of coal loomed beside the furnace, to my left. So incongruent to have this shining mountain of fuel reaching halfway to our ceiling in a closed and airless space. It made me wonder what would happen in a house fire. I placed a small hand shovel of coal on top of the kindling and picked up one of the long matches we used to light the fire. The small flame from the match licked at the paper, but the kindling sticks were slow to catch so I blew on it carefully with long, slow breaths, before I looked up from my work.

A photo of my father, in boxing gloves and full regalia, hung above his workbench. He was crouched as if guarding himself from attack. It made a strange juxtaposition to the small collection of broken items carefully stored on the bench. There were pieces of a broken porcelain cup waiting to be repaired, an old radio with the tubes lined up meticulously and the single leg of a wooden chair. Sitting off to one side was a professional set of vise grips, as if it might require such substantial tools to repair the fragile pieces set down there.

I kept glancing back at the photograph as I tore old newspapers, one by one, and fed them to the flames. They smoldered slowly, the pages curling up and turning to ash while they whispered about the dance and the betrayal, my loneliness and desire and fear. I pushed the voice away that said, "You take yourself too seriously" and allowed myself this sorrow.

In the morning, while I was packing a small suitcase to take with me on the train, Iona rushed into the room dishevelled, with her hair in sweaty curls at the hairline, from riding her bicycle. She sat bouncing on the bed opposite, watching and saying nothing all the while. After I closed the suitcase, I glanced in her direction—an invitation. She still said nothing.

Mama was mopping the kitchen floor when I came downstairs. She looked up.

"Are you ready to go?"

I swear if she'd asked me to stay I'd have reconsidered. Of course there was no way for her to know that. "Yes, I'm all set."

Her only answer was, "I trust you'll take good care of yourself," and I think she really meant it.

Iona ran down from upstairs and out the front door to avoid crossing through the kitchen. Seen through the door she looked carefree, happy-go-lucky almost, as she pulled her bike up from where she'd left it on the ground and pedalled away.

Mama asked, "Did you say goodbye?"

"I don't think she wants to talk," I replied.

On the way to the station, Mama turned around to give me some advice. "Don't forget you can go to a doctor whenever you want."

Neil interjected, "Don't forget you have Tommy Douglas to thank for that."

With that comment he pulled the car into the parking lot of the church. I'd forgotten it was Election Day. "This will only take a minute and we're early for the train."

"I'll wait out here," I said and sat on the stone wall surrounding the property. He finished first and sat beside me, looking straight ahead.

"How a person votes is their own business." It didn't sound like he was talking to me.

☙

As a rule, Mama didn't hesitate to jump into a political discussion but she'd been a bit quiet about Trudeau. Her card night stands out in my mind: the eight large and small and talkative women playing at two card tables that we'd set up in the living room. Two conversations happened at once, making it hard to keep track of the count. One of the women held the cards to her chest and said, "Did you see that one with the rose in his teeth?" and one of the others looked at her with a squinted eye because the smoke from her cigarette was bothering it. "Well, he's not Diefenbaker." For some reason most of the women collapsed in helpless laughter and the one who always peed when she laughed had to run to the washroom. Mama drew a few surprised looks when she quietly examined her cards and said, "At least he has something unusual to say once in a while."

"Unusual is one way to put it," said the smoker and they all looked at Mama as if she was a curiosity of some kind.

"What is it?" she asked when she looked up and all eyes were on her.

After they left, we were clearing up the leftover sweets and folding up the tables, when I asked her what she meant by unusual. Her answer was a riddle to me. She said, "I think he's more interested in things that matter than most of them are."

"Like what?"

"He doesn't want to punish people just for being who they are."

Her eyes were settled on the picture of the family that was hung on the wall below the piano window in the living room. It was taken when Francis was fourteen and all eight of us were lined up with Mama holding the baby.

"Even the abortion thing, you don't mind?"

"That's one part of it I have a problem with." She looked me straight in the eyes, "If anything ever happens, just remember you can bring a baby home here."

I rolled my eyes. "Nothing is going to happen."

"Good."

When Mama finished voting we all got in the car without saying a word.

Now on the way to the train station I wondered how I was going to figure out what I thought mattered. Was it something that just came to you or was there a method? It's a good thing Francis gave us jazz; I had at least one thing I thought mattered. Drawing, that mattered to me too. Somehow, it didn't seem that the things I thought mattered were really big enough to matter.

At the ticket wicket I pulled out the money I'd saved from the after-school job at Crowell's. It was just enough for one way. The ticket agent looked up from the long green form he was filling out as a part of selling the ticket. "Don't you want a sleeper?" he asked.

"I'll pay for it," Neil offered.

"No, no, it's a waste of money," I replied. "The seats lay back almost flat."

My mother, who always understood our finances better than he did, said, "Okay, but keep to yourself until you get there." Neil hugged me and said, without a trace of humour, "Don't forget to come home."

All of the young people on board were going to Montreal or Toronto or northern Ontario. They were finished with school and had expectations of work in the mines or in the bars. They were familiar looking although I didn't know them. None of them looked like the group from Halifax that had visited town on some kind of high school educational tour the previous year. Those youth were leaner and blonder and wore beautiful leather boots. The crowd on the train had the dark hair and eyes of islanders, with the occasional redhead among them, and there were no other girls. One of them had a transistor radio and the woman singing on it had a scratchy, comforting voice that made you believe her. I told anyone who asked that I was going away to work so they'd think I was older like them.

The one with the radio sometimes switched to the election to hear the results. On that warm June night, with the windows open and the countryside whistling by, we listened as Newfoundland results came in and then Nova Scotia's and finally on to Quebec. It felt as if we were racing along with the election, always in the place where the decision was being made. In the end, we were in Montreal when Trudeau and his party were declared winners. I felt that the world was no longer predictable and wondered if he was elected because everyone loved him for pirouetting behind the queen.

Things quieted down then and I grabbed one of the grey wool blankets folded on the seat and pushed the chair back as far as it could go so I could relax and maybe sleep. Some young men leaned over me as I got comfortable. "Come to the bar car. We'll buy you a drink. Let's celebrate!" one of them slurred in my face.

I pulled the blanket closer and said, "I don't drink."

"You do now," he said and threw off the blanket and grabbed me by the arm as if it was a great joke. There was one man there who was a little older than the others and he stepped in and shamed the other one, looking him in the eye and saying, "You're not thinking straight," and to me, "How old are you?"

"Sixteen."

"You go to sleep. No one is going to bother you," he said, looking with a straightforward gaze at the small crowd gathered around.

The rest of the night, as far as I could tell, they came and went from the great celebration in the bar car. Around midnight someone a few seats away turned the dial of a radio to the station where Francis had his show. I was soothed by the comfort of hearing his voice for one minute and by the whispering tones of Chet Baker. At some point in the night the man who'd been so good to me earlier came back to the car, sat on the other side of the facing double seat, and pushed his chair back as flat as it could go. I roused enough to see him and felt reassured, having him quietly lying there. In the morning he was gone.

"Call me when you stop tomorrow," Mama had called as a parting comment and I envisioned disembarking to a larger version of the small wooden building the train was leaving from. But the room I found myself in when we spilled into the station at Montreal had great inlaid arches more reminiscent of a cathedral. It was a grand and overwhelming piece of architecture, and with two hours to spare I decided to explore. A marble staircase led me down to the street below and delivered me to the sunshine on a street called Saint Antoine.

By the time I found a pay booth I was feeling worldly, or other-worldly, and terribly grown up just from the sheer wonder of finding myself there.

Iona picked up the phone after several rings, "How are you?"

"What time is it there now?" I asked.

"Do you still hate me?"

"I don't know what you're talking about."

"Well I'm going to the dance tonight," she said, "and I wish you were going with me."

"You're going alone? Who'll walk home with you?"

She fell silent.

"I'm sure you'll be fine. Put Mama on."

Mama took the phone and we talked about the trip, and the train ride and the sleep I'd had. I experienced an unreal sensation of disconnection from the present, as if I was standing a long way off in the future, watching myself on the phone.

Toronto did not turn out to be the place I expected. We passed some areas that were half rural and half factory and didn't seem to know if they were coming or going. In other places along the route, when I stood between cars with a window open, I could almost reach out and run my fingers along a picket fence or trail them through someone's laundry hanging on a backyard clothesline. Some of the backyards were filled with junk and abandoned cars. To see a small child playing among the rubble was disheartening. Only the arrival at the station was appropriately overwhelming in what seemed to be a big city way.

It was a bleaching hot day so I decided to walk instead of taking the bus. Francis had told me on the phone to take a bus up Bay Street about twenty blocks and get off at Cumberland. The bus is unbearable in the heat and it didn't sound too far. I figured if I walked, I'd know for sure where I was going.

On Bay Street a crowd of grey drifted toward me. It was made up mostly of men, although there were a few women among them. They were all wearing light grey suits, I suppose because it was summer. They reminded me of the fog in the marsh at the base of the hill, but I didn't feel the same courage to walk out into them as I had felt as a child sur-rounded by a cloud.

Perhaps I was going against the flow, because all the people on the sidewalk seemed to be walking toward me. This was more people than I was used to seeing on the street at one time, unless at a parade. Not only that, at home it was the custom to speak to everyone you met unless that didn't seem appropriate, in which case, you nodded. I had my eyes open and my head up, preparing to make contact with anyone who glanced my way, but not one person did. Instead, they kept their eyes on the ground or stared straight ahead.

I wasn't sure I'd be able to find my way back to the train station and started to count the blocks, trying to commit the names of the streets to memory in case I might need to retrace my steps. I wondered how long crumbs would last before the birds got them, if I had any to drop behind me.

A magnificently tall building loomed larger on my limited horizon. I put my suitcase down on the sidewalk to look up and up to try to see the very top, turning in circles with my neck craned back, as if I was in a forest of giant trees. A passing man laughed at me and said, "Yeah, pretty tall first time you see 'em, eh?" I was embarrassed to be caught looking so much like a visitor from the country, so I smiled and said nonchalantly, "Oh, I've seen them before. I was just trying to see the top." When he laughed again I realized this had done nothing to increase my credibility.

Cumberland Street, when I finally found it, was a canvas bursting with rebellious colour and disorderly signs. Music poured from a dozen places, and I had never before seen clothes like those the people on the street were wearing. They were painted and embroidered and patched with all manner of fabric and denim, except for the ones in black leather bike outfits. No one was going anywhere in particular. This was the exact antithesis to what I'd seen on Bay Street. Those two worlds backed up against each other, with neither having much to do with the world I'd left behind, and caused some kind of altered consciousness, nothing to do with the drugs that were swirling in the air.

The sheet of paper with the address where we were supposed to meet was somewhere in my bag and refused to be found when I stopped and put my suitcase down on the sidewalk to look for it. I noticed a beautiful boy standing to one side of the sidewalk with a broad face and high cheekbones, a wide smile and perfect almond eyes. He looked clean and clear. Propped up against the building was a piece of brown cardboard and in black crayon was written, *Hugs for Change*, and in smaller writing underneath: *It's the only talent God gave me*. When I laughed he caught my eye and winked at me.

I stopped looking for the address. I knew I was early so I tried to call Francis at home from a pay booth. The phone rang into nothing. In any case, I was sure I'd soon come across him on the street and decided to wander for a while.

About fifteen tough-looking men, with long hair and tattoos, sat on motorcycles curved around a bend in the sidewalk. One by one they nodded at me when I walked past, as if we had just exchanged some meaningful information. I was ready for someone to look me in the eye. I wondered if they were from small towns too.

I kept moving until I came upon a place that had some tables on the sidewalk and sat down, feeling this was an urban and grown-up choice. The tea I ordered came in one of those little metal pots that always make a mess when you pour. While I was sopping up the tea I'd spilled, I looked up and there he was across the street.

He wasn't as tall as I remembered but he still had his curly thick hair. Now it was covering his ears. Not really very long, but long enough to get you kicked out of school back home.

Sitting at the table with him was a woman and a man who, at first glance, I mistook for a woman, dressed in flowing white pants and a red shirt with bursts of orange like miniature suns all over it. The man's blond hair ran all the way to his shoulders in waves, and he was very thin but softly handsome in a way I'd never seen before. He and Francis were talking very excitedly, so I had lots of time to look them over. The woman also had long straight hair, a style impossible for me to achieve without an ironing board. She wore a blouse of rose Indian muslin with a swirling paisley pattern. The fabric was almost sheer but the skirt had more than one layer so that it flowed and draped around her. They all wore leather sandals.

I looked down at my sleeveless navy Swiss dotted cotton dress with the empire waist. It was from a Butterick pattern designed by Mary Quant and I was pleased with how closely it fit from the moment I basted it together. I'd been very proud of it until that moment. Now my stomach clenched in embarrassment. It was instantly and blatantly obvious to me that I knew nothing about how to dress myself.

Francis wouldn't care what I was wearing, would he? Here I was, in a breezy city with new clothes, new shoes and a small suitcase that was easy to carry. I intended to feel confidant and outgoing when we met. Instead those first moments when I saw him with his friends were a torture.

Francis glanced across the road and looked at me. Ever so slight changes registered on his face, as if recognition was being exposed by some kind of time-lapsed photography. I just kept looking and smiling and he kept looking back and forth to his friends as if they might know, although they were deep in conversation and didn't seem to notice. Finally he looked back and I shrugged so he'd know it was me. He leapt up and held his arms open and when I bent to forage for some change to pay the bill, he leapt across the road to me.

He stuttered and didn't seem to know what to say until he threw his arms around me and gave me the kind of bear hug I remembered so well. He laughed then, "You're so tall. I bet I can still lift you but I don't think I could throw you very far."

"Why would you want to?" I asked as if I had no recall of the way he and our brother Joe used to toss me around.

His friends had been watching this from the other side of the street. When we crossed they were polite in the way you'd be to your friend's family. The woman said, "It's really nice to meet Francis's little sister. I didn't even know he had one," and smiled in a way meant to be nice, I suppose, but which annoyed me terribly for some reason. Francis looked around at the scene on the street, nodded at his friends and said, "I think we'll head out."

He grabbed my bag, which was much like the one he was carrying the night he'd left home himself, and as we started off I felt giddy from having caught up with him. We walked in silence until he looked over and noticed I was practically quivering. He just started to laugh a bit and that made me laugh and soon we were full-on belly laughing, stopped on the sidewalk. I was here! Francis was here! And nothing had changed! When Francis read my thoughts he sobered.

"We should go before it rains," he said.

"What rain? I don't see any rain," I said, looking at the cumulus clouds ahead of us.

"It's just an expression."

Heat rose in waves off the sidewalk. As we walked, we indulged in one of those conversations we used to have at home after supper. Was it particles in the air that the light reflected off or was the heat bending the light, squishing it under its weight? He told me that people in Toronto come to long for the booming summer thunder and the downpour that would follow. I remembered running home from the dance in the rain with Iona and asked him what time it was.

"It's about seven o'clock back home if that's what you're wondering."

"Iona is probably getting ready to go out right now."

"Do you wish you were there?"

"Absolutely not."

The road we were travelling ended at a small city park and he said he lived there. "In the park?" I joked.

"I do get sent there sometimes when I misbehave," he replied, heading across the grass to a row of neat brick houses. The only other row housing I'd ever seen was the company houses near the steel plant. This row was statelier, though not more dignified, because of the brick. Even after many decades it held a crispness that wood does not. A windblown maritime house, permeated with sea salt and ravaged by the quick thawing and freezing of an east coast climate, is not easy to maintain.

Each home had a brick stairway that led directly from the sidewalk and under a curving arch to a broad front door. When he opened the door and motioned for me to enter, I was confused by what I found there. It looked to be some kind of gracious family home of the type I only saw in movies. It wasn't the furniture, which was almost non-existent, it was the height of the ceilings and the beautiful wood. We walked into a roomy kitchen where there was a soft, red brick wall, salvaged after the plaster and lathe had been removed.

He sang out, "We're here," but it didn't occur to me he had a room-mate until a man materialized in the kitchen, wearing a t-shirt with a picture of a bucking horse. He had a muscled body, long hair and un-smiling eyes.

"This?" he asked.

"Eileen, this is Pierce." He studied my face for a reaction. "Never take him seriously."

Later, when we got to know each other better, Pierce claimed he brought out the best in me, but on the night we met that was not the case. He offered no hand or welcoming gesture, so I said, "You weren't expecting me."

"Sure I was," he said. "I just couldn't imagine Francis with a little sis-ter. I always thought he grew out of the slimy sidewalk like a mushroom."

It was then I caught the drawl. "Are you from Boston?"

He looked at Francis, shaking his head. "Something like that."

Francis raised his hands in the air and mimicked Pierce's accent. "I don't know how everybody knows I'm American." To me he said, "Ignore him."

Pierce stuck his tongue out at him. Francis gave him a warning look. I pretended not to see any of that. It was so childish.

We walked through what should have been a dining room. It had a mattress and pillows all over the floor as if someone had come while they were out and taken away the bed. He led me to a room at the back painted a violet grey, and dumped my suitcase on the floor. The bay window had a deep seat and a thick cushion on it covered with purple corduroy. The whole place seemed exotic. "The rent must be exorbitant," I said.

"Don't worry, for you it's free for a while. Pierce and I can afford it. If you're still here in the fall you might have to chip in."

"I didn't know Pierce lived here."

"Well, he does. I'll tell you all about that later."

"Like I'm going to forget what you said between now and then? What does he do?"

"I don't remember you being so talkative. Didn't you used to be re-ally quiet? He's a law student."

"I was eight," I said.

"Right, you're an adult now."

"Not really."

"I'll try to remember that."

I rolled my eyes. He laughed.

We strolled back through the living room. Francis touched a few keys on the piano and then turned to look at all the other instruments casually strewn around on the carpet. "People like to hang here. You can make yourself comfortable." Comfort was already in the room, where light from the tall windows was filtered through well-tended ferns and philodendrons in hanging pots.

"I brought your fiddle," I blurted out, fearing I was naïve to have thought he would want it.

His eyebrows lifted suddenly but he said quietly, "I haven't played since I left."

"Why not?"

"Didn't have my fiddle."

"It's not the only fiddle in the world."

"Hah! I'm so glad you came," he said. "Let's sit out the back."

We sat on his tiny back porch, looking out at an unkempt mess of vegetation that had once been someone's cherished garden.

"Are you going to be homesick, do you think?"

"It's not as if I'm in some foreign country and can never go home." I heard the accusation in my tone and so did he.

He turned and looked at me more solemnly. "I never felt I belonged there."

"What does that mean?" I asked. "You're *from* there."

"Don't you ever feel like that?"

"Well… sometimes."

"Well, I felt like that a lot."

"You belonged there to me."

"You didn't really know me," he said.

I tapped him on the arm with the back of my hand. "I did so. I knew you very well!"

He put his hands up. "Okay, okay, you did. I take that back."

16

I sat behind a glass wall, trying to match the man on the other side with the brother I'd been missing for so long. He was there but so changed; his black-rimmed glasses made him look studious, and he was using that deep adult voice that made me laugh when I was eight. Now, in this studio, it was the only voice he used. But it was more than that. He belonged here. It was like watching him play his records in his room. The same care he took with them, the same bob of his head when he listened. Suddenly I was caught between two different worlds and not sure where I'd rather be. It was the first breath of a feeling of belonging in two places at once that has never really left me.

When we walked home around midnight there was no breeze. It was humid, sticky. Minute beads of water shimmered on Francis's forehead. Without warning, there was a crack of lightning and large drops of rain began to fall heavily on our heads. By the time we'd run a couple of blocks we were soaked through, so we slowed down and meandered home in the pouring warm rain, a sense echo of something I remembered doing as a child.

For the next few nights I went with him to the radio station, and several of the workers there stopped by my chair and asked questions I found difficult to answer.

"What made you come to Toronto? Do you like it better than Cape Breton?"

"I like them both," I said, trying to be diplomatic and not knowing why you'd have to choose.

"What are you planning to do here in Toronto?"

"Get a job, I hope."

The boss arrived on an evening shift and took note of this activity.

He put a hand up to his forehead and squeezed it a couple of times, as if it hurt, then beckoned Francis aside. They stood a few feet away with their heads together, but I could hear him say, "Who is that?"

"My little sister."

"You can't babysit your little sister here."

Francis looked across the room and could tell I'd heard it.

On the way home we walked silently for a while. Eventually I said, "I'll get a job. If I can't, I'll just stay for a visit and then go home."

I found myself standing under the shade of a blue awning in front of a red door. The sunlight outside the awning's protective circle seemed to hit the sidewalk and bounce back. In the plate glass window beside the red door there was a sign posted.

Waitress Needed Day Shift

Mama's voice popped into my ear. "Tell them you're a hard worker. That's all they want to know."

A bell above the door tinkled when I entered. The restaurant was empty, just waiting for the lunch customers to fill up the booths. The owners were a couple in their thirties, leaning at either side of the yellow Arborite counter, talking. They weren't as old as my parents but they had a grown-up feeling to them, both what you'd call good-looking, I think. But they did nothing to promote that. Short plain hair for him, no makeup for her, with luxuriously thick hair tied back in a ponytail. A far cry from Maisie Cochrane, and thinking of that made me feel quite confident.

I introduced myself. "Hello. I'm Eileen MacPherson. Do you need a waitress?"

"Hello," the woman smiled, "I'm Cici and this is Gheorghe."

Gheorghe spoke. "Do you have experience?"

I was prepared for that question.

"I had a job in a big store and handled cash, and I come from a big family so I'm used to waiting on people."

They exchanged looks.

"Sure, we need a girl right away. Start tomorrow," he said with a broad smile. The accent he spoke with struck me as Italian. The woman sounded the same. "Do you have a white shirt and a black skirt?" she asked.

"No problem, I'll get those."

"Can you work tomorrow?"

"Yes, I'd love to!"

Walking along the street, looking in shop windows, I caught sight of the reflection of a slim woman passing by. She had a large amount of dark, curly hair. She looked familiar and when I glanced back at her, I realized she was me. It was funny and embarrassing at the same time, and I was glad no one could read my thoughts.

A small clothing store a few shops away had exactly the things I needed, the black skirt and the white blouse. I was quite proud of myself for so quickly solving the problem of what to do with me.

Francis was impressed. I wouldn't let him be.

"I'm waitressing. No big deal."

I started the next day as promised. When I arrived for the lunch shift they looked surprised to see me. Their expressions stopped me.

"I thought I was supposed to start today."

They looked at each other and he shrugged. "We thought you were coming at breakfast and then we thought you weren't coming. But it's okay. You're on time for lunch."

"Sorry. I got it wrong somehow."

The first thing they wanted me to do was eat.

"Oh, no thanks. I already had breakfast."

"You don't like this food?"

"I probably like it but I already ate." I shrugged, trying to be inoffensive.

"You're young. You need to eat. How can you tell the customers you never tried the food?"

"Okay then, I'll eat."

The wife asked lots of questions as I devoured the eggs and bacon she set before me. "Where is your family? How many brothers and sisters? Are your parents still alive?" All easy to answer until she asked, "Why do you leave home so young? Are there no jobs for you there? No restaurants?"

"I just want to be independent and see what it's like somewhere else."

"Adventure. What does your mother think?"

I paused for a moment to think about that. "She thinks I can do it."

She shook her head. "You can work here as long as you like. We'll give you vacation after summer. You go to your family. Don't forget them. There's no ocean between you and no war."

She looked away for a moment before she began to gather the plate I'd emptied.

"Do you miss Italy?" I asked.

"I'm from Romania."

"I'm so sorry!"

"It's no insult."

"When did you leave home?" I asked, trying to quickly move on from my gaffe.

"Fifteen years ago. I was just your age."

"Have you been back?"

"My parents are not living. I have no reason to go back. Maybe someday." She quickly gathered the table and herself together.

Every working morning started with a meal at seven but we never had this kind of conversation again. She kept her comments to places where I could buy cheap clothing and what I might do with my hair.

I told Francis about her when I came home from work and before he left for his.

"Do you think Cici had to leave Romania?" I wondered.

"Everyone has to leave home sometime," he tossed off.

"I don't like that saying. It doesn't mean anything."

"Well… you can't live with your parents for the rest of your life, can you?"

"No, but you don't have to leave the country!" I said.

"Some people do. Ask her," he suggested.

"I'm asking you."

"If she had to leave home?"

"No. I'm asking if *you* had to leave home."

He took a deep breath and let it out in a rush. I thought he was planning to tell me something important. "I'm going to work now. We can talk about this another time."

✿

The weekend was spent in the park, an entity all its own. The yellow Frisbee whirled toward me, always out of reach. I'd never played before and when it became obvious it would take some time, Francis lobbed it gently so I had time to run and catch it. When I had to throw it back, Pierce found a way to put himself in front of my feeble efforts. He fell down a lot and it looked a bit like the way a boy tries to impress you when you're both ten or eleven years old. Lying on his back, wearing a blue t-shirt with a tie-dyed yellow and orange sun on the front, he looked full of life.

The summer evening promised to be warm for hours, so we shopped on the way home and bought a baguette, cheeses, tomatoes and some wine. They both set to cutting up the food, side by side at the counter.

I sat at the table watching. They shoved each other playfully and Pierce said, "Don't be a pig!" when Francis dropped a piece of tomato on the floor. You could tell they were good friends. They bumped into each other a lot while they cooked.

"You could set the table, Eileen," Francis reminded me.

"Don't let him boss you around," said Pierce. I really thought Pierce liked me.

In the tiny overgrown backyard there was a small table and some chairs. A sarong that had been left behind in the music room served as a tablecloth. The candle in a wine bottle seemed like a nice touch, and I found some coils in the back porch to keep off the mosquitoes.

Francis was off that night so we sat out well past dark, talking.

Pierce asked, "Have you thought about college?"

"I have no money for that," I said.

"What do you think you'll do?"

"Waitress?" I offered.

"Will that make you happy?"

"A job?"

He laughed. "Why not? Think about something to do that would make you happy every morning when you got up to do it."

"I like to draw. And if I could, I'd like to paint."

"There it is then. You're a painter."

"Maybe I'll have to be a waitress so I can afford the paint."

"You can be paid to paint."

"Houses maybe."

"Modesty will get you nowhere," he said, and I was flattered that he thought I might be able to do something, and even more so because he had never seen anything I'd made and had nothing but regard to base this on.

I didn't want the evening to end, so when Pierce got up to clear the table, I said, "I'll do it in the morning. I don't want to go in yet."

He sat back in his chair again and, just to make conversation, asked Francis, "Did you hear they're working on reintroducing the criminal code legislation?" Francis looked at him with raised eyebrows and continued to scrape a few plates together.

"Mama was talking about that," I said.

"Oh yeah? What does she think?"

"She seemed to think it's good for the most part. Except for abortion. She likes Trudeau. Says he cares about things that other people don't."

"What does she say about his stance on homosexuality?" Pierce asked.

"She's never said. I know Neil is not too keen on it."

"I can imagine that."

"What's your stance?" I asked him.

"I don't know," he said. "Francis what's your stance on that?"

"Each to his own," Francis replied as he gathered dishes and took them to the kitchen.

∂

Pierce and I spent hours in the evenings talking about the state of the world. He had a serious way with me and asked my opinion about things, assumed I might have one.

"What's your theory on why Canada isn't in Vietnam?" he asked one night, as if it was a casual question I might have thought about. I ignored Mama's advice about talking through your hat and offered a tentative opinion. "Canadians just don't seem to feel like it's their fight," I said.

"That's a bit lame, Eileen. There are Canadians fighting. And there are a lot of Americans who don't want this fight either."

"Is that why you're here?" I asked, hoping to recuperate myself.

"There are a lot of reasons to be here," he said. "How old are you again?"

"That's mean. Don't ask me any questions if you're just going to make fun of my answers."

"Chill out. I'm not doing that."

Around eleven or twelve he went out to meet Francis at the bar. When I asked to go with him, he said I was too young.

The house was perfectly quiet when I got up the next day. A letter from Iona was conspicuously placed in a ray of sunlight on the dining room table, so I knew Pierce had been up and gone. I circled it for a while before opening it, wary of whatever it might offer.

The sun on the back porch was hot and bright at that time of day and the bees buzzed the remnants of the garden. The letter was a white, accusing rectangle sitting on the step beside me. It seemed best to open it while I was alone.

Dear Eileen,

I hope you're enjoying yourself there. It's been very hot here but no humidity so we're having a great summer. I've been thinking about you and wishing you could accept my apology. I never meant to hurt your feelings. I should have told you right away that I'd run into him and that he wasn't doing well but I was afraid you'd be hurt. It's hard to know when the truth is a friend or an enemy.

It turns out that Robbie MacLean is quite a nice person. He's really sorry for standing you up but he was so depressed he thought he'd just ruin your night. I ran into him at the square dance in Marion Bridge. He would like to be forgiven too.

I'm looking forward to you coming home.
Love, Iona

She'd abandoned me. I hadn't really known that was possible. I told myself I didn't care a bit if she was going to fall in love with someone who obviously didn't have a loyal bone in his body.

A diversion was clearly in order.

Performers and panhandlers stepped into my path. Bookstores advertised peep shows in the back. So many people, some half naked, wearing wild colours, filled the streets.

A band of people with shaved heads, wearing orange sarongs and dancing and chanting incessantly, blocked the sidewalk. When I stopped to watch them, a man who was dressed the same way as the chanters and whom I assumed to be one of their group, approached me and asked me if I was a spiritual person. I thought I must have misheard. It struck me as an extremely intimate question to be asking someone before saying hello.

I said, "Sorry, I didn't catch that."

"It's not a disease," he said and smiled as if he felt a bit sorry for me.

I moved on, feeling a bit embarrassed, and was happy to turn the corner when I noticed a sidewalk café where I could escape.

This was nothing like Bay Street. The reason Francis had steered me away from Yonge when I first arrived was obvious.

While waiting for my tea, I noticed the young men at the next table sharing a few laughs and looking very happy to be in each other's company. They touched each other on the shoulder occasionally or on the back. At the same moment, a man with a good physique, wearing a tight black t-shirt and jeans, stepped off the sidewalk and started for a table under an awning. Then he noticed the two young men. He walked over to their table and stood with his arms crossed.

"What the fuck are you two doing here?"

The young men put down their forks. "Eating lunch," one of them said.

The man started shouting and pointing, "Why don't you go back to the rock you crawled out from under. We don't want your slime here!"

The manager came out quickly. "Hey. What's the problem?"

"Hey buddy. Serving queers now, are you?"

"They're not hurting anything."

The man's voice dropped to a controlled and measured timbre.

"I come here every day. If you don't get rid of them, I will find a way to shut this business down."

The manager turned apologetically to the young men, who were already on their feet, tossing coins on the table.

"It's okay," the men said.

The manager shrugged and walked back into his restaurant.

The rest of us tried to avoid each other's eyes, not knowing what we might find there.

Reading the paper at the table out back on a Saturday morning, with the finches around my feet looking for crumbs, I saw that a curfew had been imposed in Yorkville for people under eighteen. I desperately wanted to go back there, so when Francis dropped into the seat opposite with a bowl of cereal, I began to campaign.

"Take me back to Yorkville. I liked it there."

"You're too young," he mumbled.

"You know I can pass for eighteen."

He looked at me and shook his head. "You don't want to go to Yorkville. The real hippies are gone. There's a bunch of greasers there now."

I reverted to Iona's type of reasoning. "Come on! Are you really going to let me go home and say to people, Oh no, I never went to Yorkville. I have a stuffy old brother who wouldn't let me."

Never mind whether most people my age back home had ever heard of Yorkville. The argument was basically successful.

We planned for Pierce and me to meet him there after eleven. That evening I came out of my room all ready to go, wearing a newly acquired minidress with large psychedelic flowers and suns. He crossed his arms and nodded slowly.

"You hate it," I said.

"No, no, no. I'm just considering you." And after a pause, "Do you have anything else?"

"A few things."

"The first time you go out on the town, you should feel like the queen of the night." As if he was some kind of fashion plate himself.

I looked down at the dress. "People would wear this."

"All right then, man, it's your choice," he said.

I went back to my room.

All I really had in the closet was a pair of shorts, a pair of blue jeans, four t-shirts, some socks and underwear, my waitress uniform, the clothes I'd arrived in, and the dress. I looked at it a long, long time before I ripped off the thing with the flowers and suns and pulled on something that felt more like the moon over the ocean.

When I re-entered the room, he said, "Okay, that's good, you look…"

"Outstanding," I said.

"Exactly," he nodded.

The walk to Yorkville seemed shorter than it had on the day when Francis and I walked from there to his house for the first time. It always seems that it takes less time to go back the way you've come. I admired the brickwork on the houses we passed. It looked like eyelashes spread over the wide-eyed windows of strangers' apartments, as if we could be seen and the world approved of us.

On Cumberland Street, the same long line of tough-looking men on motorcycles nodded as if they knew me. This time I smiled back and Pierce grabbed hold of my arm and steered me away.

"There are limits to being friendly. Don't mess with them."

There were an enormous number of people on the street. It was nothing like the afternoon when I met Francis there at all. The traffic was bumper to bumper and moving very slowly, and there were hundreds of people crowding the sidewalks. Some of them looked like hippies, but some of them looked terribly sick. Their eyes were haunted as if they were seeing a frightening world to which I had no access. People in expensive clothes were waiting to go into a restaurant half a block from where the bikers were sitting. It felt a bit like being at a circus and I was glad to have company.

When we got to the Mynah Bird, Francis was standing outside on the sidewalk waiting for us. He let out a long slow whistle and said, "Wow!"

I laughed because it reminded me of the time when I was six years old and came down to the kitchen wearing my first communion dress. Francis gasped and said, "Wow, you're so beautiful in that dress, you're going to knock God's socks right off."

Mama had heard him and said dryly, "That doesn't even have a semblance of humour. Go get dressed for church." Then she looked at me, "That was very close to blasphemous."

Although I'd never heard the word before, it was a good introduction to the concept. I ventured, "You mean God wouldn't think that's funny."

"No, he wouldn't."

Maybe Francis thought of Mama that night too, because there was some kind of weird act going on inside and we were going to the Riverboat instead.

"You think I'm not old enough for go-go girls?" I asked, looking at the posters on the door.

"The go-go girls are topless."

"That must hurt," I said.

He laughed. "We aren't going in."

I liked the Riverboat. It had comfortable red booths and portholes and everyone seemed to know Francis. Pierce explained to me later that being a disc jockey meant that musicians wanted to know Francis because he could play their records on the air and help them to make a name for themselves. I didn't recognize the many people who stopped at our table to say hello, because I was only familiar with the names of big bands that had played on *Ed Sullivan* or local bands from home, like Sam Moon and the Universal Power.

The girl with the long, straight hair, who I'd met on the very first day I'd come to Toronto, was on stage playing a guitar and singing an unfamiliar song. Her voice was clear and clean and when I told Francis I'd never heard it before, he said she wrote it herself. I was very impressed that a girl could write her own song. When she finished she stood up with her guitar hanging from her neck and said, with a bow of her head, "Thank you for listening to me," then walked toward our table and sat down.

Her name was Lucy and she looked me in the eye and said she remembered me. As the evening wore on, she paid special attention to me in a way I had not expected. I wondered why she would be bothered with me when she seemed so much older and could write her own songs. At first I thought she was sort of taking care of me, but later I understood that she also needed a female friend. All the other women were with a man and weren't clinging to each other in pairs the way we did at home.

She'd been at the table for only a few minutes when she started to tell us a story with her hands in that same way Iona did. She said, "When I got up this morning and opened the dresser drawer a mouse with big ears jumped out." The whole time she talked about how cute it was, she mimed setting a trap with cheese, as if she couldn't speak of this for fear of warning the now-dead mouse. It was endearing and engaging and I was flooded with affection that probably rightly belonged to Iona.

As we were leaving the coffee house, she touched me on the arm.

"I love your dress," she said.

When I said my mother made it for me, she looked quite taken aback and tried to hide that with a laugh. "Lucky you to have a mother like that. Do you think she'd make me one?"

"I could ask her," I said, feeling a bit confused by the request.

She said quietly, "Thank you, that's very sweet, I'm just joking." Her eyes shifted to a young man who was coming in the door. "Daniel!" she cried out. He turned his head away as if he hadn't heard. Francis got up and said, "We should go." I wasn't able to catch her eye again.

17

I was often alone, marking time, while Francis and Pierce were out without me, and took to hand embroidering flowers on my jeans. The flowers travelled in an ornamental line, from hip to ankle and back, until I had one whole leg almost completely covered. Before starting on the other one, I decided to do some cleaning. Francis and Pierce must have done a clean sweep of the house before I arrived, but since then they hadn't emptied an ashtray.

I wandered up the staircase for the first time to see how it looked up there. At the top I found a second-floor hallway with two doors of a split bathroom in front of me. Doors to the left and right led to bedrooms. A quick little tour of the one on the right confirmed it was as neat as a pin and had almost nothing in it. The bed was made up with a white bedspread and the walls were white. There didn't seem to be any sign of life there except for the closet with Pierce's clothes in it.

The room across the hall was a disaster. There were socks and underwear all over the floor and the window seat was piled with clothing. The bed was unmade and the bedclothes were dragged halfway across the room. Even the blinds and curtains were askew. I'd seen how bad the boys' room at home could get, so I wasn't completely surprised but I thought that Francis could take a few lessons from Pierce.

I started picking up the clothes and putting them in a straw hamper in the closet. Some of them belonged to Pierce. The blue tie-dye and the t-shirt with the bucking horse stood out among the others.

All of a sudden I was up in a corner of the room, watching myself as I picked them up and carried them over to his room and put them in the hamper in his closet instead.

Still up there in the corner, I saw myself sitting on the floor, picking up things within reach, like gum wrappers and sunscreen. When a wave of nausea hit me I catapulted back into my body. The rocking back and forth calmed me enough to recognize that I was overcome with confusion.

An intuition I had been trying to drown had finally pushed its way to the surface. Now one little realization after another lined up in my mind for attention: the fact neither of them had a girlfriend, the fact they wouldn't take me along to the clubs, the conversation at the table in the garden about the new criminal code, and the fact I'd have to accept that Pierce wasn't even remotely interested in me.

Oh, and the most illuminating clue of all, which made me want to hold a hand above my eyes because it shone so brightly, was the fact you could see they loved each other. It was in the scathing comments they made and the way they always knew what the other was up to. I could see they belonged to each other.

It was as if I'd taken sunglasses off and suddenly all the colours were so bright they hurt. Then came the deep embarrassment, a cringe travelling the length of my body, followed by a steely kind of fury made of pain. I thought we were closer than that. How can someone be one of your own if they can't tell you the truth? I sank back to the floor, hunched around pulled-up knees, feeling alternately hot and cold. Did he think I was blindingly naïve? The kind of person you should hide from? Was I? Did he and Pierce laugh at me when I wasn't around? Was he afraid I'd squeal on him?

Thoughts and emotions refused to settle in any kind of pattern, and perspective was impossible to find. Back home, if anyone heard about this there would be dismissive jokes, but after seeing how they were together, I felt a bit jealous, excluded.

By the time I left the room half an hour later there were fresh sheets on the bed, the clothes were sorted and the floor was vacuumed.

Once downstairs I paced around for a while before curling up in the window seat in the living room overlooking the park. There were occasional flashes of lightning followed by thunder and I have never wished more fervently for rain.

I packed the same suitcase I'd arrived with a month earlier. Laid out the jeans with the embroidery to be ready to wear the next day and put the waitress uniform on a hanger in the bathroom where Francis would see it. When I crawled under the bed covers I pulled them over my head, needing the dark.

The dream I had that night was of floating above the clouds and looking for an opening so I could find my way down.

At dawn I found myself sitting on a suitcase in the kitchen, eating a bowl of cornflakes, looking out the back door at the non-garden. The light was coming from tall windows behind me and making the shadow of the suitcase very long. Part of it was already out the door. But the shadow of the bowl that held the cereal I was eating was a narrow oblong and was still all inside.

A morning-dishevelled Pierce came down the stairs, noticed me sitting there like some kind of tableau. "Francis is not happy," he mumbled.

"That's too bad. Are you?" I asked.

"Never mind about that. How are you doing?" he asked when he noticed the suitcase.

"I'd be doing a lot better if you fellas treated me like someone with a brain in my head."

"Oh, man!" he rubbed his forehead with the palms of his hands while saying, "Okay then. You better sort that out with Francis. I'm going for some grub." Then he left, grabbing a windbreaker as if it was cold outside.

When Francis walked into the room he didn't even glance in my direction. His body was tense and his eyes were downcast. He turned the radio on. The program was a repeat of what he'd done the night before and he always listened in the morning. Nat King Cole's velvet rendition of "Nature Boy" eased into the room.

I watched him for a while as he pulled out cereal and milk from the cupboards and fridge, and then proceeded to eat them, standing at the counter with his back to me.

Finally I said, "I'm sorry I went in your room. I thought it would be useful if I cleaned up."

His shoulders relaxed the smallest bit as he turned around and glanced at the suitcase. "I wanted to tell you but there was no good opportunity. It seemed to go right over your head. I was afraid you'd cry and go home or something."

"What makes you think I'd cry?" I asked.

"Isn't that sort of what you're doing with your bags all packed?"

I stood so that I'd have my feet under me.

"No. Do you see me crying? That is your interpretation of me," I said. "Maybe I'm leaving because it's the best thing to do."

"I knew you wouldn't be able to handle it."

"There it is again. You're attributing attitudes to me that I don't even have. I don't mind!"

"You do mind," he said. It's a little far-fetched to say you don't mind. Everyone minds."

"You used to ask me what I thought! I was eight years old and you made me feel like an equal somehow. Most people talk down to you when you're a kid. Very few people talk straight across. But you did. So why am I your *little sister* now?"

"Okay. I'm sorry. I didn't want to hurt you."

"The only thing that hurts is that you don't trust me to understand! You think I'm too dumb to get it."

After a large intake of air and a soft expulsion, he said, " I don't think that."

"Mama knows, doesn't she?"

"Yes, she does."

"She didn't say a thing," I told him.

"I asked her not to."

"Why?!"

"I wanted to tell you myself."

"Well you did a great job of that," I said.

"Why should my sex life be a topic of discussion anywhere but between me and my friend? Isn't that the way you'll want it?"

"It doesn't matter!" I said. "Most people only think about other people's struggles for about ten minutes before they get back to worrying about their own!"

He paused a moment. "You don't know how ugly people can be. I can just imagine the talk back home."

"But I'm right here. You could help me grow up a bit. I'm not as narrow-minded as you think. Don't give up on me!"

Francis looked away and shook his head with the smallest movement before he looked back. "When you were eight years old I thought you'd probably grow up to be the smartest person I ever knew. And you are. I'm sorry. I didn't recognize you."

We looked at each other for a long moment before I found the proper thing to say. "I guess that's two of us then. I'm sorry I didn't recognize you either."

When he held his arms open wide, I walked into their circle, feeling great relief.

We found Pierce lying spread-eagled on the grass in his blue tie-dyed shirt with the big sun. He sat up quickly as soon as we arrived and stood above him, but when he saw us together he said nothing. I couldn't tell if he was squinting against the sun or smiling. He lay back down on the grass and Francis and I lay down on either side of him, making a row that in winter would have looked like snow angels watching the clouds drift by.

The worthless nature of my insecurity became obvious. It had never occurred to me that Francis and Pierce needed my support as much as I needed theirs. I'd had my own picture and I just laid it on top of reality so that the world always looked good. That day in the park it felt like my little picture of the world was tossed aside and the whole totality of real things was laid out there to see. It was a bit frightening but exhilarating, and it felt better.

⁂

The next morning I phoned Mama, before Francis and Pierce were up. I told her that I wanted to stay as long as I could and had even thought about finishing my schooling there. Of course I hadn't talked to Francis about that, but I was pretty sure I could win him over to my way of thinking.

Mama said, "I don't think you should do that. You're too young to stay away." Then when I said nothing she went on, "Think about it really hard, Eileen."

"I have."

"Say hello to your father then." The phone was put down and I heard her call out. "I have her on the phone."

His footsteps were quick before I heard his quickened breath. "How are you, dear?"

"I'm good. The weather's been hot and there are a lot of thunder storms but I like it."

"It would be good to come home before the fall," he said. "You have to finish school and then you can always go back to Toronto whenever you want."

"How is everyone there?" I asked.

"Well, things are pretty good. Iona is moping around though. I think she misses you."

"I'm pretty sure it's not me she's missing." She broke up with Robbie is what I assumed.

"Come back, Eileen. You remember we agreed to that." The tone of his voice alarmed me.

"Is something wrong with Mama?"

"Everyone is fine." His tone was decisive and left no room for further questioning of that sort. I assumed he didn't believe I was old enough to be on my own, but I knew that both he and Francis had left home at the same age and I wanted to believe I was capable. In any case I was with

Francis, so I said, "Don't worry, Francis will take care of me." There was a long silence before he said, "You do what you think is best."

That night I didn't want to go to the Riverboat.

"Take me where you go when I don't go with you."

"Those clubs can get a bit rough," Francis said.

"What do you mean? Fights?"

"When the cops show up it doesn't usually go well."

"Really?"

"Really," he said.

"I want to go with you."

"Why?"

"Because I want to see for myself!"

He looked at Pierce. "What are we going to do with her?"

"Let's start with The Maison de Lys."

It was on Yonge Street and was a good choice with male and female couples. Francis said that when the cops came, people who were dancing just changed partners so they couldn't be arrested for indecency. Sounded practical to me.

The bar was crowded and the dance music loud. Gender seemed a bit harder to pin down than it did outside. Both the men and women were flamboyant, and for the most part the women who flirted with me weren't trying very hard. A woman with a Mia Farrow haircut engaged me in conversation for half an hour, and when she reached over to push the hair out of my eyes, Pierce was right behind me.

"We're on a roll," he said. "Never stay anywhere too long." He smiled, offered his hand, and we were out the door.

"I called Francis," Pierce told me. "He's going to meet us back in Yorkville at Lucy and Daniel's place. We're going to stop at a place or two along the way."

"I'm with you."

"People might be smoking hash at Lucy's. Francis told everyone that he will personally punish them if they offer you any drugs or booze, so you have to co-operate."

"He's not responsible for me," I said.

"He is and he has me for backup."

"That's perfect. I have my jailors with me."

"More like bodyguards."

"I'm sixteen!" I protested.

"Yes, and you're with us."

When we came to a break in the street where a narrow and poorly lit alley opened to our left, Pierce took my arm without speaking. We quickly turned the corner and hurried along the brick tunnel. He didn't look at me and seemed to know where we were going, so I didn't resist or ask why. We came upon a door, painted black, halfway down the alley.

"Here it is," he said proudly.

He opened the door and we descended a long stairway with a single bulb at the bottom and top. When we opened the door below, a large, smoky underground alternate world was revealed. The shimmering gold and leopard skin clothing of the women circulating in the bar gave it a carnival atmosphere. Men were dancing with each other and the large, heavily made-up woman on stage was singing "Happy Birthday, Mr. President" to some imagined lover. She stopped often to make sarcastic comments about some of the costumes worn by other performers who were waiting to appear. It took only a minute to realize that none of the women standing near the stage were really women. Some of the costumes were excellent. One woman wore a red, sequined, strapless gown with breasts pushed up high. Her long hair was blond but the eyelashes were black and swept her cheeks when she closed her eyes. She noticed a woman wearing a fairy costume, like Tinker Bell without the wings, and called out, "Tink! It's you!"

My favourite was a very tall person wearing high heels and a slinky black dress with a generous chartreuse boa. She was both beautiful and imposing. Everyone was talking and drinking and exclaiming about how great everyone looked.

A friend of Pierce's saw us and hurried over. He had chin-length black hair and beautiful eyelashes. After kissing Pierce on both cheeks, he held me at arms length and said,

"My *gawd*! Look at the dress! You are a vision, my dear. Pierce, where did you get her?"

"Francis's little sister."

"Okay! It's a Shirley Temple for you, sweetie," and he winked at Pierce before he rushed off to the bar.

"I wanted to bring you here," said Pierce. "But we can't stay. Francis would kill me."

"Why not? Come on. It won't hurt."

"If the police show up, it will."

"Are they a threat every night?"

"They're always a threat after eleven o'clock, but they don't always show up."

When we got to Lucy's apartment the party was in high gear. She seemed different that night, off in space somehow. Ten of us sat in a small second-floor room on cushions, listening to music. Every time the curtains fluttered, Lucy would have to get up and leave the room, then come back two minutes later. At one point I asked her what was making her so restless. She searched my face and whispered, "I dropped some acid."

Something akin to an electric shock made me jump from my chair and leave the room myself. Acid was stories of people jumping off buildings because they thought they could fly or roasting babies in the oven by mistake. Standing on the front verandah of the house on Cumberland Street, I wondered what Iona was up to right at that very moment. Maybe there were dangers I had never considered. Maybe I would spend the rest of my life worrying about people who were elsewhere. What kind of perspective is it when the people you love are not even in the picture?

A small group of hippies came up the stairs toward me. I moved aside to let them pass, and one who wandered in behind them looked different somehow. He was really from India and not just wearing made-in-India clothing. He seemed to be the same age as everyone else, but when Lucy came through the front door, she greeted him and introduced him to me with some reverence. "This is Baba Ganesh." She passed a pipe filled with hashish to the group now gathered on the verandah. When I turned down the offer of the pipe as it made its rounds, Baba Ganesh nodded and said, "Smoking hashish changes the frequency of your brain waves but you can learn to do that without it." I nodded and didn't bother to tell him I'd just had my brain frequency change all on its own.

Soon after, Francis found me wandering in empty rooms and asked what I was doing in a cautious kind of way.

I said, "Don't worry. I didn't try it. But I might the next time, and I don't want you hovering."

"Let's get out of here," he said. "This scene is getting a bit strange. Pierce wants to stay but I'd rather go to a coffee house."

Later, in the coffee house where I'd first met Lucy, a young man stood at a microphone in the corner and read a poem. I could make no sense of it.

When he came to our table, after he read, he asked, "What do you think?"

"Good one," said Francis.

I said, "It sounds beautiful but I didn't understand it completely."

"It was inspired by one of Blake's."

I bluffed. "Which one?"

I didn't know who Blake was and he could tell.

He turned to Francis. "You better take this girl's education in hand." Then he excused himself and moved to another table.

On the walk home I asked Francis if he had read Blake.

"Don't worry about that. You're sixteen," he said. "You have a bit of catching up to do." After we got home and made some tea, he went to his room and came back with a thick volume called *The Romantic Poets*. "Start with this." I took it to bed with me and read for half the night.

There was a poem that recalled a night when we were children, when I confessed to Iona about having what I called three-second flashes, moments of fleeting illumination when it seemed that I could remember something vitally important. The only words I had to describe it were to say, "Sometimes I feel the fog that surrounds us, and keeps the light from getting in, lifts for just a moment and I can see what the world really is and I remember that I knew." Iona said she felt that too, sometimes.

So the day after I stayed up late reading poetry, I momentarily put aside my anger and called her from the phone booth outside the restaurant when I arrived for work. I didn't want to share an intimate conversation with my co-workers. It was a scorching day so I held my arms close to my body and didn't touch the hot glass walls of the booth as I told her about the poem. I thought she'd be excited to hear something that legitimized those strange and beautiful moments that we had never found reflected anywhere else.

"Do you remember three-second flashes?" I asked.

"Yes," she said, although she sounded a bit reluctant.

"Well, other people have them too. I just read a poem by a man named Wordsworth that describes it perfectly." I recited a bit of it to her.

Not in entire forgetfulness and not in utter nakedness
but trailing clouds of glory do we come from God
who is our home.

She sounded tired. "Oh, Eileen, you're too much."

Perhaps I was, but I'd always thought when it came to her and me, the situation fell the other way around.

"You know how Mama says, 'We trail more than clouds of glory.'"

"Not to me."

"How are things going, then?" I asked.

After a brief pause, she said, "Mama says you want to stay in Toronto."

"I was thinking of it."

"I guess you made a lot of friends."

"The people here are all really nice to me."

Then before I got to ask her if she was okay, she said in a rather high-pitched voice, "I have to go. Someone is here to pick me up." I was sure she meant Robbie.

She handed the phone back to Mama who, after a moment, spoke very quietly. "She thinks you left because of her."

"Well, tell her that's not true."

"She's upstairs sobbing on her bed right now."

"I doubt if that has anything to do with me."

"Don't become hard. It's not good for either one of you."

I arrived a bit late for the lunch shift. The booths were already full of customers and Cici was busily running back and forth to tables. "You take the counter," she said. The customers were the usual. One of them was an older hippie who said he was a poet when I asked one day what he did. He was lonely, I guess, and started leaving little notes under his coffee cup for me, saying things like, "You dwell in a place of light." I felt sorry for him. I had just put his coffee down with a smile and registered his longing expression, when Cici came to the counter and called me aside. She was agitated and spoke under her breath so as not to be heard by the customers.

"There are two men in the back booth. Ask them to leave, please." Her breath was a bit uneven.

"What did they do?"

"Just tell them."

"Why can't you tell them?"

"If I do, I might spit in their faces."

Her face was flushed and she tapped her pen on the fingers of the opposite hand.

"What did they say?" I asked, fearing they had been horribly rude to her.

"They said nothing. When I brought the coffee, they were holding hands. They pulled away but I saw."

She looked away as she said this. A long silence followed and my heart beat faster.

"Why do you care?" I asked.

"What kind of crazy girl are you? You want people to think we are that kind of place? I'll get Gheorghe but he'll be so mad, I'm afraid of what he'll do. It's better if you do it."

I looked around the restaurant, and couldn't see the men in the booth from where we were standing. After I pulled the apron off over my head, I pushed it into her hands.

"Keep it," I said quietly and headed for the door.

She yelled after me, "What's wrong with you?"

The door tinkled when it closed behind me.

Lucy was standing on the doorstep of the house when I answered the knock. I had my dress on and was waiting to go out with Pierce, but she said, "I really need to talk to someone. Can we hang out for a while?"

"Yes, of course," I said. I was happy to avoid Pierce and Francis. They still didn't know I quit.

While I set a fire in the fireplace and lit some candles, she talked about her trouble with her boyfriend, Daniel. I put an Aretha Franklin record on the stereo, thinking that might be appropriate. Pierce came in at one point and said, "I'm going to meet Francis. Are you going to come?"

"No, we're fine."

He looked back and forth at us and nodded. "Okay."

The door closed behind him and Lucy started to cry.

"He asked me to find a place of my own for a while. He thinks we both need to do some growing before we settle down."

"What will you do?" I asked.

"I don't know. I have no money at all."

"Maybe you can find a job."

She didn't acknowledge that idea.

"He loves me, he's just afraid of commitment. He's been hurt in the past. If I can convince him that I really love him, I think he'll be willing to try."

Something about that didn't feel right, but I couldn't put my finger on what it was.

"There's no way I'm giving up on him," she said.

When I made no response, she asked, "Wouldn't you be loyal if you loved someone?"

I thought about those I loved for a moment and wondered if I would. "What about your family? Why don't you go home?"

"I can't do that," she said. "If I go back it will be a prison and they'll say 'I told you so.'"

"How old are you?" I asked her.

"Seventeen." I was surprised because she seemed so much older and more sophisticated. We talked a while longer about her family and why she could not go back to them. She said they never liked her and if she went home, they'd kill her, but we both understood that was not meant literally. Eventually, we became sleepy and there seemed nothing more to say. "Would you like to spend the night then?"

"Yes, I think I would."

It was better for her to take my bedroom because she didn't know Francis and Pierce like I did, and I thought she'd be embarrassed if they passed her in the night while she was sleeping. I made a bed for myself on the mattress in the dining room. When I got ready for bed, I hung the dress on a hanger in my room and she remarked again how much she liked it.

There was a dry storm that night and slamming thunder made the house shudder on its moorings. In a flash of lightning I thought I saw Iona standing at the door of my room. I fell back to sleep and dreamt of a girl in a blue silk dress, walking alone on a sidewalk at night, running her fingers along a picket fence. In the dream, drops began to fall in splashes on the dress and she stopped under a street lamp as if it could protect her from the rain. In the light she felt completely exposed to the truth.

It took me a minute, when I woke with a start, to recognize where I was. I could hear the rain falling in a steady rhythm. When I went to check on Lucy, she was missing. Perhaps I'd dreamt of her leaving. The bed had been scarcely disturbed, and what I noticed right away was that the dress was no longer in its place. I rushed out into the rain as if I might catch up with her. Standing on the front lawn with the cool water running over me, I realized it was me under the street lamp in the rain.

18

When the plane touched down at home, we had to wait for the technicians to pull the stairs alongside. I picked my way down the steps and crossed the tarmac to my mother and father, who stood behind the open doors of the one-room airport. Mama's eyebrows were a mile high as she looked for me, and Neil held his cotton fedora in his hands. The first thing I asked when the hugs were over was, "Where are the kids?"

Mama said, "They're home making cupcakes."

We pulled up to our house and it looked even smaller than I knew it was. I pulled on the handle to get out of the car, searching the verandah for signs of anyone else. By the time I was standing in the driveway, the front door sprang open and Iona flew toward me and jumped into my arms in one fluid motion, as if she was a much younger child. I'd forgotten how petite she was and how light to hold.

There were only the five of us at supper. Joe was working away and only came home every few weeks. Murdoch seemed glad to see me, but like any ten-year-old boy he didn't have a lot to say except, "I have a whole new box of hockey cards."

I accepted his comment as an invitation to offer some of my own observations.

"The Toronto airport is huge," I said.

"How many planes an hour, do you think?" he asked.

"I have no idea."

After supper he turned on the television to relieve me. Mama looked at Iona and me still seated at the table.

"Lots of time to go for a walk," she offered.

The water in the pond could be counted on to be low at that time of year. Our pants were tucked into our rubber boots and we sloshed out to a large exposed rock where we could sit to take in the full view in utter privacy. We sat side by side with our knees pulled up and surveyed the white birches at the shore as they reflected the sun glinting off the still water in sparkles and flashes of light.

"I didn't want anything to do with him at first," she began. "He asked me out and I said no. But you never gave me a chance to explain and then you left. He walked me home from the chip wagon one night. He said it wasn't my fault and I didn't do anything wrong, and he was so sorry if he'd hurt your feelings and would do anything to change that if he could. Sometimes he said he just couldn't help himself when he was around me." She couldn't meet my eyes and bent to examine something in the water.

"What did Mama think of him?" I asked.

"She wanted me to feel happy. She knew I missed you."

I wanted her to get to the story of how they split up, because I thought it might show me some way I'd been wrong. I wanted to be wrong. I wanted to forgive her.

"I had sex with him right over there." She looked away. "I don't even know why. He wanted it so much and he kept saying that he loved me and he'd never leave me. He put his coat down on the path for us to lie on and pulled me down so gently. He was so passionate and it happened so quickly. I didn't know what to feel. Afterwards, he jumped up and walked away along the path and just sat on his heels and looked at the water. When I said, 'What's wrong?' he said, 'Nothing, don't start that.'

"We didn't talk much for a few days after. He was busy helping his brother move. We walked down to the chip wagon late one night and, just to make conversation, I told him I was worried about Mama because she seemed to be dizzy, and he said, 'Look, I'm really sorry your mother is sick but it's getting to the point where that's all you talk about. I'm tired of it. I think we need a break from each other for a while.' I felt so stupid, like I'd made some big mistake and I didn't know what it was or how to fix it.

"Two weeks went by and he didn't call anymore. Another week and my period was late. I was in a terrible panic, walking back and forth, back and forth in the bedroom. Mama could hear me and wanted to know what I was doing. I told her I was practising a dance step. After that, I spent a few days down here at the brook, throwing stones in the water and trying to figure out what to do.

"In the end, I called him because I just needed someone to tell who might keep it a secret. When I asked him to meet me somewhere, he said, 'I just can't. I'm pretty busy.'

"I just had to tell him outright. 'I'm pregnant,' I said.

"There was a long silence at the other end of the phone before he said, 'Are you accusing me?'

"I said, 'No I'm just telling you! It's your baby and I need help dealing with this.'

"'Look. I have no money,' he says. 'I'm sorry but I just can't get dragged into this. How do I even know it's mine?'

"When he said that, it felt like the blood started pounding in my brain. I thought my eardrums might burst.

"'You can't say a thing like that. You can't say that!' I started yelling at him. Then he said he'd meet me somewhere no one would see him, so I said, 'Okay then, the pond, today, this afternoon.'

"I waited for him a long time. Must have thrown a hundred stones into the water, harder and faster, until I did some kind of damage to my arm. It was days before I could use it again."

While she spoke she stared at the rock that jutted out from the marsh. When she turned to me, the pain in her eyes was both recollected and immediate. "I guess it's no surprise he didn't come."

I finally realized it was me who needed forgiving.

My heart beat hard just imagining her disappointment and her terror. I found myself thinking that she clung to those she loved the way a butterfly settles on a branch and hangs on even through a gust of wind. I wanted to be the branch.

"Why didn't you tell me?" I asked, although I really knew the answer.

"I was afraid you'd tell Mama."

I imagined the upstairs back room office and the vicious tools used on her to end it. "How...?"

"I begged the baby to go away. Every minute, I promised it that if it would go, it could come back when I was ready. I told it, 'I can't take care of you now. They'll take you from me. My life will be ruined and God knows what will happen to you,' I begged it. Then, when I started throwing up, I pretended I had the flu and spent a couple of weeks in bed. Mama was so nice to me I almost told her. Thank God I didn't. All I remember is waking up in the middle of the night in pain. When I lifted the covers there was a pool of blood on the sheet and on my nightie.

"I made it to the bathroom but it took a long time to clean myself, and the toilet and the floor were covered in blood. I was standing in the middle of the room naked, in a daze, when Mama knocked on the door. I said, 'Don't come in. I just started my period. I need a clean nightie.'"

"So she came back with one and opened the door a crack and handed it in.

"After she went back to bed I went back to the room with a load of towels and covered the bloody place on the sheet. Early in the morning I must have gone back to sleep, because before I knew it Mama was standing by the bed, feeling my forehead, checking for fever. 'That was a heavy one,' she said.

" 'Just surprised me,' I said. 'It's a bit early.' "

"She offered to pour a bath for me and when I heard her banging the stove covers around downstairs, I got out of bed. The warm water made me dizzy but I got over that and the water turned pink at first so I pulled the plug and let it all escape, then filled it again. Mama must have wondered what was going on. When I went back to the bedroom the sheets were changed and the towels were taken away.

"After supper when we sat at the table and the boys watched TV, she said quietly, 'Are you alright, dear?' with that look in her eyes that makes you want to tell her everything but I couldn't. I said I was feeling fine."

Iona sat beside me silently for some long minutes while I searched for words and didn't find any.

"I saw it. It was just a small lump but I saw it. I watched it swirl down the drain. I wish I had done something else with it."

Trying to comfort, I whispered, "It wasn't really a baby then."

"Yes it was," the fierceness in her tone surprising me. "I begged it to go and it did. It was the only one who helped me."

"I didn't know."

"You would have been embarrassed by me and I couldn't go back to school and I'd always be that slutty girl who got pregnant! You'd have wished you didn't even have a sister."

"That's not true!"

She quieted down then, staring out at the marsh with her face resting on her pulled-up knees. "I can't wait to get out of here," she said into her jeans.

"Wait! Don't go now."

"I can't go now! I'm only fifteen!"

I was so glad to hear the familiar pragmatism in her voice. Somehow it signalled a belief in the future, a wish to carry on.

"Will you wait for me?" she asked, without a trace of pleading in it.

"Yes, I will. I promise. I will. You can be sure of that."

"Okay then." She got up and stepped off the rock and into the marsh with her boots sloshing as she quickly moved back to shore.

Mama glanced up from her paper when we arrived back home. Iona passed by quickly and went upstairs to hide her eyes.

"What happened?" Mama asked.

"We were just talking."

"Did she tell you what happened?"

"Yes, she did."

"She thinks I don't know."

"Why didn't you ask her about it?"

"I tried. She didn't want to tell me and I didn't want to make her."

Then she folded up the paper and went out to the kitchen to finish cleaning up. I followed her, wanting to talk a little more, and found her looking out the back door window with one hand on the door handle.

"Mama?" I asked, "why didn't you tell me about Francis?"

"Did you tell Iona?"

"No, I didn't."

"Well then don't."

"Why not?!" I asked.

"Iona's had enough to deal with."

"It's not a sin!"

"In the eyes of some people it is, and it's illegal."

"Not for long," I said.

"It's his own private business."

"It would have been nice to know before I went. I felt so stupid!"

"I'm sorry," Mama said. "I couldn't find a way through it. This has never happened to one of us before."

"Not that you know of."

"No one ever talked about it."

"Does Stella know?" I asked.

"Yes, she does. I had to tell someone."

It took a moment for the meaning of that to sink in.

"I'm not someone?"

"When he told me about it, you were ten years old. How was I supposed to tell you?"

"I'm not ten anymore!"

"You worshipped him!"

It was a shock to think she might have kept him away to protect me.

"Is that why you never wanted him to come back?"

Tears spilled over the edges of her eyes and she pushed past me to grab a Kleenex off the counter.

"He could have been anything he wanted to be. He's never going to have children. I want him to have a better life!" She looked up at me. "What's wrong with that?"

"He already has a better life." I said, thinking she was the one missing out.

"I'd like to believe that."

"What does Neil think?"

"He's heartbroken."

"What good is that?" I asked.

19

A plume of dust was unsettled as I retrieved a book from the top shelf. Holding my breath had become a habit while I waited for Iona to grow up, and the bookstore I worked in had become a sanctuary of sorts. Strange thoughts, like throwing the clock into the toilet when I looked up and saw that only ten minutes had passed when it felt like an hour, had begun to intrude on my composure. The sameness of everything made me think about running into the snow naked.

Histrionic thinking, of course, but I was having too many conversations that never were heard by anyone else. Sitting in church with the whole family, I held my breath to keep from blurting out things like, "Why would God let people suffer and starve if he loves us so much?" I knew they would all say, "It's because we have free will." And I would say, "Not so free if you burn in hell if you don't get it right." I couldn't say a thing like that.

In my mind I was always searching for the people, who must be there, who might see the world from my perspective. I never let on I felt that way. I wouldn't be able to stand the way Mama would look at me, or look away.

After work I planned to meet Iona at the dance. It would be the same boys walking around in a circle examining the girls standing by the walls and waiting to be asked. It was bad enough before I finished high school but now it was unbearable.

I called Francis to get a break from this kind of thinking. It was before the show and I knew he'd be on his supper break. I was allowed to call him at the studio at times like that.

"I can't bear the dance anymore," I said.

"Of course not. You're too old for it."

"There are boys there who are twenty."

"Boys, did you say?"

"It's hard waiting," I said.

"Well, come to Toronto and wait here. Iona will catch up."

"I don't want to go that far, and I promised her I'd wait."

"So what's the plan?"

"We don't know yet."

A silence at the other end of the line suggested I could change the subject.

"Did Pierce get the job?"

"Yes, he did. He's going tomorrow."

"I'm sorry," I said. "I guess it's his big chance."

"He's a brave guy. Taking a big risk."

"If it goes really well there, will you go?"

"I don't think there's much room for a Canadian music show host in America. Could never get a green card anyway. We're going to try to make it work. New York is not very far from Toronto."

"You two are like brothers."

"I don't know about that. I think you're more like family if you stay together than if you blow apart."

We both were silent for some moments, feeling the soft reverberations of that statement rolling over us.

I wanted to make light of it and offered, "It's taking quite a bit of courage to stay here, in fact. There's always the risk of running in front of a bus."

"That's a bit morbid."

"Is that what it is?"

"Are you painting?" he asked.

"Not since school finished."

"Get the old man to set you up downstairs."

"You know *him*," I said.

"Not really."

"Whose fault is that?"

"Whoa, okay, this is bitter," Francis sounded hurt.

"I'm sorry," I said. "The dance does that to me."

"You better go," he said gently. "You're supposed to be working, I guess."

Outside the windows of the store the swirl of snow had picked up speed and I knew there would be whiteout conditions on all the roads. The store felt safe and warm, with the books adding a six-inch layer of insulation to every wall. I went back to the book I had left sitting on a table by the window near the stove. As I picked it up again I had to acknowledge that my life was better than Anna's in the *Anna Karenina* I was reading. I thought that she and her husband were a bit full of themselves, though. Willing to sacrifice a little boy just so they could both have what they wanted—her freedom and his pride.

The book fell out of my hands when the door to the bookstore slammed open, banging against the wall, and a cold blast of wind burst through the gap it left in the wall. The storm took the form of a wildly dishevelled woman who was blown in with a drift of snow. Or so it seemed. I ran from behind the counter to grab the banging door as the driving sleet threatened to damage the books. If you could have seen me from above, or felt the pounding of my heart, you would have thought there was a life at stake.

It took leaning hard on it to get the door to close, and dealing with her long coat when it got caught only added to the struggle. Once we got it shut, and her safely in, the room settled. She pulled off a red cloche, letting her long, dark, wavy hair swing free, and stamped her tall leather boots on the doormat.

"Thank God you're open! I'm surprised."

"Me too."

I was so relieved to have shut the door and pulled her in.

"Are you looking for something or are you just coming in from the storm?" I asked her.

"Isn't that always the question?"

I took that to mean she didn't want anything.

"I have no clue how I'm going to get back to my hotel in this. There are no cabs."

"It will blow over," I told her.

"Well, you're a philosophical little thing!" she said with some exasperation.

"Would you rather if I said you'll have to spend the night in the bookstore?"

"That's better," she said, rather approvingly. "Do you own this store?"

"No, I don't. I'm the manager."

She looked around slowly. "Do you manage books or people?"

I felt myself back inside my body. "Both books and people come and go," I said.

"I see. How old are you?"

"Eighteen, how old are you?"

"Oh! It's quite different for someone my age to ask someone your age how old she is. The other way around is not really polite."

We both laughed.

"You're not that old," I said. "Can I get you a cup of tea? There's no going anywhere for a while."

Light bounced and reflected off the high walls of books on the way back to the nook where I made tea. I loved the store, but it was nice to have a little company. When I returned she was sitting at the small round table in the front window. People normally sat there for a while to examine a book, but she was fixated on the violent storm as it bent the trees into grotesque and unfamiliar outlines. She accepted the tea with some relief when I handed her the cup and saucer, and she looked at me closely.

"Why are you still here?"

"It's Friday. I'm here until nine unless they close the roads."

"I mean here, in this town," she said.

"I like it here."

"Where else have you been?"

"Toronto."

She nodded slowly. "Toronto is not really representative of the world."

"Where are you from then?" I asked.

"Chicago. My husband has business at the steel mill. None of that is really representative of the world either."

The blizzard stopped blowing abruptly and, in the space of a few minutes, the sun broke through so that the world donned a glamorous dress, every car and rooftop clothed in white velvet and flashing diamonds.

"Don't get me wrong. I love it here." And then, with a smile, she was gone.

⁂

The soft new snow I waded through covered my boots up to my ankles. My hands, even double gloved and jammed in the pockets of a navy duffle coat, grew numb. The hall where the dance was held that night glowed as I walked toward it, and in between the dance and me was a huge parking lot so I had a good long point of view. It was a big, square, brick building with the bottom floor lit up. The church was on the second floor, with the hall below it, a step or two down from the sidewalk. When I opened the door, the music and the warmth pulled me in.

Coming in from the bitter cold to the warmth inside, an array of images from other times passed through my mind: the classroom after waiting in line to come in; the church after wading through snow drifts to get there on Sunday morning; our kitchen after walking home in my skates because my fingers were too cold to remove them when I finally dragged myself off the rink.

In summer, with the big double door thrown wide open to the parking lot, and the high windows all cracked open, the hall felt breezy and spacious, but on this night, with the door closed, the ceilings lowered themselves somehow, and the room took on the feel of a winter lair.

The band was covering "Bell Bottom Blues." This was a favourite because of its passionate plea for romance, "Do you wanna see me crawlin' across the floor to you? Do you wanna hear me beg you to take me back?" All the dancers swayed as if a gentle wind was blowing through the darkened room. In a far corner, Iona was telling a story, gesturing wildly with her beautiful small, pale hands, surrounded by spellbound boys, who listened as if it what she told was of great import. It felt like standing in front of a painting of my former life. I didn't want to ruin it.

She saw me at the foot of the stairs and waved. When I didn't move she walked straight through the circle, as if the dancers were not there, and came to stand beside me.

"I'm not going to stay," I said.

She thought for only three seconds before saying, "I'll come with you."

As we walked toward home our breath surrounded us and, fleetingly, through the clouds, we could see the moon was full. After some minutes she asked, "What are we going to do?"

"I want to go away," I said.

"Right now?"

"No, I want to make a plan."

"You want to go back to Toronto."

"I want you and me to go away to college."

"Yeah, right. Dream on."

"If someone can go to the moon, surely we can leave Cape Breton."

She rolled her eyes a bit. "Where will we get the money for that?"

"Student loans," I said, more than prepared to slip into a life of debt if it meant an expansion of my world. Any change at all will do in some circumstances.

"Where do you want to go?" she asked.

"We'll have to work too," I said.

"We can waitress," she agreed.

"I bet you could sing in the bars."

I knew she wanted to sing. Jazz seemed more possible for a woman than rock and roll, and we had Francis to thank for that.

An overhanging branch of a pine tree let go of its load as we passed under. The snow fell and completely covered our coats and hats and some of it fell into our boots. We shrieked but not from the cold.

Newspapers were spread over the living room floor in folded sections where they had been tossed after Neil and Mama finished with them. They both looked up when we came in, and Mama said, "I made pie." She assumed we'd rush to the kitchen to find it, but after we pulled off our outer layers of snow-covered clothing we sat down on the chesterfield side by side. When they could no longer ignore us, Mama asked, "What? What is it?"

I would have liked to hold Iona's hand for this but realized it would not project the picture of independence for which I hoped. Leaving, this time, had to be different. This was not about the summer job or being sixteen. This was about becoming ourselves. "We're going to apply to go to college in Halifax."

They both sat quietly for a moment, looking at us.

"How will you get by?" Mama asked.

"We'll get jobs," I said.

Neil, understanding the assumption in that, replied, "What if you don't find work?"

Iona jumped in. "Of course we will. Someone will hire us."

He looked at us for a moment. "You'd think so but not always."

"Will you come home if it doesn't work out?" asked Mama.

"If it doesn't work out, I'll shoot myself," Iona said with a grin.

"That's not a bit funny. Are you going to live at the residence?"

"Oh no," I said, "we're going to get an apartment." She looked at us with her head tilted to one side, "When I was a young girl," she said, "I thought I'd go to college too. A cousin of my mother's offered to pay my way but Mama didn't want to be beholden."

This seemed to turn the tide, and the next words Neil spoke settled it.

"Make sure you stick together. Family is the most important thing."

20

The men working on the road hailed Neil down on a day he went to school hungry. One of their crew had been hurt the day before, so they were short a man to dig and had an extra shovel. "Mr. MacPherson," one of them called to him. "Why are you carrying those childish books when you're such a big strapping fella? There's a wage to be made here if you can work like a man." Neil hesitated only a moment. He was fifteen years old.

The men suggested they would pay him according to how long a trench he could excavate, so he threw his books in the ditch, picked up a shovel and furiously began to dig. By the end of his first working day he had enough earnings in his pocket that it was worth walking the long distance to the village to buy meat for supper. The sun shone through the trees on the way home. His mother smiled and quietly said, "You make me proud of you," when he handed her the meat.

When his brother, Frank, who was older and not going to school anyway, heard the story of the work on the road, he looked at Neil with a new respect, saying, "Do you think they'll take me too?"

"I don't even know if they'll take me again, but I'm going back tomorrow to look so you might as well come."

The trip to the roadwork site the next morning was carefree and they horsed around, pushing and shoving each other, trying to knock the other one off balance. But when they arrived, the men could see that Frank was older and they said, "Ah, we better take the older one. You go back to school."

"No, I will not," Neil said. Frank knew him well enough to know he was distraught, but said nothing, fearing they might both be sent home. Neil looked to Frank in disbelief when he picked up the shovel and began to dig as if there was not a deep betrayal in his actions.

"Go home now," the men said to him.

He felt treated like a stray dog, walked away to hide his tears and snuck into the barn at home, where he furiously shovelled out the stalls, the deep smell of manure stinging his lungs while he wept.

His mother found him wildly flinging the manure out of the stall into a heap behind him, muttering and crying to himself.

"You're a good worker and a strong one. There will be another job," she said.

He knew he was too old for it, but he let her put her arms around him and lay his head on her shoulder, because he felt she understood how it was for him to lose his chance to make their life better.

"Frank is eighteen. You can go back to school for a while."

"No, I will not," he muttered into the warmth of her sweater. "I already do math and read and write. There's nothing left for me to learn there."

His mother had no real answer for him because she also believed this to be true.

The whole situation came to a head one night when the boys and their mother were finishing supper. Jack had been gone for a few days playing fiddle and gambling in the bars, but he came in as they were clearing up the table.

"I need some supper," he declared.

"There are potatoes but the meat is finished. I was expecting you to-morrow."

Jack was furious that they had saved no meat for him.

"The least I can expect is meat on the table when I come home from trying to earn us a living."

Neil couldn't keep himself from saying, "If you brought some home occasionally maybe we could freeze a little of it in the ice box for when you show up."

Jack hollered, "You have no respect at all!" and struck Neil on the back of the head while he still sat at the table. Neil got up in a rush and shoved him hard so that Jack fell and hit his head on the cast iron stove and lay there unconscious. All three of them stared, unmoving for a moment. His mother broke the spell by running to Jack and kneeling at his side.

Neil asked, "Is he dead?"

"No, I think he's just drunk," she said, looking up at Neil as if trying to comfort him.

"I'm not sorry."

She sought his eyes and held them before turning away. "Frank, help me get him into bed."

They dragged him, a lifeless and heavy sack, into the bedroom and Neil could see Frank awkwardly bend to pick him up and lay him on the bed. He told himself he would rather be dead than lend Jack Fisher a hand.

Frank came back out and said, "You've got her crying now. Are you happy? I don't know why you always have to have your say."

Neil rushed him from the other side of the room and leapt upon him, throwing them both against the stove and knocking the table so that the burning kerosene lamp began to rock on its base. Neil had Frank in a bear hug and was too angry to let go, but they froze in that position and watched the teetering lamp, not breathing. When it finally rested without tipping, they wrestled themselves out the door and landed on the frozen ground. Frank got an arm free and walloped Neil in the face. The gushing blood startled them both and they jumped up, but Neil tried to kick at Frank, who wheeled away from him. Neil stood glaring accusingly at Frank, with blood running down his face.

Frank said, "Go clean yourself up. You're acting like a madman."

That night Neil slept in the barn rather than return to the room they shared. In the early morning he crept into the house and gathered a few things in a sack, then walked away from the house alone.

He was in and out of lumber camps for most of the next year. They were disorganized places. Rough tarpaper shacks thrown up until the job was done, and then the men dismissed with almost nothing to show for their work. There were never enough jobs and they never lasted long. Only his mother knew about the times when he hid in the shed for shelter. She brought him boiled potatoes and pretended to the others that she ate them herself. She told him, "It's a good thing that you come home once in a while. If you didn't, I'd get terribly fat."

Late in summer he sat on a tree stump outside a bunkhouse and was deep into a story in the *Workers Voice*, about a march being planned elsewhere in the country, when a man called out to him from across the clearing, "Neil, your brother is here." Neil looked up to see Frank picking his way through the remains of the violated forest with a brilliant sunset at his back, and yelled, "Wrong fella. I don't have a brother." He turned back to the paper he was reading. Frank walked toward him anyway and stood over him, saying nothing at first. When Neil did not look up, he offered, "You'll get nothing out of reading that nonsense. Probably get yourself shot, more likely."

Neil jumped up quickly so he was on an even footing and eye to eye with Frank.

"Wait now," said Frank, "I didn't mean to be telling you what to do."

"That's good then," said Neil without relaxing his stance at all.

Frank struggled for words and looked away and then back before speaking. "I have some food back at the tent. Would you like to come back with me?"

"No, thank you," said Neil, "I think I'd rather read."

Frank stepped back, standing very straight, and said, "Alright then. When we finish here, I'm going out west to look for work. You could come with me."

"No, I don't think so," said Neil as he looked down at the paper he still held in his hand. "There might be only one job and it would obviously be yours."

That was where they left it. There was no wave or signal between them when Frank walked back into the woods.

An older man who had overheard the whole exchange asked Neil, "Is that your brother?"

"I'd say not," said Neil.

"Sweet Jesus," said the man, "he must have done something awful to you or you must have an awful lot of brothers if you're willing to throw one away."

"I don't have any others," said Neil.

He felt encased in a cold and brittle anger but resisted letting his blood run warm to melt the thing. It was much the way he felt in the woods when his feet began to freeze and he finally found himself close to a fire. The thawing made him fear he would whimper in pain, and the important thing was to never allow that.

21

On a sultry day in August, Iona and I took the bus to Halifax. The windows were open and the cross breeze kept us reasonably cool, blowing the hair away from our faces. Iona pulled hers back in a ponytail and stuck hair pins at the temples. It made her look even younger than her years.

We had the address of someone's older sister, and the note said it was not far from the Acadian bus station. We asked directions and found our way to her apartment building, a divided-up house really, but when we knocked she opened rather hesitantly and said, "Oh, hi! What are you fellas up to?"

"Could we possibly stay for a couple of nights until we find a place to rent?" She looked at us for a moment before saying directly to me, "Did you two run away or what?"

"Don't be rude," Iona said. "Just say yes or no."

"You'll have to sleep on the floor then. Good thing it's warm." She gave us sheets and pillows and that night we slept with our heads sticking out the doors of her balcony in an effort to find some air.

The next day at the public garden, the ducks surrounding our park bench were intent on getting a piece of the hot dog we bought at a vendor's cart. We were intent on circling the waitress jobs and the cheap apartments in the newspaper, and passing the hot dog back and forth, holding it out from our clothes. The mustard started to drip before we realized the ducks were looking for a bite, squawking and scolding us. By this time they were right up against our legs and starting to shove. There were so many of them it was almost frightening. Iona raised her eyebrows, let out a little burst of a laugh, and hefted the last bite onto the grass some fifteen feet away so that they all scurried after it.

The apartment on Cunard Street was a walk-up with two bedrooms. Perfect, we thought. The landlady, a very old woman with a heavily lined face, lived on the main floor.

"Sisters?" She looked a bit suspicious. "I don't rent to no students."

"We work," said Iona.

"We'll see if that's true."

After we moved in, she muttered comments as we passed by and peered out through a chained door as we made our way to the second floor. We hid our books in grocery bags. For some reason, we found this hilarious and could hardly contain ourselves until we got inside our own apartment. But it wasn't as funny when I was alone. She held the door to her dark apartment open a crack when I brought her the cheque. Through that slit, I saw the outline of furniture—dressers and armchairs—piled one on top of the other as if she was storing it or planning to move.

We told ourselves our apartment was charming because it had a little pot-bellied stove that reminded us of home. The wall behind it looked scorched. We were probably lucky to get out of there alive on more than one count.

On the first early morning walk to the school, skirting around the commons and the Citadel, catching sight of the ocean, I felt like I knew exactly where I was going. I'd been told to watch for an unobtrusive side door, on a steep street leading down to the harbour, with the name of the school in square letters on the door. I had a strange sense of recognition, finding home, when I first saw it. Inside the door was a set of wooden stairs leading somewhere I wanted to go. I took it slowly, one step at a time, and met no one else on the way. Paintings on the walls in the hallways were white on white with a minute speck of grey. It was a conceptual school but I didn't really understand what that meant when I arrived. They let me in based on the painting I'd sent them of a child at twilight drawing with a stick on a dusty road in front of an isolated house in a field that ran down to the ocean. An ochre and crimson sunset reflected off the house's grey, sun-bleached walls. It was my best, but it didn't belong with these others at all. I suspected these painters were far more sophisticated than I could ever hope to be.

An upper hallway led to a maze of studios with towering windows. It was early but most of the studios had at least one or two people who looked as if they'd been there for hours. The intaglio studio was empty, so I sat on the sill of a ten-foot-high window with the sash thrown open and felt the ocean air drift over me.

Iona came to an opening with me the first week in, and she stared for a while at a piece of white canvas. The long explanation printed down one side of it suggested that every observer would project her own picture onto this empty space and that paintings themselves meant nothing. Each one was simply a vessel to deposit our own ideas, values and beliefs as they pertain to an unstructured reality. It implied that we always impose our own limits on a world without constraint, our own reality on the space that we inhabit.

She said, "I guess you'll have to learn how to talk about it."

"Analyze it, you mean."

"A little analysis wouldn't hurt, you know."

"I know, I know, I know. But I don't have to like it," I said.

"There's no analysis in music. Most of the guys read comic books when they aren't practising their instrument."

The bar where Iona wanted to sing was one of those dark places with wooden chairs and tables, where they put down as many draft beer as you want at one time. I went along as some kind of backup the day Iona tried to convince the owners they should let her sing for them. The afternoon light, filtered through yellowed windows, settled on her open face as she made her argument. The two owners looked skeptical at first, but I watched Iona convince them she'd be good for business, just by singing "Georgia" a cappella at the bar. Her voice was so much larger than her stature implied it might be.

The man with the tie deferred to the larger man in the black t-shirt.

"That was impressive. But we can't pay you."

"Don't have to," she said. "I'll pass the hat."

They exchanged looks and the one in the tie shrugged his shoulders, "Let's try it."

The other one thought for a moment. "You have a band, right?" he asked her.

"Oh yes, of course," she said without hesitation.

For the next few days she put up signs at the college music department: *Bass Player and Jazz Pianist needed. Must be available to practise in the week before Friday Oct. 15 and prepared to play on that night.* She put our address on the bottom.

Five people showed up at our place at different times of the day, all of them young men. The first one was very sweet, terribly shy and not a very good bass player. We listened to him play, then Iona said it was great to meet him and that she had some other people coming and would let him know. The next guy said he played piano, but we didn't have one, so Iona said she'd meet him at a piano room in the school tomorrow. He was a bit cocky but you could tell it was something of an act.

At suppertime, a few of them arrived together.

"So you have a band?" one of them asked.

"No," she answered truthfully. "I have a regular gig."

"Thought that might be the case. You're going to need a drummer. This is Carl. I'm Barrie, your pianist, and that," he said, pointing to a long-haired man with a decided slouch, "is Greg, your bass player. We've been looking for a singer, so if you can sing, you can have us. Not for free but we'll get to that."

She came home the next day from the school where they had practised and said, "They're perfect."

The customers at the bar cheered and clapped wildly the first night they played. Her jazz standards were different from most bar music, which was usually very loud rock bands or rock and roll piped in through wall speakers. She acquired a sizeable group of fans over the next few weeks, and we had a sense that we'd found the right place to be. The crowd put to rest any fears the owners may have had that she'd scare their beer drinkers away, so they began to give her and the band free booze. Most of her admirers were other students, but there was one old veteran who fell in love with her just because she flashed her wide, red smile at him. When she walked by between sets, he nodded and held up his beer in salute, then followed her around the bar with yearning eyes. Every night a small number of young men sat in the back and stared at her, entranced.

There was one she agreed to go sit and drink beer with in between sets, but she never left the bar with him. I was her cover when he offered to walk her home.

"Eileen and I always go together. She's kind of like my agent. We have things to discuss."

Then she laughed to show she was joking.

He looked at her in a hard way and said, "If you two weren't sisters, I'd think you were lesbians."

"Or maybe friends?" she replied with raised eyebrows.

Her casual response to the world cloaked a great passion. She wrote poetry on little scraps of paper and sang songs in a way that spoke of innocence betrayed and a great impatience that it should ever have been so. When she did date someone, she seemed to grow weary of him easily and one night she flung herself on my bed with her face down so that her voice was muffled. "I've found a perfect way to break up with someone. You just stop laughing at their jokes until they decide you're boring and they never feel rejected." I slapped her on the arm for her duplicity, but didn't have much energy behind it. She lifted her head and looked at me. "No, it's way better. They have to be nice to me later because they broke up with me. It's a friendlier way to do it."

One of her psychology professors took a special interest in her. She was so curious and so engaged in every conversation that he began to invite her back to his office to discuss the reading. She ran up to see me at the studio one day on her way to work. She was breathless and seemed excited. "I'm going out to the country tomorrow with Laurie Johnston. Do you want to come along?"

"Why are you doing that?" I asked, gently pulling her hand away from the edge of the acid bath. "Does he have some experiments to conduct on you?"

She ignored me. "He has an old place out in Herring Cove. Could be fun to get out of here for the day." She paused, and I looked at the intaglio piece I was about to dip.

"If you aren't too busy searing metal plate," she said.

We drove out with a friend of Laurie's, one of the other young professors who were from Oxford or U of T or Harvard and had moved to Nova Scotia to teach part-time and live on the land for the rest of it. The drive along the coast brought our home to mind, but I would never have admitted such a childish thing.

Many of the farms in that part of the world have always required that the men work off the farm somewhere. This was no different for hippies from New York and elsewhere. They learned to farm by making themselves useful on the neighbouring properties when the sons and daughters had moved on to urban pastures. There was not enough cash to be earned on the land alone.

Laurie Johnston was out in front of the house admiring his garden when we arrived. He had blond curly hair and wore yoga pants and a beatific smile. He was very proud of living on a farm and having a garden. Others at the college saw him as a serious, high-minded person because he'd made that choice. I'd never thought of gardening that way before.

A group of about twenty students sat on the floor of the kitchen on cushions. Some of them on the chaise lounge. I'd love to know what Gran would say if she saw a thing like that. Some of the faces in the room were familiar, others from back home studying to be teachers and lawyers and artists, all of us engaged in the process of reinventing ourselves.

Laurie's friend handed out beer to anyone who wanted one. They had a fridge full of the stuff. I said, "No thanks. I don't drink," and Iona rolled her eyes at me. Once we were settled, Laurie and his friend sat on kitchen chairs facing us, as if in some alternate classroom, and launched into their project. "We're doing some research on Cape Bretoners."

We all burst out laughing. "Oh good," one of the boys said immediately. "Let's study how much beer a Cape Bretoner can drink on a sunny afternoon given an unlimited supply." We laughed again and they joined us in the joke.

"Cape Bretoners are so interesting," Laurie said.

Secretly we were all thinking, "We knew that," even if we didn't. Outwardly, we'd become a sea of blank stares.

"I'd like to be a Cape Bretoner but it's not possible. Unless you were born there you can't be from there. No matter how long you live there. You can be a New Yorker just by living in New York."

"Clannish, it's called," someone sang out.

"You tried living there, didn't you?" Iona asked.

"I lived there for a year."

"Takes a bit longer than that to be part of the team."

"It's not just that. Gaelic? Bagpipes? Strathspeys? I want to know how you did that in the middle of North America."

"You need a map," someone else suggested.

I tried to switch things around. "Where are you from?"

They looked at each other to decide how to answer and one of them finally said, "From all over really, but can I ask you a few more things? Is that okay?"

He began again when he could see we were not going to give an opinion on the okayness of this.

"What religion do you follow?"

I replied patiently, "Well, about half of them are Protestant and half are Catholic."

He paused a moment and then said quietly, "None of you ever say "we" when you're referring to Cape Bretoners. Are you ashamed to be one?"

The room grew quiet and no one had much to say to the questions that came after. He and the others must have been aware of the undercurrent of feelings he'd stirred up. The room was smoldering with anger, or maybe that was just defence. It's possible it was just me.

We stood out in the yard as we left, with a bruised sunset vividly painting the sky and the field in purples and blues with an undercurrent of vermilion. It was distracting in its beauty and may have been why we didn't respond when Laurie suggested to the whole group, "Next time you get to lead the conversation and tell us anything you want. So think about it."

None of us ever went back.

As soon as they dropped us back at the apartment after a strangely silent drive, I put the kettle on the boil for tea, "Laurie Johnston is an idiot," I said.

"He is not! He's just curious."

I didn't press it, not wanting to hurt her feelings.

When the kettle whistled and she got up to pour the water into the teapot, she said, "He makes me laugh. All the time."

I didn't see her much during that time. We were both busy working and studying. My waitress job conflicted with her song nights so I didn't get to the bar as much. The night they broke up she leaned on the door jamb of my room and said, "There's something wrong with me. I just don't really like sex."

"Don't even think that. Maybe you just don't like it with him."

"If I was going to like it with anyone, I'd like it with him."

"You're not ready."

"You think so?"

"I'm sure."

"Trouble is I may never be."

I looked down at the book I'd been reading. "Have you ever heard of hermeneutical phenomenology?"

"Sounds like some kind of disease," she said.

"It's pretty complicated, but it has something to do with understanding our being in the world from the inside instead of from the outside."

"Subjectively, you mean."

"No, it's not that simple. It seems to mean something underneath subjectivity. The book is called *Being and Time*. It's an ungodly brain teaser."

"I'm reading *Be Here Now*. Maybe it's about the same thing."

"Maybe. I don't really think so," I said.

The next day a torn-open envelope was sitting on the hallway stairs with a poem scribbled on the back.

She was a tree growing upside down
Roots in the sky, branches
Struggling to reach warm rich earth.
Finally she made contact with cold hard ground
And found herself buried there.
Now she asks all her children
To remain seedlings of the air.

Iona was somehow both younger and older than I was.

22

The coming eclipse of the sun was a big topic in the bar and everyone had an opinion about the best place to watch it. The group at the table I'd joined was also engaged in conversations about politics, or commiserating with each other about broken hearts. The atmosphere was totally relaxed until someone foolishly lit up a joint. The handsome bouncer, on whom I had a bit of a crush, came over and leaned in close to the young man holding the joint and said quietly, "If I see you do that again, I'll have to kill you."

As if to punctuate his comment, a fight erupted in the corner where the drug dealers sat. When a chair was thrown against a wall, most of us stood up as one, and I anxiously looked toward Iona, who had stopped singing. She tilted her head toward the open door, so those of us who hoped to avoid a fracas moved outside just as a table was upended and a couple of the fighters grabbed each other and fell to the floor. Standing out on the sidewalk, the men from our table half-heartedly complained about not being allowed to take their drinks, but we'd all seen this kind of excited nervous brawl and knew it would be short-lived. We stood well away from the doors so that when they swung open and one of the fighters angrily pushed out, we were able to give him some room. He yelled behind him to someone in the bar, "You watch your back, buddy!"

The good-looking bouncer finally arrived. "Free beer," he said and we all flooded back to our seats.

Iona was singing Annie Ross's "Twisted," when the form of a man filled the door to the street. It was hard to see details with the waning light behind him, but he was tall and had hair that hung to his shoulders. After scanning the room, he finally settled his sights on our table. The room was very dark, but his shape was so familiar that I found myself holding my breath. The man took a few steps closer into the light and there he was. It was him, right there, my brother Francis.

I jumped out of my seat and threw myself at him before he even reached the table. "When did you get here? Why didn't you tell me? Oh, my God. Mama is going to be so excited. Is Pierce with you?" I almost had to shout to be heard above the racket of talk and music in the bar. He hugged me hard and said, "Let's go outside."

I suppose that was a bit of a spectacle and others wondered who he was, but it was Iona's eyes I noticed. She kept the song going but her eyes were all questions as she sang the words, "My analyst told me that I was right out of my head," as she watched us go.

"That's Iona," I yelled in his ear.

It stopped him cold. He stood and stared for a moment. He shook his head as if to clear it and then took my arm to continue out.

"What are you doing here?" I asked him.

"I've come to see the eclipse of the sun." I may not have been able to hide my disappointment, and he said quickly, "Don't be ridiculous. I came to see you."

"How long are you staying?"

"Just a few days is all I could get. I drove straight the last twenty-four hours. I'm pretty bleary-eyed."

"I'll drive home with you," I said, imagining the pleasure of driving onto the island and up to our parents' front door with him at the wheel.

"I'll call them tomorrow. I'm hoping they'll meet me here."

"They never come up here," I said.

"I came more than halfway. If he wants to see me, he can come here."

"I suppose you grew that hair just so he could cut it for you, too."

He started the laugh that always got me and we stood on the street with our arms linked, holding each other from falling. When we regained control, we went back in for a beer and to wait for Iona. I waved to her and, as we sat, she put the mike down. "That's it for now, folks." She walked, smiling, over to our table.

He had the advantage. I'd already told him it was her. But she was all curiosity and no recognition at all. She hadn't seen him since she was six years old. There were very few photos of any of us at home. We had a Brownie camera, but we were always careful of how often it was used because the film was so expensive to print. The only picture we had of Francis, besides his first communion, was of him, Stella and Joe, all thin and shorn, arms draped around each other's shoulders and wearing blue jeans and short-sleeved t-shirts. This would have been from about a year before he left home and he bore no resemblance to the man who stood before us now.

"Very cool set," he said.

"Thank you. Who are you?" she smiled and looked at me, wanting more. We looked back and forth among ourselves for a moment before he replied. "You're listening to jazz on late-night radio."

Her eyes grew large and she took a step back.

I said, "This is probably what they meant by cognitive dissonance," referring to complaints she'd made about her new psychology class. She knew his radio voice in an instant, but her reaction was a bit disconcerting. She stared and remained immobile until I said, "It's him."

"I know," she said, holding her hand palm up, and froze again in that position. The puzzled look she wore as she looked back and forth between us made it seem as if she didn't know me either.

Perhaps from her perspective, he was more a dream to her than a reality, the familiar late-night radio murmur, an iconic centre of her music world, the whole reason she was singing. Or maybe all she had was a remnant of some dream she had lived when she had a flesh-and-blood brother named Francis. Come to think of it, maybe that was *me* standing in her shoes and she didn't feel a bit like that. I was used to blending our thoughts, but I remembered, as if it was a lesson I had to continually relearn, that the assumptions I made regarding how she felt about any given thing could be all wrong.

"Let's go," he said. "Can I park the van at your place?"

"Sure, there's a driveway with nothing in it."

We were living with four other students in a nice old house on Princess Place with six bedrooms and a verandah to sit on in the evening. It was the kind of rundown, gracious old place that was still possible for students to rent before they became character homes and were renovated and improved by the addition of several bathrooms. There were so many layers of paint on the trim of the windows and doors, and who knows how many layers of wallpaper, that the whole place had a rounded, relaxed, wrinkled feeling to it—deeply comfortable.

People often stayed over, but I got up early on the weekends to have a bit of time alone. When I came down the next morning Iona was already sitting with Francis and full tilt in conversation. "I knew it was you."

"Bullshit. I deserve a point for that."

"Depends on how you define a point."

"You travel a thousand miles and not only surprise someone, you completely fool them into thinking they don't know you and leave them standing with their mouth gaping, that's how."

"I'll cut the hair if you want," she offered.

"How do you know I want it cut?"

"Don't you?"

"Okay, it's too warm in the summer," he conceded.

"And Neil would be happier."

"Like I care."

While she worked she sang the first verses of the song "Nature Boy."

There was a boy
A very strange, enchanted boy
They say he wandered very far
Very far, over land and sea
A little shy and sad of eye
But very wise was he

And then one day,
One magic day he passed my way
While we spoke of many things
Fools and Kings
This he said to me

When she got to the last line she just hummed it, but we all knew it and sang it silently to ourselves. "The greatest thing you'll ever learn is just to love and be loved in return."

She said, "The note on that last line is hard to get right." It was difficult to know if she sang it as a lullaby or a challenge. His dark hair fell to the floor in great, long, shining pieces and the click of the scissors was the only sound for some moments.

"Let's take tomorrow off and go home," I suggested.

"I have no time for that," said Francis.

"What do you mean? You haven't seen them in over ten years." Iona's eyebrows pulled into wavy curves that resembled the mathematical sign for "approximately."

Francis exhaled quickly as if he'd been holding his breath. "I need to talk to him on neutral territory."

"You can talk to him anywhere," I said.

"No, I can't."

Later that evening he called home and asked Mama if they would drive up to see him. He intended to confront Neil about the past in the hope of engaging him in an argument they could finish. One of his worries was that Neil might think his being gay had to do with their relationship. Francis didn't want that. He didn't want Neil to think it was some reaction to him, as if he had that much power. In any case, he knew he would have been gay regardless of what kind of a father he had. All of this was explained in a rush as if speaking made him breathless.

There was a pause at the other end of the line before Mama said, "It's a long drive for one day." Francis held the phone to his chest, "Is there room here?" he asked, then turned back to the phone without waiting for an answer. "Of course there is. Come up for a couple of days, both of you. We can watch the eclipse. You know you'd love that."

She didn't speak for a moment until he asked, "Are you still there?" Then only her murmuring tones could be heard for a few minutes before he replied, "He never accepted anything about me. Why should this be any different?" When he got off the phone I asked him where he was planning to talk to Neil. He looked around the kitchen and said, "Right here, I suppose."

I was home alone two days later when Mama arrived by herself in a red and white taxicab. I ran out to meet her and to grab her bag. One side of her body seemed weak. She wasn't exactly limping but she leaned more heavily on one leg than the other when she stood. The yellow piece of paper she held, with our address on it, had been folded and refolded several times.

"He wouldn't come?" I asked.

"He couldn't do it."

Once we were settled at the kitchen table with a cup of tea, she spoke quietly as if this was any private conversation, but I wished Francis could hear the urgency underlying her words.

"I tried to convince him. I said, 'He just wants to tell you. What harm can it do?' But he was convinced that Francis wants some kind of confrontation like he always used to do. The worst thing is that your father thinks the whole thing is his fault." She paused for a moment. "Or possibly my mother's."

"That's exactly what Francis wants to change. There's no fault to it."

"He's from a different generation. People aren't used to it."

"There have always been people who were gay," I said.

"Not that we knew of."

"Francis has a good life."

"Yes," she said. "He seems to. Neil just couldn't be budged."

I noticed that she sat heavily in her chair, as if it would be too much effort to lean forward to replace the cup in its saucer. She lost energy easily now, and the trip must have been exhausting.

"You look tired, Mama. Do you want to lie down?'

"All the way up on the bus, I went over and over the conversation with him. I might have robbed them both of a chance to get over it."

"I think he should have gone to you."

"How could he when he didn't know what kind of a reception he'd get?"

It took a moment to realize the object of my anger was Francis, not Neil. She'd made a six-hour trip, alone on the bus, because he had a point to prove.

"They certainly don't spoil a pair," she said.

When Francis arrived home she rose from the chair with a new energy that she must have been saving just for him. He walked into the room, smiling his bright, toothy smile and swept his long arms around her. She looked deeply relieved.

"You smell good," she said. "The same as ever."

While she held him, he looked over her shoulder and, when she finally let him go, he asked, "Where is he?"

She shook her head. "He couldn't come."

There was a short exhale of breath and a pause before he said, "Alright then. I guess that's it."

"That is not it. You're just as stubborn as he is."

"I'd accept an apology," Francis said.

"Why does it have to be like that?"

"How else could it be?"

"I tried to convince him to come and told him you wanted to talk to him," Mama said.

He turned his back to remove his coat before he spoke.

"I'd have liked to tell him myself," he said as he sat down at the table.

"Yes, I know. I really am sorry. I thought it might be too hard on you. I thought he might say something hurtful." She leaned forward and tried to search his eyes. Francis looked away and leaned back in his chair.

"It's okay, Mama, I'm not afraid of him hurting me. I'm twenty-nine, not nine years old."

"He thinks you want to blame him for the way things turned out."

"For what? Being gay? Is that what he thinks? There's a few things to blame him for but being gay is not one of them."

"No, he just can't talk about it. He knows he'd say the wrong thing."

"I can't believe it's all about being gay. Do you think it always was? Even when I was five?"

"No, I don't! I probably just stood in the way."

"You can't take credit for every messed-up thing, Mama."

The plan had been for all of us to watch the eclipse at the harbour. Iona was already there waiting.

"I'll go find Iona," I told them. "Why don't we meet up after you two have some lunch?" I wanted them to at least have some time together.

"You'll sleep in my room tonight." I said to Mama before I left.

"Oh, I don't think so. I should get back. There's a three o'clock bus. Your father will pick me up at the station."

"That's such a long ride," I said, looking accusingly at Francis.

"Oh no," she said. "I'll read."

I wondered if she felt it would be an abandonment of Neil if she stayed away without him.

The hour of the eclipse was nearing as Iona and I waited for them at the harbour. Vendors were hawking viewing lenses and people were trying them on and fitting their children. We bought a pair to share. There was still no sign of Mama and Francis. It occurred to us that they might have the wrong meeting place so we split up to look for them, agreeing to meet back at the wharf in fifteen minutes. The light began to fade as I hurried to another gathering spot at the water's edge. When I looked up, I expected to see clouds crossing the sun but the whole sky was an iron grey. Everyone was staring at the sky, wearing the safety lenses or a pair of welding goggles. I didn't have the lenses with me and knew better than to look at the sun. Leaning into the doorway of a warehouse, I tried to get my bearings. There were no streetlights, but there was light coming from the stores on the hill behind us. The people in the crowd were no longer talking or walking, and when the sky grew darker, the birds stopped singing and the cars on the roadway crawled to a stop. The silence spoke of fear and I had an urge to run. In my brain, the question, *Why is this happening?* kept repeating itself. It didn't matter at all that I knew this was the eclipse.

When Iona and I got home that evening, he was gone, leaving us a note that said he'd taken Mama to the bus and rambled on about the eclipse. The note, or maybe it was the tone of it more than the words, made it clear to me that the man who'd left home at sixteen and become a folk hero to everyone we knew, the man who loved a man and made that work, the man who made music his life and gave me and Iona the courage to pursue our dreams, was also a man who had no peace of mind.

He wanted Neil's approval and Neil wanted his.

Iona wept. "What's wrong with him?" she kept saying. "What is wrong with him?"

"Which one?" I asked, not being sure if she meant Neil or Francis.

"I don't see him for over thirteen years and he blows into town and leaves without saying goodbye?"

At least that settled the question, but it seemed unfair somehow.

Then it was herself she turned on. "I don't fit here. I never did."

"Oh, come on. I don't understand how you can say that."

"You do so. You just pretend you don't so that you won't have to face the fact that no one here ever talks. They just hide away in their own proud, silent world and pretend everything is fine."

"We talk about everything!" I protested.

She was pacing, emphatically counting things off on her fingers. "Do we talk about Mama being sick? Do we talk about the fact that Francis left home and never came back? Why were we so poor? How is that possible? They never explained anything. Do we talk about the fact you don't like boys?"

"I do so!"

"Oh yeah? Where is he then?" She looked around the room expectantly.

There was no talking to her at all, so I went out for a walk by myself.

This kind of thing, when she became so critical and disillusioned with life, happened a few times in the next months. But it wasn't until the following spring that she got smashing drunk at the bar. She didn't fall down but she started slurring her words as she sang at the microphone. Her bandleader shut the song down as inconspicuously as he could, nodding at the other players and looking at me with a question in his eyes. "Will you take her?" is what I assumed he was saying.

She spoke loudly and repetitively while we crossed the bar, heading for the doors. "I really love that song. I really love that song. I do, man," in the same way I've heard some friends, when they are truly drunk, slur out, "I luv you guys. I really luv you guys. I do, man." I was grateful it was music she'd settled on that night. The bar patrons smiled, and one of them called out, "It's never as good as the first time." The others joined in laughter that did not feel friendly.

Our conversation on the way home was my first experience in talking to someone I cared about who was drunk. This one was memorable mostly because Iona never remembered any of it.

"I get so tired of being a nice girl," she said, as she fell over on one heel.

This is better? I thought, but didn't speak, and walked very close to her so that I might catch her if she fell. As we crossed a back lane, she suddenly had to throw up and leaned over in the gutter so as not to make too big a mess on the street. "That was not nice," she said, after she straightened up and I'd wiped her mouth with a Kleenex.

"Do you think you can keep going?" I asked her. "It's not far."

"I'm going to go for ever. I'm just going to keep going." We passed a group of young men standing in front of another bar. By this point I was pretty much holding her up and they started laughing as well.

"Are they laughing at me?" she asked.

"No, no, they're just saying, 'Good luck.'"

She tried to focus on my face. "Do you wanna go away?"

"We already did."

"I mean rilly, rilly, rilly away."

It's a good thing there weren't too many stairs to climb when we got home. It was hard enough just to get her to come in. She kept pulling away from me, saying, "No, no, you go in. I'm gonna keep walking." Once we got up the four steps to the main floor, I had no intention of trying to carry her up another flight to the bedroom. Anyway, she collapsed on the sofa as soon as she saw it. The blanket I covered her with folded around her and in that condition, lying on her side, she looked perfectly well.

The next morning, when she padded stiffly into the kitchen, she had deep sleep creases on one side of her face and was licking her lips as if they were very dry. "My head is pounding. I drank too much."

"I hear water helps a lot," I said and got up to pour a glass.

After drinking it in two long drafts, she said, "I'm going to take an aspirin and go back to bed."

At noon she woke and seemed completely recovered. I made hot dogs because that was what we had. She was pretty intent on eating and didn't mention the previous night at all, so when she finished I asked, "Do you remember how we got home?"

She thought about that for a moment and decided to look me in the eye and lie. "Sure. We walked." A pretty safe bet as we usually did walk.

"Do you remember what we talked about?"

"Not really. Are you grilling me?"

"No, no."

"Well, then you tell me what we talked about last night."

"We talked about how much we love it here and would never want to leave."

Skepticism washed over her face and passed on. "Oh yeah. That."

A few weeks later she announced one morning at breakfast that she was applying to universities in Toronto and in England. "Come with me," she said.

"I'm already in the best school there is."

"This town is so small," she said. "I feel like I know everyone."

"Why move? Why not just travel?"

"Did you ever think people might be more open-minded in other places?"

"No, they're not," I said, remembering my own time away in Toronto. "Just a hunch."

"There are open-minded people here. Look at you and me."

"I'd like to spend some time in a whole crowd of them. Have you ever done that?"

I admitted I had not.

"There you go. Not going to happen here."

The day the letter came from the University of Toronto music department, inviting her to audition, I figured we were coming up to the end of an era. A small gnat of envy fluttered around in my brain and eluded my efforts to swat it.

"Do you have to go there to audition?" I asked as casually as I could.

"No, they come here. I'm not the only one applying."

Lentil loaf with about a pound of cheese in it had just come out of the oven on the night of her audition, when the phone rang. They wanted her. The whole time she listened she looked at me with her eyes opened wide in exclamation. "Thank you! That's exciting. Wow. What do I do now?… Okay. Yes, of course. Thanks. Goodbye. Goodbye."

She put down the phone, wearing a wide grin. "Oh my God! I won! I feel like I just won! I wasn't supposed to find out for a couple of months."

The envy gnat became stuck in my throat. It was not that I wanted anything but love and glory for her, but I was so drawn to go along, even though I was committed to making art in the place I already stood. Some part of me thought her lucky to be going and I didn't want to think that way.

She was sitting with me in between sets, days later, when she leaned closer, to be heard without shouting, "I'm not going to go to Toronto right now."

"What? Why not?" I asked.

"I'm going to go travelling."

"What about the music program?"

"Since when do you need a degree to be a singer? Or a painter for that matter."

"You're going to give it up?"

"I'll travel for a few months and decide after that."

"Where?"

"Don't know yet."

"Who with?"

"Alone."

"Why?"

"Give me a little room! I don't know. You're the one who said I should travel! I just have to go somewhere no one knows me and see if I can survive."

"And if you can't?" I asked.

"Very encouraging! You could always come."

"I can't leave right now."

"You could so. You're just stuck."

"I started it, I'm going to finish," I said. It was only a stubborn streak that buoyed this position, because really I agreed, but it cost so much money and represented so much work.

Travel guides, open and stacked, soon covered the surface of the kitchen table. I found her there in the middle of the night, poring over them. When she started playing "Marrakesh Express" all the time, I realized she'd settled on Morocco. The map of the world that she pinned on the wall began to grow a line of blue push-pins plotting her route.

On the weekend in late May when she left on her travels, we went to catch the train together. There were a number of tracks leading out of the station. I looked for the one going to Sydney and she looked for the one marked Montreal.

I'd booked an earlier train home so that I could pretend she was seeing me off. The Montreal platform was several tracks away and she was going to take her leave when I boarded mine. It was the first warm day of spring and the blue wool coat she carried over her arm was suddenly hot and heavy. She looked at it with some panic before holding it out. "Will you take it home for me? I'm not going to need it."

I hesitated. "It might be cold and wet in London."

"I'll be in the airport. I'll have no use for it in Morocco."

I took it because there was nothing else to do. My own jacket was lighter and I had no heavy knapsack. She smiled and hugged me. "Thanks, I'd hate to lose it." We both knew she meant that as some kind of olive branch. She would return, her wave suggested.

There was no window seat left so I sat beside a woman who was turned to the window and focused on the platform. Her white hair was tied back in a braid. The soft, bulky coat was a weight on my knees as the train pulled away.

It was warm enough, when we arrived, that I thought to walk home so I took the back streets and kept saying to myself, *I'm from here. I'm from here*, alternating the emphasis between *from* and *here*. The coat was beginning to chafe where I carried it under my arm, when Neil and Mama met me on the road with the car. She rolled down the window and smiled, her eyebrows pulled up as if she was surprised to see me, which she was not.

"We thought we'd catch up with you here."

I climbed in behind her awkwardly, kissing her from the back seat.

"How did you know I was coming?"

Neil looked at me in the rear-view mirror. "We had a call from Iona."

When I offered no reply at all, he looked over at Mama and then again to me, "Did you two have a falling out?"

I couldn't believe he was asking me that. He usually didn't want to know if there was emotional trouble afoot.

"No, she's just leaving." I shoved the heap of blue wool away from me to the other side of the car. "She wants you to keep her coat."

"She'll be back," Mama said, staring straight ahead at the road. "People come and go."

"I went and came back myself," Neil offered. "I went to Europe once."

"That was quite different," Mama said.

"I don't think it was so different," he said, then added as an after-thought, "Anyway, it's not as if there's a war going on over there. I'm sure she'll be perfectly safe." He stopped and seemed to be listening to what he just said and added quietly, "She just wants to do something and that's all she can think of right now."

23

The first time I laid eyes on Findlay he arrived late for English class, thumping the book he was carrying onto a table and slamming himself into a chair that was too small. His sleep-swollen eyes were those of a child and belied the message he was sending with his combed-back hair and the black leather jacket with so many buckles and studs. The professor noticed him too and within minutes asked him if he'd like to read from the heavy text he was toting around. He said, "No, I don't care for how it sounds in English."

"Why don't you tell us what it's about then?"

"It's about a guy who falls in love with a monster and then discovers the real terror is the monster's mother. Kind of a soap opera." We were studying *Beowulf* that month and apparently he'd actually read it. He looked across the aisle at me and raised his eyebrows. I found him irresistible, and thought it might be best to have nothing to do with him, so when he caught me staring I quickly turned away.

Later he brushed by me in the library without a glance. Fine with me. On Saturday morning, just as I reached the door of the Claire de Lune, he came striding out of the place, jumped on his motorbike and roared off into the city. The next day he was sitting in the laundromat reading something when I arrived with my load. For an hour and a half we both pulled and pushed clothing in and out of machines and folded every piece carefully. Apparently he didn't notice me. He left just as I was about to say something.

In class, on a day when I expressed an opinion that countered his, he finally looked at me. I raised my eyebrows to invite a reply. He said nothing. Clearly not an easy person to get to know.

It was disconcerting when he pulled up beside me a few blocks from the university. "Excuse me, miss. I think you're in my English class. Would you like a lift home?"

"Have we met?"

"I believe we have. I'm Findlay."

"I'm Eileen.

"Good then. Hop on."

What could I do? It would have been rude to say no. I'd forgotten I'd have to hang on to him with my arms around his waist, and it felt like a strangely intimate thing to do with someone you've never touched before. He drove the bike too fast but when we got to my apartment house, once the home of a wealthy Halifax merchant, we sat outside on the wide, curving staircase and talked for a while. I didn't ask him to come in and he never suggested it.

Before he left he said, "You're a good listener."

"You're a good talker," I replied.

He looked surprised. "Sorry if I went on too long."

"That's not what I meant," I said, too quietly.

"It's okay. You're right."

I found him hard to read and wondered if perhaps he'd never really noticed me before and if I was making it up in my head that he'd been ignoring me.

I wished Iona were there to help decipher him. She'd gone to Toronto after her fling in Morocco and a three-month love affair with India. When she came back she said India had felt like coming home and I really couldn't see that at all.

They were still happy to have her in the music school so she just picked up where she left off. I understood, for the first time, that she was going to be okay.

I called her right after the bike ride with Findlay. When she picked up the phone in her bed-sit, I didn't even give her a chance to say hello.

"I met someone."

"Thank God."

"Not funny."

"Do you like him?"

"No, I've decided to go out with someone I can't stand," I replied dryly.

"Just tell me something about him."

"He reads *Beowulf* and rides a motorcycle."

"Oh my!"

"No, it's not like that. He can pull it off. He's a nice guy."

We spent the next few days meeting at coffee houses, not pretending it was any accident. At the end of a week we met at a Bergman movie playing at the college, but in the middle of it he leaned over and said, "Let's get out of here." We slunk out the back under the disapproving eyes of our fellow students.

The September night was summer warm, with a foggy haze turning the streetlights into great orbs of light. We walked aimlessly, or so I thought, until we ended up in the warehouse district on the harbour. He stopped at one of those rundown buildings and said, "I live here." I thought he was joking but sure enough he had a key. He opened a door adjacent to the sidewalk and I followed him up several flights of stairs. His living space was bare and open but he'd made a couple of areas for eating and sleeping. At the centre of it there was a rope dangling from the ceiling and when he pulled it, a ladder descended. He gallantly extended a hand as if to say, "You first," so I scrambled up the ladder and through the opening to the roof.

The world up there was enormous, with the ocean stretching far away and the low-lying mist covering much of the land. The freighters in the harbour were just lights competing with the stars. The smell of the ocean was profound.

"What is that?" I wondered. "It's not just salt."

"I think it's seaweed and other low-tide factors."

I laughed. "It's impressive up here."

"I sleep here sometimes," he said.

"Lucky you."

When he reached out and touched my bare arm, I shivered.

"Hey, are you cold?"

"Ah… maybe."

He picked up a yellow sweater of his own that lay in a heap on the top of the wall we were leaning on, and wrapped it around my body with his arms.

When I kissed him I wanted it to be the best kiss anyone had ever had or ever would. Lingering made the difference. Those beautiful soft lips and clean mouth. No pulling away until I was dizzy.

"Where's the bed?" I asked.

"We can pull one up from below," he suggested.

In a quiet frenzy we created a bed for ourselves by covering a space on the roof with his straw mats and then dragging his foam mattress up through the hatch door and piling it with pillows and blankets.

There we stood, one on each side of the makeshift bed, not quite knowing what was next. At least I didn't. It struck me as funny and I started to remove my clothing one piece at a time, throwing it carelessly and dramatically to one side as he watched. When I stood naked and questioned him with my eyes, he hurriedly followed my example, until both of us were only wearing wide grins.

Once we fell onto the bed, permission granted, it was all rush and closed eyes, as if he couldn't possibly wait one more minute to be united. My own body was overwhelmed with a pulsating energy, but I wanted to say, "Wait, slow down." I didn't, because it was my first time, or maybe because it's never easy to give directions in the middle of a passionate embrace. It was not what I'd imagined it to be, although I'm not sure I ever imagined it all the way through to the end anyway. It seemed so unlikely. I was a bit embarrassed that my fantasies had all been kissing and touching, and hoped my inexperience was not too evident to someone who so obviously knew what he was doing.

Once he was spent, he lay face down on top of me and then rolled off to one side, sat up, and fumbled in the pocket of his pants lying beside the bed. He came up with a hand-rolled cigarette and his Zippo lighter. The light that flashed when he lit it was no match for the open sky. He took a drag and offered it to me.

"Hash oil in it," he said, holding his breath.

"No thanks. Too strong for me. Makes me paranoid."

He let the smoke escape in a whoosh.

"Do you have a lot of fears?"

"No, but I try to avoid imagined ones."

He put down the joint, and lay back down with me.

"You're beautiful," he said.

His earlobe smelled like the earth, in a forest, on a wet day, and I fell asleep while the mist drifted over us.

When I awoke he was twenty feet away, leaning on the wall of the rooftop, wearing jeans, no shirt, his body so slim and long. I dressed while he had his back turned, looking at the harbour below. When he turned I was standing by the mattress, gathering my things. He looked surprised. "Are you leaving?"

"Will you walk me home?"

"Sure, but you don't have to leave."

"It's better, I have an early class."

He shrugged as if that shouldn't matter.

On the way home he grabbed my hand and held it. "I don't want to lose you in the fog."

The next time we met at a café, I asked him what he wanted to do in the next few years and he said he wanted to travel. He was from up north on the island and his family had given him his grandfather's house and said they would keep it warm for him in winter in case he ever wanted to come back.

"They don't understand that I'm not materialistic. I'd never let a house anchor me. It's just a bunch of wood nailed together."

"They just want you to know there's always room for you." This sounded to me like an echo of my own grandmother's voice, not exactly the right tone for a first love affair, so I added, "Not that you'd want to put anything in the way of freedom." That statement ricocheted around the room and bounced off the inner walls of my brain. It sounded like the truth, but I could not find a place to store it, this thing I'd said but didn't believe.

"What about you?" he asked.

"I don't know. I'd like to paint, have a family. Not sure you can do both."

"You can do anything you want."

"Have to make a living somehow," I said.

"What's wrong with waitressing?"

"Nothing," I said, although I didn't really believe that either. I was turning into quite the liar, it seemed. This was new territory for me and in the following months I tried to make it an insignificant one.

By the time the student loans arrived in October, we were spending almost every day and night together. He was using my address, to avoid detection at the warehouse, which wasn't a legal living space, so I brought the mail to him when we met downtown. We sat on the library wall under the orange and wine turning leaves, the filtered autumn sun dancing over us. He said we should take the student loan money and go to California.

"There's a revolution going on and I'm not planning to miss it."

"Isn't the revolution supposed to come to you? I mean, I don't think there are travelling revolutionaries."

"There is no other kind," he said.

"I wouldn't know. I never met one."

He took offence to that. "I guess you wouldn't know one if you met one."

"I'm sorry…"

He got up and left without a word and didn't come to my third-storey walk-up at suppertime as we'd planned.

In English class the next day, he acted as if he didn't know me, re-fusing to catch my eye and speaking in an earnest and absorbed way with another woman about how an analysis of all modern western political dysfunction could be found in the writings of William Blake.

Blake again, I thought to myself, remembering the poet in the coffee shop in Toronto on my first visit there.

On Gottingen Street, the motorcycle roared up beside me and stopped.

"Ride?" he asked.

I had too many books with me, so he had to stop and help me put them in the saddlebags. Our elbows and hands kept finding each other as we stored the books, and once I was on the bike it felt like going to the warehouse was an obvious choice.

We took turns sleeping in each of our places, neither one of us wanting to lose our autonomy, it seemed. I needed to study more than he did, and he liked to drink Kahlua and write poetry.

One morning in December we opened his street door and discov-ered two feet of snow blocking our way. The door was jammed at an angle, and even if we could have got through, it would have been hard going.

"Let's check the radio," I said. "Bet the college is closed."

"Let's just assume it is." So we broke apart some cardboard boxes he had, and set out to trudge up to the Citadel through a glittering white world of unplowed streets, with householders and business owners shovelling sidewalks. Everyone we met smiled as if we shared something to celebrate.

The stone fortress above us was dusted with snow and did not seem as formidable as it should. The trek up the untracked hill was exhilarat-ing, regardless of how often we sank to our knees in the deep, soft snow. Once we were near the top we placed our cardboard side by side, held hands and grinned at each other while we prepared to shove off. The co-lour had risen in Findlay's face, as it must have when he was a child and excited about a day spent sledding. His lean, long body seemed to belong to a boy who'd recently had a growth spurt. I was reminded of the day when Francis took Iona and me out to the hill behind the house and set us on a toboggan, both nestled between his long legs as we hurtled down that steep incline.

The first ride down the Citadel Hill was wildly out of control and it almost seemed we'd fly right off it and continue through the streets until we landed in the wide ocean below us. Instead, we arrived at the bottom in a heap of cardboard. We each grabbed a piece of the board and raced to the top again. Findlay won, but only because his legs were longer.

Near the top, where we stopped to catch our breath, we turned to survey the sea and shore and the city below. McNabs Island stretched below us at the mouth of the harbour.

He put his arm around me and pulled me in to him. "Maybe we should go live out there. Build a little cabin."

"Nice idea. But no grocery store."

"We could plant a garden."

"I honestly don't think you're allowed to squat there."

"I was talking about an adventure, not the rest of our lives!" He pulled away.

When I turned to look at him, his forehead had a crease in the middle and it was not from the glare.

"Sorry. I didn't know we were having a serious conversation."

The sparkle had gone off the day and he suggested we walk down to the water. A freighter in dry dock in the harbour loomed above us as we stood passively observing the activity on its deck.

"It's just that whenever I talk about leaving here to do anything else, you treat it like it's a joke," he said.

"I don't mean to. Where do you want to go?"

"Somewhere people are more into change."

"I already did that and I landed here."

"You can't call Halifax a big stretch."

"Where would be better?" I asked.

"Let's go live in Mexico for a couple of years."

"You think people are more open-minded there?"

"Well, they won't be so tied to the profit motive that governs everything here. They live a more simple life."

"They have lots of babies, I hear."

"Is that what you want?" he asked.

"I'd like to start with one."

"I'm not ready for that."

"Do you think you'll ever be?"

"Don't even think about it."

That afternoon, having consumed too many beers at the Piccadilly, he started ranting, "You're afraid of everything."

"Excuse me?"

"You just want to have a baby and hide out from real political responsibility."

"Are you suggesting I'm a coward because I want to have a child someday? That might take a bit of courage I think."

"You want the white picket fence and the guy who brings home the bacon. Well, I'm not him."

"I can take care of myself, thank you! If I was looking for a man to take care of me, you'd be an unlikely candidate!"

"Sure."

He signalled the waiter for more beer.

That night I called Iona.

"You think he's vain," she said.

"Nooo. It's just insulting for him to think I want him so much."

"How much do you want him?"

"Quite a bit," I admitted.

"Maybe he's just smart."

"I'm not sure about that."

"Just don't get pregnant."

"Don't worry," I told her. "We're taking precautions."

The next day I couldn't tell if he remembered our argument about having children. He was his usual talkative self, theorizing about identity and how we decide who we are. "You don't have to identify with the group of people you were born into. A person is free to identify with any group you choose or to identify as a totally free-thinking individual."

"We aren't born into a vacuum," I asserted, thinking of the long line of people who had come before and somehow were a part of me.

"I'm just saying that if you believe in free will, you have to believe you get to choose. It's about taking risks, Ailee, you just have to leap."

"But doesn't it matter what you're leaping from? A trampoline or a diving board or the top of a cliff?"

"No. All that matters is the way you jump."

A week home with Iona at Christmas was a chance to get her perspective. We'd dug ourselves out of our parents' house and set out to find a store open where we could buy some candles, as we were all anticipating the power failing. The banks on either side of the road were six or seven feet tall, so there was more of a wide path than a road. Most of the time we walked through this canyon of snow side by side, only climbing the banks a little to let a passing car go by.

"Do you think I'm a stick in the mud?" I asked her.

"No, I don't."

"You don't think I'm a coward?"

"What's going on with you?"

"Findlay says I'm those things."

"Don't let that guy convince you of something you know isn't true."

The problem was in not knowing.

Findlay had wanted me to stay in Halifax over the holidays and, when I couldn't do that, the compromise was coming back early and spending New Year's Eve with him. I half expected him to be gone but when I got there, his bike was parked outside.

He had bought vegetables, rice and fish and had it all prepared to cook together in a wok. "This is a surprise," I said.

"Don't let the domesticity fool you. I'm just buttering you up so you'll come with me."

"On a motorbike in freezing weather?"

"No. I can wait until spring."

The meaning of the look that passed between us then was probably no easier for him to puzzle out than for me. Did everything we believed have to be sorted out in the middle of a dispute about travelling? Were we just intellectually, politically and emotionally incompatible? Was this a power struggle? These were the questions that we tested in the next few months. There was little relief from the push and pull of it.

On the ferry to Dartmouth in early May, on our way to our favourite chip shop, with the weather warming and my courses finished for the summer, the conversation veered in his direction.

"I say we go on the Queen's birthday. We'll just plan for then. If the weather is bad we can hold off a few days. You can give notice today."

"Whoa! Where are we going?" I asked, looking out across the harbour as if this place might be somewhere on the horizon.

"We're getting on the bike, driving to Yarmouth, taking the ferry to Bar Harbour and then driving for six days until we reach the Grand Canyon. Then we're going to talk about it over a campfire when the place cools down at night."

"I have to save some money."

"I didn't pay my tuition. I have the whole thing in the bank. We can just take it and go."

"You're going to have to pay it sometime," I told him.

"I don't care about sometime. I care about now."

"Give me a few months," I said. "I'll save some money. I'll sublet the apartment for August and I'll come with you. In September I'll come back to finish my degree.

"You're talking about going on vacation and I'm talking about radically changing our lives."

"In September you can keep going or come back with me."

"Time's up, Ailee," he said quietly. He seemed more angry than sad when he stomped away.

"Findlay, wait a minute!"

He kept walking away on the dock.

My voice was thrown back to me by the breathtaking wind. "I didn't say I wouldn't go!"

Still nothing.

The wind lapsed for a moment and my cry, "I'll meet you back at my place!" came out as a shrill and desperate plea.

He turned but he never stopped walking.

Late that evening, reading in bed and fully dressed in case he still might arrive, I heard a terrible racket that sounded like some kind of construction. I had moved back into one of the old mansions that were cut up into apartments and bedsits where students tended to congregate. This one had a broad, main central stairway that funnelled noise up from the street if the door was opened. It was likely something was happening just outside, but when I looked out the windows to the street below, I could see nothing. There was no one else home on a Friday night, so I hesitated before I opened my door to investigate. It sounded like a backhoe was digging up the foyer.

The noise continued while I made my way to just above the first landing and looked into the stairwell below. From there I caught a glimpse of his motorbike struggling up the broad and shallow circular staircase. What I saw was a wild and courageous warrior fighting his way through the rough terrain of an old and storied place. I thought my grandmother would have liked such a man, even one with so much leaving on his mind. Maybe she would have understood him.

He braked on the landing and turned off the key. "Jump on," he said.

"It's okay. I'll meet you on the sidewalk."

"It'll be a thrill going back down."

"You're out of your mind."

"What if I am?"

"How about if you be out of your mind all you want, and I won't be out of mine at all. It'd be a good balance."

He looked me in the eye for a long moment in a way I couldn't interpret and then turned the bike and bumped back down the stairs without turning on the gas. I ran to get a coat before following him down, expecting he would wait for me. When I arrived on the sidewalk it was empty, and I could hear the receding sound of his bike climbing a hill in the distance. I could no longer distinguish it from other vehicles when I finally retreated from the street.

I lay awake in the silent apartment, listening to the traffic through my open bedroom window: a car with a bad muffler roared by, then a pick-up truck with a bunch of teenagers or college boys in the back literally whooping it up. There might have been a motorcycle out on Coburg. By two o'clock there were no vehicles to be heard at all, and sometime around sunrise the chickadees' repetitive calls lulled me to sleep. In the following days, I didn't play any music in case I'd miss the sound of his return.

When the phone rang I snatched up the receiver. Iona's voice was unexpected but a welcome intrusion into the silence enveloping and threatening to overwhelm my apartment.

"How's it going?" she asked.

"Findlay's gone."

"What do you mean? You broke up or he's dead or what?"

"Neither! He's just gone away somewhere. I haven't heard from him for a week. I checked his place and he hasn't slept in it since the last time we were there together. There was a note."

"What did it say?"

"'Wait for me. I'll look for you when I get back.'"

"That's original. Is he asking for your commitment as he runs out the door?" She paused. "Did he ask you to go with him?"

"Sort of."

"Why didn't you?"

"I don't know. He's just so serious all the time. I wish he'd laugh out loud sometimes."

"You're looking for someone just like your gay older brother?"

"Your point is?" I asked.

In the silence it was obvious that she was feeling less than generous, and perhaps had called for reasons of her own.

"How is everything with you?" I asked.

"The program is demanding. I lost my job. There's no food in the place. I have a date tonight and I'm hoping he plans to buy me supper. Everything is good."

"You're okay then."

"I think we both are."

"Try the Riverboat. That's a good spot to pass the hat."

"Okay, I'll call you on the weekend."

"Thanks for calling, Iona. It's good to hear you."

"I love you too," she said.

That night I turned the radio on to listen to Francis's show. The theme song from *Summer of '42* was playing and I couldn't stand it. Its romance didn't match my mood. When I quickly turned it off, the pain eased just enough to allow me to fall asleep.

24

He called from California a year later. My friend Mark, another painter, who lived in the apartment below me, was up visiting and answered the phone. He handed it over to me saying, "Very official sounding." I took the phone with some hesitation and said a tentative hello. Mark mouthed, "Should I go?" When I realized it was Findlay I put my hand over the phone, "It's okay. Don't go," and turned away in case my face betrayed too much emotion.

I'd had one letter from him, in which he talked about the people he was meeting and how creative and alive he found them to be. He said the cultural revolution was happening right there and every standard and norm of behaviour was being turned on its head.

He wrote, "No one owns anyone or anything. I hope you are experiencing the same freedom." He said he missed me and would someday come home when he finished the work he was doing on himself.

Now here he was on the phone. "How's your world?" he asked.

"I'm pretty busy. Grad show in two weeks."

"You're graduating."

"Yes, I am."

"Good for you. You must be pleased with yourself."

"Is there some reason you called?" I glanced back at Mark. "I've got a friend visiting."

For a moment I thought the phone had gone dead. "Hello?"

"No need to get defensive."

"I think I'm going to go now, Findlay."

I put the phone back in its cradle and looked up to see Mark studying me. "Is it a bit more crowded here than I originally thought?" he asked.

"No, no, that was a guy I met in English class. Just a kid actually."

When Findlay arrived at the door a few days later, we were listening to "Dark Side of the Moon" turned up high. It was one of those not-so-cheerful tunes I'd taken to listening to in the previous months. *You run and you run to catch up with the sun and it's sinking.* The apartment was one of those narrow places where all the rooms are to one side of a long hall. The front room was directly to the right of the door, followed by the bedroom and bath with the kitchen opening out at the end.

Mark and I were in the kitchen discussing turning the front room into a bedroom so that we could share the apartment and split the rent. His apartment was identical and one floor down. Mine was cleaner, so there was no question of who would move.

We didn't hear the knock, if there was one, and when Findlay walked into the room we both jumped. "Findlay!" was all I could say.

He was even thinner than he'd been and had let his hair grow longer and wilder. When he looked at me he just nodded his head and it was all I could do not to embrace him. But he spoke directly to Mark, "Do you live here?"

"Not yet. We were just discussing that possibility. I live one floor down."

"That's cozy enough. Why double up?"

"Cheaper."

"Right."

"Mark, Findlay, Findlay, Mark," I said as introductions and in the hope of slowing this down.

"I'll make some tea. How was the trip up?"

"I hitched all the way from San Francisco in three days. Slept on the side of the road in Oregon the first night."

Mark quietly interrupted, "Eileen, I'm going to head down."

"Okay, I'll talk to you tonight."

But Findlay intervened. "Can I come down for a minute? Maybe if you're moving I could rent your place." He looked at me. "I'm planning to stay for a while."

"Sure." They walked to the door together, but when Mark glanced back before leaving, he looked puzzled.

Half an hour later, when I opened the door to Mark's knock and held it wide for him to enter, he stood rooted in the hallway. "He says you and he are soulmates."

"That's ridiculous."

"If I asked you to completely put him out of your life so you and I can live together, what would you do?"

"What are you saying? I thought we were friends. I wasn't even sure you were really interested."

"Okay. Well, I am. If anything changes, let me know."

"You're acting as if this is a competition without even consulting me about whether I want to be the prize!"

"That's bitter."

"Yes, it is."

"I guess you could have told me about him." He left without saying any more.

Findlay arrived sometime later through the fire escape window. The four-by-four landing served as my balcony so I was used to him coming and going that way. For his part I think he loved the quirkiness of the window as an entrance. When his tall, angular frame bent to come through it, he reminded me of Francis. Once he was inside he paced, stopping occasionally to address me. "I started moving right after you hung up on me. One ride today all the way from Portland. It's so obvious I'm meant to be here."

"You told Mark we were soulmates."

"I did not. He may have thought that's what I meant but I said we were destined to be together." He passed along the length of the hall, looked at the front room and then came back to the kitchen. He stood in front of me again. "I'm sorry Ai, I was wrong to go that way. I didn't realize how much I needed you until I thought you might be gone."

"So tell me why."

"I needed to reach out and grab life and it seemed so safe here."

"Boring, you mean."

"No city with you in it could be boring."

He was still irresistible to me and I think some part of me wanted someone to claim me. Findlay did the claiming so well. Much later I realized that I might have confused his persistence with devotion.

The opening reception of my grad show was in a tiny storefront gallery, crowded with friends of mine and patrons of the gallery. The paintings were a series I'd worked on for a year of different kinds of roads leading away from someone in the foreground. The gallery curator had suggested I include the one of the boy in front of a house on a lonely road that had gained me entrance to the school. The night of the opening, the owner put an arm around me. "Good turnout. People are interested."

Findlay arrived late in full leather, carrying his helmet under one arm. In public I was usually more aware of the beauty of his eyes. I could see the effect they had on others. But that evening they were red-rimmed and cloudy. He strode into the small gallery and immediately came over and kissed me for a rather long moment. It made me uncomfortable in public and I wasn't sure why.

He turned to the small crowd I'd been talking to and said, "This is terrific. Tomorrow I get my girl back. Can we smoke a joint in here?" They all laughed, except for Mark.

He quickly became the centre of attention and answered questions about what he'd been up to by telling the story of his months in California, the political action and the naked parties on the beach. That night, as we lay in bed, he said, "I love you. You made me proud tonight."

We had to have some money coming in, so waitressing seemed to be my best option and living with Findlay made it bearable. When he picked me up at the end of my shift to walk me home, the Greek maitre'd was skeptical. "Be careful who you lie down with," he advised. It seemed there was no knowing Findlay without forming an opinion. Even the guard in the public gardens glanced away and smiled secretly when he saw us sitting on a bench, drinking wine from stemware.

I loved having him to come home to. It helped when I'd had a rough day. One night the manager in the restaurant yelled at me for removing someone's side plate at the wrong moment. "What kind of an idiot are you? You act as if you've never even eaten in a good restaurant before, let alone worked in one!" I silently agreed he had something there.

Findlay heard me coming as I bolted up the stairs after work. The door to the apartment opened before I reached it. Behind him the kitchen table was covered with his papers. He intended to be a poet but I knew he'd probably spent the day looking for work. There never seemed to be anything for him and he always tried to put a good face on it.

"No paid work for poets today," he said as he took my coat and hung it up for me.

Finally some friends put a good word in for him with someone who hired for the big ships that came into the Halifax harbour and left again for Florida and points farther south. They promised him work the next time one of their ships came in. It fit for both of us that he would travel out to work occasionally and that I would be there when he returned. That was a story we knew well. When we lay cozily in our bed on a Monday morning and I brought up the idea of children, this time he laughingly agreed they would be beautiful and smart. But when I suggested, "Maybe they'll inspire you to write children's books," he fell silent and I was afraid I had offended him.

⬬

In July I went home to see Mama and Neil as I always did in summer, and a few days into the visit Findlay arrived on a balmy evening, in full throttle, wearing his leathers. Neil and Mama came outside to greet him even though he was unexpected. Neil shook his hand and when Findlay said he was sorry to come unannounced, Mama smiled at him. "No trouble at all. Always room at the table for one more, especially these days."

There were none of us still at home then. Murdoch was in Alberta working on an oil rig. No one had heard from him for a few months. Mama had been feeling well, not showing any symptoms to speak of for several months, and seemed happy to have guests again.

Findlay took off his helmet and ran his fingers through his sweaty mat of hair.

"Come in and have something cool to drink," Mama said. "Eileen, grab some ice cubes out of the freezer, will you?"

I went in ahead to the kitchen with Mama and while I poured a pitcher of water she pulled a pie out of the oven and set it on a cooling rack.

"Did you know he was coming?" she asked me.

"No, I didn't. Sorry."

"It's alright. I was enjoying our visit, but I suppose he was missing you. He can sleep in the boys' room."

After supper that night, we sat for a long time at the table after the dishes were cleared and Mama had served up her best lemon meringue pie. Neil brought up the bike again. "I guess you need gear like that in case you fall off, but it must be awfully warm in this weather."

"It's cold on the bike. I never fall off."

Findlay smiled at me with very slightly raised eyebrows as if we were complicit in sharing a tolerant understanding of my parents. I never granted him a flicker of agreement in that regard.

"I drove a bike in Spain," Neil said, "during the war. We used them to deliver medical supplies and the Spanish preferred if the Canadians or Americans did those kind of jobs. I never did fall off, either."

Findlay's eyes widened. "The Spanish War?"

"That's the one."

"What did you do there?"

"Anything and everything they told me to. That's the way it is in a war."

"That's impressive."

"I never wanted to go to war. It was freedom I was looking for, a chance to stand up and be someone instead of waiting forever to be thrown some crumb of work. My brother, Frank, had gone out west before me and I thought I'd do the same. Jumped on a freight car and felt pretty good when I landed in the rail yard in Halifax. I remember the snow melting as it hit the ground. Perhaps the warmth put me in an overly receptive frame of mind. I was skipping from one rail to another, looking for a car headed for Ontario, when I saw a fella coming up the tracks toward me in a flimsy jacket and bundled in a scarf. He had no gloves and his hands were tucked into his armpits. When he came within a couple of feet of me and stopped he said, 'I'm Charlie. You're new.' 'A bit ragged around the edges to be new,'" I said.

"So he offered me a smoke and I told him I was headed out west. He had a story about the works camps, and the awful food, and the lice in them.

"We spent a few days together, him paying for the beer, and it turned out he was a union man and recruiting men to go to Spain. He found passage for me on a Cunard liner to France."

Findlay was obviously impressed and surprised by this story. As was I, having never heard it before.

"Big decision. Took a lot of courage."

"It seemed important at the time, but we didn't really accomplish much."

Mama always seemed to get anxious when conversations about war began. As a way to change the subject, she asked Findlay, "Where are your people?"

"You mean where am I from?"

"Yes, I do."

"Inverness."

"And are your parents still there?"

"My parents are in Inverness. Yes, they are."

"Are you going there from here?"

"Not on this trip. It's a long drive up the coast."

"That's too bad," she said softly.

To cover any awkwardness, Neil offered, "Some of our own are far away."

"Yes, I know." When he looked at me and we shared a small smile, I saw Mama breathe. I knew she'd be happy I talked to him about family.

He left the next day. When he revved up and rolled away, all that leather made him seem more vulnerable than he looked on the day he climbed my staircase with the very same bike. His twenty-two years looked younger. This may have been because in the presence of Mama and Neil, I saw how young he really was.

I was working on another painting of a woman standing on a vanishing road, when a friend called to say there was a job for Findlay on a freighter working the coast from Newfoundland to Jamaica.

I wanted to go with him.

"You could get me on as your wife! The pay for kitchen work is ten times what I earn as a waitress."

"Women don't work on the boats," he said.

"Says who?"

"All the men who work on them."

"That's so tacky."

"It's just reality. Women are believed to be bad news on a big ship like that," he said. "No point getting in a snit about this one."

"You think I'd be bad news?" I asked.

"It's not up to me."

"You could fight for it."

"Yeah, and maybe all of a sudden there's no spot for me after all."

"You won't stick up for me?" I asked.

"You'd get raped."

"I can't believe you're saying that. You're making all men out to be animals."

"No, just some."

I hated that he might be right. I loved the idea of going off to sea with him and facing the hard work and the elements together. A better wage, so we could put aside some money, was certainly another motive. But I understood, having never discussed it, that he didn't want to be the only man, in an all-male group, who had a woman with him.

There is only one way to be in this world when you are living like a single person and need the company of others, but are not available. Your friends are other women and, if you're lucky, a couple of gay men. Great company, but then they go home and leave you to paint. So I found a job in a graphic art supply store, turned the front room into a studio, and felt the first real freedom of painting for myself, no assignments, no expectations to fulfill, no distractions.

It went well, I thought, until the day I realized that the nausea caused by the smell of the paint was more complicated than that. The chair beneath me felt hard and cold, but when I touched my belly I could sense the child within me before any blue line told me she was there. Our precautions had failed me. There was no address to write to tell him.

The sheets and wool blankets were twisted around my ankles and I woke feeling trapped and panicky. Cold air drifted in from the open bedroom window and a line of snow sat on the floor and on the windowsill. The clock by the bed claimed it was only midnight even though it felt as if the dream I was emerging from had lasted hours. I'd been running, frantic to reach my mother, but I couldn't tell if I was me or the baby in the dream.

Iona answered the phone with a group of people laughing and yelling in the background. "Hey! How are you? It's noisy here. Hang on, I'll take this outside." I could hear the door opening and closing before she said, "Oh my God, it's cold out here. What's it like there?"

"There's a blizzard."

She knew right away there was a problem and her voice took on a different note. "Eileen, what's wrong?"

"I'm pregnant."

"Oh no! How did that happen? Oh, sorry sorry, that was stupid. Oh my God, what are you going to do?"

"I guess I'm going to have a baby."

Silence and then, "What does Findlay think?"

"I don't even know where he is right now but we've talked about it before and I think he'll be okay with it."

"Do you want me to come down?"

"*Nooo.* What could you do here? And don't tell anyone else."

"Where are you right now?"

"In bed under the covers."

"Okay, that sounds good. I have to go in before I freeze to death but I'll call you tomorrow."

"Okay, goodnight."

"Eileen?"

"Yeah?"

"You'll be a really good mom."

It was a week before I got up the nerve to call Francis.

"I don't know how I'm going to tell Mama. She'll be so embarrassed."

"She loves you. And she loves babies. She'll get over it," he said.

"Easy to say."

"The truth is, I'm a bit jealous."

"You wish you were pregnant?"

"Very funny. But I do wish I could have a kid. And I guess that's not in the cards."

"You can be a good uncle. She's going to need that."

"You'll be okay. You'll both be okay. We'll all be there for you."

"Metaphorically, you mean."

I heard him take a deep breath before responding. "Do you want her?"

"Yes, I do."

"How do you know it's a she?"

"I can tell."

"I see."

⊅◎

I'd already quit my job and was living on savings when I met Findlay at the door in April, wearing a tight blue t-shirt and a wraparound skirt tied low under my large belly. The door opened just enough for him to get a glimpse of me, and he reeled and walked a few steps back down the hall. Then he stopped and returned.

"I… didn't recognize you."

"Oh come on."

"This is just so strange."

"If you kiss me, it won't seem so odd."

"I've never kissed a pregnant woman before."

"Come in out of the hall." As I backed up into the apartment, I wasn't sure he was going to follow.

When he finally was able to communicate, he had many concerns. He had fought with the first mate and had no job he could go back to. He felt he couldn't be a good father until he had resolved more of his own issues with his parents. He was too young to be tied down in that way.

"I'm sorry to have sprung it on you, but there was no way to reach you."

"You could have written. I got mail when we came into port."

"You could have called when you were in port."

After he slept on the sofa overnight, he got up and made the tea as he liked it with lots of sugar in the pot. He explained that he wanted to be supportive but he wasn't prepared to be part of something like a shotgun wedding.

"I can give you a year," he said.

"This is your baby you're talking about here." I intended our child to have a father.

☙

The night I went into labour I was alone at home. I lay on the bed on my side, there being no other way to lie down at that point in a pregnancy. I felt my whole being tighten and should have been on high alert, but I'd expected to feel pain and there was none at that point. I was afraid this might be the kind of false contraction that Mama had warned me about. My mind contracted too. The whole world was contained in my body. The walls of the room seemed a galaxy away.

At some point I felt like getting up to walk, but once I was on my feet, one of the contractions sent me downward, squatting with my hands on the floor in front of me. When I came out of it, my mind expanded enough to figure out I needed help. Within seconds of banging on the floor with a shoe, to alert Mark and Kate, the woman who was living with him, I could hear them running up the stairs. They both carefully pulled me off the floor and supported me until I was standing.

Kate took charge. "You hang onto her. I'll call a cab."

I was grateful for the care they took. She stayed with me in the hospital and Mark went to look for Findlay. He found him at the Piccadilly so he got to us before she was born. We'd planned for him to be at the birth, but he couldn't stay in the room. It made him too anxious. Early that morning, she came out in one piece and was so healthy and normal that they sent us home the next day.

I called home. Neil answered.

"I have a baby girl!"

"Well, well. Congratulations! I'm very happy to hear that. Did you get married?"

"You know very well I did not."

"Why is that, I wonder?" he asked.

"Maybe we're just free-thinking people."

"I see, well, I'll hand you over to your mother then."

When Mama came on the line she wanted all the details. There weren't very many though, and after a few minutes she offered to come up to help a bit after we'd had a week or so on our own.

"Call Stella and Murdoch and Joe, will you?" I said. "I'll call Francis and Iona but that's probably as far as I'll get."

When I got off the phone, Findlay said with some humour, "Does he hope I'll make an honest woman of you?"

"I think he just wants to know you're in for the long haul."

"I'm right here. That's all that matters, isn't it?"

Findlay was very good to us in those first days. He insisted I just focus on Maira and he would do the rest. He made food and went to the store for more groceries. He cleaned up and swept, and it kept him busy. He'd come in the room and lie down beside me sometimes, but if Maira was in the bed with me he shied away. On the third day, when it couldn't be avoided any longer, he picked her up to cradle her and she turned her face toward his body, looking for a breast. He looked bewildered and couldn't see the humour in it when I laughed. Her warm body smelled like powder and something remarkably new when he put her back in my arms.

"I think I'll go do some research at the library," he said.

"Or maybe at the bar?" I smiled so he could see I didn't mind.

A couple of days later, after I'd been up and at least making sandwiches and cooking breakfast, I called Mama. "Would you like to come visit?"

"I'd love to come help for a week but I don't want to be in the way."

She came, bringing wisdom and compassion, homemade biscuits and date squares. She was not in the way. The old, overstuffed sofa we'd bought at the Salvation Army became a bed for her. I found her one afternoon lying on her side curled around the baby, who was tucked in at the back. Mama seemed to be sleeping and Maira had her hands in the air, examining them as if she'd never seen them before.

Findlay went out to buy groceries, and after Mama napped for most of the afternoon, she cooked supper. I was completely free to look after Maira. She even helped rinse the diapers and set them in a pail, but then Findlay had to take them on his bike to the laundromat.

He said, "Those diapers have a kind of eau de baby poo smell when I put them in the washer. Yesterday a woman at the next machine said, 'Aren't you a help?' We're going to have to move somewhere with a washer and dryer. We can't keep this up."

I worried sometimes that this helping was too much work for Mama, though she was in a kind of remission and didn't seem to be leaning to one side at all. "Don't be silly. When I feel good I like to do things I can't do otherwise." When she left a week later she said, "I'll come back to keep you company sometimes when he has to go out again," referring to the boats.

"We have some savings. He won't have to go for a while."

"That's good then." Her eyes met mine and she hugged me hard before she left in a bit of a flurry, with the cab waiting.

After that, if I was up late alone with Maira I listened to Francis, who sent me messages along the airwaves. "This one is for mothers everywhere," he said and played anything by Ella Fitzgerald or, if he thought a lighter mood was wiser, he dished up Annie Ross.

Maira was about four months old when Findlay woke up one morning with her in the bed between us and rolled her around and pulled at her feet to make her laugh. I was sure we'd be okay then, and for quite a while we were. We settled into a routine; he got up when Maira let out a yell in the morning and brought her in to me. Then I gave her the breast while he made tea. When she'd had her fill, I called Findlay and he came in and played with her on the bed while I had a shower. We had breakfast together and one of us cooked it while the other one watched Maira. She was entertaining, as are all infants, so that was no trouble. He usually went out to the library after that. She and I went for a walk.

After a few months, he switched to a novel and left the poetry behind. He was happy to have a project. "I need something I can sink my teeth into," he said.

At eight months old, Maira was a messy eater and her food often left her spoon unexpectedly. One morning Findlay got up while she was still eating breakfast and stood in the doorway to the kitchen with those same sleepy eyes I'd first fallen in love with. Maira was so happy to see him she moved every part of her that she could and her spoon struck the metal tray of her high chair. The rice cereal flew off the spoon and landed in his hair. We both found it funny. It was a good moment in our lives.

"How's the novel going?" I asked.

"Good, I think. I've settled on a way to tell it. If I use just one character's perspective, I can focus on what I'm trying to say."

I knew it was about a man who hitchhikes continuously for a year, looking for meaning in the world as he comes across it. I wondered if he was aiming at a version of *On the Road*, the book I found after Francis left. Perhaps they had something in common, but it seemed they had very different issues to resolve.

Writing the novel kept him home more and, when the money from his savings and mine was all used up, I called the owner of the art supply store, who agreed to take me back. The money was not as good as waitressing but he let me take Maira to the store with me and the customers didn't seem to mind. She was a smiling and gurgling sort of baby.

Findlay seemed happier and I felt we could take care of everything else. But life is never so simple. He began to feel burdened by the trek back and forth to the store when he had to pick her up for her afternoon nap. He would just get going on an idea and felt he could never get back to it if he was interrupted. And then he felt terribly rejected if I worked an evening shift, because he had to put her to bed and she fussed and asked for me.

He grew even more unhappy when the novel stalled.

"I'm living this narrow life filled with baby food and diapers. No wonder my imagination has totally deserted me."

Sometimes he flew into a bit of a rage. One night he kicked the pillows around the living room, saying, "This place is a disaster! We're living in a hovel that smells like shit, pretending it's what we want."

To me, it seemed an overreaction. Maira was out of diapers by then and the place smelled fine. It was small but there were the remnants of a painting studio and his writing desk and books. It didn't seem so destitute to me.

Still, I was surprised when he shared his new plan with me one evening when I got home from the store with Maira on my hip. The oven was on and he pulled out a pizza he'd been warming for us and opened a couple of beers.

"I'm going to circumnavigate the globe," he said. "It's the only way I can really write this book."

I suppose I looked somewhat stunned. I certainly felt that way.

"I'm not leaving you. I want you to come with me."

"Me and Maira?"

"Of course," he smiled. "I wouldn't expect you to leave our little friend behind."

I nodded. "I thought we were over that. I thought you meant to stay."

"I'm asking you to come with me."

"For how long?"

"Maybe a year."

"Will we ever come back?"

"Well, maybe not to this exact place," he said, "but North America for sure."

"It's too fast. I need time."

"Okay. We can talk some more when I get home."

Sitting in the kitchen late that night, after he'd gone to the bar and Maira was asleep, I called Iona.

"You think I should go, don't you?" I asked her.

"Only if you can go and take all of you along. It's no good going anywhere and leaving a part of you behind."

"Isn't some part of you still here?" I asked her.

"People I love are there, but I think I'm all here."

"I don't know about that," I said and we both laughed.

Findlay came home a bit drunk and tried to explain his reasons. "It's what I need to do if I'm going to write this novel. It has to take priority. It's the only way I'm ever going to grow, Eileen. Come with me; people in India love children."

"She's too young."

"There are babies all over the world."

"Yes," I said, "but they aren't travelling. They're at home with their families."

"This is important to me."

"Can't it wait a year?"

"Sometimes children just have to learn to roll with it," he said.

"I don't think it's good for her to go."

"You're always going to put her first, aren't you?"

"She's just a baby."

"I didn't mean you shouldn't. I think it's good that you do."

"It's good if you do, too."

He took a deep sigh, as if he was dealing with a child who couldn't understand him.

"I'll be back by Christmas. This journey is not a statement about how much I love you. Don't make it about that."

"Don't you think there's some way to grow right here?"

"I'm stuck. I can't write. I can't think."

For some reason when he left that time, he didn't feel so much like one of my own.

Francis was not much comfort when I called him looking for sympathy.

"I'm sorry," he said. "What are you going to do?"

"There's a woman downstairs who can babysit sometimes and I'm allowed to take her to work with me."

"Findlay will be better when he gets back. He needs to reinvent himself."

"So do I! I'm trying to do that. Why does it always have to be the geographical solution?"

"Sometimes it's the only option."

"What about Maira?" I said.

"She has you."

⁂

He'd been gone five months when Mark and his girlfriend moved out. The night before they left, they came to my apartment for lasagna and wine. Mark was quiet and Kate was friendly as always. They said they regretted going but Kate was accepted at Concordia and they liked the idea of a Montreal adventure. None of us mentioned Findlay.

"I'm sure going to miss you," I said. "I hope you come to visit before Maira gets too big."

Mark nodded. "Oh, we will." But I didn't believe him.

A couple moved in who never smiled when we passed on the stairs. About three weeks after the move, voices grew loud at night while Maira was sleeping. There seemed to be two men with the woman. Then the woman was screaming and there was the sound of glass breaking. Someone was trying to get into *our* apartment, knocking and kicking at the door. I could hear a drunken male voice yelling, "Let me in. He'll kill me."

I yelled back, "I'm calling the police." The people left right away and when the police came I opened the door to talk to them. The hallway floor and walls were smeared with blood and there were broken beer bottles on the stairs.

Maira was still sleeping when I went to check on her. It was important to me that she never had any recall of this incident. We moved within the month to the main floor of a house in the north end.

Findlay came home soon after and went to look for us at the apartment. The woman managing the place opened the door a crack and looked out through a chain.

"They're gone. Sorry, buddy."

"Do you have an address?"

"Why would I give it to you if I did?"

He never liked to be questioned and no doubt this conversation was a little taxing. "I'm her boyfriend."

"If that's so, where have you been, and why didn't she give it to you herself?"

It was the weekend and he was not able to find us until Monday when I went to work at the store. His eyes were piercing and he spoke in a muffled whisper, as if he was trying to contain his fury, when he told me the story of searching for us. I stepped out to the back storage area so that we wouldn't make a scene, and amid the cases and stacks of romantic novels, he hissed from between clenched teeth, "You could have left a message for me. How do you think it felt to come all the way back here and not be able to find you?"

"You found me."

"I called your parents."

"How did that go?" I asked him.

"What did you say to them about me?"

"There was nothing to say."

"Don't ever do that again."

"Don't ever go away again," I said.

"That's extortion. Every time I go away, you're going to disappear?"

"How does that hurt you?" I asked.

"I have a right to know where you are."

"If you ever find another woman who loves you, don't abandon her. Then you'll have a right to know where she is."

"Is that what this is all about? You're splitting up with me?"

"There's nothing to split." I said.

When he realized I was serious, he just nodded and left without another word. He wasn't as relieved as I expected him to be. I thought I was letting him off the hook.

Home for him became a rented warehouse space with rough wood floors, high wood-beamed ceilings and big windows. He put a mattress in one corner and set up a kitchen that did not likely comply with any municipal bylaws. Maira was somewhat shy with him, as little ones are with strangers, but she got used to him and went with him to his place. He said she liked it there, running up and down its long length. On one of these occasions, when he'd brought her home, I asked him for money to help with her shoes. He said, "You're just asking for that to be hurtful. You know I have no money."

He called a week later.

"I'm going west. I'm obviously no good to you here."

"What about Maira?"

"I'd like to pick her up this afternoon so we can say goodbye."

He arrived on a motorcycle with a helmet for Maira that had no face guard. She was so excited to hear him say, "Wanna go for a ride with me?" she jumped in the air.

"She can't hold on," I said.

"Don't spoil this. I'll put her in front of me."

I shouldn't have, but I let them go. For the next hour I sat on the front steps and waited. When they arrived back I thought my heart would explode.

Maira's eyes were shining and her smile was beaming. She had chocolate ice cream all down her chin and the front of her jacket.

I pulled her off the bike and set her down on the sidewalk. Findlay got off too and bent down to her level to say goodbye.

"When I come back, I'll take you for a ride again."

She ran a little excited circle around him.

I smiled at her and met his eyes. "We'll see," I said.

This time we both watched him ride away.

Perhaps we should have gone with him. Perhaps he was right and I had no courage.

When I spoke with Iona about it by phone, she said, "You just don't love him. And there's nothing to be done about that."

"I would have gone if I'd thought we were going toward something instead of just away!"

"Sometimes you don't know which one it is. Sometimes you just have to move."

The weekend after Findlay left, Maira and I went home for a visit. The train ride was different than the first one I'd ever taken on the trip to Toronto a lifetime ago. Even the most disrespectful characters show deference to mothers with small children. They pride themselves on it. We were quite comfortable for the eight or nine hours it took to make the journey. Maira was fascinated and engaged by everything she saw and studied people as if they might be someone she knew. It seemed too early to teach her that staring was considered rude, so I let her do it.

As we stepped down from the train I saw them waiting: Mama with her raised eyebrows looking as if she expected a miracle to appear. I had Maira on my hip and when she saw Mama she started jumping and laughing so that it was hard to keep hold of her.

That weekend, Neil took Maira out to pick blueberries at the edge of the woods. She stood on an anthill while they picked and soon was covered with ants climbing up her legs under her pants and biting her with quick sharp stings. She shrieked and pulled at her clothes, so he picked her up and ran back to the house with her in his arms yelling, "Pour a bath! She's got ants in her pants!" He handed her over to Mama and me and we put her in the bathtub and pulled off her clothing while the water ran. The ants floated away from her body and swirled into the drain.

Eventually she stopped crying and came down the stairs dressed in her pajamas and trailing the blanket she was wrapped in. All of this drama on a sunny afternoon. By the time she reached the bottom of the stairs, Neil couldn't resist teasing, his smile a mile wide. "Here's the little miss with ants in her pants."

Maira laughed and did a little kick that was reminiscent of a jig. "Ants in my pants, ants in my pants."

There was great freedom in the way I loved her.

25

Culturally imperative migration was an idea that Francis introduced to me when he came home to the island after living away for so long. It was the first time it crossed my mind that we were meant to leave, or that leaving has taken on a place of honour, because for generations there has been no other choice. It may have been framed as adventure but there is no disguising the mourning in the songs that are sung here. Even the new ones echo verses from the Hebrides, songs of loss. It may be that buried in our cultural subconscious is the deeply held belief that to travel away is to come into our own and that mourning for home is inevitable.

Francis pulled up to the front of the house in early evening while I was sitting in a second-storey window seat overlooking the street. He didn't notice me sitting there, so I had a good chance to watch him undetected. He had a new Volvo, very trim and solid-looking. I thought he belonged in a movie from another era when he got out of the car wearing a suit and tie. It was so unlike him. It seemed designed to say, "You see, I'm doing very well now. I'm in complete control of my life." But he was wearing gossamer layers of self-respect and seemed a bit transparent at the edges. I wondered if he was well. Now I see that the attempt at solidity made more sense than I would allow at the time, and was necessary if he was to maintain his dignity.

Then the doorbell was ringing and I was running downstairs, forgetting I ever thought there was anything awry. When I opened the door, and he stepped into the front hall with that grin of his, he brought so much light with him I didn't see the fragility. Maira ran down behind me and hung back because she didn't know him. "Hey! Who is this beautiful girl?" he asked. "Is this Maira? Wow. Hi, Maira."

"Hi," she said quietly. "Are you coming to Gramma's with us?"

"You bet. Are you ready to go?"

"Not *now*," she said, thinking he was teasing.

He looked at me. "Why not now?"

"They aren't expecting us until tomorrow," I said, "and it's a five-hour trip and Maira is already in her pajamas."

I knew it would be best if we could arrive in early afternoon when Mama would still have some energy to visit. Or maybe I just wanted him to myself for a while.

"Okay, okay. I can adjust."

"Let me get your bag from the car," I offered.

"Let's leave it there, it weighs a ton."

Maira offered her hand and he raised his eyebrows at me as he followed her upstairs.

After I got her to sleep, I brought out the steak I'd bought for him that afternoon at the butcher. "You must be starved."

"You know, I ate a big dinner on the road. Just some toast and jam for dessert would be good."

I wondered about his health one more time.

"Is Mama okay?" he asked.

"It's up and down but she doesn't complain."

There was no mention at all about him talking to Neil. Everyone but Mama assumed he simply wouldn't. They both used her as a go-between. Francis would talk to her for half an hour on the phone and only at the end send his formal regards to Neil. She believed Neil loved Francis with a fierceness he could not express, and by then she would have welcomed an explosion if it meant the lid coming off the vessel that contained his heart.

We left at sunrise the next morning and as we sailed through the countryside in his solid new car, I imagined Neil and Mama were eating their breakfast and silently reading the paper. I supposed Neil was worrying about it being too late for him to ever reconcile with Francis, and that Mama was harbouring hopes that Francis's homecoming was a healing balm that only needed application for the family wound to close.

That August day in 1984, when we crossed the causeway to the island, Francis described how we would look if we could be seen from above, gliding through the blue and green forest. As he spoke, he took one hand off the wheel and used it to describe his view of us from somewhere up above.

"We're part of some great migratory trend that stretches from island to island all over the world, heading for a destination that may not even be there anymore. I certainly can't picture it."

"It's there, all right. It didn't disappear because you went away."

"There wasn't much choice about leaving, was there? That was the story. We're a leaving kind of people."

Maira was in the back seat, at six years old looking almost exactly like my sister Iona, which lent a strange, timeless aura to our travel. When we approached the causeway, Francis got her giggling by speaking in a tour guide voice. She'd been thinking a lot about humour and asking me questions about it, and she could tell this was meant to be funny,

"Okay, folks, straight ahead you can see what used to be an island in the Atlantic Ocean. It's tethered to the continent now, but it will never give up its wild and solitary ways. It has a very long memory." Maira laughed at what she thought was his exaggeration and said, "That's the way it goes, Bud."

He looked at me. "What kind of conversations do you carry on with this child?"

"Is that sarcasm?" she asked.

"No, it is not," he said, "it's total confusion," which sent her into peals of laughter as she picked up on his tone. The way she joined him gained her a special island of her own in his affection.

He had only once before crossed over the man-made spit of land that separated island from mainland, and at that time he was travelling in the other direction and too young to really get his bearings. So he showed some excitement when he saw the island's landscape rising into view. "Wow, I do remember. It looks just the same. I thought I didn't remember."

"I don't know how that would be possible."

"It was a long time ago. No real connection anymore."

We drove in silence for some time until we realized Maira was asleep and we could talk without an inquisition. I remarked on the strangeness of his staying away from the island for so long, but he rebutted that.

"I knew I could see my family anywhere in the world. I didn't need to be here to do that." We'd been having this discussion for a long time and I was glad it was finally going to be over. In fact, for years, whenever anyone would suggest he might come home for a family reunion, he claimed to be more pragmatic about family connection than the rest of us.

That day in the car I couldn't let him get away with it. "I don't think that's pragmatism. I think that's something else."

"Like what?"

"Like some kind of stubborn pride, or maybe fear."

"Oh well!" he threw his hands up while driving, "Thanks for the encouragement!" he complained. Then he started laughing and almost put the car off the road. I tensed without crying out, not wanting to wake Maira. She stirred but settled as soon as the car was on track, and I didn't have much to say for a while. I suppose he had a right to be a bit on edge. He was the only one who knew to what extent his life was in transition.

His musings on the nature of connection, or lack of, caused me to recall a recurring vision I had as a small girl. I imagined gossamer threads of light that grew from the tips of my fingers so that everywhere I went, I left a fine white filament of energy behind and, if it could be made visible, the picture of my life, over time, would be a great tangle of luminous yarn connecting me to all of those I'd touched.

When I tried to share this vision with Francis he responded by saying, "You were a very odd child."

"I suppose you were so normal," I replied.

When Mama fell and landed in hospital in the previous June, Francis had offered to come home to see her. This time she said, "Yes. Yes, come for the reunion in August. We're celebrating our fortieth. I'll be better by then." She was always determined she would recover quickly and sometimes she did.

She wanted Neil to call Francis to confirm it. I was home with Maira and while I was putting her to bed, I heard Mama quietly chiding Neil, who remained intransigent in his refusal to reach out. "Why would it be that I had to ask my own son to come home to visit me?"

"Just to let him know he's welcome."

"When did I ever imply he wasn't welcome?"

"You never accepted him the way he is," she replied.

"I never rejected him! He just has a chip on his shoulder." The strength of feeling and the catch in his voice when he made this declaration stopped her from further attempts at convincing. It was another glimpse into the anguish he felt over his broken relationship with his eldest son. She didn't reply and he spoke again. "It's up to him now."

Later that night we drank tea while Neil was in the basement. I suggested the problem with both Neil and Francis was pride. Mama agreed with this theory.

"Pride is a black hole. Sucks all the light in."

I'd called and asked Francis to pick me up in Halifax with Maira because I wanted to see what his mood was and because no one had been able to tell him that Mama had fallen again and that she hadn't really got up. She was using a wheelchair but she'd sworn us to secrecy because the nature of her illness sometimes granted a quick turnaround in symptoms, and she didn't want him to be imagining her sick. So Iona, who was coming for the festivities anyway, agreed to arrive home early the day before the party to try to prepare our father for Francis's coming. My job was to drive across the island with him and try to break it to him that Mama couldn't walk.

Iona was living on the Gulf Islands on the west coast at that time with her extended family. She had a partner, Jim, who had two kids, and Jim's mother and father, and the kids' mother, who lived in a cabin on the property. It sounded complicated but when Maira and I visited there the previous summer it had all felt quite normal.

I did have an unnamable feeling on that trip that the ocean was in the wrong place, always on the wrong side of me regardless of where I was standing. This was a physical sensation but felt strangely delusional. Later when I tried to explain it to Mama, she had her own theory. "Probably wherever the sun was rising was where you expected to find the sea."

When she'd had this most recent relapse, Maira and I made the trip by bus from Halifax to see her every weekend. As soon as we arrived, Maira climbed up beside her with a book and read to her while the young woman who helped on weekdays took me aside and told me how she had been.

"Her temperature was all off this week. She sits outside under the apple tree with her feet in one pan of water and her hands in another one on her lap. She seems to like that. Your father says she's fine, too much of a lady to sweat, that's all."

"Don't listen to her," Mama told me after she left. "She's a worrier."

She was very ill on some days. One weekend when we arrived she could barely speak but the way she looked at us and the one word she uttered slowly, "Youuu…" expressed more love than can be found in many lengthier assurances. She couldn't get up for more than a couple of hours.

Somehow she managed to remain grateful. As she lay on the verandah daybed in the cool part of a July evening, after she'd regained her speech, she said, "So many parts of me have failed, but my eyes were never taken. It was my worst fear." That summer there was never a sense that the best days were gone. In fact, she seemed to have found a new sense of the future, planning to have the boys' room painted and hanging new curtains in the girls' room to accommodate the visitors who were coming. It may have been the upcoming party that lifted her spirits but, more likely, it was because Francis was coming home at last and we would all be in one place together again.

Aunt Effie was in charge of the reunion and when I told her on the phone that Francis was coming, she asked, "Do you think he'll have a fella with him?" and I knew she said it so that I would not feel I was the keeper of a secret. Family members often tried to ask about him, thinking I knew more than they did about his life and loves. But for all of his good nature, Francis was a very private man and never prone, as some of us are, to gossiping about himself.

We decided to stop for tea in Port Hawkesbury and pulled in at a roadside phone booth to call and say we'd be another couple of hours. Iona answered the phone and spoke to me in that slow, steady way of someone who is in shock and has no idea how she feels.

"Mama's gone, Eileen."

"Where?"

"She died very early this morning. We called, but you'd already left."

The night before, she'd asked to be taken out to the verandah to watch the August stars as they leapt from their places and plunged to some unknown destination in a final streak of light. Although I could never have admitted this possibility at the time, perhaps as the last stars winked out at sunrise, she decided to go with them.

Neil was there with Joe and Iona. "It was a seizure," she said. "It was so awful, Eileen. It looked as if her soul was struggling to tear itself away from her body." Iona was weeping inconsolably by then, so Stella took the phone from her. "Hello, dear, I'm sorry you have to hear this when you're on the road. Drive carefully now. Tell Francis we love him."

Before I got back to the car he had already jumped out, asking, "What's wrong?" I put my arms around him and said, "Mama." Maira looked more worried than a six-year-old ever should, staring at me through the rolled-up window from the back seat.

After we started back on the journey, the radiator obliged us by boiling over. We were able to pretend we were much dismayed but in truth it allowed us to focus on something that was entirely of this world and so to calm ourselves a little. For Maira, it was a fascinating event and I'm sure if someone asked her now about the day my mother died, she would relate in detail about the steam rising from the hood of the car somewhere near Mama's family farm and cruising into a garage on the side of the road there, as if we had all the time in the world. The man who ran the garage knew us and tried to tease us about having to get a couple of rooms at the hotel because it would take so long to find the parts for an exotic car like that, but he looked puzzled when he could see our nods were tinged with some kind of panic. Francis said quietly, "Our mother died this morning and we really are hoping to get home tonight to be with the rest of the family."

The man's whole demeanor changed then. "Go next door to the restaurant and have some tea or some lunch. We'll find the part in Hawkesbury or bring one from Sydney and you'll be on your way in no time after that."

The smiling, white-haired woman who stood behind the counter wearing a blue print apron was the man's wife, who was known to us and, of course, knew our mother. "You poor things. Come inside to the kitchen," she insisted. "I'll make you some breakfast. Don't think about a thing." We sat in a kitchen booth intended for family meals and special restaurant guests. Maira ate pancakes with strawberries and whipped cream, and kept suggesting that I eat the scrambled eggs sandwich that lay on my plate.

"Eat, Mama," she said. "You'll get cranky if you don't eat." The kindly woman asked if I'd like something else, but when I looked in her eyes and said the sandwich was perfect, she nodded in understanding.

"She died watching the stars," I said.

"She told me once when I was just a girl that it was a woman astronomer who discovered stars were made of hydrogen. Up until then I never knew a woman could be an astronomer. I think she would have liked to be one herself."

"I think you're right," I said.

When we finally got on our way, she gave Maira a Cherry Blossom chocolate bar. A few miles down the road she spilled the sweet liquid on her dress and wanted to stop and change before we got to the house because she knew there would be a lot of people there. She was tearful and insistent, and I could see that the day had been a strain for her. Francis quietly pulled over to the side of the road and she and I rummaged in a suitcase in the trunk of the car until we found a dress she wanted. Before she got back in the car she hugged me and brushed my face with her hand, as if she was the parent comforting her child. Somewhere on the road, she fell asleep again and Francis and I said almost nothing until we pulled into the yard at home around nine o'clock.

Even though she'd been unwell, Mama had refused to delay the re-union because she said that she might not get another chance to see everyone together without it being someone's funeral. We were arriving just two days before the date set for the event, so most of the family was already there. There were thirty-five people milling about the house and the yard that evening, some of them sitting on the verandah or under the tree, and although I appreciated their kindness and warmth, I felt I would rather sink into the grass and disappear completely than have to speak to anyone.

Neil slowly opened the screen door and came out onto the verandah to greet us. You could tell he'd been crying and the slump of his shoulders, as if he was carrying a huge weight, belied the vacant, emotionless face he was presenting to the world. When he saw Francis he took a sharp intake of breath and his eyes filled. When he could speak he put his hand out to shake Francis's and all he said was, "She really wanted you here."

Our sister Stella rescued us from the moment by emerging from the house and throwing her arms around each of us in succession and saying how glad she was to see us. It occurred to me she was playing Mama's role for us. I was grateful to her because it was obvious someone would have to do it if we were going to survive the week or the rest of our lives. Never mind that she was living in Calgary and married to a fellow who was always too busy with his business to come out for a visit. She had her three teenagers with her, so there was every indication that her life was full and she would have the strength to fill in some missing piece of mother love for the rest of us. I don't know who did that for her.

One by one, we were greeted by the others who had arrived already from across the country. Joe, who was living outside of Halifax with his wife and five kids, running a motel business, came down early to help with the rental of tables and other things for the hall where they were planning to hold the big do. That afternoon he'd called his wife to say he could not drive back for them, and she would have to come on her own with the children before the wake planned for the next day. Iona had arrived days earlier and I'd seen her when she stopped with me in Halifax on the way. Murdoch came from San Francisco, where he was working for an investment company, and we'd all been thrilled he was coming home because we didn't get to see him so often either. He was twenty-seven and had no new family yet.

The wake was held the next day and all of Aunt Effie's good grace could not keep it from being a sharp and piercing thing. The comments were repetitive if meant well. "She looks so good. Doesn't she? She could be sleeping," but inside I was screaming, "No, she does not. She doesn't look good to me at all." The hardest part was the receiving line, when the right thing to do is to stand in a line, press hands and search the sympathetic eyes of others at a time when all one wishes to do is hide under a bed somewhere, preferably your mother's bed, while you wait for her to wake up. One of Mama's old card-playing friends held my hand in both of hers so that I could not escape, even in my imagination, and whispered, "It's probably a blessing. Who could blame her if she just gave up? It was harder than most of us knew."

Just those three little sentences, uttered with such well meaning, caused me to feel so nauseous that I barely made it to the bathroom in the funeral parlour before throwing up. There was velvet wallpaper in there and it seemed a contradiction to me. How could Mama be dead in a place with velvet wallpaper? The idea that she would give up and leave us to avoid her pain was unthinkable. I held on to the sink and felt wave after wave of nausea pass over me.

Eventually my brain stopped burning and I could breathe again, but when I returned to the wake I was no longer able to keep up with the expectations of civility. Stella could see that I needed a break and suggested that Francis should walk me home, but I insisted on going alone. It was incredibly quiet on the streets and I thought perhaps the whole town and even the birds were in mourning. I refused to recognize the skeptic who shares my mind when she weighed into the conversation and suggested I was being melodramatic in my grief.

It was a great relief to shut the door behind me when I arrived home, and I thanked God for giving me a moment alone. I locked all the doors and wept and wept and after an hour was no closer to being drained than when I started. Mixed in with the grief was a shame, one I'd never really acknowledged before, that it could have been too much for her. I couldn't bear the idea that her life may have been so painful she wanted to get away from it, because that would mean I didn't really know her and that she had been able to conceal herself from us.

I climbed into her wardrobe and rubbed the threads of the folds of one of her dresses and examined all the cuffs and small pockets of her clothing, trying desperately to find her there. When I stopped crying, all that was left was a clicking feeling in my mind where my thoughts should be, like a record skipping. Under this annoying tick, a barely audible phrase kept repeating like a prayer, "Please, please, oh, please. I'll do anything."

When the others came home I was pretending to sleep and didn't rise until they'd all talked themselves out. After midnight I managed to open the door and wander out into the yard. The slender moon did not interfere with the visibility of the stars falling from the sky, and I knew I was looking at something similar to her last vision of earth. Over the next few hours, there was a continuous rush of falling, streaking cosmic debris as the night gradually moved toward what she would have called "the fullness of its glory."

The strongest image I am left with from the funeral is of Francis crouching by the grave, after the priest had said the words, as the rest of us stumbled off through the uneven cemetery ground to the cars. Neil was leaning heavily on a tree, as if it was all he could do to stand, watching him. I sent Maira back to get Francis, so we could all go home.

In the days that followed they pretended they had reconciled, but in the face of her death they both felt a great shame that they had clung to their disagreement for so long. When Francis and I got back into his car to return to Halifax, there was more like a vacuum between them than a wall. Every time I saw Neil in the year after, he would get around to saying, "All she wanted was to see Francis at home."

I couldn't find the cruelty it would have taken to say, "All she wanted was to see you together."

Christmas that year was as it always is in the year after a loved one has died. Hollow. There was pretended surprise and pleasure on all sides when we opened the gifts, and the meal was fine, although we said it wasn't as good as Mama would make. But it all rang false and even, or especially, Maira could tell. "How long are we going to be sad?"

Neil replied, "I think that will be different for each of us."

When I came down for my habitual glass of milk around midnight, I found him standing in the dark with his arms folded on top of the radio and his head resting on them as I'd seem him do so many years before. Francis's quiet voice extolled the virtues of Etta James.

26

There was always some kind of intensity about Neil, unless I am mistaken and we all, both the loved and the unloved, feel this way about our parents. As we were driving home from grocery shopping on one of my weekend visits in the spring, he asked, "Do you think it's okay to leave Maira next door for a few more minutes?"

"Sure, I think so. Why?"

"Do you want to see where I first met your mother?"

"Yes, I would. I would."

It was raining and perhaps the swish of the wiper blades and the greyness of the day made us both especially well disposed to contemplation. When we pulled up to a softened brick building in Whitney Pier, he jumped out of the car and quickly moved around to the other side to open the door for me. Then he stood and waited for me to join him in staring up at the steps and the closed, locked door of the empty building.

He wore a canvas fedora that day and it flew off in the wind as he crossed the yard and would have been lost, except that I saw it lifting from his head and ran to catch it as if it was a Frisbee that had been tossed about among my friends. He didn't replace the hat and stood facing the wind and speaking above it, as if to a crowd of people. "She was standing right there the first time I saw her. She was beautiful, you know." He said this as if I might not have known that, but of course he was thinking of a time in her life when I did not exist and she was, no doubt, even more beautiful then.

He'd changed in a lot of unusual ways, even developed an interest in visualization, saying it was a way to paint without all the mess. When Mama was alive she was determined to keep our lives stable in the face of our poverty and his unpredictable spells of "sleepwalking." Perhaps her intense desire for normality had caused him to avoid opinions and actions that might be thought eccentric. With all of us gone, and the rages cooled by time, he no longer felt the same compunction to keep his dreams and unorthodox theories to himself. Perhaps he had always been a complicated man masquerading as a simple one.

We retreated to the car and sat for a while with the engine off, listening to the rain and waiting for something. He finally said, "I didn't deserve her. But she never held that against me." Then he turned to me and asked, "What happened between you and Maira's father?"

"I don't know. I guess I gave up on him."

"Dear God, I'm glad your mother never thought of that," he said. Then he smiled a little so I'd know he'd meant it as a joke on himself and not a criticism of me.

After some time spent watching the rain fall quietly on the windshield, Neil turned to me as if he'd read the undercurrents of my thoughts. "The important thing is to find some place to be and stay there. Don't keep turning away or you'll never find yourself anywhere."

I didn't know how to tell him how it was for me right then, even though his advice suggested he already knew. The year before Mama died and after Maira had started school full-time, I'd applied to do a show in Toronto and been accepted. It was the only solo show I'd had since graduation and the only one that mattered. Now, as a result of that show, I'd been offered a job teaching art in Toronto in the fall and there would be time to paint during the day while Maira was at school. If I took it, I'd only see him between semesters.

Somehow my world no longer fit its boundaries and I could feel myself being torn in two by the desire to be there forever and the need to travel away. I'm sure he experienced or at least understood this straining toward two different perfections: on one side the perfect loyalty to a people and a place, and on the other the powerful, almost mythic, imperative to leave. He must have known that the yearning for a place to begin again and the mourning for the place left behind were bred into my bones.

When Maira and I were all packed up and ready to leave, standing on the verandah before we got in the car to go to the train station, he said something like, "There's lots of room for you. You don't need to be on your own in Halifax when there's a home for you here." My heart contracted and expanded too quickly and all I could do was nod.

Maira fell asleep in my arms before we reached Halifax, so I carried her from the passenger car and a porter carried our suitcase along to the street to hail a cab. She didn't wake up on the drive to our apartment until I drew her out of the taxi. While I stood with the fare in my hand, waiting for the driver to haul our bags from the trunk, she stood on the sidewalk, looking up at the house. She pulled on my skirt for attention and when I looked at her she said, "We're home, Mama."

"Yes, we are."

"Do you think Daddy will ever come home?"

I turned to face the driver, who was standing with our bags, pretending not to hear, and handed him the fare.

"Do you need some help with those bags?"

"No, no, we're fine."

When he turned away, I bent down to help Maira with her small backpack and said, "He may never live here. But he always thinks of you. And you'll see him again."

"He's going to take me for a ride on his motorcycle."

"Yes, he is."

∞

It was closer to summer when the call came.

"I had to steal Francis's phone book to get your address because he doesn't want you to know he's sick. He has cancer. I think he'd like to see you."

I felt a flush of nausea.

Maira was sitting at the table practising her printing. The ray of light that fell across her paper was particularly steady and warm and held a million motes of dust. I wanted to fling the phone across the room, but instead I put it down carefully and let it go quickly as if it was a thing that might burn me. A disembodied voice from somewhere inside of me spoke: "So this is how he'll come home to us."

Maira looked up at me when she heard the phone rattle on its cradle, so I turned to leave the room in case my face might show the pain.

"Who was that?" she asked, bending to her printing again.

"It was Corry, a friend of Francis's. He says Francis wants to see us."

"Why didn't he call himself?"

"I think he… might be too sick."

She quickly raised her head again. Perhaps my tone betrayed me. "Want to go to the park?" I asked.

∞

The wait, in my own doctor's office the next day, was agonizingly long. It was a clinic near our apartment that served the community. There were ten people in the waiting room when I squeezed myself into the last leather chair with wooden arms that kept some bit of space between us. A dog-eared copy of a *National Geographic* about Africa sat on the side table and wide-eyed children beckoned me from its cover. Reading it distracted me while people came and went. I was hoping for a place where they could fit me in, but after an hour and a half I could hardly keep my tears at bay and knew more than I really could absorb about the crisis of hunger in those children's lives.

When I finally got up to tell the receptionist, "I have to go now. I'll come back soon," she sprang into action.

"No, no, don't go. Let me tell her you're going." When the doctor heard what was happening she decided to see me next. It was all I could do to not hug the receptionist when she told me. I wonder now what she thought was wrong with me.

The doctor was a young woman who had attended Maira's birth and I trusted her to be honest with me. Her dark hair was pulled back in a ponytail and she sat very straight in her chair when she confirmed my fears that this kind of cancer, Kaposi's sarcoma the friend had said, was linked to the new disease we were hearing about. "He may have AIDS," she said with her clear-eyed gaze. "You should ask him. You won't catch it. You must be careful if there's blood for any reason, but it's not airborne."

An hour later, on the phone talking to Neil, I managed to keep the tears and the truth at bay.

"I'd like to bring Maira down to stay with you for a few days. Do you mind?"

"Do I mind having a cherub in the house, you're asking me?"

He always loved to see her and even in his sadness could still stand strong when she leapt into his arms.

After I put Maira to bed that first evening at home, I sat down at the kitchen table with him, waiting for the kettle to boil for our evening tea. I started with, "I had a call from Toronto."

He nodded his head in a listening posture as he always does when he listens for something he may have misheard, so I continued, "A friend of Francis called to say he's sick."

He stood up suddenly. Then went to pour the tea. With his back to me he asked, "What kind?"

"I think he probably has AIDS."

"No, no, no."

"Yes."

He silently bent his head and rubbed his forehead for a long moment before he spoke. "Give me a few minutes," he said. "I need to think." Then he rose and went to stand in the field outside, staring into the distance as if he was waiting for someone to arrive.

27

"My darling one, my darling one" were the words Neil's mother spoke over and over in the moments when he first came home from war. Neil felt a shock to his somewhat fragile nervous system when she first opened the door. She was so very thin and her complexion so sallow, she seemed a faded copy of the mother he had known.

It was the smile that lit her face when she saw him, and the tears she shed while she held him, her arms encircling him completely, that finally allowed him to breathe as if he had access to all the air in the world and not just the small bubble he'd grown used to occupying.

While she went out to the yard to fill the kettle from the pump, he sat in the kitchen and looked around him. The house was little different from the ones he'd seen in Spain, especially in the way the pall of poverty had fallen equally on both.

His mother set the tea to boil on the back of the stove and sat down with him. "You're not hurt?"

"No," he said, "I have no injuries at all."

Then, looking around, motioning to the bedroom door off the kitchen, he asked, "Where's himself today?"

She couldn't look at him and gave her head a shake, then motioned with one hand toward the closed door. He got up quickly and impatiently, thinking he would find his stepfather passed out in his own vomit, and was unprepared for what he confronted in the tiny darkened room. Jack was lain out on the bed like a corpse, hands folded on his chest but with his eyes open and watching Neil when he moved toward him. The room smelled of stale breath, urine and fear. It was an odour that he'd learned to live with in the trenches in Teruel. Jack looked much older, shrivelled, and didn't speak when Neil said to him, "Looks like they got you too."

He stood there for a long moment, looking into the stricken eyes of this man who had caused him so much pain, then turned and went back to the kitchen, where he leaned with both hands on the table and for the first time in ten years wept inconsolably. When he managed to stop himself by taking great gulping breaths of air, he looked at his mother, who said, "Jack had a stroke but refused to die."

"Isn't that just like him," said Neil and his tears turned to uncontrollable laughter that shook his body and made the teacups on the table rattle. His mother joined in after a moment and the two of them shared this rollicking laughter, wiping their tears and saying, "Oh my, oh dear, that's terrible," and then starting again. When they sobered up, he asked, "How long has it been like this?"

"Since August," she replied.

"Are you all alone then?"

"I haven't heard from Frank. He seems to have fallen off the face of the earth."

"How are you surviving?"

She looked at her hands and said quietly, "I sold the house," then looked up, saying, "I'm so sorry but we had nothing and they are letting us stay here as long as we want. It was good of them really, and they pay me every month with food and wood and five dollars that the boys scrape together at their jobs. They've said they'll pay me the five dollars every month even if I leave here."

Neil looked through the kitchen window to his neighbour's field.

"I suppose they wouldn't want it to go to anyone else," he said.

"They act as if I'm one of their own."

He had to look away, eyes to the floor, when he answered, "I'm sorry."

"What could you have done?" she said, bringing his eyes back to hers.

So he stayed. He slept inside until the weather turned warmer and then made up the shed behind the house into a kind of bedroom with a little cot and a table where he could read. He helped with Jack, feeding him soup and wiping his face when it dribbled out of his mouth and onto his clothing. He even carried the frail, child-weight body, with the always-searching eyes, to the outhouse in the morning and at night and cleaned him up when they didn't make it on time. He understood the irony that this gave him a reason to live when he so desperately needed one.

One morning after he'd settled Jack in the bed, his mother appeared in the kitchen, having walked back from the village. She was winded and held a letter in her hand.

"Frank has enlisted. He's joined the RCAF."

"I suppose that's a better place to be than on the ground."

He pushed his chair back and went to stand outside.

In the spring, Jack died in his sleep. Neil stood beside the bed, holding his mother's elbow as if they were about to cross the road.

He told himself he felt nothing. *Okay then*, he thought, *I have no one but myself to blame now.*

His mother packed Jack's things off to the neighbours a bit more quickly than was polite. He understood that well, but shuddered when he came home for supper and found the rooms cleaned and bare of small possessions. She heard him come up the outside steps and open the screen door to the kitchen. When he entered, she stood in the middle of the room where the table should be and spoke immediately. "I heard from my brother in Pictou. I'm going to go there."

"You don't need to go. We can get by."

"You've done enough," was all she'd say. "I'm sorry about the house."

"No, really, we'll be all right. I can get some work. It will be good to be home."

She looked through the window to the field.

"The neighbours have asked me how long I intend to stay. They always thought I'd go to Pictou when Jack died. They want the house. One of the boys is getting married."

"Ah."

"It was reasonable of them to think it. They knew I wouldn't stay alone and I hadn't heard from you. They own it now."

"They took advantage of you when you were alone."

"They've been very good to me. I don't know how I would have managed without them the last few years."

There was not a great deal to sort out. They packed up her things, leaving the bigger pieces of furniture to be shipped later depending on what her brother might want. The rest was his to keep. "Take your father's tools. He'd want you to have them." They agreed that anything in the shed belonged to him.

He drove the neighbour's truck to the station and she sat beside him with a rose-patterned silk kerchief tied under her chin.

Looking sideways at her, he asked, "How old were you when I was born?"

"That's a roundabout way to ask your mother how old she is. Twenty years ago I was twenty-two years old. I had a three-year-old and a baby. It was the happiest time of my life."

He helped her down from the truck and carried her bag past the curious stationmaster, then through to the platform.

"Wait here. I'll get your ticket."

"Take some money," she said, opening her purse.

"No, I don't need it."

"You will."

He accepted the money. When he returned from the wicket she held him close and said into his ear, "I know they won't mind if you stay in the shed."

"I'll come to visit you after I get on my feet."

She let him go. "I would love to see you whenever you come."

At the door of the train, a porter helped her up the step. "Don't worry, boy, I'll take care of her for you," he said.

Neil drove slowly along the road to the home that was no longer his and tried to take stock of what seemed to be a destitute and solitary life. No house, no job, no family. The neighbour was standing in the yard, pretending to check a fence post, when he pulled in.

"I've good news," he said. Then he looked away to the distance as if expecting someone to come along the road.

Neil followed his gaze and saw nothing.

"They're opening up the colliery. Jobs for young fellas like you."

Thank you," said Neil.

"We're not rushing you. The shed is yours as long as you need it."

It was a long year later that he walked along the village road, having survived the winter. He could not bring himself to go into the mine. He knew that with the arrival of spring he would have to make a change or die of loneliness. It was so difficult to contemplate how to begin again. The devastation of war had left him with no faith in his judgment and no faith at all in a just or good world.

The earth was a brown and muddied mat but the air still winter clean. Robins pecked at the ground in the field beside the road. He entered the general store more for warmth than anything else. There was no money in his pocket but he still had flour, sugar and tea in the shed. He needed nothing else.

The man behind the counter looked up. "Neil," he called out, "I have a letter here with a Pictou postmark." Neil held the small white envelope, addressed in the long, sloping script of his mother, and would have liked to rip it open but the eager eyes of the store owner reminded him that it was a private conversation he wanted with her. He tucked it in his pocket and started home in a better mood than when he'd begun. Arriving back at the shed, he touched the stool that sat outside the door and found the sun had warmed it, so he settled there to read.

My dear boy Neil,

I have very bad news for you and feel quite sick with grief myself. I have heard from the military that our boy Frank is dead. They have sent his number to me as some kind of proof I suppose and two medals that tell us he was a brave soldier. His plane was shot down and he was trying to help his comrade when he was shot himself. It is difficult to continue.

I'm sorry I didn't write to tell you he was going. He wrote from a training base in Portage La Prairie. I wrote back that you fought the war in Spain and were not participating in this one. Please promise me that this is true.

I had no idea he was going out so soon. Perhaps he was not allowed to tell. At least I gave him my love.

My love to you,

Mother

The letter dropped from his hand and he walked out into the field with a weight in the pit of his stomach that caused him to collapse to the muddied field.

Over and over he whispered, "I'm sorry, I'm so sorry."

28

Standing in the small field outside the kitchen door, my father did not appear to be looking at anything in particular—not the star-filled sky or the low berry bushes that surrounded him or the road that passes so close to the house, even though he stared into the distance along its disappearing path. He'd been standing there ever since I broke the news and I wondered if perhaps I should go to him. I wanted to allow him the time he needed to make sense of it all, but I suspected that was more time than the evening held.

When I lifted my head from my own thoughts, Neil's body was filling the frame of the doorway. He looked around the room as if trying to decide where he was before he came forward and sat down slowly on the kitchen stepstool. He kept his arms folded across his chest and he looked at the floor as he spoke.

"Go get him and bring him home. I don't want him to die in some hospital room without his own people around him."

"I have to work."

"They'll give you the time if you tell them why, and you know Maira loves it here in the summer."

Then he raised his head with a question in his eyes, "Are you afraid you'll catch it? Is that why you're leaving her here?"

"No, the doctor says there's nothing to worry about as long as you're careful about blood."

"Then we should ask him to come home."

"I thought you wouldn't want to see him," I said.

"Of course I want to see him! He's my son!"

"Then why didn't you?! What was wrong between you?"

"We got off to a bad start," he said. "I drove him away. No excuse..."

He bent his head. There was a long pause as he contemplated the green and black linoleum, his mouth twisting while he tried to contain his feelings. I wanted to comfort him but didn't want to interrupt.

When he was able to gather himself, he tried again.

"The other night I was sitting alone imagining my own life as a child. All of a sudden there was the face of Jack Fisher coming at me with a rock in his fist. He kept coming and coming until a voice came from inside me, clear as a bell, 'That old man can't hurt you anymore.'" He looked up at me. "I've been braced for a blow my whole life."

Another pause while I took in what he'd said.

"Jack crawled inside me at some point. When I used to hit the boys, I could feel him in the room. When he died I was too cold-hearted to tell him I forgave him."

When he rose to get the tea, I noticed his breath was laboured and he stumbled slightly so that he had to catch himself by grabbing for the edge of the counter. Neither one of us acknowledged this weakness.

For a few minutes the only sound was of cups clinking on saucers. There was the break of tears in Neil's voice when he spoke again.

"I made a botch of the family. I'm sorry about that."

"No you didn't. We're all okay."

"I love all of you."

"I know," I said.

"Then bring him home."

"I'm not sure we can really look after him."

"If I only have a few years left, I'd like to make the most of them. It won't be the first time I took care of someone sick."

That night he called Francis. "I just want to make him an offer," he said.

He went to pick up the wall phone receiver in the kitchen, and then stopped with it in his hand before dialing. "You better get on the upstairs extension. Help me out if I get in trouble."

I lay on the bed in my parents' room, as I used to do with Mama, and spoke into the phone cradled at my ear. "Okay, I'm ready," I said.

The phone rang several times but he persisted and didn't hang up until Francis answered in what seemed to me to be a weakened voice.

"Hello!" Neil spoke loudly into the phone as if he could make himself heard across the distance. "I hope I'm not waking you."

"No, I'm up."

A silence and then, "I heard you're sick."

Francis paused a moment before answering, probably wondering who had betrayed his secret and to what extent. "Oh, I'm all right now, how are you?" he asked Neil.

"I've been worse." Then, after a pause, Neil continued, "Well, you're not sick then, that's good. You could come home for a visit." Perhaps because he wanted his words to be a trail of crumbs that would lead his son back home to him, he said, "I have Eileen here with me on the line."

"Hi, Eileen. Are you eavesdropping?"

"Whenever I can," I said.

He laughed and Neil sounded hopeful in pushing his case.

"Why not come for a week?"

"It's awfully hard to get the time off," Francis said.

"Oh, I understand that," said Neil, finally accepting that Francis was not going to give him this chance to repair the damage and hoping that I would have better luck when I got there. "Well, it's good to hear you and we'll talk again. Think about a visit home."

"I'll do that," said Francis.

"Good then, goodbye, goodbye," Neil said as he hung up.

"Are you still there, Eileen?" Francis asked.

"Yes, I am."

"What's up with him?"

"He'd like to see you, I guess."

"It's been a bit of a rough winter. I don't really want to travel right now."

"What do you mean rough?"

"I'm not that well."

"How so?"

"I was going to call you."

I felt so at a loss for what to say. I didn't want to impinge on his privacy but he seemed to have given me an opening.

"What is it?" I asked.

"They say it's cancer."

"Oh no. Francis. Are your friends helping?"

"They try. Most of them work evenings. They come by in the afternoon but they all go home to sleep in their own beds at night."

"Are you able to work at all?"

"No. They're probably going to fire me any day now."

"I'm coming," I said.

"You don't have to."

"I'm coming."

The Air Canada agent was sympathetic when we arrived at the airport and told her about Francis having cancer. She said the red-eye flight to Toronto, leaving at midnight, was full but I should stick around for standby. "This time of night you can always depend on someone staying too long in the bar." Sure enough there were several empty seats, and Neil patted me on the shoulder when they called my name.

"Try to get some sleep," he said.

The trip to Toronto takes a few hours but we were only forty-five minutes in the air when the speaker began to crackle.

"Good evening, passengers, or should I say good morning. I'm afraid our indicators are telling us we to have to put down in Halifax for a brief check of our electrical system. Everything seems to be working perfectly so this is no big concern, but your safety is paramount. We'll only be delayed about half an hour."

"Famous last words," the man behind me uttered quietly.

We sat on the tarmac for an hour. Outside the windows, the dark sky was filled with stars that were not diminished by the lights of this small airport. A lone baggage cart travelled back and forth from another plane to the terminal. When they started to unload ours and the captain could be heard saying we'd have to clear out and wait for another plane that would be leaving in four or five hours, my temples started to throb.

They let us take the blue blankets with us and we all tried to find a bench or chair of some kind to fold up on. Ours was not the only delayed flight and the small airport was full of people trying to endure the night.

There was a large family from India, who had missed their flight, sitting and lying down in an open area. I counted fifteen including adults and babies and a grandmother. Perhaps they too were travelling to a loved one who was ill. They didn't seem happy but were perhaps just unhappy to be in a foreign airport at night. The softness of a language I didn't understand comforted and lulled me into something resembling sleep.

Even when we finally boarded the plane at sunrise, I was in a soporific trance until the drone of the small aircraft set my nerves on edge as it landed. I took long, deep breaths to control my impatience with the woman who stood in my way in the aisle and took so long gathering her things. She chatted the whole time about the weather in Toronto. "I hope you're staying a while," she said. "This is going to be a fantastic summer. I feel it in my bones."

By the time I got outside, the lineup for cabs was long, so eventually I gave up and found a small shuttle bus going downtown. When we passed through Yorkville, I was in a headache fog and happy to get off the bus and walk part of the way to the same apartment Francis had lived in for years. The friend who'd called to tell me Francis was sick let me in. He had a key because he often came by in the morning. He said, "He's been sleeping ever since I got here. Didn't want to wake him."

With that, the door to the bedroom opened and I tried, no doubt unsuccessfully, to conceal my shock at the way Francis looked. He was emaciated, and wearing layers of pajamas, a housecoat and blanket on a warm day. The hardest thing was that he kept his arms by his sides instead of holding them wide to invite a hug as he always has in the past. I went to him too tentatively and made a circle with my arms around his fragile, leaning body. I hoped he couldn't feel the pounding of my heart against its walls and buried my face in the scratchy wool of his blanket.

We sat in his small kitchen that evening after I'd gone out to the deli for take-out. He tried to eat the Oka cheese that was his favourite but the crust of the baguette seemed to be a bit of an effort. When he wasn't eating, he kept his arms across his chest and rocked gently forward and back. I'd never seen him do that before.

"Have you seen Pierce lately?" I asked

He was startled. "Sorry, Eileen. Pierce is gone."

"What do you mean?"

"He called me from San Francisco six months ago. Said he had cancer and asked if I'd come to see him. I met his father. He was different than I thought he'd be. Pierce always talked about how formal a guy he was, but he seemed a lot softer than that to me. When I got there he was standing in the middle of the living room holding *The Pedagogy of Oppression* that he'd picked off Pierce's bookshelf, and I felt a bit sorry for him. I think he was relieved when I introduced myself and he could put the book down. He had a kind handshake. It made me wonder if my father would come if I was sick." He stopped for a moment. "Guess he sent you."

"Do you wish I was him?"

He laughed out loud—a glimpse of his healthy self. "Just think about that now. What do you think?"

He fell back to a more serious attitude almost immediately.

"Anyway, Pierce died that night. I got to see him, though. The morphine had him all over the place but he told me his father had come back and he knew he would. He was so happy about that. About 4 a.m., after they closed his eyes, his dad and I were standing outside the house on the sidewalk and his dad said, "I think it was you he was waiting for.""

I was just trying to be good, so I said, "I think if it was me, I'd be waiting for my father," and right away he said, "Do you see him?"

I said, "Occasionally."

"I wonder if he knows that if you were dying, you'd wait for him."

Francis's knee began to twitch in that unconscious way some people have of dispelling anxiety. "I didn't really mean that in terms of me but I've been thinking about it since."

*

The flight home was excruciating. There were a few lesions on his face and people gave us a wide berth, as if even being within a few feet of him could affect their health. But when we arrived and crossed the tarmac, Maira came running out from the crowd. She stopped short when she was near enough to really see him, because he was so greatly changed. With some vestige of his usually infectious grin, he said, "It's all right, I promise I won't hurt you," then looked up at Neil without saying anything more.

Neil was awkward, fedora in hand. Francis was just as bad. Then Neil patted his back and said, "Okay, let's go home now." So we gathered up his bags and walked, with more resolve than was really necessary at that point, to the car.

When we entered the house, Francis stopped in the hallway and stood for a moment as if he was listening for something. His eyes turned upward to the ceiling but it was drywalled now and the knothole in the wood could not be seen.

"Let me take your bags up," I offered.

"Sure, I'll come with you. You coming, Maira?"

Neil busied himself in the kitchen.

It hadn't crossed my mind until that moment how strange it would be for Francis to sleep in his childhood room. I don't remember where he slept when Mama died. The door swung open with a touch and the cotton curtains blew lightly in the breeze coming through the open dormer windows. The floor was covered in a soft rose and blue area rug that looked like something Mama would have chosen, but I knew it was brand new. A wooden double bed, with a green and blue plaid blanket covering it, was tucked under the slanted ceiling created by the eaves.

"It's a different place," he said.

"He's tried hard to make it nice." I replied, taking his bags and setting the big one on the trunk. "Do you need help to unpack?"

"No, no, I can easily do that."

"Okay then, I'll be on the verandah."

After an hour or so I came back in looking for him, and I heard him and Neil talking in the kitchen. My father's voice was steady and calm.

"I'm sorry for the way I was. I wanted to say that for a long time."

"I never gave you much of chance, did I?" Francis said.

"I suppose we didn't spoil a pair in some ways."

"You saying I'm like you?"

"I'd like to think so," Neil said.

After a moment of silence I showed myself at the door. They were sitting there quietly, my father on the stepstool and Francis straddling a chair. Francis looked up when I entered.

"Do you want to go for a walk?" he asked.

When we left the kitchen to head for the path, he looked back at Neil.

"Would you like to come with us, Dad?"

"Oh no, no, you and Eileen go ahead. I have some things to do here."

Francis nodded and when their eyes met, the old animosity was gone.

The vegetation at the brook was more lush than it had been on the day Iona and I rescued a bird and put it back in its nest. Francis sat on the bank, a bit spent from the walk down the hill, but I had an insurmountable urge to climb the tree and found my footing easily. The branch I shimmied along stretched farther over the water than it used to, but it was more dependable and strong. There was less chance of falling if one were to risk travelling along its length to save a life. I yelled down to him, "You look very small from up here."

"Careful," he said. "I'm still bigger than you."

After I climbed back down, it was an easy walk across the shallow pond to sit side by side on the rock at its centre. "I haven't been here for twenty-five years," he said, looking around as if it was all new.

"Why is that?" I asked him.

He didn't reply right away. I wasn't sure he was even going to acknowledge the question as he gazed across the pond. But then he looked directly at me with one side of his face in sun and one in shadow.

"I couldn't figure out who I was meant to be here."

"Is that all it was?" I asked.

"All it was?"

"Because you were gay?"

"Maybe partly. But I didn't even really know what to think about that then. You know how Gran always said we take care of our own? I didn't know who I belonged to."

"I've always thought if you and Neil had got along..."

"I was just mad at him. I thought a father should have your back. No matter what."

"He wants to make up for that now," I told him.

"I know he does."

"Are you going to miss everyone in Toronto?"

"They'll call. It was too hard for them to watch anyway. They've lost a few people lately."

"You lived there longer than you lived here," I said.

"When I first got there I was ecstatic. Completely reinvented myself. But I had to leave behind the guy who liked kids and goats and played the fiddle. Used to laugh about that with people. Never admitted I missed that guy."

"I missed you when you went away," I said offhandedly, as if it is not the one thing I have wanted to say to him my whole life. In that moment there was no assurance of another chance.

"You were lucky to know where home is. It wasn't that easy for me."

"I'm still trying to figure out who I belong to."

His smile was full of regret.

"You're putting yourself on hold for me. I know that. You're only thirty-two. You have so much life to live."

"I had a dream last night," I said. "Music surrounded me and I was held in a dance embrace so perfect that I became totally calm. I have the same feeling here right now."

⁊○

Boxes of his belongings arrived by truck. Maira and I came home from downtown on a sweltering July day and found him standing in the middle of the living room, wearing a baseball cap and a heavy jacket and swinging to an upbeat version of "Summertime" by Oscar Peterson. The speakers on Neil's old player lent the music a slightly used quality. Records lay in haphazard piles at his feet. The minute he saw us he said, "We need a new stereo."

Neil appeared at the door, having heard our conversation from where he was reading the paper in the kitchen. "You'll have to get it, Eileen. I won't know what to buy. I'll come along though." In the end we all went because it was a wonderful thing to bring the possibility of music home together.

In town the word had got out that he was home and he was sick. When we walked down along the main drag we ran into neighbours and old friends. Everyone stopped, including Francis's old schoolteacher. I remembered him as an imposing man with a receding hairline, but now he was a bald man with a quieter aspect.

"Let me tell you, I was very disappointed when you dropped out, but you have given me a whole world of music I would never have known. I owe you a great deal. I suspect a lot of people feel that way." He patted Francis on the arm before he walked away.

When he did, Francis winked at me.

We found a small portable system at Eaton's that he thought was okay. There was not a lot to choose from. The sales girl was perturbed by his heavy clothing. "God, aren't you sweltering in that jacket? It's eighty degrees out there."

"I have a bit of a chill," he answered with a smile. I think he was pleased she didn't recognize he was so sick.

At first we set the stereo up in the living room and listened to pieces that we'd heard before in kitchens and bedrooms, late at night and on Saturday mornings, Charles Mingus and Chet Baker—Francis music. Neil shook his head in wonder on more than one occasion. "One time, after Mama died, you played a song on the radio about flying that I found very moving. I don't suppose you have that?"

"Do you remember the name, Dad?"

"Oh sure, I think it's called 'I Believe I Can Fly.' It helped me out that night. It was something about believing you could go on."

"How often do you listen to the show?"

"Pretty much whenever I can."

Francis looked at the floor, trying to absorb that idea, and then reached for Etta James.

At first he played music for hours every day. It became part of the atmosphere, often quietly there when I awoke and still a soft hum when night fell. Sometimes I came across him swaying to it with his eyes closed. There was hope in that.

Then we moved the stereo into his room, where he could more easily listen while he was lying down. We moved a TV in there, too. I knew it was a good day if we had Miles Davis instead of *Jeopardy!* as background.

From the early days, he slept erratically and everywhere, and I could never be sure if he was simply dropping in his tracks or making every inch of the house his by experiencing its movements, smells and echoes while he slept. He collapsed in sleep on the stairs one night and I found him there when I went down for a drink of water. I sat on the stair beside him listening to the night richness of frogs and crickets playing their own symphony. The sound of Neil washing dishes in the kitchen added a soft percussion. When he woke, he grinned up at me in the old way.

By then we were all sleeping anywhere and nowhere. Somehow the term "bed" lost meaning and become interchangeable with chesterfield or verandah or easy-boy chair.

We let Maira stay up late with us and watch anything she wanted. She liked *Dynasty*, especially the clothes. One evening Francis spoke out loud to the TV son whose father would not accept his homosexuality. "Don't get sick. There has to be a better way to get him to take you back." Maira, who was sprawled on the rug, resting her chin in her hands as she watched, raised her head and looked back at him with inquiring eyes. He replied, "Ignore me, honey, I don't know what I'm saying anymore."

"Yes, you do," she said. "But I don't mind." He looked at me and said in mock conspiracy, "You're never going to keep a secret from her. She knows things." Maira crawled up on the bed, pulled his arm around her, and curled up with her head on his bony shoulder. His eyes, when they met mine, held a deep sadness.

We spent a lot of hours in his bedroom as the days ran into the fall and it became too cold for the verandah. He needed to lie down most of the time, so we made the room as cozy as we could with a comfortable chair and extra cushions. The television stayed on all day and night. When I tried to convince him that he would sleep better without it, he said, "Sometimes when I wake up, I have bad thoughts and the TV distracts me." So we never turned it off again.

"It's all right, I promise I won't hurt you," is what he said to us when it was time to take him to the bathroom. He dragged himself there with the little help we gave, grabbing at furniture and falling against walls. He refused a bedpan.

A notice of a package waiting to be picked up at the post office arrived on a day when he seemed to be in great pain. We all hoped it was the experimental medicine that was still illegal in Canada and had been shipped to him across the border from the States. Neil rushed out to pick it up and brought it home, which to me was some kind of miracle. My father is not a man who likes to flout the law. But after he opened it and prepared the syringe, he sat bravely beside Francis, wearing rubber gloves, and said, "I had to give Mama a few needles. She said I was good at it."

Francis developed an acute sense of hearing in those days, or at least that's how I explain to myself the fact that he heard every movement in the house, and knew if someone had come in, even if it was beyond the awareness of others. He'd say, "Dad is home," and I would say, "No, he's downtown," and then Neil would walk into the room and I'd feel that perhaps it was me who was losing touch.

We took turns making sure he was never left alone and keeping the rest of the family caught up on the latest development or medications. Iona called during the week to see how he was and I spoke as quietly as I could on the phone in the kitchen. "He's okay. He can't eat much, though, and he refuses to take his painkiller sometimes because he hates being in a fog, but other than that he seems in good spirits... we're all looking forward to you coming."

When I returned to the room after this near-whispered conversation, Neil was sound asleep on Francis's bed, lying on top of the covers. Francis lay beside him, wide awake and with the TV on but the sound turned off. He said, "When is she coming?"

A morning came when I brought him tea first thing and found him sitting up in bed, something he hadn't done in days. His eyes were wide, dark pools. "When I woke up there was a warrior angel standing at the foot of my bed in full regalia. She was carrying some kind of shield. I felt like I was going to have a champion to keep me safe along the way."

To me, it felt as if time had stopped and I could absorb every detail of the room at once and from a great distance: the blue and green blanket, the flutter of the cream-coloured curtains, all the light that surrounded him.

"I think it was Mama," he said.

"You think so?" I managed.

His words rolled out quickly and tumbled over one another.

"For a while after she died she was always in the room with me, even when I took a shower and especially when I lay in bed at night. She didn't want to leave. But it was making me miserable and one morning while I scrounged around making coffee, her presence was so strong I could almost see her. There was the weight of a stone on my chest so I put up my hand and begged her to go. She left, but I think she just went somewhere out of sight so she wouldn't bother me. I think that was her this morning. I couldn't tell for sure."

"I would have liked to see that," I offered.

The rest of the day was intensely alive. He heard the train whistle from down at the shore and thought we were leaving home.

"There's no need to go. I could just stay here."

I heard no children playing outside but he did.

"I love that sound they make whooping and hollering," and then, "I have no child," he whispered.

"You have me," Maira said from the doorway.

He must have thought she was Iona when he said, "You're a fine singer."

I left the two of them curled up when I ran outside at dusk to indulge an obsession with twilight I'd developed. For some months I'd felt a sense of panic if the light was fading and I was shut inside. I couldn't bear it if the night should fall without me as a witness.

After waiting on the verandah for complete darkness to descend, I came back inside and headed straight back up to Francis's room. Both he and Maira were asleep so I covered her with a small blanket and turned the TV down a bit. My father was nowhere to be seen when I looked around downstairs and in the yard, but when I came back in and called to him, he called back from the basement, "I'm here."

He was at his bench, standing in the circle of light shed by the overhead fixture, bending to some task with a single focus. The picture from his boxing days, with him in a defensive crouch, still hung on the wall, an artifact of a previous time. He didn't look up as I approached.

In the middle of the work surface sat a partially repaired china cup in a place he'd cleared amidst the clutter. I recognized it as a teacup that had sat on the bench for years in the same broken condition, a few large pieces with the handle still intact on one of them. Two of the pieces were already affixed but there was one still sitting on the table. His jaw set while he carefully applied a fine line of glue where the missing part should be. The light above shone through it and the cup appeared to come alive when he positioned the piece in its place and held it there for a long time and with a deep concentration. Finally he set the whole cup down and quickly released his hands. He let out a lengthy sigh, as if he had been holding his breath, when he saw the glue was strong enough to hold the thing together.

ACKNOWLEDGEMENTS

My thanks go first to the people who made this book possible. Vici John-stone at Caitlin Press shared her confidence, expertise and kindness from the first moment we spoke. She and her publishing team dedicated meticulous care and attention to the process of bringing the novel to light. Of those many who supported the writing process, I would like to thank Betsy Warland as a mentor and friend who supported the work in its early stages and shared her wisdom and advice over dinner conversations in the ensuing years. I am extremely grateful to Marion Quednau and Patricia Wolfe for their editorial guidance and keen eye.

Alistair MacLeod generously read and commented on the work more than once. I hope he would be pleased. Of the others who read and commented on this novel and to whom I am deeply grateful, I would especially like to thank Shaena Lambert and Patricia Kells. They provided beacons of hope when I couldn't see a way to land the novel. To all of my wonderful friends, who encouraged and pushed me on, you were the wind at my back.

The Writer's Studio at Simon Fraser University made this novel possible in too many ways to name. My thanks go to the mentors and writers in the program whose friendship and enthusiasm never wavered.

My generous and tolerant family gave me all the room I needed to write and still were there whenever I needed them. My love and gratitude go to my first reader, Colin MacNeil, whose insight and humour always sustain me.

Note: The translation of the Gaelic phrase in Chapter 6 is by Donald A. Fergusson as written in *The Hebridean Connection*.

Photo James Loewen

Ethel Whitty was born and raised in Cape Breton and emigrated from there to the West Coast in her early twenties. She wrote *The Light a Body Radiates* in stolen moments and occasional weeks of solitude while working for twelve years as the Director of the Carnegie Community Centre in Vancouver's Downtown Eastside. A graduate of the Simon Fraser University's Writer's Studio, she currently lives in Vancouver.